2018

THE
MAW

THE
MAW

A NOVEL

TAYLOR ZAJONC

Skyhorse Publishing

Skyhorse Publishing books may be purchased in bulk at special discounts for sales promotion, corporate gifts, fund-raising, or educational purposes. Special editions can also be created to specifications. For details, contact the Special Sales Department, Skyhorse Publishing, 307 West 36th Street, 11th Floor, New York, NY 10018 or info@skyhorsepublishing.com.

Skyhorse® and Skyhorse Publishing® are registered trademarks of Skyhorse Publishing, Inc.®, a Delaware corporation.

Visit our website at www.skyhorsepublishing.com.

10 9 8 7 6 5 4 3 2 1

Library of Congress Cataloging-in-Publication Data is available on file.

Cover design by Erin Seaward-Hiatt

Print ISBN: 978-1-5107-3240-7
Ebook ISBN: 978-1-5107-3243-8

Printed in the United States of America

For Sammy, whose adventure has only just begun

CONTENTS

PART 3: SYNTHESIS

PART 4: GENESIS

PART 1:

THESIS

Because the eye has seen, thoughts are structured upon images and not upon ideas.

—David Consuegra (1939–2004)

CHAPTER 1:

RELATIVE CONCEPT

4,500 feet above sea level

The Land Rover bucked along the washboard road, plumes of fine dust and scrubby green trees rising in sharp contrast to the impossibly blue African sky. Now far into rural Tanzania, Milo Luttrell could no longer see Mount Kilimanjaro's white-domed peak in the distance. Even the ever-present smell of sulfuric diesel and cooking fires had faded along with any trace of other people, leaving only clear, dry grasslands. He winced as his driver caught a deep rut under one of the thick tires, violently bouncing the truck to one side. Recovering, she steadied the wheel with her well-manicured hands and glanced at Milo with a reassuring smile. Milo shook off the jolt and tried to smile back, wondering why flat savanna still made for such desperately rough road.

Milo considered himself well traveled and a bit of an adventurer to boot. Even so, he felt a twinge of concern every time she reached a fork and invariably picked the fainter of the two roads, winding ever deeper into the endless plains, the tracks before them now barely distinguishable from the red earth.

He wished he could remember his driver's name. Three hours ago he'd been confident—now he wasn't so sure. Jody? Jordan? Jet lag was a bitch, and the name, ordinary as it was, had simply fallen out of his brain. He still didn't know quite what to make of her—she'd greeted him at the international receptions gate with a sly smile, a placard reading *Luttrell*, and a demure, unexpectedly posh British accent. She was black, perhaps five years older than he, but wore it well: elegant though not stunning, well-spoken but unapologetically reserved. When he'd asked their destination, she answered with such charm he almost missed the absence of an actual answer.

"Can you tell me what this is all about?" Milo asked now, clearing his throat. The dust was everywhere—even with the windows up, it had formed a thick layer on the dashboard and black leather seats, on his clothes, his face, everything. "You found something out in the savanna, didn't you?"

She winced as she shook her head in answer. "I find this just as awkward as you. But my employer was quite clear—I can't tell you a bloody thing until you sign the non-disclosure agreement. We'll get all the paperwork sorted out just as soon as we reach camp, I assure you."

"Are we close?" asked Milo, not entirely willing to accept the issue as closed. "Can you at least tell me that?"

"We're in the bush." She smiled as she took her eyes off the road for much longer than Milo would have preferred. "*Close* is a relative concept out here. Have you been to Tanzania before?"

"No," said Milo, rubbing his eyes as he tried to consciously reset his internal clock. "First time in Africa."

The Kenyan highway they'd initially taken southbound had been smooth and new, nothing like this rough road. Designed with one lane in either direction, highway traffic was often three abreast: shoulder, main, and passing. Waves of smoke-spewing trucks and minibuses had advanced toward each other like charging tank battalions, only sorting themselves out into recognizable lanes in the last possible moments before collision.

Milo had marveled at the ballet-like precision exercised by the apparently suicidal drivers. He told his driver—what was her name again?—that it was amazing there were no accidents, but was quickly corrected. Collisions, she said, were frequent and often fatal. Milo had decided he'd rather not think about it, resigned his fate, closed his eyes, and tilted his seat back. He'd slept intermittently until they turned off the crowded highway and into the wilderness.

The border crossing from Kenya to Tanzania had been no less surprising. When he saw the lines—nearly a mile of unmoving tractor trailers and overfilled, sputtering minivans—he prepared himself for another interminable wait.

His driver had pulled over to the shoulder, slowly parting the crowds of fruit sellers, candy hawkers, water-bottle vendors, and beggars. Men and women pressed against the Land Rover, tapping the glass, chanting *mzungu, mzungu*, trying to get their attention. Gravel crackling under the tires, the truck crept forward with unassailable deliberateness until they were at the front of the line before a perplexed border guard and his soldiers, ignoring the glares from the long convoy of semi-trucks behind them. A smile, a few spoken words, a many-stamped letter handed over, then handed back with equal speed—and they were through, freely passing the opposite stacked-up traffic waiting on the Tanzanian side. Milo realized he hadn't even presented his passport for inspection.

"You're the last to arrive," the driver said, sighing as the Land Rover crawled over a low rise and dipped down the other side. "I picked up the rest of the team yesterday. Bloody inconvenient, all this driving. I suppose your flight was delayed?"

Milo shook his head. It didn't seem possible that he was the last one in—he'd left the very same day he'd received the phone call from his department chair. His superior at Georgetown University didn't even know the destination, but insisted Milo take the opportunity all the same. After some brief argument, the chair admitted that a significant departmental donation had been placed in escrow pending the young professor's acceptance. It wasn't enough money to put him on tenure track, but it would grant Milo another yearly contract in the Darwinian publish-or-perish department. The subtext of the demand was clear—if the escrowed money went elsewhere, so would Milo.

A well-dressed chauffeur with plane tickets had arrived at his apartment with a town car shortly thereafter. He'd barely had time to stuff his oversized backpack and locate his passport. The timing wasn't great; mid-February meant his spring classes were in full swing, and he doubted any of his colleagues would appreciate being saddled with his students. He'd had a few minutes at the airport gate to Google the name of the company that had paid for the ticket, but came up with little more than a Bahamian-registered shell company with no published corporate officers or directors.

"Where did you depart from?" asked the driver. "Before Nairobi?"

"Washington, DC," said Milo. "Then to New York, then Dubai."

"I understand you're a professor of sorts?"

"Yeah," said Milo, unsure if she was making conversation or genuinely didn't know. "An adjunct history professor—Georgetown University."

She smiled and nodded, signaling her approval of the prestigious institution. Still, many of the faculty he worked with probably wouldn't have appreciated the name-dropping. Milo took pride in being a bit of an oddball in his field, often quoted in popular blogs and magazines but published in too few academic journals. Though he had joined the department with top honors and a record of innovative publications— to say nothing of his popularity with students—he'd quickly become an outsider among his peers. His superiors among the old guard regarded him as a bit of a failure, a promising mind who couldn't hack a proper academic career.

Even his field of study was consciously unconventional. Rather than limiting his focus to a specific time period or civilization, Milo analyzed the exploratory and migratory expeditions of all peoples, from

Everest to the Amazon, Columbus to Doctor Livingstone, Polynesian rafts to the lunar landing. Interesting as it all was, more than one of the faculty had quietly taken him aside for some frank advice—his career demanded either academic publications or rainmaking with private endowments. Keep on with his current path, he'd been warned, and he'd eventually be searching for a new position with a much lesser institution.

"How about you?" asked Milo. "What do you do?"

"I'm a trade law barrister," she answered. "I work out of Birmingham. It's all *terribly* boring, which is why I try to get into the wild as often as possible. The firm hates it, but what can they do? I arranged for a yearly block of uninterrupted vacation time before signing on. It was my only non-negotiable stipulation."

"Into the wild?" repeated Milo. "I haven't seen another car in hours— where are we going?"

"You *really* don't know, do you?" She laughed.

"I *really* don't," said Milo, trying to quell his rising irritation.

"Do you have a wife? Girlfriend?" she asked, again changing the subject without so much as missing a beat. "I bet the secrecy is driving them positively *mad*."

Milo shook his head. He'd recently begun casually dating a foreign aid worker he'd met through a mutual friend. She'd been surprisingly nonchalant about his sudden and mysterious departure. The fact that she worried so little made him wonder if she even cared, a suspicion he'd confronted her with in a series of rapid-fire text messages from the Air Dubai gate of New York's JFK Airport.

You're a historian, she had texted in response to his admittedly neurotic interrogation. *How concerned should I seriously be?*

He supposed it was true; it wasn't as though he was going to one of the poverty-stricken war zones she frequented. And she didn't owe him her worry; they hadn't even had the exclusivity conversation yet.

All this left Milo to fill in the blanks as best he could. The best explanation was a privately funded archaeological dig for artifacts from a

historic European expedition, probably from the pre-colonial or early colonial period. Maybe an amateur had gotten in over their head, needed
someone to evaluate the site and their initial findings from a fresh perspective. It would certainly explain the money, the secrecy, and why his
thus-far-unnamed benefactor would involve him. But he still wished he
knew enough to bring the proper reference books.

"I appreciate the ride," Milo said now, preparing to gently probe for
information. "But aren't you a little overqualified to play chauffeur?"

"You're wondering what you're doing in a car with a British attorney
and not a Tanzanian guide or local fixer?"

"I wouldn't put it like that—"

"There are 120 tribes in Tanzania," she said. "Each with a complex
set of family ties and obligations, networks of dependents, and ancestral relationships. To call it *impenetrable* would be an understatement.
But none of them are quite sure what to make of a black British woman.
You could say it brings out a certain cultural helpfulness. They call it
undugu, which means something along the lines of hospitality, family,
and so forth."

"Uh-dugu . . . ?" repeated Milo uncertainly. He thought he'd read
something about that in the guidebooks, but couldn't quite remember
the context.

"I find it all quite appropriate that such a romantic concept arose
from the cradle of humanity. After all, this area has been populated con-
tinuously since the dawn of the first people. In fact, we're not terribly
far from Olduvai Gorge, one of the most important Stone Age sites on
the entire planet. But I suppose you might know more about that than
me—being a historian and all."

"What does *mzungu* mean?" asked Milo. "At the border crossing—
those people kept on saying it when they were trying to get our attention."

"It means *those who walk in circles*. It's a term of respect."

It had to be an archaeological site, probably that of a lost European
explorer. What else could explain the need for a history professor with
such specific expertise? Milo racked his brain for possible explorers

as the Land Rover clattered over another low hill. No good candidates came to mind. Obviously not Daniel Houghton's disastrous expedition of the late eighteenth century; it was well established he'd been abandoned to starve on the other side of Africa. Same for Edward Vogel sixty-odd years later; he hadn't made it much past south Sudan before his murder at the hands of the local sultan. And the lost DeWar expedition was just an old cock-and-bull story, at least as far as Milo could tell.

His mind wandered as she muscled the wheel, cutting through a sandy river-wash. Rounding a corner, the Land Rover skidded to a halt, the road blocked by a milling herd of brown cattle. At a great distance, two tall, slender men in red plaid *shukas* guided the herd from behind, each carrying a long, iron-headed spear over their shoulders.

"Bollocks," the driver said, shaking her head as she rolled down the window. "When the cows start to outnumber the people they become very *bolshie* indeed. Move! Get out of the way!"

The livestock lazily parted as the Rover pushed through, its brush guard inches from their branded haunches.

"The elephants are even worse," said the driver. "We saw some yesterday. This is their migration trail. They could care less if you're trying to get by or not."

"At least you have the right vehicle for the job." Milo gestured to the well-appointed interior of the off-road SUV.

"Maybe, maybe not. Land Rovers are nice, but not always right for the bush. I personally prefer the Toyota minibus."

"Really? This far off-road?"

"Absolutely!" She smiled. "The Landy has big tires, four-by-four with locking differentials, the whole package. But if it breaks down, you can't get parts to save your life. Have to be shipped all the way in from South Africa or Britain—by air, no less."

"Come on. No way a minibus does better on a trail than a Rover."

"Not so!" she said, waving her finger in the air. "Land Rovers were designed as the ultimate off-roader, mountain-climber, river-crosser, a real go-anywhere vehicle. But in the real world, all it takes is one larger-than-average mud puddle and you're stuck."

"And the minibus?"

"Minibuses never get stuck or break down, not truly. When the wheels start spinning in the mud, or the engine blows—everybody just climbs out and pushes! Try *that* with a Landy."

Milo allowed himself a genuine chuckle, appreciating the lesson. She waved as they passed the tall tribesmen, her eyes drifting from the road to their handsome, muscled statures.

Silence fell and he lost track of time, watching the dirt and small stands of trees go by for hours. The sun lowered in the sky, and eventually the Rover turned off the last hint of a trail and into the untamed wild.

W aking suddenly, Milo's eyes snapped open, the sleep-inducing stillness of the open savanna now broken by the gathering roar of a cargo helicopter as it descended from high above. The heavy aircraft slowly passed, a massive generator dangling from its undercarriage in a cargo net like a raindrop hanging from spider silk. Cresting a hill, the Rover made a careful final descent down a steep bluff, turning onto a freshly bulldozed triple switchback above a pastoral tree-lined dry valley. Their view was blocked by the descending helicopter as its rotor wash kicked up massive clouds of grit. A scramble of local porters unhooked the bulky cargo net and cable from the helicopter, which then broke from hovering to soar away. The red dust settled as they drew closer, revealing a sprawling encampment of trailers, olive-drab tents, off-road vehicles, and people hurrying between equipment and temporary structures.

Milo scanned the scene for a marked-off archaeological site or anything else that could tell him the purpose of the mind-bogglingly vast encampment before him. He saw no test pits, no marked-off areas.

He was briefly annoyed—without basic protocols, the trailers and trucks could destroy irreplaceable historical treasures.

"Where's the dig?" shouted Milo over the *whump-whump-whump* of the departing helicopter.

"What dig?" asked his driver as the aircraft disappeared into the distance. "We're not going to a dig."

"Then why am I here?"

"You honestly don't know? I thought *somebody* would have had let it slip into the academic rumor-mill by now."

"I still have no goddamn idea."

The Englishwoman smiled and leaned toward him conspiratorially. "You ever explore a Cretaceous-era supercave before?"

CHAPTER 2:

STAGING CAMP

"But I'm not a caver," protested Milo as the Land Rover lurched down the last steep switchback to the encampment below.

His driver laughed. "Then I hope you can cook!"

Milo's mind did a couple of backflips trying to parse the absurdity of it all. Maybe it was some giant cosmic fuckup, his coming here. Maybe there was some other Milo Luttrell worriedly checking his email inbox for a missing invitation to a secret spelunking mission. But expedition backers had to know exactly who they'd hired—though the question of *why* remained another issue entirely.

The Land Rover clunked over a patch of dusty potholes and rumbled into the motor pool, parking alongside two identically equipped off-road SUVs. From this new vantage, Milo could see the symmetry of the camp, small domed personnel tents stretching down one side in a long line, three helicopter-transported trailers and twin temporary pre-fab structures on the other, a newly bulldozed dirt road between them. A pair of mess tents rose from the center of the row, complete with an open-air kitchen. Chemical toilets stood a respectful distance down a narrow footpath. Towering piles of bar-coded Pelican-brand cases lay in uneven stacks beside the motor pool, some still wrapped in cargo netting or strapped to lightweight plastic pallets.

Local porters and coverall-clad foreigners worked side by side as they set up the last of the trailers and equipment. Others sat in folding chairs near the small personnel tents, talking as the last rays of the sun disappeared behind a distant grassy hill. As darkness fell, high-efficiency LED poles slowly glowed to life like streetlamps, bathing the camp in artificial illumination.

Staggered by the size of the encampment, Milo stared openmouthed before turning back to his overqualified chauffeur. But she was gone, along with his baggage.

"Thanks for the ride," muttered Milo. Now abandoned, he had the distinct sense he should report to someone, but who?

As if on cue, Milo heard the sound of a clearing throat behind him. He swiveled around in the leather seat to see a young blonde woman standing beside his door. She held a tablet computer like a clipboard as she waited patiently for his attention. She wore an expensive safari-chic outfit and flirty smile.

"Mr. Luttrell?" she asked, cocking her head slightly as she spoke. Milo could see she'd pulled up his profile picture from Georgetown University's website; the question had been entirely for his benefit.

"Milo, yeah," he said, awkwardly extending his hand through the open window. She shook it, then opened and held the Rover door for him to step out. Her manner reminded him of a flight attendant; the only thing missing was the uniform and a drink cart.

"I'm Kylie, and I'll be showing you around today—how was the trip?" she asked, her voice cheerful and clipped. "Did Joanne take good care of you?"

"The trip was long," said Milo, quick-stepping to keep up with her, but glad he didn't have to ask the driver's name. He promised himself he wouldn't lose it again. "And a bit sudden. But Joanne was . . . the drive was fine."

He shivered—with little to no humidity to hold heat, the temperature had already begun dropping quickly. Kylie cocked her head like an inquisitive bird, then without waiting further led him down the central camp avenue at a fast gait. It felt good to stretch his legs; he hadn't realized how stiff he was.

"Do you have any luggage with you?" she asked.

"Had a backpack with me," answered Milo. "But I think the driver took it."

"Sign this," Kylie said, putting the tablet into his hands along with a digital pen. The screen held a one-page agreement that he quickly skimmed. Milo couldn't help but be impressed with the sheer volume of legal threats that had somehow been fitted into such a short document.

"Done," said Milo, handing the tablet back after affixing his signature.

"Your luggage will be waiting for you in your assigned tent," she assured him. "I wanted to know if you have any special items with you now, or if you might expect to have something delivered separately . . . books, equipment, things of that nature."

Milo briefly felt a pang of overwhelming dread, like the first-day-of-school dream where he was missing a pen or pants. "Not much beyond my digital camera and a laptop," he finally mumbled. "No books—nobody told me what to bring."

"You need a few minutes?" she asked sympathetically, though still ignoring the larger point. "Wash up, change? Eat something? Dinner isn't for a couple of hours, but we do have some very nice snacks."

"Couldn't eat even if I wanted to," answered Milo. "Still no appetite from the flight. I'd rather go ahead and meet whoever's in charge, if that's possible."

"Good," she answered with a smile as they passed the mess tent without stopping. "He is *very* eager to meet you as well."

"Can I make a quick phone call first?" asked Milo. "Let my folks know I've made it in one piece?"

"I'm afraid not," she answered. "The communications equipment is not yet ready for use. But if you give me their names and contact information, I'll pass word on your behalf once we establish a secure connection."

"This is quite the setup," Milo said, gesturing to the expansive camp. "I've never seen anything like it—very impressive."

"*Believe* me, I know," Kylie said with a slight laugh. "Three days ago, this was all just empty grassland. Not even the cattlemen make it this far out."

"You part of the logistics team?" asked Milo, trying to figure out her role beyond that of helpful camp guide.

"I'm the head of the logistics team," she corrected. He briefly worried that he'd offended her.

"Big job," said Milo, still somewhat stumbling for a response.

Kylie just shrugged. "Easier than Kandahar or the Sudan," she said. "Nobody's shooting at us here."

Milo thought about making a lame *not yet, anyway* joke but decided against it. They passed the main section of the camp with three large trailers on adjustable aluminum jacks. The first seemed to be some kind of laboratory, the second a windowed office, and the last a sophisticated communications setup complete with multiple satellite dishes and radio antenna. Milo found himself doubting that it was non-operational—lights and screens within the cloudy windows flashed, and he heard a faint hum coming from unseen computer servers. How hard could it be to place a simple phone call?

"Dinner will be *wonderful* tonight," she said. "Your choice, lasagna Bolognese or strip steak with salad and breadsticks, all made on site. New York cheesecake for dessert. And the wine pairing is *always* excellent."

It all sounded much better than the frozen pizza Milo would have had if he was still home in Washington, DC. Again he found himself pondering the cost of it all.

They passed the last trailer. Through wire-reinforced glass, he caught a glimpse of a sophisticated medical bay, not unlike a mobile operating theatre. Biohazard suits hung from hooks at the side of a double-airlock entrance. From the look of the facility, it could have handled just about any procedure up to and including major surgery.

"May I ask how you know Mr. Brunsfield?" Kylie asked. "He was *so* insistent that you join us."

"I don't," answered Milo, unable to place the name. "Know him, I mean."

She turned to face Milo, openly surprised. "Maybe he knows you," she finally said, unconvinced. "But even if you've never met, there's still a good chance you'll recognize him when you see him."

"Or you could just tell me," said Milo. But his guide just gave him another smile as she pointed toward the largest shelter at the end of the personnel row, a waxed canvas Bedouin-style tent held up by old-fashioned wooden pegs and hemp rope.

"Anything I should know?" asked Milo as he ducked through the entrance.

"Just one thing," she whispered with a sly smile. "Don't be afraid to kiss his ass."

She did not follow him into the tent.

Milo stepped into the opulent shelter. The interior was a lovingly recreated Victorian-era safari bivouac—gilt fixtures, soft leather, blown glass, colorful woven rugs, lacquered wood, and rough cottons. But then there were the modern touches, namely the bank of frameless monitors mounted against the fabric wall that displayed a grainy black-and-white view of a stark cavern moonscape, robotic tank-treads barely visible at the bottom of the screens. A white-haired man sat on a low couch with his back turned to Milo, intent on the screen as he gave instructions to a joystick-wielding technician.

"Back!" he exclaimed. "We're not stuck yet—just give it a little more gas!"

Milo's gaze shifted back to the monitors. It was difficult to get a sense of scale; the black-and-white video might well have been taken from a distant rocky planet. The white-haired man grumbled and placed his face in his hands with frustration. The robot couldn't free itself from between two rocks and the backseat driving wasn't helping.

"Goddamn robots," he boomed. "Back it up! Get it loose again!"

Milo looked at the technician with sympathy. The robot wasn't going anywhere.

"We should have sent in a goddamned canary instead," he complained. "Useless!"

"What am I looking at?" asked Milo, no longer able to restrain his curiosity.

The white haired man swiveled to face him. Milo felt his first inkling of recognition. "The cave has been sealed up for a long time," he said. "We needed to check the atmospheric composition for noxious gases. The little bot survived the fifteen-hundred-foot winch down the main shaft—"

"Fifteen hundred feet?" interrupted Milo in disbelief, wondering briefly if he'd misheard an order of magnitude.

"That's right, more than a quarter mile straight down. We're looking at the deepest pit cave in Africa, maybe the second or third deepest on the planet. It's going to rewrite every geology textbook and record-book, *if* we can get it mapped—which we obviously can't do with our goddamn *robot*, because it can't do *shit* once it reaches the bottom!"

Milo pursed his lips and nodded, not sure what to say. The technician frowned but kept his mouth shut as well.

The older man stood, turning his back to the screens. "I think it's safe to say the future of caving is *not* with robotics," he said as he extended an open hand toward Milo. "I'm Dale Brunsfield. Welcome to Main Camp, Milo. I'm so thrilled you finally made it all the way out here."

"Pleasure to meet you, Mr. Brunsfield," said Milo, confirming his recognition. Brunsfield was a fixture of Wall Street and was well known to the adventure community as a generous benefactor, using high-dollar corporate sponsorship to bolster the rugged image of his hedge fund and the luxury apparel brand he'd acquired as a hobby. Rich safari-goers, mountain trekkers, and would-be jungle explorers often began their travels with a stop by his upscale stores, selecting from the expensive olive-drab and khaki designer clothing and handbags.

"Call me Dale," he said. "I'm a big fan of your work on Richard Halliburton's 1939 *Sea Dragon* voyage. Top notch. The conclusion that the shipwreck found off San Diego wasn't Halliburton's reproduction Chinese junk? All deduced from a single nail? Made me a believer, no question."

Milo wasn't surprised. Rich men like Dale Brunsfield *loved* Halliburton and his exploits. After becoming the first man to swim the length of the Panama Canal, Halliburton's bestselling book *The Flying Carpet* (the story of his eighteen-month, 34,000-mile global circumnavigation aboard an open-canopy biplane) was, to some, the first true modern adventure travelogue. Halliburton played the part of romantic adventurer to the hilt, becoming legendary for his parties and bohemian lifestyle. Guaranteeing himself a place among the iconic adventurers, Halliburton was lost at sea in 1939. The particulars of his disappearance were not unlike those of Amelia Earhart. With no trace found, he'd been similarly mythologized into speculation and legend.

Despite the lofty reputation, Milo wasn't Halliburton's biggest fan—one of his most-relayed stories was the purchase of two child slaves in Timbuktu as entertainment. As loathe as Milo was to judge the historic figure by the standards of a modern era, he regarded that unsavory decision as legacy-defining and nothing short of reprehensible.

"Thanks," said Milo now, reflecting on his obscure article. "I'm glad you found it interesting. I didn't think too many people had read it."

"Well, I for one *loved* it," said Dale, eyeing Milo suspiciously. "So, I have to ask . . . have you sniffed out what I'm up to?"

"Not as of yet," admitted Milo. "Something about a cave, I hear?"

"You've heard nothing? No journalists poking around? Or other interested parties? Anybody try to contact you about me, Tanzania, or a lost cavern?"

Milo shook his head. He didn't think he knew any other "interested parties," whatever that meant, and the importance of the cave itself remained a complete mystery.

"Good," exclaimed Dale with uncomfortable volume. "Tight ship, that's what we're running here. A tight ship."

Milo could only figure Dale Brunsfield was on to something big, or at least thought he was. The size of the camp all but confirmed it—either a legitimately monumental find or Dale was exceptionally rich and crazy.

On the four-screen bank, the feed from the robot winked out into choppy video blocks, then a blank blue disconnection screen that clashed against the muted earth tones of the tent's interior. The tech mumbled a long string of expletives and smacked the controller without effect.

"Hell," said Dale, shaking his head at the monitors. "We're done for the day with the robot. Reel 'er back in."

"You'll have to forgive me," said Milo before he lost Dale's attention for good. "I still don't know what you want from me."

"Thought you'd have figured it out by now," said Dale with a sly smile. "I should make you guess at it, but we're short on time as is."

Dale paused, squinting as he eyed Milo.

"Milo, we didn't just find the largest cave in Africa. I'm on the trail of DeWar's legendary lost 1901 expedition. They weren't planning to climb Mount Meru. That nonsense was just their cover story. They disappeared *into that cave*, never to be seen again."

Milo stared back at the blank screens, confused.

"I've read up on you, son," said Dale, grabbing Milo by the shoulders. "You're no caver, but you're a regular Sherlock Holmes when it comes to historical expeditions. You know your stuff—usually—and I know your DeWar obsession almost tanked your career."

Dale released Milo, who wavered on his feet.

"This find will be bigger than Stanley and Livingstone," he said, stabbing his finger toward the now-dark screen. "When we map this cave, we're going to discover DeWar's lost expedition down there—we'll be the ones to solve a mystery more than a century in the making."

CHAPTER 3:

MIGRATIONS

Milo had to choke back an open scoff. The DeWar expedition? What a waste of time and money. All these people and equipment hauled out to Tanzania for nothing more than a myth, albeit one he'd once entertained himself. Yes, at one point the English aristocrat was hailed as the next great mountaineer and explorer, a maverick of yet-unexplored mountain peaks and polar lands. Lord Riley DeWar cut his teeth on the French Alps, ridden dog-sleds across the Canadian wilderness, studied winter survival with Nordic reindeer herders. He'd even accompanied the Adrien de Gerlache expedition to Antarctica in 1896, enduring seven months of scurvy-ridden hardship in the clutches of pack ice.

Supposedly DeWar's destination was the summit of Mount Meru—Kilimanjaro's volcanic little sister—assuming he ever had any intention of reaching the peak. Most historians theorized that he'd simply stolen his backer's money. All that was known for certain was that Riley DeWar, six comrades, four servants, and a dozen porters marched out of Dar es Salaam, never to return.

Dale Brunsfield was right. Milo's DeWar fixation had almost ended his career. Shortly after graduating with his master's degree, he'd been the first to make a connection between a set of bones recovered from the marshes of a Kenyan lake and oral history of an ambushed convoy of whites and porters. But Milo didn't just make the connection—he staked his career on it, with a published paper, popular news articles, and a book deal well underway, even ending a serious romantic relationship over the newfound demands of his budding notoriety.

The heady days all unraveled when a respected French anthropological forensics laboratory took on the case pro bono, recovered sequenceable DNA (which Milo had been told was impossible), and definitively declared the bones as those of a family of nineteenth-century German farmers. Almost every professional relationship Milo had painstakingly garnered over years was instantly shredded, leaving him with little more to rebuild his career than a handful of reluctantly loyal advisors and professional contacts.

Maybe DeWar got sick and died en route, or maybe he was ambushed and killed by a local tribe; either outcome wouldn't have been unknown to the region. More likely, Lord Riley changed his name and bought a plantation—or spent his final days in an opiate-laced stupor, the logical outcome of his chosen vice. Fading into the heady two-decade "Scramble for Africa" would have been an easy exit from his ongoing financial troubles.

DeWar's fame persisted, even after the age of colonies came to an inevitable close. His good looks, boastful tales, and trails of bad debt assured this notoriety—as did rumors of two jilted fiancées. Even so, his backers, likely duped, never stopped believing his intentions, many concluding he'd been kidnapped or murdered. It would have been a considerably more romantic ending for the Victorian sensibility than deeming the young lord a con artist and thief.

Rumors and sightings bolstered the theories, local legends and the occasional imposter kept the story alive for a time. But over the years, the dream of Lord Riley DeWar emerging alive from the plains of Africa became increasingly remote until, embroiled in the Great War, England simply forgot their missing son. DeWar was left to the historians. The near-end of Milo's career was little more than an ironic footnote.

Dale Brunsfield dismissed the tech with a wave of his hand, leaving the pair alone in the luxurious safari tent.

"I have to be blunt," said Milo, looking Dale square in the eyes. "DeWar and I have a *very* troubled history. I know you spent a lot of time and money getting me all the way out here, but as far as any of my peers are concerned, my opinion on DeWar won't be worth the paper it's printed on."

"I don't care about your reputation with the ivory tower," said Dale, returning the look with equal intensity. "I care about your expertise. You're right, I paid an awful lot to get you out here—I think that buys me a five-minute pitch for your time, if nothing else. If you aren't convinced, I'll put you on the next truck back to Nairobi."

"Let's hear it," said Milo, raising his hands in mock surrender.

"The locals don't know about the cave," said Dale. "It doesn't even have a name as far as we can tell. This area was barely settled in DeWar's time. Not even the nomadic herders passed through with any regularity."

"That's surprising," mused Milo. "My knowledge of this region is rusty at best—but didn't certain tribes maintain cave shrines in this area?"

"That they do!" Dale agreed, nodding enthusiastically. "Used them for fertility rituals, mostly. But the low profile of this one is good news for us, heads off some potential problems. Locals have a way of thinking we're out here to steal gold or disturb the spirits of their ancestors, that sort of nonsense."

Milo nodded. Dale's enthusiasm was infectious; the older man could hardly keep still as he talked. One minute he'd be on the couch, then standing up and pacing as he spoke. Maybe the explorer persona was more than corporate posturing after all.

"Like I said, the locals don't know about any caves in this valley," Dale continued. "But what they do know—and you're going to love this, I promise—is that the elephants visit this area."

"Elephants? Why?" asked Milo.

"Nobody has an explanation," said Dale with a shrug. "They don't appear to actually *do* anything here. Every migration, they'll stop in this little valley. They won't eat, won't breed, won't do anything special as far as anybody knows. They just stop for no particular reason, have a look-see, and leave."

"But you have a theory," said Milo with a smile.

"Damn right I do!" answered Dale, grinning almost ear to ear. "I think they remember this cave—or at least what it used to be. It's all collapsed now, but the original entrance would have been *massive*, big as a house. We'll learn more when my workers finish tunneling the new entrance and we actually start getting people inside."

"Collapsed? How long ago?" asked Milo.

"Hard to say," answered Dale. "Maybe a century? But like they say—an elephant never forgets."

Milo folded his arms, thinking, as Dale watched him with intense gray eyes. "But a cave? The DeWar expedition? It still feels like a long shot; I've never seen any evidence that Lord DeWar was doing anything but climbing Mount Meru or perpetrating a fraud."

"It's all circumstantial, I'll give you that," said Dale, unaffected by Milo's doubt. "But think about it in the context of the time. Kilimanjaro was conquered in 1889, more than a decade previous. And Mount Meru? Nobody even knows the name; she's the beauty queen's plain-Jane sister. Hemingway never wrote about the snows of Mount Meru. Toto didn't write a song about it. Lord DeWar staked his reputation on this expedition, and he wasn't the type to go after anything but the prettiest girl in the room . . . figuratively speaking."

"I suppose," said Milo, still unconvinced. He liked theoretical musing and cocktail-napkin calculations as much as the next historian, but the key to reasonable conclusions was a dispassionate, unattached outlook, which Dale clearly lacked. The CEO was nothing less than smitten with DeWar.

"Look past Kilimanjaro for a moment and give some thought to the other notable geological feature in this area—Amboni Caves, the largest natural caves in Africa," Dale continued. "They've been the source of myth and legend for centuries. A popular refuge for hoodlums, revolutionaries, and would-be Robin Hoods alike. Some believed that the underground passages crossed from the coast of Tanzania to the slopes of the great white queen herself. One writer claimed that a dog went missing in one of the caves and was found two hundred kilometers away, supposedly emerging from some other hidden entrance. The mapped caves—the ones the tourists and the religious pilgrims visit—never quite measured up to the legends. But I think this one just might."

"I'm afraid I'm just not familiar enough with caves to comment," admitted Milo. He hated coming across as so fundamentally useless on the subject, though it hardly seemed to dampen Dale's enthusiasm. Milo wished he'd been briefed on the expedition—or given any indication of the purpose for his visit, for that matter. At least then he could have brought some books and studied during the thirty-plus-hour journey across oceans and continents. Maybe then he'd have more to offer.

"No matter," said Dale, flipping the main screen away from the dead robotics feed to a series of false-color aerial images of the valley. The camp itself was rendered in muted blues, with a cluster of yellow and green plumes seeping from the ground about a hundred yards further down into the valley.

"What am I looking at?" asked Milo.

"I'll give you the short version," said Dale. "We had to establish that this is a bona fide cave and not some itty-bitty hole in the ground, right?"

Milo stepped closer to the display. He couldn't make sense of it, not quite, but could recognize the layout of Main Camp, the motor pool, and the main thoroughfare down the center. The plumes looked almost like geysers, roiling puffs of clouds spilling upward from a hundred tiny crevices. Was this a live feed?

"There are only fourteen mountain peaks in the entire world that rise over 8,000 meters in height," Dale began. "All fourteen are situated on the perimeter of the Indian subcontinent. There are even fewer known supercaves in the world, none of which are in Africa. Just like with mountaineer expeditions, exploring these super-caverns requires large, costly expeditions and multiple camps over multiple weeks. A massive undertaking. When first presented with the idea of supercaves, astronaut Buzz Aldrin said, 'I never thought there could be an environment as hostile as the lunar surface. No more.' That quote has always stuck with me."

"But how did you establish that you were looking at a supercave?" asked Milo.

"We do this through measuring air exchange," said Dale. "This is live infrared heat-mapping, by the way. We have a small drone circling overhead on a holding pattern, collecting data for the egghead types. Basically, all caves 'breathe'—they maintain a constant internal temperature while the outside temps fluctuate due to the weather, day-night cycle, seasons, and so forth. During the warmth of the day, she 'inhales,' and then 'exhales' at night when the temperature drops—like you can see on the screen."

"And then you use that information to get an idea of the cave volume," concluded Milo.

"Precisely," said Dale with a sly smile, leaving Milo to suspect he'd sprung one of Dale's little conversational traps.

"So how big?"

"I'd give you an estimate," Dale replied, "but she never stops breathing. The best my analysts have come up with is 'unquantifiably large.' A supercave, no doubt. The analysts have never seen anything like it. No supercaves have ever been discovered on the African continent. We scanned for ten miles in each direction; there are no other plumes, no other way in or out. She's a rare bird, Milo. A rare bird indeed, unprecedented on this continent. We know it—and I think Lord Riley DeWar knew it too."

"Incredible," breathed Milo as he leaned toward the screen, trying to visualize a city-sized system of underground chambers beneath his very feet.

"Riley led me right to it," Dale whispered. "I own a great deal of his collected letters and documents, some purchased at considerable expense from distant heirs. Initially I was only interested in his reputation, a persona I do admit admiring in my own way."

Milo had heard about the estate sales at the time; the purchaser had always opted to remain anonymous, leaving historians to speculate as to the identity. Dale pointed a remote and quit the live infrared display, flipping through a collection of archival photos to another display—a faded parchment map composited with modern Google Earth satellite imagery.

"This was hidden with his estate ledgers—taxes, milk delivery expenses, that kind of thing. My researchers almost missed it. They didn't know what to make of the map at first. After considerable investigation, we discovered that it shows the entrances to the entire Amboni cave network. But DeWar mapped an extra entrance unknown to modern cartographers, quite far from all the others—the entrance at the base of this camp. I had a plane fly over the area with an infrared camera and discovered the plume of humid air seeping out of the soil, *right* where the map was marked. Not sure where Riley got his information—local tribesman, one can only assume."

Dale sighed and leaned against the back of the couch as Milo processed a flood of thoughts. The CEO was no dummy, and circumstantial evidence was still evidence of a kind. Milo couldn't believe he hadn't found the map during his time with the documents, kicking himself for overlooking it. Still, he didn't have the funding for a team of researchers like Dale did.

"But this all begs the question—" began Dale.

"What happened to Lord Riley DeWar?" whispered Milo, finishing the thought. Silence hung between the two men for a moment as Dale collected himself.

"I think you can help me with that," said Dale. "I know this is tough for you, but I want you to climb back into Lord DeWar's mind, son. Get all cozy in there. When we get inside that cave and start finding clues—and I promise you, we *will* find clues—*you* will be our guide. Let's make some history together. Let's put you back in the good graces of your peers. What do you say?"

Milo barely remembered making his way back to the personnel tents, his mind wandering as he walked under the deepening reds of the sunset sky. The amount of information he'd absorbed was almost overwhelming. It wasn't hard to find his tent, helpfully marked with a small placard on the front flap that read *Luttrell, Milo*. He unzipped it and stepped through into the cramped interior. Though a far cry from the ornate interior of Dale Brunsfield's tent, the inside still boasted a comfortable low cot with an unrolled sleeping bag and enough leftover room for his backpack.

He clicked on the LED lamp hanging from the ceiling, illuminating the tent. A small tablet computer lay on top of his backpack, no doubt a gift from Dale. It was hard not to marvel at the remarkable efficiency of Main Camp. Curiosity took hold, and Milo turned on the small electronic device.

The tablet was loaded to the gills with research data. Six different biographies of Lord DeWar were saved to the home screen, as well as an unpublished PhD thesis and multiple books on the geology of Tanzanian caves. In addition to Milo's own papers on the subject, the entire contents of Lord DeWar's personal archives had been lovingly digitized and uploaded to the device in ultra-high fidelity. The implication was clear—Milo was expected to re-familiarize himself for the expedition, and fast.

Milo sighed. Maybe the long flight hadn't been a waste of time after all. Dale certainly had a way of making him feel like a critical part of the expedition, a partner even. Despite the promise of scholarly redemption,

Milo still suspected that any resulting glory would be Dale's and Dale's alone.

He opened his backpack and fished around for a clean set of clothes, intending to change before dinner. His appetite had returned, a good sign, though the jetlag still gnawed at his tired body and fuzzy mind.

As he dug in his backpack for a clean pair of jeans, Milo realized something felt entirely wrong—like coming home after work and realizing a stranger had been inside your bedroom. Everything in the backpack was as he'd left it, but not quite.

Then it struck him.

His digital camera, smartphone, and Macbook Air were all missing. Someone had searched his bag and taken them.

CHAPTER 4:

CONVERGENCE ZONE

Milo sat alone at the long table in the mess tent, trying to ignore the one-woman camera crew scrambling to capture footage of Main Camp. The small, energetic producer with a brunette bob had been at it since the last light of the day started to fade, alternatively asking on-camera questions of cornered team members or hurrying around the camp looking for attractive people with interesting things to say. Now, in the early hours of the night, she'd set up powerful lights at the other end of the table for one-on-one sessions with various expedition members, none of whom Milo recognized. The blonde logistician followed the producer in virtual lockstep, ensuring those attractive people weren't saying anything they shouldn't.

Served late, dinner was not yet prepared, but the mess tent was the best-lit area in the camp and a good spot to read. Besides, Milo had to admit that his own tent was a bit claustrophobic, a little concerning if Dale wanted him to accompany the cave expedition once the entrance was reopened.

Tablet in hand, Milo skimmed the six Riley DeWar biographies to re-familiarize himself with the explorer. It all came back to him quickly.

Stories about DeWar's lost loves and noble Scottish heritage were romanticized studies of the era, revealing little of the man himself. As he suspected, Riley's disappearance remained a question mark, a gap glossed over with various degrees of authorial prerogative and credulity.

Milo then tried to absorb the caving guides, finding them full of geological analysis and practical caving techniques. It was all but impenetrable. *Abseiling, colloids, cavernicolous, epiphreatic zones, kernmantle ropes* and *carabiners, spitzkarren* and *stromatolite* . . . it was like trying to learn a foreign vocabulary in one sitting.

Dale Brunsfield's digitized DeWar archive held a great deal more promise. Soon Milo found himself lost in Lord Riley's letters, inspiring pitches to potential financial supporters, correspondence with backers and advisors—and more than a few florid love letters. The lattermost held to a remarkably predictable pattern, and once a new conquest entered Riley's sphere, the letters would begin as an overwhelming flood of affection and emotion. But his interest in the Rose or Grace or Mary (sometimes several simultaneously) would inevitably peak within a year, then drop off with both frequency and passion until it ceased altogether.

The explorer wasn't what Milo had expected. Far from the square-jawed picture of unassailable will, DeWar was often vulnerable, even insecure. Though sharp-witted and decisive, many of his letters portrayed a man who desperately wanted to live up to his family name, despondent that his finances (or even his life) might end before he made his mark on history. Themes of irrelevancy and inadequacy were revisited with ever-greater frequency as his supposed Mount Meru expedition approached.

Strangely, Lord DeWar had come to believe that the golden age of exploration had ended. Milo was baffled by this. In 1901, the poles had not been reached, manned powered flight was unachieved, the oceans were largely a mystery. Everest was a half-century from summit, to say nothing of feats of aerospace. Milo pondered the thesis, wondering how much of a similar arrogance might be reflected by his own generation.

"Hey you," said a warm, familiar voice from behind him. Milo looked up to see a woman sitting across from him on a folding chair, a woman he'd never expected to see again in his entire life. She was as beautiful—no, more so—than when they'd last spoken nearly a decade prior.

Milo smiled, half-baffled and more jolted than he cared to admit. "Hey yourself," he finally replied.

"I was going to lead with a Doctor Livingstone line," she said. "Or something out of *Casablanca*. But I figured seeing me here would be enough of a surprise."

She wasn't wrong. In fact, Bridget was rarely wrong at all.

Bridget—no, not Bridget, it was Dr. Bridget McAffee now, wasn't it? In any case, they'd first met when he was a newly minted undergraduate instructor and she was a premed student at UNC Chapel Hill. It was his first job after completing his master's. She'd been a tennis prodigy—one ill-timed ankle injury away from going pro—and a brilliant scholar. With her tennis career over, she'd trained as a triathlete before becoming an early adopter of the CrossFit fad; the constant training paid dividends in her strong shoulders, muscled arms, and easy confidence.

Their relationship was volatile and lasted well beyond its natural expiration date, the turmoil made all the more consuming by its semi-secrecy. Despite all odds and good sense, they'd stayed together for nearly three years.

It only took a few incriminating text messages to blow up the floundering relationship. Milo left UNC Chapel Hill and eventually wound up in Georgetown. Bridget became Dr. McAffee, ultimately landing her dream job as a trauma surgeon with Emory University in Atlanta.

Now, the only evidence of their relationship—he'd tossed or deleted all the photos and emails—was the awful pang he still felt in his chest every time her face flashed in his memory. At that precise moment, Milo just wished he didn't find Bridget so goddamn gorgeous.

"I'm not even sure where to begin," said Milo as he stared at Bridget, trying not to look like he'd just been smacked in the face. The world was small, but not *this* small. "Why—when did you get here?"

"Two days ago, when they were first setting up the camp," answered Bridget with a half-smile. "But it's my third expedition with Dale. Emory lets me take up to two months a year. Thought I'd spend them on vacations, but traveling solo gets pretty dull after a while. I eventually found out that archaeological and scientific expeditions are always looking for a volunteer doctor on staff."

"Wow," said Milo. "How often do you get out into the field?"

"As often as possible," Bridget replied. "I've been to a Polynesian archaeological dig in the South Pacific, helped excavate a lost Buddhist cave temple in Myanmar . . . even cruised to the site of the *Titanic* with a documentary film team that dove on the wreck. Spent most of that trip sick in my cabin."

Milo couldn't help but feel a wave of profound envy wash over him. He remembered the adventures they'd promised each other; it pained him to learn how many she'd had without him. She seemed so maddeningly *unaffected* as she spoke, as though they could pick right back up as reacquainted friends.

"You always had the best summer vacation stories," responded Milo, struggling to return her smile. Despite her friendly tone, her words still felt distinctly competitive, a direct shot at his identity and aspirations. Of course she knew his of romantic obsession with exploration, but he couldn't tell if she had co-opted his dreams to memorialize their relationship or to throw it in his face.

"I really do," agreed Bridget. "Some of my superiors think it's a bit much; they hope I'll eventually outgrow it."

"I hope you don't," said Milo. It was an honest statement—whatever the motivation, she clearly loved the adventure, his irrational jealousy notwithstanding. "And how did you meet Dale?"

"Oh, this is a good story," said Bridget. "You won't believe this— we met rappelling into an Incan cliff tomb in the Peruvian Andes. He asked me out immediately; I told him I wasn't at all interested. Ended up friends anyway, and he always brings me on his expeditions. This is the biggest one by far, of course."

"I don't doubt it," said Milo. Part of him really hoped she wouldn't ask him about himself, force him to reveal how uninteresting a life he'd led since they parted. Meanwhile, she sounded like she'd just stepped out of a glossy *National Geographic* cover story.

"Still, this one feels a little different," she added. "Dale had me study up on exotic viruses. Strange, right?"

"That's a little concerning," said Milo. "But why? Wouldn't he be more concerned about falls?"

"Fair question," sighed Bridget as she absentmindedly ran her hands through her long, dark hair. "I suppose he's a bit paranoid when it comes to diseases. Caves are classic convergence zones where cross-species viral jumps occur. Bats and their guano, sheltering mammals, human hunters all passing in and out of a confined, humid, temperature-neutral space. Diseases love to make the first big leap from animal to human in caverns. Did you know the first major Ebola outbreak was ultimately traced back to a single cave in central Africa?"

"I didn't know that," admitted Milo.

"It's legitimately scary stuff," she said. "Emory handled a couple of Ebola-stricken US aid workers after the 2014 outbreak. Still, why not take the invitation? This is a long shot, but I think there's a chance that we can trace the yellow fever outbreak that devastated Central and Western Africa in 1900 back to this cave. I'll take some samples and see if anything comes of it. Could make for a hell of a paper. And how cool are supercaves? Some people even call them the eighth continent—that's how vast and unexplored they are."

"Seriously? Yellow fever?"

"Like I said, it's a long shot," she said. "But still worth checking out. Did you know yellow fever is a hemorrhagic? Same family as Ebola."

"I didn't know that," he said again.

"You manage to get a call out?" Bridget asked, changing the subject. "Tell the family you made it?"

"No," said Milo. "They said it wasn't set up yet."

"Not set up? Fat chance," she said, laughing. "I left a message with that lurking blonde girl. I can't even look up without seeing her with that clipboard computer thingy, asking me if I need anything. Your family good?"

"Everybody's fine," said Milo. "Mom still asks about you sometimes."

"Pass along my love. You've probably heard enough about me—what have you been up to?"

"Teaching," said Milo. "Blogging a bit. Get some interesting contract work once in a while."

"Still studying the great explorers?"

"Yeah."

"Rich guys do love their historical icons. I know Dale does."

"Speaking of whom, what can you tell me about Dale?" asked Milo.

"Probably not much more than you already know," said Bridget.

"Don't be so sure."

"I don't know much more than what's on his official bio," said Bridget. "Wall Street tycoon, activist investor. He's deep into pharma conglomerates, like investing in the development of ADHD meds, neurotransmitter reuptake inhibitors, and the like. Family money has been in it for a generation; they've been involved in the launch of a dozen or more extraordinarily lucrative product lines."

Milo nodded, again chastened by how little he knew about his sponsor.

"Glad it keeps him smart about the cave," said Bridget. "Like I said— classic viral convergence zone."

"I suppose the early archaeologists knew it," reflected Milo. "You know about the mummy's curse—opening up old tombs and getting sick. Most of those stories are bullshit, of course. But it was known to happen."

"But if it gets a doctor from Atlanta a free safari, why not?" said Bridget, grinning. "So, are you going to do it?"

"Do what?" asked Milo.

"Join the caving expedition! Go inside with the rest of us!"

"I don't know," said Milo. "Maybe Dale wants me to consult from up here—analyze photos, do tabletop historical scenarios, that sort of thing."

Bridget sat silent for the longest time, considering Milo until he felt uncomfortable.

"You really have no idea what you're getting into, do you?" she finally said. "Milo, this is a *supercave*. We could be down there for weeks. There aren't going to be any photos or tabletop theories going back and forth. We'll be completely cut off from all contact, entirely on our own. I think you should come—it's going to be unlike anything you've ever done."

CHAPTER 5:

EXTREMOPHILE

I t wasn't camp food; more like a visit to a gourmet cafe. Dinner was fresh salad, warm bread rolls, and a thin but expertly prepared New York strip steak. Milo even had a slice of cheesecake, baked in a solar oven and drizzled with a home-made strawberry reduction. Still foggy from the flight, he had selected the far corner of the mess tent, a couple of empty seats down from the next nearest person. Awkward small talk could only serve to remind him how little he belonged in Tanzania compared to everyone else.

Sitting apart from the rest of the group made it that much easier for the blonde logistician to pick him out. She'd stepped up to the edge of the tent, swiveled her head once, and instantly spotted him, marching over to his bench with great intent as he swallowed a last bite of the dessert.

"*You're missing it!*" she said, leaning over and placing a hand on his shoulder. Milo struggled and failed to not look down her shirt.

"Missing what?" gulped Milo, unconsciously reaching for his water glass.

"The technical team meeting—it was on the white board."

"The what? Where?"

She smiled at him and theatrically grabbed him by the hand, pulling him up from his seat. "You're coming with me," she said, pretending to drag him away.

Part of Milo's mind consciously realized his palms were sweating. Another part couldn't quite shake his desire for another slice of cheese-cake. She led him past the other diners and down the narrow path to Dale's oversized tent. Reaching it, she stuck her head in through the flap to look inside.

"Shoot," she said, her voice faint from the other side of the fabric. "I seem to have lost Dr. McAffee in the interim." She pulled her head back out.

"You going to hold her hand too?" asked Milo.

"Get in there, smartass," she said, playfully patting Milo on the shoulder, then shoving him in through the entrance and into the dark-ness. Milo desperately wished he'd remembered her name.

As his eyes adjusted, Milo realized he was looking at the sitting form of none other than YouTube star Charlie Garza. The Internet celebrity wore a perfectly curated four days' beard, immaculately styled to appear reckless and unintentional. Milo's gaze was drawn to his $300 haircut and the compression shirt he'd tucked into his khaki pants. The rugged image was completed by a subtle tribal bicep tattoo peeking from be-hind a shirtsleeve and a simple seashell necklace.

Though somewhat of a backbencher in his previous career—a nomi-nally sponsored backcountry skiing, rock-climbing adventure junkie—Charlie had made quite a name for himself on his online channel, Extreme History. In his fast-talking, enthusiastic—and prominently muscled—style, he was a favorite of twelve-year-olds cramming for his-tory tests, and his view count reflected it.

The online series had started out with a bang, the damage from the first episode alone totaling one wrecked aircraft, two broken wrists, and a shattered ankle—and a full week of breathless cable news coverage during a slow news cycle. Under the tagline "History is Dangerous," Charlie had attempted to duplicate the Operation *Eiche* raid in Italy, Hitler's daring commando rescue of a temporarily deposed Mussolini from a castle in the Italian Alps, complete with a period-replica Nazi glider (albeit with the swastikas tastefully redacted.) Charlie's re-creation didn't quite live up to the original, ending abruptly when the glider crash-landed into the side of Gran Sasso D'Italia mountain. Charlie survived the crash and landed a hat trick of major corporate sponsors, much to the delight of his bankrolling father.

Rumor had it that Charlie was a contender for the next cable adventure/documentary hosting slot, despite remaining a minor figure to few but the most craven of academic historians.

"Hey!" said Charlie, looking up from his phone. "You're the guy with the expedition blog! I read it all the time! Milo, right?"

"Great to meet you," Milo responded, stepping into the darkness and offering his hand. Charlie took it in both of his, shaking Milo's entire arm in a gesture that bordered on violent.

"Exciting, right?" said Charlie, waving around the impressively appointed tent. "This is all so *cool*—and I'm *pumped* to finally meet you! Been reading your posts for *ages*."

"Yeah, nice to meet you too," answered Milo, though he was physically unable to muster the same degree of enthusiasm. "Love your YouTube channel."

Milo tried really, really hard to dislike Charlie but couldn't. So what if Charlie wasn't particularly original? At least he was memorable, and he really did seem to have a deep love of history. In person, Charlie wasn't so much a prima donna as an overgrown kid.

"Where's Dale?" asked Milo, glancing around the room.

"Not here," came a voice from the far side of the tent. In the midst of Charlie's gregarious introduction, Milo hadn't even noticed the man in the corner fixing himself a well-aged bourbon from Dale Brunsfield's impressively stocked wet bar.

"That's Logan Flowers," said Charlie, pointing toward the bar. "Doctor Flowers, I mean. Doc—it's Milo Luttrell, the guy I was telling you about."

Logan didn't smile, just walked over, wordlessly shook Milo's hand, and sat down on a folding chair, drink in hand. He didn't sip it, just held it in one hand, condensation collecting at the rim. Logan had an unkempt, bushy red beard and thick black glasses and was noticeably overweight. If it weren't for his piercing, intelligent eyes, Milo could have pictured him hanging out at a bus station in a bad part of town.

"Nice to meet you," said Milo, breaking the silence. "Are you another historian?"

Dr. Logan Flowers snorted and shook his head. "No, not a historian," he said. "Geologist."

"At least one hard science guy in the bunch, right?" said Charlie. "Keep the rest of us in line?"

Nobody answered him; Logan was characteristically silent. Milo sat down, putting Logan between himself and Charlie.

"What's your specialty?" asked Milo.

"Speleology," Logan said. "I study caves. I focus on speleogenesis and hydro-morphology. Basically means I try to understand how caverns are formed."

"Don't stop there," interrupted Charlie. "I looked this guy up—he's been with NASA for years. Studied the lava tubes they discovered on the moon. He's the real deal—spends days, sometimes weeks underground."

"And he explores alone," came a feminine voice from the entrance flap. Milo gulped as Bridget stepped in and found a seat across from the three men. "That's his reputation, anyway."

"Hardcore," said Charlie, nodding in appreciation. "*Wicked* hardcore."

"I think it's quite suicidal," said Bridget as she shot a glance toward Logan. Milo noticed she wasn't smiling—Bridget wasn't teasing.

"What is darkness to you," quoted Logan, more than a little defensive in tone, "is light to me."

"Dante?" asked Charlie.

"Jules Verne," corrected Logan.

Bridget didn't respond, but instead crossed her legs and flashed Milo a thin smile. He didn't return it.

"I'm pretty psyched about this whole expedition," said Charlie. "About as extreme as history gets, right?"

"Nice to do something outside the norm," admitted Bridget. "I love Emory, but it has a tendency to get all-consuming."

"I've been dying to ask Milo this question," said Charlie. "You really think we're going to find Riley DeWar and his guys?"

Milo let the silence sit for a moment as he thought about it. "It's certainly what Dale believes," he finally said. "And I have to say, the evidence he's put together is highly compelling. Circumstantial, yes, but compelling nonetheless. The find would rewrite history—and prove DeWar didn't steal money and disappear, but that he died taking on a challenge decades ahead of his time."

Barely paying attention, Logan stood from his seat and booted up the monitor bank, playing back recorded footage from the earlier robotic penetration of the first chambers. Milo couldn't make any sense out of the film—the diminutive robot could barely capture more than the crushed and shattered stones immediately before the camera. The onboard light source couldn't so much as reach the nearest cavern wall.

Milo wasn't done talking, but he could tell Bridget and Charlie's interest was already flagging, especially now that he was in competition with the video feed.

"But if he's in there," said Milo, trying to wrap up with some confidence and swagger, "we'll definitely find him."

Logan just snorted.

"I take it you disagree?" snapped Bridget, reflexively coming to Milo's aid.

"We're not talking about a single missing caver," said Logan. "We're talking about an entire missing *expedition*. Every last man gone, vanished. One, two guys I can understand. Somebody falls, gets hurt, maybe their buddy panics, doesn't keep a level head, and turns a simple screwup into a catastrophic fuckup. But an entire expedition, nearly twenty men vanished into this cave? I don't think so. Something happened down there—something we haven't accounted for."

"Could have been a cave-in," said Charlie. "Trapped 'em."

"This cavern formed 150 million years ago during the Jurassic age," said Logan. "It predates humanity itself. It has survived submergence in an ancient sea, continental drift, multiple ice ages, severe earthquakes. A significant interior collapse is very unlikely."

"Carbon dioxide poisoning," suggested Bridget. "Or toxic levels of sulfur dioxide, ammonia . . . maybe even methane."

Logan shook his head. "Those gases are found in *volcanic* caves, not limestone. Look at the video feed—there are none of the crystalline structures associated with volcanism. Besides, our probe's sniffers are capable of measuring down to the parts per billion. I've seen nothing alarming in the readings."

"They suffocated," said Milo. "Camped out in a small chamber. Maybe lit a fire by mistake."

"Suffocation? Not with the amount of air exchange we've witnessed," said Logan. "But let me stop you all there. You're all using a conventional understanding to try to understand the unconventional— I don't think you really get the environment we're dealing with. Think about hydrography, the weathering forces that turn mountain ranges like the Rocky Mountains into smoothed-over Appalachians. These forces are turned on their heads underground. Water hollows out the earth like an acid, carries away particles by friction and gravity. While on the surface, weathering turns mountains—vertical features—into plains—horizontal. It's exactly opposite underground. Gravity and friction dictate morphology. Horizontal passages are narrow and squeezed, where acidic waters collect between sedimentary layers, slowly eating away a lazy, narrow path downslope. But vertical shafts are swallowing and massive."

"Those vertical drops are called pitches, right?" asked Charlie.

Logan nodded. "This is a classic pit cave. We'll have more rope by weight than the rest of our gear combined," he said. "It's called riding the nylon highway—dropping pitch by pitch into the center of the earth, figuratively speaking. It's incredibly dangerous. It's said that everything about caves is the antithesis of life on the surface."

"Extremophiles can survive in those conditions," said Bridget. "Not just bats and bears. Sightless fish . . . albino spiders and snails . . . to say nothing of single-celled fungi, bacteria—"

Logan snorted. "Evolutionary dead ends," he said. "Organisms that discovered an uncompetitive, temporary niche. Leftovers from the dominant ecosystems."

"You certainly have a diminished view of biology," snapped Bridget.

"Even if we don't find the DeWar expedition," interrupted Charlie, "we'll still accomplish something truly extraordinary. Imagine, we will be the *first people* in more than a century to pass across the threshold of this virgin cave—"

"Not exactly," said Logan with a smirk.

"What do you mean?" asked Milo.

"*Please* tell me I'm not the only one who sees this," said Logan, rolling his eyes. "Somebody's been inside. Recently. Well, recently in geologic terms. And *not* the DeWar expedition."

"Another expedition?" demanded Charlie. "The fuck are you talking about? Dale says this is a virgin cave—"

"You ought to just say exactly what you mean," said Bridget, losing patience.

"Just look at the footage!" said Logan, pointing at the grainy, grayscale imagery on the screen as if it should be self-evident. "See the shattered rock formations? The broken hanging stalactites? Someone was in here, probably within the last sixty years. I'll have to take some samples for verification, but it looks like this entrance didn't collapse—it was brought down with high explosives. By the looks of it, whatever munition they used would *not* have been available during DeWar's time."

Charlie shook his head angrily, stood up, and left the tent, not bothering to close the flap behind him. Harsh light streamed in from the high-efficiency LED lights outside.

"What do you think happened to the DeWar expedition?" asked Milo quietly.

"How should I know?" said Logan. "Assuming they were ever down there to begin with? You're the historian, you tell me—maybe they all killed each other."

CHAPTER 6:

THRESHOLD

Bridget and Milo followed Logan out of the tent and into the night. Above, the bright stars glittered over the savanna, the Milky Way a bright ribbon against the moonless sky. On the well-lit main thoroughfare of the camp, a pair of fuzzy desert foxes slunk past, their oversized triangular ears sharp and attentive as they scurried across the dirt road. In the stillness, Milo felt a sense of awe wash over him. He could see why the plains of Africa had captured the romantic imagination of explorers and poets alike.

At the far end of the road, one of the bright LED lights had been wheeled away from its orderly position to a grassy flat spot. Dale Brunsfield crouched under the illumination, intently organizing an immense spread of ropes, carabiners, scuba regulators, and shiny aluminum air tanks. Piled separately was the largest collection of rechargeable lithium-ion batteries Milo had ever seen.

"Looks like we found Dale," said Milo. "What's he doing?"

"Don't know," whispered Bridget from behind Milo. "But I hear he's leading this expedition personally. I've been told he's trained under some of the most accomplished cave divers in the world. He told me he was the one that first cracked the Delgado sump."

"What does that even mean?" asked Milo.

"I have no idea," admitted Bridget. "But Dale made it sound like a pretty big deal."

"I can't believe the sheer number of batteries we're bringing," said Milo.

Bridget just shrugged. "Light is life in a cave."

Milo stopped to look. Dale must have known he was being watched but didn't react; his intelligent eyes remained focused on his task.

"Should I say hello?" asked Milo.

"I wouldn't bother," drawled Logan without turning around. "He won't appreciate being interrupted."

Milo took one last glance toward Dale as Bridget and Logan turned to walk back to their tents. In the corner of Dale's collection, he noticed a half-opened cardboard box filed with what looked like thick black vinyl sheets. He recognized the unique packaging and shape.

They were body bags.

M ilo woke the following morning to the unfamiliar sound of his tent unzipping. Dale stuck his head in through the flap, then held up a small thermos of hot coffee with two cups. Rubbing his eyes, Milo waved him in, appreciatively took his cup, and mumbled a thank you. He sat up in his sleeping bag and let his feet off the cot and onto the fabric floor, briefly wondering if he was late for another meeting.

"So, what do you think?" asked Dale, sitting cross-legged and facing him, uncomfortably close in the tiny tent.

Milo thought about it for a moment. "This is still all new to me," he admitted. "Supercaves . . . supercaving . . . I've never done anything like this before."

"There's a first time for everything," said Dale. "You're out here with the best of the best. Listen to me and the guides; we'll take care of all the heavy lifting. I need you down in that cave—*if* you can handle it. Any serious issues with heights? Claustrophobia? The dark?"

"No more than the average guy, I guess," said Milo. He tried to remember the last time he'd encountered any situations that would have brought out such fears. Flying was fine, but it wasn't exactly the same thing as standing at a cliff's edge. And as far as the dark went, the only fear he'd ever had was of stubbing a toe during a late-night trip to the bathroom.

"Just let somebody know if you want to talk it out before we go in," said Dale. "One of our staff has a background as a counselor—he can teach you some breathing exercises, visualization, that kind of hippie stuff."

"I'll let you know," said Milo, giving Dale a tight smile as he took the first sip of his coffee. Vitality flowed through his veins, shaking off the fuzziness and sending a little jitter of excitement right into his bones. Dale just sat there, looking at him with a faint smile on his face.

"And how about Dr. McAffee?" added Dale, asking the question with a bit of a wary tone. "I understand you two have a bit of a history. We'll be in close quarters for extended periods—should I anticipate any problems?"

"We're both professionals," said Milo, answering almost by reflex. "We'll be fine."

"Glad to hear it," said Dale. "Go see Duck to get geared up. We're going in today."

The entire mess tent had been taken over. Crates spilled out over the tables with an assortment of boxed gear of all sizes. Bridget stood beside Milo wearing a long-sleeve thermal shirt, tight jeans, and tennis shoes. She yawned and stretched—Bridget was never a morning person.

Dwayne "Duck" Spurlock had buried himself halfway in a crate, humming a tune as he loudly dug through it. Finally he found what he was looking for, yanking out a small ukulele from underneath a pile of silvery emergency blankets and giving it an experimental strum. The chord was painfully off-key, but Duck just grinned at Milo and Bridget before putting it aside.

"*Now* we can get you guys fitted," said the cave guide, drawling out the word *now*. In his early twenties and with an unruly crop of blonde hair, he looked more surfer than caver. But Milo had heard he was a top pick for Dale's team.

"I suppose everybody else has their own gear already," Bridget whispered to Milo. "Except us."

Joanne—Milo's driver on the journey from the airport—appeared beside the young man and popped open a box on the far side of one of the tables.

"Thank God for corporate sponsors," she said. "We got a *brilliant* kit this time."

"You guys remember Joanne," said Duck. "She'll be giving me a hand today."

Joanne gave a friendly wave to everybody.

Late, Charlie Garza came marching up from the personnel tents, trailed by a short, energetic, brunette-bobbed woman. Milo remembered seeing the woman the previous night, and had since learned Isabelle was an experienced camera operator and producer of adventure and exotic reality television shows.

"I got him suited up yesterday." Isabelle pointed to Charlie as if the Internet celebrity were her pet poodle. "But didn't get it on film—going to have to reshoot. Sorry we're so behind schedule *again*."

"No prob, no prob," said Duck, giving her a big thumbs-up. Dressed in a safari outfit straight out of central casting, Charlie stood next to Bridget, the pair fully occupying the frame of Isabelle's already-recording camera.

"Head protection first," said Joanne, lugging over a box of differently sized and configured caving helmets. "Milo—you look like a medium. Doctor McAffee . . . maybe a women's small?"

"Doc McAffee," said Duck, bobbing his head. "Trauma surgeon at Emory, I hear. So much brains for such a small helmet, am I right?"

"Ignore him," whispered Joanne to the trio. "He may sound like a teenager that just smoked himself stupid, but he's actually a damned fine guide."

"What'd she say?" Duck jerked his head up.

"I'm telling them you're not actually stupid," answered Joanne loudly. "You're just from California."

"Santa Cruz, baby!" said Duck, flipping another thumbs-up as he grabbed a set of heavy headlamps with rechargeable battery packs. He piled them next to Bridget and Milo along with a big stack of chemlight sticks. Duck busied himself with a few other items—toilet paper, eye drops, personal first-aid kits—before stopping and squinting at the trio.

"Okay, pop those tops off," said Duck, gesturing with his hand.

"Seriously?" asked Milo, glancing around uncomfortably.

"Yeah," said Duck. "Pants too. We're going to be real cozy with each other down in that cave, so start getting comfortable now. Got to get you fitted for some skivvies."

Bridget shrugged, slipped off her shoes, pulled up her thermal top, then shimmied out of her jeans, stripping down to boyshorts and sports bra. She looked even better than Milo remembered; her grueling training regimen had done wonders for her body. He simultaneously couldn't stand to look at her, nor could he tear his eyes away. An intense wave of jealousy shot up his spine, an emotion he knew full well he had no right to possess. For the first time, he reflected on how incredibly difficult the coming days could become—not so much for the grueling expedition, but the fact he'd be faced daily with such a profound source of unresolved pain.

"Right on, Doc!" Duck gave yet another thumbs-up. "Gettin' with the program!"

Milo shot a glance over to the camerawoman. Isabelle had gone completely silent, training the unblinking glass lens on Bridget as she captured every moment.

Charlie Garza took a deep breath, flashed a blinding smile to no-body in particular, sucked in his stomach, and flexed as he peeled off his shirt. Consciously or not, he made certain the morning light caught his pectorals and thick arms.

Milo reluctantly took off his T-shirt and pants without the showy en-thusiasm of the other two. He wished he'd worn a newer pair of boxer shorts. And that he'd been to the gym more often. And that he'd caught a little sun once in a while.

Duck eyeballed the trio for size and flipped each a set of poly-pro base layer, heavy synthetic pants, stretch shirts, fleece zip-ups, and water-resistant coveralls.

"You get what you need?" called Charlie. Isabelle nodded and put down the camera, letting him say a goodbye and slip away.

Milo and Bridget put on the new clothes and glanced at each other. They were starting to look like twins. Duck brought out thick socks, boots, kneepads, and rubberized gloves next. Finally, they were both fit-ted for a heavy-duty rappelling harness.

"Either of you wear contacts?" he asked as they sorted through the expensive bounty of clothing.

"I do," said Milo. Bridget shook her head.

"You bring glasses?" asked Duck.

"They're in the tent. I can grab them in a minute."

"No can do," said Duck. "That's how critical gear gets left behind. Joanne?"

Joanne popped up to her feet and jogged down the path to Milo's tent. Milo really hoped he wouldn't have to wear them often—they were years old, the frames unfashionable and the lenses badly scratched.

"That'll about do it," said Duck, pulling a long roll of stickers out of a final crate. "These are RFID tags—how we manage the entire in-ventory in camp. I'm going to need you to grab the roll, take it down to the Communications trailer, and dig through the boxes. Anything you might need for the expedition—waterproof notepaper, condoms, cameras, Toughbook laptops—slap a sticker on it. Name it and claim it, the gear is here for a reason. If it's got a sticker, we'll make sure it's waiting for you at base camp once we're set up in the cave."

"I thought *this* was base camp," said Milo as the group began to break up.

"Condoms?" asked Bridget, bewildered.

The team assembled at the bottom of the new road, a few hundred yards down the valley from the camp. The entrance looked like the rest of the landscape, an inconspicuous depression in the earth like a dry oasis, surrounded by a stand of scrubby trees. Mid-morning, the heat had already begun to build, sending the marmot-like rock hyraxes into the shade beneath the dusty stones.

Porters had stacked Pelican cases, dry bags, and scuba tanks on the ground, an assortment of equipment so large that it dwarfed the team itself. They faced a massive metal hatch door built into the earth, a battleship-gray steel door with a hefty metal wheel in the center, the result bearing more than a passing resemblance to the entrance of a nuclear missile bunker.

"They're keeping it sealed," explained Logan, adjusting his backpack. "The entrance has been collapsed so long that the interior has reached homeostasis. Can't just open it back up again without destabilizing the upper passageways. They put in an access hatch before tunneling into the main cavern. We're probably looking at the most expensive cellar door on the continent."

Milo nodded as he surveyed the team. Eight people in all. Two guides—Dwayne "Duck" Spurlock and Joanne Gatewood—stood at the ready. Producer Isabelle kept her attention on Charlie.

"What's she doing?" asked Milo.

"I think she's shooting a pilot," said Bridget, nodding toward Isabelle. "Probably for one of the big cable education networks. Maybe Extreme History has some legs after all."

Dale Brunsfield had ditched his safari wear for a brand-new technical spelunking outfit. Logan was looking at the pile of caving equipment with a strange mixture of skepticism and approval. And Bridget was right there next to Milo, close enough to grab his hand. Every once in a while she'd shoot him a little nervous look.

Dale cleared his throat and stepped into the middle of the assembled team. "We're going to take things easy on day one," he said. "We're scheduled for a two-week mission, so don't get ahead of yourselves. Move deliberately, move slowly. There's going to be a bit of a learning curve here, not just for the new people but all of us. This is an unmapped, unknown cave. Our first—and only—priority on day one is to get inside and find a suitable location for base camp at the bottom of the main shaft. Once that's done, porters will start rolling in all our gear."

Dale shifted his weight from one foot to the other, lost in thought. He looked up and spoke again.

"On days like this, I reflect on a favorite quote," he said. "It was said by Ernest Shackleton, legendary explorer and savior of the disastrous Endurance expedition. He said something like this—*I vowed to myself that someday I would journey to the region of ice and snow and go on and on until I came to one of the poles of the earth, the end of the axis upon which this great round ball turns.*"

Dale looked around, allowing his gaze to settle on each team member in turn, meeting Milo's eyes last.

"If this cave is what we think it is," Dale continued, "we're not just visiting the axis upon which the globe turns; we're plumbing its deepest secrets. In doing so, we may well solve a century-old mystery and clear the tarnished name of a great man."

With that theatrical declaration, Dale turned away from the camera and twisted the wheel on the front of the steel door to the cave entrance. Hydraulic actuators flexed, prying the door open against incredible air pressure. Milo felt a ripple in the wind as the cave breathed in, gently at first, but quickly building to hurricane force, the now-open mouth sucking air through the doorway and into the earth with a harsh, guttural whistle. Steadying himself against the wind, Dale was first to disappear into the darkness, followed by the two guides.

"This is a good sign," said Logan, shouting to be heard over the noise. "Very significant volume of air exchange."

"Close the door," ordered Isabelle. "I want to get a shot of Charlie opening it."

Charlie nodded, spinning the wheel and allowing the hydraulic pumps to slowly squeeze the steel portal shut. He waited for Isabelle to get into position with the camera as he posed in front of it.

"We're the first ones into this legendary cave in more than a century," said Charlie to the camera with a stage-whisper before opening it again. The whistling howl drowned out the rest of his words, forcing him to start over. Milo wanted to cover his ears, protect himself against the awful sound.

Milo heard Logan groan from behind him. "Was he even listening to me yesterday?" Logan complained over the din. "We are *not* the first people inside."

"Why are we here? To solve a mystery a century in the making," shouted Charlie, crouching before the opening cave entranceway again. "And in doing so, to clear the tarnished name of a great explorer. Folks, this is extreme history in the making."

With that, Charlie ducked through the metal doorway and vanished into the darkness, followed by Isabelle.

"Is he seriously going to repeat everything Dale says?" grumbled Bridget. "Because that's going to get *really* old."

Bridget too passed into the void.

"This is why I cave alone," said Logan, following her.

Milo said nothing as he, last in line, stepped into the darkness and shut the steel door behind him. The last thing he heard before the door clanged shut was Logan.

"Little caves whisper," mumbled Logan from the darkness, barely audible. "Big caves shout—but supercaves scream."

PART 2:
ANTITHESIS

But delirium is the antithesis of death; it is the body's struggle to survive.

—CORNELL WOOLRICH (1903–1968)

CHAPTER 7:

GALLERY

41 feet below the surface

Milo stumbled through the darkness, tripping over loose stones as the steel door groaned shut behind him, extinguishing the last of the wind and sunlight. The passage was bored through a muddy mix of shattered limestone. Feeling one wall, he ducked through two dozen feet of virgin tunnel. He could see the intermittent dance of headlamps and flashlights as the party made their way into the interior of the cave before him. Milo held out his hand in front of his face but couldn't see it in the suffocating darkness.

As he passed from the tight entranceway to the cool stillness of a wide, dark chamber, he felt a hand on his shoulder, then pressure on his helmet. His own headlamp flickered on with a geyser of light, momentarily overwhelming his still-adjusting eyes.

"Do be careful!" Joanne took him by the elbow and pointed his entire body away from hers. "Caving etiquette dictates *not* blinding everyone. In close quarters, keep the lamp pointed *down*, at your feet—that's where you need light the most."

"Sorry." Milo kept eye contact with the guide as he averted the angle of his head. "And thanks for turning it on for me."

"You must start doing that yourself," she scolded, her aristocratic accent turned sharp and chastening. "Even in total darkness—*especially* in total darkness. You might not always have a guide with you."

"Yeah, I know," said Milo. "Sorry."

Milo unconsciously looked back at the closed steel door. It was shut tightly, but had a wheel on the interior side as well. He appreciated the importance of the hydraulics system; no human muscle could open it against such howlingly powerful air pressure.

The helmet lamp was more than adequate, but the fixed light barely reached his peripheral vision. He could only see forward, and was blind in all other directions. He successfully experimented with exaggerated head movements, but directing his eyes too far in any one direction revealed only darkness or the haphazard flashes of others' lights.

Logan had not made it in very far. The geologist had stopped at the entranceway, examining the walls of the newly dug tunnel and the rocky debris field at its terminus.

"Look at this." Joanne pointed to a skeletal menagerie of bones covering the cavern floor. "I see rock hyrax, antelope, dik-dik, gazelle, eland . . . oh, that's a kudu."

"How did they get in here?" asked Milo.

"Dragged in by predators, probably over thousands of years."

The remains were broken and scattered, pulled apart, some splintered, all with toothy indentations. Some of the skull variations appeared primeval, from species long since extinct, the oldest among them covered in a drizzle of calcite and fused to the cave floor. Milo tried to shuffle around them, but the most fragile—the graying remains of birds, bats, rodents—crunched beneath his feet with every step.

Milo could see that the entrance had once been massive, large enough to fit Dale's theoretical herds of elephants—a ceiling twenty feet above, thirty feet across, with a flat dried-mud floor. The walls were wavy, multi-hued brown with a texture like sandpaper, a passageway carved through hundreds of millions of years of hard-packed sediment turned stone. A thin layer of dust clung to the air, glittering in the beam of his headlamp.

"This is incredible," breathed Milo, soaking in the confined, alien world.

"Not really," said Logan with a sigh. "It's a dead cave, at least this section. No moisture to speak of, and the features—columns, stalactites, stalagmites—all dried out."

"What's a live cave like?"

Logan smiled for the first time. "Dangerous—but beautiful," said the geologist. "Slick with wet crystals and growing calcites everywhere. Rushing subterranean rivers. See, native peoples believed that caves were sentient. They breathe, circulate, digest . . . even excrete. They can even become sick and heal. But not this dusty, broken passage. You'll know a living chamber when you see it—unforgettable."

"I can only imagine." Milo returned the smile.

"This may seem like an odd question," said Logan. "But do you know anything about bombs? Controlled demolitions?"

"No more than the average former fireworks-obsessed teenager."

"Something is bothering me about the entranceway," said Logan, thinking out loud as he ignored Milo's droll comment. "At this point I'm completely positive it was brought down using explosives. Just look at this place. Whoever did it collapsed the entire entrance."

Milo glanced around the caved-in chamber. "They did a thorough enough job of it, all right."

"Thorough, yes. But inefficient."

"How so?"

"Standard operating protocol would be to drill about three to six feet into the ceiling, pack, and detonate. It's a universally utilized technique dating back to the 1700s. But whoever blew this passageway looks like they just threw everything they had into the chamber and set it off. Like they were in a hurry, couldn't be bothered to do it right."

"Just lit the fuse and walked away," guessed Milo.

Logan frowned. "Not necessarily," he said, speaking more to himself than Milo. "More than likely wasn't set off using a fuse . . . the main charge was probably paired with a precursor explosive . . . or maybe they used an electrical charge with an ignition plunger . . ."

Milo tried to follow the train of thought, but soon Logan was simply mumbling to himself as he tapped at the collapsed rock with a small hammer. He was probably making too much of it all. A hurry? Maybe the last visitors simply broke their drill and couldn't get another one. This was Africa, after all.

The chaotic jumble of rock soon gave way to smooth walls and a flat floor as Milo crept further into the cave passageway. With no more blast-scarred walls or collapsed ceiling, the cave almost resembled the long central gallery of an abandoned museum, a grand chamber complete with small alcoves and side passageways. Milo's light fell upon loose, broken potsherds, broken flints, strings of coins and animal teeth: the first evidence of ritual practices. His heart leapt into his throat, trembling at the significance of the discovery.

Ahead, Bridget stood facing a smooth section of cave wall, her light reflecting off the surface and softly illuminating her wonder-filled face.

"Look," she whispered, motioning Milo to stand beside her. Milo gazed at the cave wall, and before him materialized a tall mural of petroglyphs. Elongated figures shone in the artificial light, hunting stick-legged buffalo and elephants, the ancient stories cast in vivid red pigments against the stone. The pair traced the wall deeper into the cave, staring as their lamps fell across alcove windows. Ivory and stone idols stood within, some flat and broken from the blast, others standing defiantly tall. Carved African faces stared back at Milo, the figurines flush with rounded bellies and full, drooping breasts. Before them lay empty grit-filled dishes, the food offerings within long since turned to dust.

"They must be goddesses," breathed Bridget, barely able to speak. "They're so intricate."

"The carved figures are relatively modern, but these paintings appear ancient," whispered Milo, matching her reverence. "When the first

Egyptian step pyramid was under construction at Saqqara, the paintings could have been already thirty thousand years old. Some say the
emergence of cave art marked when we became human—when we first
transitioned into a species unlike any that had come before."

"Incredible."

"This could be one of the greatest finds of this decade. It's hard to
fathom, but stone art from this region dates back 40,000 years. Mumba
Cave in South Africa has signs of human activity from 70,000 BC."

Together, Bridget and Milo stood frozen in wonderment, almost
as if a single spoken word between them would desecrate the sacred
space. From behind them, Milo could hear the crunching footsteps of
Logan and Joanne. Milo couldn't understand why, but the other six,
Dale among them, had already crossed the threshold to the next chamber, nearly a hundred yards distant.

"It's very vaginal," said Logan, pointing at one of the sacred alcoves.
"From an artistic perspective, I mean. Would make sense given the fertility ritual artifacts."

"Let's not dally," said Joanne, interrupting Logan. "This is just the
entrance; we have a great deal of ground to cover before we make it to
the main shaft. I don't want to be left behind."

"We'll come back, take photos of everything," said Milo. "There's a
dozen publishable papers in this chamber alone—we'll all get credit for
the discovery."

"Dale will get credit, at least," said Logan.

"I thought you just studied expeditions," said Bridget, ignoring Logan's cynicism. "How come you know so much about cave paintings?"

"The San people were the first explorers," answered Milo. "They
were the first people, the ones who left Africa to colonize the entire
world. If hunter-gatherers worshipped in this cave, it's overwhelmingly
likely that they were San."

"Their art is incredible," said Joanne from behind him.

"It's not art," whispered Milo, gently correcting her. "It's magic. Imagine these images by torchlight. They'd be given life. Ritual practitioners

danced into a hallucinatory trance-state, and the paintings danced with them. See the eight-legged animals? It's a lenticular effect—between the flickering firelight and the tricks of the human mind, these animals *ran*. This isn't a rock wall; it's a veil between our world and the spirit realm."

Milo leaned in, looking even closer, as though he could bridge the separation of 40,000 years in the space of a single breath.

"Trance-dancing?" asked Joanne, shaking her head.

"The shamans would dance for hours until entering an altered state, during which their spirits would leave their bodies and travel the breadth of the earth. They could sink into the earth and swim the great subterranean river. At the end of the river, they would find threads of light, which they could climb into the sky."

"What would they find in the sky?" asked Bridget.

"Depends on the interpretation," said Milo. "Some would plead their case before God—ask Him to spare a sick member of the tribe, grant favors, rain, fertility, that sort of thing. Others said they'd commune with the trickster demon, the first shaman."

"The devil," said Joanne. "You're saying they'd see . . . the *devil*."

"Or they'd simply traverse the cosmos," said Milo. "Explore the universe—free of their earthly bodies."

Bridget shivered as she turned away from the cave paintings. "Anyone else get the feeling of being watched?"

Joanne led the way deeper into the cave, the lights before them having already vanished into the next chamber. Milo adjusted his headlamp downward, letting the illumination play across the dry mud floor.

"Dale was right about one thing," said Milo, pointing down as he kept pace with the other three. "Check it out—elephant tracks."

"Amazing they made it this far into the cave," said Bridget, bending down to trace the outline of an oversize imprint. "Look at them—all these jumbled footprints on top of one another. The pilgrims could have visited this site for centuries, even thousands of years."

Milo felt a hand on his shoulder, pulling him aside as Bridget and Joanne continued toward the next chamber. Logan stood beside him, unflinching even as Milo accidentally blasted him in the face with his headlamp.

"All these observations—very important, very important, no question," mumbled Logan.

Milo felt a sudden tingle of worry; Logan seemed restless, or even agitated. "What's up?" whispered Milo. "Are you okay?"

"All these things we see," said Logan, eyes darting, his voice too fast and low. "But what do you . . . *not* see?"

"I really don't know what you're talking about," admitted Milo. An experienced caver acting in such a squirrelly fashion worried him— what was so unsettling?

"Where is everybody?" asked Logan. "It's been bothering me from the moment I rolled into camp. Where are the Tanzanian archaeologists? Interpreters? Guides? Government representatives? Local porters? I don't think Dale has told the authorities about this expedition—which means everything we're doing down here is unsanctioned and illegal."

CHAPTER 8:

THE ELEPHANT TOMB

300 feet below the surface

T hough the rest of the party had disappeared into the second chamber, their echoing voices remained. Milo could only assume they were waiting for Joanne, Bridget, Logan, and himself. Milo glanced up as he passed beneath the mammoth fossil-impregnated limestone archway separating the chambers, his headlamp playing across the multi-hued sedimentary layers and the mineralized shells of primitive aquatic invertebrates. The division between the two rooms was stark. After a distinct and immediate rise up three wide stone steps, the second chamber more resembled an auditorium, with a high, domed ceiling and vanishingly distant walls. The larger of the hanging stalactites and growing stalagmites had long since met, foresting sections of the chamber with thick columns like that of an ancient temple.

The walls around Milo glittered with crystals as he traced the circumference of the room with his light. Unlike the flat mud floor of the previous chamber, tectonic forces had cleaved the auditorium in two, leaving a deep, gaping crevasse ten meters wide and four times as long in the center of the chamber. There were no more shrines—though the gods had graciously received their worshippers in the gallery, the auditorium was now the uncontested domain of the underworld, devoid of even the faintest human fingerprint.

"Look at the walls," said Logan, guiding Milo's attention to the crumbling earth at eye level. He moved closer, his light revealing a bas-relief of endless crisscross scrapings stretching from his boots to far above his head.

"What am I looking at?" asked Milo, brushing his fingers across the rough crosshatching.

"This chamber was formed biomorphically," said Logan. "Elephants used their tusks to dig rocks out of the walls; they'd grind them up with their molars and swallow them for the salt. They would have continually hollowed out this section over a hundred thousand years or more."

"Incredible—creating a room of this size, one mouthful at a time," marveled Milo, imagining the two thousand successive generations of the massive animals making their way through darkness and silence. He wondered if they too treated this as a shrine, a sacred place.

"The climate has changed a lot," added Logan as he absentmindedly picked up a loose conglomeration of petrified elephant dung and squeezed it. It gently exploded to dust in his hand, the glittering fragments slowly drifting to the cave floor. "They probably liked to wallow in the mud outside when this region was wetter. We're in a true wild cave now."

Charlie had posed himself in front of Isabelle's camera at the edge of the room-cleaving chasm. Dale and Isabelle prompted the host with questions as the two guides set up powerful lamps in various parts of the chamber, illuminating it throughout. With each take, Charlie leaned closer to the camera, conspiratorially pointing out dubious sources of danger and shoehorning the phrase "extreme history" in at every opportunity.

Milo recognized—and hated—the style. It was the same artificial, self-serious tone adopted by any number of interchangeable media personalities, making a mockery out of rigorous scientific and historical study. Still, it was hard to fault Charlie for his genuine earnestness. Milo concluded that Charlie would have made the world's best middle school instructor, but had the unfortunate luck of family fortune and handsome features and would thus never satisfy his true calling.

"If this is all illegal, should we be filming everything?" asked Milo, feeling a little stupid for broaching the subject again.

"It wouldn't be the first time Dale has asked forgiveness rather than permission," said Bridget. "I'm sure he has a plan. Hell, the fact that it's illegal will probably only increase interest in Charlie's pilot."

Logan couldn't take his eyes off Charlie; he shook his head and grumbled every time the man said something particularly stupid or inflated. Bridget seemed to not hear him at all; she studied the walls of the cave as though enraptured, a look of pure marvel across her wide eyes and open mouth. Watching her, Milo tried to bury a familiar twinge of longing in his stomach.

Separating from Logan and Bridget, Milo traced his way along the far wall, away from the glare of the camera. The earth beneath his feet crunched louder with every step until it felt almost soft, like thawed grass underneath a thin layer of spring ice.

Milo bent down, casting the light of his headlamp at his feet.

Dead bats.

Thousands—no, tens of thousands—lay piled beneath his thick boots, mummified to little more than wispy pelts, brittle skin and dried, yellow bones. Their thin membranes had long since withered away, leaving the rat-like bodies with frozen, open mouths and empty eye sockets, the wings now long, delicate claws.

Milo slowly backed away, retracing his steps, wincing each time he crushed the fragile skeletons beneath his feet. The layer of bodies was easily six inches deep, more in some sections. He imagined the entire ceiling was once alive, rippling with movement as the bats slept and groomed and raised young. He thought perhaps some had died from the initial blast at the distant entrance, the concussion ripping down the confined gallery and spilling into the elephants' salt mine. Others would have perished from stress, their sensitive eardrums ruptured by the terrible noise. Any survivors would have futilely sought an exit for weeks, only to starve and die; a feast for the insects that preyed upon their bodies and guano, until the insects too succumbed in the now-sealed environment.

Bridget met Milo at the edge of the mummified carpet, bending down to take a closer look. She'd freed a ballpoint pen from a pocket, speared one of the tiny mummies, and held it up to her headlamp, slowly rotating the corpse before her intent, inquisitive eyes.

"I hate bats," she finally said, sliding the body off the pen and wiping it on her trousers before replacing it in her breast pocket.

Across the chasm, Isabelle had finished filming and unhooked her camera from the tripod. Warm from the hot lights, Charlie Garza wiped sweat from his forehead and adjusted his form-fitting cotton shirt. Dale and Isabelle paced the length of the chasm, speaking in low tones as they discussed the next shot. The two guides had left already, hauling rope-stuffed dry bags across the auditorium chamber.

"Get a load of *this*," shouted Charlie. All seven turned to watch as he removed a powerful LED floodlight from a camera bag and aimed it into the chasm. Milo and Bridget cautiously approached and leaned over the edge from the other side of the seemingly infinite abyss. Below, the vertical walls led down just forty feet to a flat mud bottom almost entirely obscured with thick, splintered bones and flaking brown elephant leather. At first the bodies looked like a haphazard collection, a half-hidden mass grave, but the longer Milo looked the more he could see order of it all, the complete skeletons piled atop each other. He shivered—the skulls were tusked and cycloptic, like the massacred young of some prehistorical elder god.

"Elephant bones," Bridget murmured. "Calves and juveniles by the looks of it. Maybe a dozen?"

"Maybe more," said Milo, pulling back from the edge. "We don't know how deep that mud is."

"The babies must have fallen in the dark, couldn't get out," said Bridget.

"Somebody get me a harness and rappelling gear," demanded Charlie from the other end of the chasm as he pointed at the grave. "We could get some *killer* shots down there. Never mind that—I could just down-climb."

Milo turned to see how Bridget would react, but her face had gone ashy and cold, her mind vanishingly distant.

"Charlie!" Isabelle snapped her fingers at the host. "Go find one of the guides to help. Is anyone going to care if we rearrange some of the skulls?"

"We can do this gonzo." Charlie lowered himself to a sitting position and dangled his feet over the ledge. "Maybe a GoPro helmet mount? Get the POV look?"

"Everybody stop what you're doing *right now*," Bridget shouted, raising her arms. "We need to get out of this chamber—we're in danger."

CHAPTER 9:

SHAFT

650 feet below the surface

Bridget didn't drop the shirtsleeve from her mouth and nose until after the cavers squeezed through a fifth elbow passage, worming their way between jagged boulders and tall columns. A strange ambient noise increased as they descended deeper into the cave—with every step the silence of the elephant graveyard gave way to a mounting baritone roar that reverberated through the tight, intersecting tunnels. The dull, ceaseless noise and claustrophobia were almost overwhelming—Milo felt as though he'd held his breath for hours.

The team formed a line as they continued their escape. Lagging far behind the cave guides, Dale led the troupe, followed by Charlie, Isabelle, Bridget, Milo and finally Logan.

"Are we safe now?" Dale demanded, turning around from the head of the line, inadvertently dazzling everyone with his powerful headlamp. Milo closed his eyes and saw dancing black spots.

"Safe from what?" wheezed Charlie, sweat running down his forehead and into his eyes. "What were we even running from?"

Isabelle again mounted the camera to her shoulder and was now pointing the lens at face after worried face. Milo caught a glimpse of his reflection in the clear glass and saw his own dread.

"I can't *believe* I didn't get the doctor's freakout on camera," complained Isabelle, having now caught her breath. "Maybe we could re-shoot from the other side of the passage, splice it back up later?"

"Not a freakout." Defensive anger crept into Bridget's voice. "And save your bullshit stage direction for Charlie—I will *not* be repeating myself, on this or any other matter."

"I *still* don't know what happened back there." Charlie huffed as he pulled himself between two wet columns. Everyone else had removed their backpacks at the section, but Charlie did not, muscling himself through the narrows with brute force.

"You were running from Marburg," answered Bridget, ducking under a particularly low stalactite. "I'd have to run tests to be sure, but that chamber was a perfect convergence zone—tight quarters, animal remains, the constant temperature and humidity required to preserve viral RNA structures. It was *clearly* inhabited by bats, elephants, and probably some other mammals as well, all with overlapping feeding, breeding, and migration patterns. If the virus ever passed through this region, it could still be hibernating there."

"Marburg?" asked Charlie. "What the hell is Marburg?"

"Marburg *virus*," said Bridget, "causes internal hemorrhaging with an eighty-percent-plus fatality rate. It's in the same viral family as Ebola and yellow fever. Nasty business; basically melts the infected victim from the inside out. Ever hear of Uganda's Kitum Cave?"

"Kitum is a non-solutional *pyroclastic* cave," said Dr. Logan Flowers. "Predominantly formed by Mount Elgon's volcanic activity. The geology has *nothing* in common."

"In viral terms, the geologic makeup is far less important than animal habitation." Bridget sighed and unclipped the chinstrap to briefly remove her helmet, pausing to run a hand through her long hair before re-buckling it. "The bats could have passed the virus from cave to cave, as could elephant migratory routes. Marburg virus—which bats carry, but are now immune to—twice escaped incubation in Kitum, killing dozens in 1980 and 1987, almost igniting a 2014-sized pandemic in both cases. It is a *highly* infectious virus. Without the proper protocols, any contact with bat remains, powdered guano, or a deceased elephant presents an unacceptable risk.

"Once the local Ugandans found out about Kitum and Marburg," Bridget continued, "they put a machine-gun nest above the entrance and shot any elephant that approached. Reduced a herd of 2,000 down to just seventy. The few survivors scattered across Uganda and joined other herds; the tusks disappeared into the ivory trade. The elephants won't return to Kitum. 'Mining' behaviors are learned, not instinctual."

"Two thousand elephants?" repeated Charlie. "That's horrible. Did anybody try to stop it? My father's foundations deal with *exactly* this sort of—"

"Bottom line," interrupted the doctor, "if I wanted to catch Marburg, I'd have jumped into that crevasse with Charlie. Doesn't matter that the cave was sealed for decades—a dormant virus won't die because it was technically never alive to begin with."

"How was I supposed to know?" griped Charlie, more irritated than embarrassed.

"That's the problem," mumbled Logan. "He doesn't know what he doesn't know."

"What's that?" asked Dale. "I couldn't hear what you said."

"Just keep Charlie away from me over the next couple of days." Logan shimmied between two rock walls, his headlamp gently bumping against rock. "Especially if he starts barfing up congealed blood. It's one of the first symptoms."

"Seriously?" A note of fear entered Charlie's his voice for the first time.

"He's messing with you," said Bridget. "But even so, I want everybody to remain cautious. Marburg isn't the only thing to worry about down here. We'll need to keep an eye out for histoplasmosis as well. It's a fungal infection of the lung tissue that can be fatal if not treated promptly. Then you have your run-of-the-mill bacterial infections."

"Rather have histo-whatever than Ebola," said Charlie, still far from consoled.

"Dead is dead," said Logan. "And histoplasmosis is a pretty ugly way to go."

"Again—infection risks should remain low," said Bridget, "so long as everybody avoids the worst concentrations of fecal residue and osseous matter."

"Stay out of shit and dead bodies." Isabelle laughed as she put her camera down. "Don't have to tell *me* twice."

"Ivory may pose a temptation," mused Milo. "Assuming there are porters or other support personnel coming in after us."

"It's a good point," said Logan. "Once we establish supply lines, there will be a steady stream of diggers, riggers, and Sherpas. If it was up to me, I'd burn it all—but I'm a geologist, bones are not my area."

"That's enough of that," said Dale, stopping dead to turn around and address the entire line. The party came to a jolting, awkward halt. "Nobody's burning anything. You can trust my people without reservation. Even if there wasn't a disease risk, they all know they are *not* to touch anything."

"Milo does bring up a good point," said Bridget. "I didn't even think about the tusks—somebody might see ivory and think dollar signs—"

"Dollar signs? Not these days," interrupted Logan. "Stacks of Chinese yuan, more likely."

"I said, *that's enough*," snapped Dale, waving the group to follow him further down the tunnel. "*Nobody* in the support team is going ivory-hunting. So drop it already."

The rushing roar in the far distance gained in strength with every twist. Dale turned the final corner, exiting the passageway with the team shortly behind. As the party entered a massive chamber, the surrounding sound level exploded in volume. The wet, mist-filled room dwarfed the elephant graveyard in every dimension and sensation; with a distant, angled ceiling overtop a narrow lip ringing an oblong, 250-foot-wide shaft. Looking down, Milo felt a little dizzy, as though he were standing at the edge of an ancient, impossibly deep well, the lights of their headlamps unable to permeate the gargantuan, churning depth.

Though the top of the shaft far above them was dry, the first waterfall burst through the wall just fifty feet below. More waterfalls joined every hundred feet as the pit pierced older and older geologic levels, eventually pouring incredible volumes of white, foamy water into the abyss.

"Those aren't just waterfalls," said Logan to Milo, shouting over the noise. "They're artesian springs—the uppermost falls are siphoned right out of the topsoil, may have fallen as rain just a few days ago. Further down are fossil water tables, trapped thousands, even millions of years ago as the geology of this region changed."

Milo nodded, amazed. Duck and Joanne had beaten them there, and were busy setting up piles of ropes and equipment at the far side of the shaft where the narrow lip was the widest. Seeing the rest of the party, Dale waved them over. Everyone followed, side-shuffling along the wall and being careful not to step too close to the slippery edge.

Inspecting the new arrivals, Dale grinned as he reached into his pack. He withdrew a taped bundle of eight road flares, the grouping resembling dynamite but missing the Looney Tunes wires and Acme wind-up clock. Flipping open a Zippo lighter, Dale held the flame to the end of the flares. The first flare touched off with a hiss, dripping flames as the others burst to life. A flickering red light grew to an overpowering, molten white core in his hand as he held it over the edge. The frothing water below turned blood-red in the harsh illumination.

Milo shielded his eyes against the onslaught of liquid light, the interior of the misty chamber now bright as daylight.

"Duck—Joanne," said Dale. "You ready?"

"Yes." Joanne held her finger to her wristwatch in anticipation. Duck picked up a bowling ball-sized rock and nodded as well.

"Three . . . two . . . one . . . mark!" Dale dropped the flares to the simultaneous beeps of Joanne's watch and the release of Duck's rock. Though the stone disappeared, the light from the flares plummeted into the shaft to the sound of a faint, echoing *whoosh* as the flares tumbled end over end, never hitting the sides, the hissing lost in moments to the bellow of the angry waters. In the initial seconds, Milo saw that the massive shaft below them actually *increased* in width, like the inside of a Coke bottle, growing to over four hundred feet in width before he lost all sense of dimension. Milo expected the flares to disappear, but they didn't—the light seemingly hung in midair as it fell ever deeper.

After an eternity, a ringing *boom* rang out from below, louder than even the waterfalls, the sound of Duck's rock impacting the bottom of the shaft. Milo backed away from the edge, not brave enough to peer into the depths a moment longer.

"What'd you get?" asked Dale to his guides. His voice was almost lost in the awesome noise.

"Thirteen-point-five seconds." Joanne grinned as she looked up from her digital watch.

"What does that make for depth?" asked Duck.

Dale and the two guides huddled, mumbling and interrupting each other. Milo caught bits and pieces about air resistance and falling objects as Duck furiously scribbled numbers into a waterproof notepad.

"Puts us at about . . . fifteen hundred feet," said Duck.

Milo felt a wave of incredulity wash over him. Fifteen hundred feet— the sheer height of the shaft was almost impossible to visualize. He tried to put it in terms he could understand. Fifteen hundred feet? That was longer than a quarter mile, higher than one-and-a-half Eiffel Towers. Milo felt a little nauseated just thinking about it.

Dale nodded. "That's about what we expected," he said. "We spooled out about the same for the Rover."

"Better be right," said Duck with a bit of a frown. "Rope lines are sixteen hundred feet. Wouldn't be good to come up short, get left dangling above the bottom."

"True, true!" Dale nodded enthusiastically. "But we'll have to make a note to come back with a laser survey—we'll set the African record for pit caves for certain."

"Probably not the only record we'll set today," added Duck.

"Think we might find any bodies at the bottom?" asked Charlie. "In some cultures they performed human sacrifices into pits like this."

"That's revolting," said Joanne, wrinkling her nose.

"Pick six independent anchor points for the descent ropes." Dale pointed his guides to a set of massive stone columns. "We'll set up three systems—each one with a main line and a backup line. Duck, Joanne, and I will each take one or two people and as much gear as we can carry per trip. Logan can rappel on his own if he wants."

"As long as I can use my own gear," said Logan.

"You got it," said Dale, only halfway listening as he tied off the first of six ropes to a mammoth stone column.

Isabelle broke away from the rest of the party, moving over to another part of the ledge, getting a better shooting angle as the camera panned back and forth across the entire troupe, zooming in and out under the illumination of a portable floodlight.

Finished, Dale looked at his guides, to the group of inexperienced cavers, and back again. He nodded curtly and stood up to formally address everyone for the first time since they entered the cave.

"I suppose this is as good as time as any to set some ground rules," boomed the CEO. "You may know me as Dale, but down here I am God Almighty. My word is scripture. And if you listen to me about footwear, I'll even save your sole."

A chuckle rippled throughout the group and Milo caught a knowing smirk flash across Dale's face.

"But unlike God," shouted Dale, an edge entering his voice, "I will *not* forgive you if you fuck up. So don't. This is a phased mission. The two-week first phase will, if possible, establish the location and circumstances of Lord Riley DeWar's disappearance. Listen to your guides; follow their instructions and you'll be fine. Then the geeks go home and the second phase begins—where my team spends two months mapping and diving the entirety of this cave. With a little luck, we'll officially establish this system as one of the largest in the world."

Nearby, Duck crossed his arms and nodded with pride.

"Expect suffering," continued Dale, his voice rising. "Caves are not for wimps. We will easily lose a pound or more of bodyweight every day. You have two weeks ahead of you, two weeks of rappelling and climbing, difficult drops while wearing heavy packs, extended crawls, malnutrition, light deprivation, sleep deprivation, and the very real potential of hypothermia."

"And diarrhea," added Duck. "Don't forget diarrhea."

Milo glanced over to see Bridget frowning. He knew for a fact she'd worked for each and every pound of hard-earned muscle and didn't relish the idea of losing any of it.

"We're going to do this slow and steady," said Dale, looking up from his first completed anchor-point, the thick nylon rope secured to a massive column with a series of knots and carabiners. "Duck will need two of you to accompany him. Don't kick anything loose, but if you do, yell *rock* as loud as you can so anybody further down can get out of the way. Who's first?"

Charlie Garza took a step back from the rim and sucked in a deep breath as Isabelle's camera trained toward him.

"I'm first," he said, winking at the camera.

And then he threw himself over the edge, plunging headlong into the abyss.

CHAPTER 10:

CONTROLLED DESCENT

725 feet below the surface

Chaos erupted. Bridget stifled a shriek and grabbed Milo's arm. His vision went dizzy and sickness welled in the pit of his stomach. Nearby, Joanne turned away, burying her face in her hands as Logan and Duck dropped to their stomachs, aiming their powerful flashlights into the shaft. Adding to the confusion, Isabelle swept back and forth with a camera, blinding everyone with a floodlight as she filmed.

Far below, an audible *poof* sounded just as a flashlight caught the edge of a colorful parachute disappearing into the misty abyss. Charlie's joyful whooping and hollering echoed throughout the chamber.

Logan looked up from the deep well with dawning realization, briefly training his furious gaze from Milo's horrified expression to Isabelle's running camera. The geologist's face reddened, cheeks flushing as a large, twisting vein in his forehead engorged itself on his anger.

Smiling, Dale lifted a walkie-talkie to his mouth. "Charlie, come in," he said. "You okay down there?"

Milo began to mouth incredulous words, but no sound came from his lips. Silence and crackling static buzzed from the radio, shrill against the churning waterfalls.

"You okay down there?" repeated Dale. "Charlie?"

The radio crackled to life suddenly, making Milo jump. "Goddamn!" came Charlie's voice, now distant and high-pitched over the transmission. "What a rush! All good down here. Shit, man . . . I'm still shaking. May have rolled my ankle a bit on the landing, but I'm fine."

Unable to listen to another second of the self-congratulatory report, Joanne stormed over, yanked off her leather climbing gloves, and aimed a finger at Dale's face.

"That man is a *fucking arsehole*," she shouted, jamming the digit into the center of Dale's chest. "He is *done*, bloody well *done*."

A flicker of annoyance crossed Dale's face before disappearing, replaced by a wide, conciliatory smile as Duck interjected himself, physically pulling Joanne back.

"Oh, don't be so hard on him," said Dale, ignoring the jabs and placing a fatherly hand on Joanne's shoulder. "Charlie has been base-jumping for years. Just last month, he was at the Cave of Swallows in Mexico. You think I would have permitted this if I didn't have total confidence in his abilities?"

"I'm going down that shaft," said Joanne, her voice cold with anger. "And once I'm at the bottom, I'm sending him back to America. Hogtied, if need be."

Hearing raised voices, Isabelle swiveled her camera to the arguing pair, pouring harsh light over them both.

"No, no, no," said Duck, pointing at Isabelle. "Do *not* even start with the camera right now. Are you for real?"

"Put 'er down," said Dale, waving apologetically to the producer. "Take five. We'll pick back up in a minute—maybe do some interviews. I want to reshoot Charlie on the radio; give you a couple of takes to choose from."

"You're the boss." Isabelle shrugged as she flicked off the camera to conserve the battery. "Won't be as dramatic as *this*, but your call."

"I can't have this cowboy nonsense on an expedition," said Joanne, her voice now whisper-quiet as she leaned in to Dale. "You know it—I know it. Completely unacceptable. You know what happens if you break your leg back home? Paramedics come in ten minutes; you're at hospital inside twenty. Think about what happens out here. First we have to carry you out of the cave. An hour to abseil, an hour to package the patient, maybe four or five to get back out to basecamp. Then *ten hours* and a border crossing to Nairobi, which *still* doesn't have a proper trauma center. God forbid he got a serious head injury on the way down, Dale. The closest treatment option isn't even on this bloody *continent*."

"I hear you," said Dale, raising his hands in mock surrender. "Message received. But I need you to see this from my perspective. I'm backing his television series—just like I'm backing your firm's charity foundation. His first episode needs excitement, something nobody has seen before. This was his moment, the moment that will sell the entire show. Nothing else will happen without your say-so, I promise. No more surprises."

"You should have warned us." Joanne scowled as she looked up from the rope anchor she'd tied at the base of a particularly large stalagmite.

"Yeah," added Duck. "Seriously not cool, man."

"Everybody," said Dale, addressing the group with open arms like a circus ringmaster. "I'm sorry for the surprise jump, I really am. But I promise we'll all laugh about this soon."

Bridget, Logan, and Milo all looked at each other uncomfortably as Logan mumbled something that sounded like *doubtful*.

The anger had drained from Joanne's face, replaced by ice-cold resolve. "Nobody's laughing, Dale. Most of us thought we'd just watched a man jump to his death."

"I'll make you a deal," said Dale, trying but failing to match Joanne's deadpan intonation. "Get us down to the bottom of the shaft. If you're still mad when everybody's safely below, we'll send Charlie home, okay?"

"You'd better be serious about that deal," said Joanne, breaking away from the older man to return to the other guides. "Because this is *not* over. He's going home—or I am."

Dale folded his arms and frowned, absentmindedly nudging at the muddy cave floor with his boot as he collected his thoughts.

"Take a moment and look around," Dale finally said, total earnestness filling his voice. "What we are already doing is groundbreaking, record-setting. I can understand why Charlie's little stunt—well-planned as it was—bothered you. Like I said, no more surprises, we'll follow your lead and stick to the rules from now on. Can you back me up, Isabelle?"

The producer nodded in agreement. "No more stunts," she agreed.

Joanne just swore under her breath and shook her head furiously, returning to Duck and the rest, checking their knots and set up the last of the ropes and carabiners.

The guides finished their work on the three rope systems while the rest of the party milled about in awkward silence.

"Dr. McAffee and Ms. Christian," commanded Dale, waving Bridget and Isabelle over as he finished. "You two are on the first trip down with Duck."

"Aww yeah!" said Duck, breaking the tension. "Ladies first!"

Each woman was tied into their harness with Duck in the middle, Bridget and Isabelle carrying small backpacks while Duck hung two hundred pounds of stuffed backpacks and duffels from the seat of his own harness. For safety, each was linked up to a main line, a safety line, and then roped again to Duck for good measure.

"How much weight can these ropes support?" whispered Bridget, her eyes cast over the dizzying array of carabiners, harnesses, and synthetic line.

"Each of these lines can hold about two Batmobiles," said Duck as he leaned back in his harness, testing the elasticity of the line and preparing to lower himself down the fifteen hundred feet to the bottom. "It's more or less a standard unit of measurement."

"Excuse me?" said Isabelle, nervously adjusting her helmet for the tenth time. "What does that even mean?"

"It's, like, super technical," said Duck. "You know that crazy car from the Batman movies? The one that looked like a tank made a baby with a Lamborghini? Yeah, so each of these ropes could support the weight of two Batmobiles, plus Batman. It's eleven millimeters thick. That's good for, like, five tons apiece, probably a lot more under ideal conditions. Awesome, right?"

"It's somewhat reassuring," admitted Bridget.

"I've had a lot of gear break on me, but never one of these rope systems," said Duck, winking. "I got you."

"It's not the rope I'm worried about," said Isabelle. Those were the last words Milo heard as the trio leaned back against the taut lines and disappeared into the darkness.

Milo couldn't get used to the hurry-up-and-wait pace of the expedition. With Bridget, Isabelle, and Duck over the edge, there wasn't anything to do but sit on a rock and wait for his turn as Joanne did the final adjustments for Dale and Logan. Milo could tell Logan felt more than a little insulted about the amateur-hour treatment. But after Charlie's parachute plunge into the shaft, Logan had wisely decided not to push Joanne's patience.

He couldn't help but imagine what DeWar would have used more than a century ago. Without the benefit of synthetic ropes, wall anchors, or rappelling racks, his expedition would have been stuck with rope ladders, maybe even a mule-and-winch setup.

A few minutes later, an all-clear sounded over the radio. Soon Dale and Logan went over the edge as well.

Joanne was too busy to talk, leaving Milo in silence. He'd just failed Joanne's pre-rappel checklist due to an improperly secured climbing harness—the same test everyone else had passed with flying colors. It suddenly occurred to Milo that he was the only one that had never been rappelling before.

"We Brits call it *abseiling*," said Joanne as she tied the last knot to his harness. "I first learned how from an ex-SAS commando I was dating at the time. We went over the edge of St. John's Head, the tallest cliff in Scotland."

Milo nodded, listening as intently as he could through his growing fear.

"You are linked to me," continued Joanne. "Even if both your main and safety lines fail—a near impossibility unto itself—you'll still be safe as safe can be. But please—no mucking about, and *especially* no swinging as we make our way down. If these ropes fail, you'll be falling at a speed of 200 kilometers an hour when you hit the bottom. So go at my pace at all times. Got it?"

Milo nodded as Joanne finished tying up his harness, trying to imagine what that much velocity would do to a human body upon impact. He felt a little uncomfortable with the sheer level of mental intensity directed at his crotch as she manipulated the rope, but appreciated her thoroughness nonetheless.

After what felt like hours of waiting, the all-clear call came in over the radio, allowing the final duo to slowly back up to the open chasm, waiting to descend. The last one, Milo leaned back, allowing the rope to take his weight little by little, until he was almost horizontal hanging over the edge. And then he allowed the rope to gently slip through his gloved fingers, lowing himself inches at a time into the pit. The entire sensation was alien, nerve-wracking. Everything about it felt so *wrong*.

"Speed up," said Joanne from below. "Smooth and steady. You'll take hours at this rate."

Milo nodded and allowed the rope to slip through his rappel device at a greater clip. In an instant, he disappeared into the mist, sucking in the cool air one ragged breath at a time. As he blinked back moisture, the reverberating waterfalls took on a new intensity, as though he were on the inside of a massive drum. Beneath him, a wind gathered, swirling through the chasm.

A foot turned into five, into twenty, and then a hundred as Milo spiraled into the depths. Soon he was lost in the darkness and wet, seeing only the cave wall before him, the entrance and the bottom lost to the lightless mist. The sense of floating, of freedom, was incredible, his truncated senses revealing no true conception of the sheer length of the drop. The shaft widened as he slowly spun on the rope, creating a lazy helix with his rotating form.

Clinging moisture seeped into every layer of his clothing, chilling him. The falling waters gained force as he descended, transforming the gentle pattering sensation on his helmet to a hard, gravel-like impact.

A crackle came over the radio, and Joanne held up her hands for Milo to stop. Milo held the rope tightly against his hip, not allowing it to slip through the metallic friction device on his harness. In the silence, he slowly swayed back and forth in his nylon seat, a weight at the end of a thousand-foot pendulum, the glistening, craggy wall just inches away from his furthest reach.

"We must hang here for a tick," said Joanne, turning off her headlamp to conserve the battery. "Bit of a logjam at the bottom, a couple of the ropes became tangled."

Deciding to leave his own on, Milo took a moment to consider his situation, hoping to bury his still-burning fear with another layer of rationality. The rope suspending him was hardy enough to heft a truck, and it was secured to a million-year-old limestone column. Then there was the safety line, the safety-safety line, and Joanne's emergency line. On balance, the descent was likely safer than an average bicycle commute through Georgetown.

But without warning, Milo's mind seized on the nothingness below him. He couldn't tell if he was a foot or a thousand feet above the bottom of the endless yawning maw. The mask of reason was violently ripped away, leaving Milo with short, gulping breath. Sweat poured from his face, mixing hot and salty with the cool water vapor. His hands tingled and the onions from his last meal bubbled up into his raw throat.

With his feet dangling in the air, Milo was clenched by a single, unshakable thought.

I'm going to die down here.

CHAPTER 11:

THE ANCHOR

1,100 feet below the surface

P ain radiated down Milo's chest and legs, as though his heart had turned to ice and now pumped freezing liquid throughout his body. His heartbeat thumped deafening in his ears, louder even than the cascading waterfalls. He tried to force air into his lungs but could only manage little hiccups. He was choking, his vision gray. He needed to *run*, but was trapped as the walls of the shaft dropped away, leaving him hanging in nothingness, hard droplets slamming against his plastic helmet like hail.

Milo breathed a wheezing gasp of air, barely enough to keep himself conscious. The rope in his hand slipped and he slid one, three, five feet before catching himself.

"Milo!" shouted Joanne from below him. "Stop fucking about!"

He tried to say something reassuring like *yeah, sure, no problem*, but just loudly coughed.

"Milo!" said Joanne again, but this time Milo couldn't even speak, his jaw and mouth clenched in fear, flashes of heat all over his body overpowering the freezing spray.

But then in front of him, a sparkle of refracted light pierced through the void and the fear and the pain, a delicate pinpoint almost lost behind a sheen of moisture. Milo fixated his entire attention on the glint, trying not to think about the fact that he couldn't *breathe*, couldn't *think*, couldn't *move*.

He had to reach the glint.

Pulling in a single jagged, uncertain breath, Milo wiggled his frozen, tingling legs back and forth, swinging toward the wet, rocky wall of the shaft. The glint came almost close enough to touch, then fell away.

"Bloody hell, Milo!" shouted Joanne. "What are you doing? I told you to stay put!"

"Have . . . to reach . . . the *wall*," murmured Milo through gritted teeth, each swing placing him a tantalizing inch closer to the glint. The rope snaked through his stiff hand, abruptly dropping him another three feet. Kicking against the wall, he swung back, hard, and slammed bodily against the slippery rocks.

The rope harness went loose as Milo held himself up on an inches-wide ledge, allowing feeling to rush back into his twitching, unsteady legs. The drop had put him a few feet below the mysterious glint. He'd have to climb to reach it.

"Milo!" yelled Joanne, fear entering her voice for the first time. "We must get to the *bottom*—please!"

Ignoring her, Milo pressed his face against the rock wall, limiting the spread of his headlamp to an intense circle just inches across. Unable to see his hands or feet in the misty darkness, he felt around for handgrips and footholds until he could drag himself up another precious few inches.

"Oh God," said Joanne, gulping. "Milo, please, please, *please* stop climbing. This is *static* line, not an elastic climbing rope. A drop of even a few feet could cripple you, even *kill* you."

"I'm . . . I'm not climbing out," protested Milo, finally finding his voice. "I just saw something—I need to get a closer look."

He found another handhold, grunting as he dragged himself upward another few inches. The glint was finally within reach. He extended a trembling hand and brushed across its cool surface with his fingers, feeling a small metal anchor bolt secured into the wall. Experimentally, he pulled against it, feeling it just slightly loose in the slimy rock.

"Milo!" pleaded Joanne. "Whatever you're doing is *not* worth it. Talk to me, you *must* talk to me."

"It's a metal anchor," shouted Milo down to the others, feeling the last of his sudden fear slowly slip away as he fumbled in his pocket for a small folding knife. "It's loose—I think I can get it out."

"If you can *talk*, you can *listen*," said Joanne, her fear turning to outright anger. "And if you can listen, you can *bloody well* follow instructions."

"Just give me a second," protested Milo, digging the blade of the knife between the wall and the bolt.

"You'd better not be getting that blade anywhere *near* the rope, Milo," said Joanne. She too kicked back and forth until she reached the wall, clinging to the rocks underneath him.

Without warning, the anchor popped free from the wall. Milo watched in slow motion as it tumbled through his field of vision, corroded stainless steel glinting in the harsh glare of his headlamp, slipping through his outstretched fingers and into the darkness. The sudden jerk had thrown him off balance, and he felt his tenuous grip slip loose.

And then Milo fell.

CHAPTER 12:

BASE CAMP

2,150 feet below the surface

Profound relief washed over Milo as his feet touched the bottom of the shaft. His vision still narrow and gray, he focused all his attention on steadying his shaking hands as he untied the ropes from his harness. Joanne watched him for a moment, dropped her harness with a swift, elegant motion, and strode off purposefully toward Dale.

Descent rope now freed from his harness, Milo took in his surroundings. The base of the shaft opened up to a large chamber, its domed, stalactite-thick ceiling a hundred feet above. The egg-like shape almost resembled a stomach at the end of a long esophagus. The waterfalls joined at the base of the pit, slamming against loose rocks and pooling in a small subterranean lake that drained along a deep, narrow crack spanning the entire length of the new chamber. The mists of the waterfalls fell to the glistening floor, leaving the majority of the colossal room dry and untouched. The noise was almost overwhelming—Milo felt as though he were standing on the deck of an aircraft carrier, a choir of jets throttling their engines for takeoff.

Feeling rushed back into his legs as pent-up blood released from below the straps of the climbing harness. Milo lifted his knees up past his waist, rotating his ankles, feeling the pins-and-needles of nerves coming back to life. Part of him felt relieved at the firm ground now underneath his boots. The other part desperately tried to think of anything other than the over quarter-mile between him and the surface.

At the far end of the auditorium-sized chamber, Joanne had found Dale and was speaking to him in low tones, the pair pausing to take a long, stern look at Milo every few moments. Whatever conflict remained regarding Charlie seemed forgotten, at least for the moment. Nearby, Duck had surveyed a flat, muddy area a good distance away from the waterfalls where he'd begun setting up the first of the tents. Milo was no geologist, but could tell the camp was on a floodplain—but whether the last flood dated from a month or ten thousand years previous, he could not tell.

He took a closer look at the flat bottom of the chamber. It almost resembled a river delta, with thin, snaking lines carved into the smooth bottom and filled in with mud, but only the central crack now serving as a natural aqueduct. The crack ended at an impenetrable, billion-year-old rock layer at the end of the chamber, draining into a lattice of small subterranean passageways.

Milo watched as Duck created a miniature version of Main Camp. Duck had lined up four tents—the party of eight would now have to double up—and started a tiny supply depot. Finished with the tents, Duck meticulously evaluated the gear. Nothing went untouched. Working with a small penknife, he diligently removed labels from tea bags, the handles from toothbrushes, even the cardboard centers out of toilet paper rolls.

The rest of the party had spread out as much as possible. Charlie worked to repack the last of his soggy parachute as Dale watched silently, more interested than helpful.

Dr. Logan Flowers and Isabelle Christian had found themselves at a table-sized rock at the far end of the room, Logan walking the producer around it and narrating about geological compositions and cave morphology. The producer looked bored.

Not sure what to do, Milo found a spot against the wall and sat down, leaning against his backpack to rest and maybe shake off the last of the nerves. Bridget joined before long, wordlessly sitting beside him and opening up a granola bar to share.

"Joanne is not happy," said Bridget, stretching her back. "I figured we were going to see her chew out Charlie the minute he hit the bottom—at the very least, wipe that smug grin off his face—but she hasn't, not yet anyway."

"Yeah?" said Milo. "Why not?"

"Whatever Dale is holding over her must be a doozy," said Bridget. "I know she founded an international development charity through her legal firm; chances are he's funding a big chunk of it."

Silence once again fell between the two. Bridget took another bite of her granola bar and again offered it to Milo. He gratefully broke off another bit of the sweet oat-and-nut confection.

"You see anything on the ground?" Milo finally asked, breaking the silence again.

"Like what?" asked Bridget.

"Small," answered Milo. "Metallic. Looks almost like a ring attached to the end of a bolt."

"Why?" said Bridget. "Did you drop something on the way down? Was it important?"

"Not exactly," said Milo with a sigh. "Not even a hundred percent certain what it was. I spotted it in the wall on the way down. Tried to pry it out, but it slipped out of my fingers and disappeared. I don't think it came from our expedition."

From across the chamber, Milo heard Joanne say something like *he's not your concern*, but it was too late—Dale had turned away from the

guide and was stomping over toward him. Joanne followed closely behind, a furious expression on her face.

"What the hell happened up there?" demanded Dale, addressing
Milo with open disdain.

Milo stood up, if for no other reason than to prevent Dale from towering over him as he spoke.

"I don't know," Milo admitted.

"We are *not* done talking about Charlie," interjected Joanne. "Milo is
not the priority here."

"I'm not going to ask again—what happened during the descent?"
snapped Dale, ignoring her. Milo felt a wave of cold fear wash over him
as the rest of the party began to break away from their duties or distractions and form up in a circle around them.

Milo opened his mouth to speak, but couldn't.

"You panicked," said Dale, answering for him. "You tried to climb
your way out a *thousand feet*, made it up about *five* and *fell*. You hit Joanne
on the way down, probably the only reason you didn't end up with a pelvic fracture. Another few feet up and you could have permanently paralyzed yourself. You endangered your life and the life of my guide."

"But—" began Milo.

"Joanne said you lost it," said Dale, raising his voice so all could hear.
"Wouldn't obey commands, wouldn't communicate your intentions."

"We told you the number of novices on this expedition would be a
problem," interjected Joanne. "But Milo still isn't my primary concern
here."

"I got a little scared, sure," protested Milo. "Who wouldn't? But I'm
telling you—I wasn't trying to climb my way out of the shaft."

"No?" demanded Dale. "Then what the ever-loving *hell* were you
doing up there?"

Bridget stood up before Milo could answer. "He says he found something," she said, cutting off Dale. "Something from another expedition.
In the shaft. Might have been something important to his investigation."

"He found what, exactly?" demanded Joanne.

"Oh bullshit," said Dale, whipping off his caving helmet with a free hand and running the other through his white hair in frustration. "And as for *you*, Dr. McAffee—you vouched for him, so I'm holding you equally responsible for this fuckup."

An awkward silence fell over the group as Milo stewed in his own thoughts. Bridget vouched for him—what the hell was Dale talking about? He knew the world was small, but the supposed coincidence of seeing Bridget again suddenly snapped into focus.

"So, what was it?" said Dale, beginning to lower his voice and retreat from the previous angry outburst. "What'd you supposedly find?"

"It was a wall anchor," said Milo, forcing himself to not flash an angry stare at Bridget. "It had to be."

"Not possible," interrupted Dale. "We haven't placed a single bolt."

Duck broke through the ranks to step up to Milo, excitement in his eyes. "A wall anchor?" he asked. "Could it have been Lord Riley's?"

Milo shook his head. "I'm not an expert," he said, "but he would have used iron, or maybe low-grade steel. What I found looked like stainless steel, but it had been in there for a long time."

"All our carabiners and anchors are aluminum alloy," offered Joanne.

"We are getting way off track here," growled Dale.

"And this is not the first evidence we've seen of another modern expedition," said Milo.

"What are you talking about?" asked Dale, concern entering his voice. Milo suddenly found himself wondering how Dale would react if he found out he was not the true modern discoverer of the cave. Would he pull the plug on the whole expedition?

Milo just pointed to Logan. Everyone turned to look.

"Well, it's hardly definitive," muttered the geologist.

"Tell me anyway," insisted Dale.

"The collapsed entrance," said Logan. "I believe it was brought down by explosives. I developed the theory initially after seeing the first of the robot's footage. The state of the first chamber confirms it—I took samples, but they'll need to be tested in a proper lab."

"I don't understand," said Dale. "You're saying Lord DeWar . . . blew up the cave?"

"No," said Logan. "Whatever was used likely did not exist during his time. Just think about the size of the blast and fracture pattern. It couldn't have been just gunpowder or TNT. This was done using a modern high explosive. If the entrance was the only evidence of modern intrusion, I'd say it was done by farmers or herdsmen years ago, maybe to keep the local cattle from wandering in. But if Milo thinks he found an anchor . . ."

The geologist's voice trailed off as the party considered the implications.

"What happened to the anchor?" asked Dale, his voice barely above a whisper.

"I pried it out of the wall," said Milo. "But then it fell—I lost it."

"You dropped it," concluded Duck. "Well—that's, like, good news, right? If you dropped it, it has to be around here somewhere. Let's start looking!"

"Maybe later," grumbled Dale, thrusting his hands in his pockets as he turned around. He went to the base of the shaft, where the supplies would be lowered down from the surface.

"I'll help look," said Bridget. Logan nodded as well, and soon the four began to poke around the rocky patches of the pit bottom. Joanne just rolled her eyes and walked away.

Milo had only been searching for a few minutes when his headlamp fell across a crumple of metal struts and tank-treads wedged between two large boulders. Excitedly, he waved Duck over.

Half-smiling, the guide pointed his flashlight into the gap, already knowing what he would see.

"That's what's left of our robot," explained Duck, letting the light play over the broken wires, shattered camera glass, and exposed circuit board. "Seventy-five thousand dollars trashed, man. Cable snapped near the upper terminus, probably fell at least a thousand feet. I'll come back and yank all this shit out in a bit—possible we can salvage a few parts, at least."

The searchers broke off from one another, each picking their own areas to carefully examine. At the ropes, Joanne radioed to the porters at the top of the shaft as crates and boxes were lowered one at a time, growing the equipment dump ever larger.

M ilo kept searching long after the others had stopped, even Bridget. Having received the last of the supplies, the guides busied themselves with the latrines, digging long, muddy trenches some distance away from the tents. Working on the theory that the anchor had bounced—all the main areas had been searched, even the pool—Milo focused his efforts on the small pockets and chambers directly adjacent to the main shaft, most too small to even fit much more than his head and shoulders.

He entered the largest of the side chambers, an alcove not much bigger than a small closet. His flashlight fell across a small object. Flush with excitement, Milo bent down to examine it, but was disappointed to only find the small knife he'd dropped during the descent. Somehow it had bounced to the side as it fell, tumbling into the tiny chamber. Milo sighed and turned off his light, wishing he could sink into the darkness and disappear.

Dale was going to be pissed. The last of Milo's credibility was gone, as vanished as Lord DeWar himself. If Dale decided to send anyone home, Milo knew he'd be on the first ascent back to the surface.

Stretching, Milo tried to think of anything but what the next few hours would bring. With too little room in the chamber to reach out without touching both walls, Milo felt the fingers of his left hand brush against something entirely unexpected. Not smooth, like the calcified stalagmites or rough, limestone walls, but a series of deep grooves.

Curious, Milo flipped his headlamp back on and aimed it toward the wall. The grooves were not natural; they instead formed elegant, carved letters in plainly scripted English.

R. DEWAR
1901

CHAPTER 13:

THE ANTHILL

Dale was a picture of barely restrained jubilance. Milo had the distinct impression he was used to working larger gatherings than the eight-person expedition; he paced as though he wanted to tell someone new the good news, issue further congratulations, but had cornered each and every person already. In some cases, he'd spoken with them twice, three times, as if he were still somewhat unconvinced of the find.

Though anybody could have found the inscription—and Milo was convinced someone would have, eventually—he still felt like he'd secured his place in the expedition, however tenuously. Almost everyone had come by to say something nice at some point, though Logan had waited until he'd verified the inscription himself. Milo didn't take it personally; he wouldn't have expected anything less from Logan.

Duck stood in the center of the chamber, inflating large, spherical balloons from a portable helium tank. Once full, the balloons were easily three feet in diameter. Unlike the shiny, high-tech look of the rest of the equipment—aluminum alloys, carbon fiber, advanced plastics—the balloons were made from an old-fashioned, cotton-like

fabric. Once four were inflated, Duck aimed a small directional remote at each, turning on a bright LED light from within. Now illuminated, their brightness adjusted to a pleasant level, the balloons
served almost like bright moons, filling the large chamber with voluminous light. Duck walked out from the center of chamber and
released each one in turn, watching as they rose to the ceiling like an
arctic sunrise.

Joanne had unpacked a laser scanner from one of the larger crates,
attaching the football-sized, lens-studded head to a bulky tripod. She
took the tripod to each corner of the room and pressed a button on
the scanner. Each time, it would beep loudly and begin to rapidly spin,
sending faint green bolts of laser light in all directions. The head whir-
ring to a stop, the device would beep again and download hundreds of
millions of directional data-points through a thick computer cord to a
rugged, waterproof laptop on the cave floor.

With the balloon lights now casting a homey glow throughout the
entire chamber, Milo and the rest of the cavers felt comfortable in taking off their helmets, headlamps, and harnesses, stacking up the equipment in tidy little piles next to their assigned tents. Duck handed out
bunk assignments and earplugs, placing Milo with Logan. Milo hoped
the large geologist didn't snore, though he doubted he'd even hear it
over the ever-present roar of the waterfalls.

Duck collected stacks of batteries from the camera equipment and
headlamps, hooking them up to a portable methanol fuel cell for rapid
recharging.

A top-to-bottom search of the chamber had revealed no other carv-
ings or artifacts, no further clues of DeWar's—or any other—expedition.
Nor was Milo's missing anchor discovered, though he suspected everyone had forgotten about it but him. The carving was vindication
enough.

Though the inscription had now been photographed, laser-scanned,
chalk-rubbed, and prodded, Dale made a special little detour to visit it
whenever he went marching around the chamber. He would look at it

from several different angles, holding up a flashlight to catch the relief of the etching before eventually moving on with no further clues gathered.

The last of the dangling crates reached the bottom shaft. Duck and Bridget carefully landed them on the cavern floor, unhooking and dragging them to the makeshift depot. A note was taped to the plastic lid of the final box. Duck pulled it off and carried over to Dale, who read it while frowning.

"Everybody circle up," said Dale, waving the scattered party to come join him at the entrance to the row of five tents. He held out the letter in front of him, showing a black-and-white computerized weather map of northern Tanzania. "I've just received word that the surface is expecting a bit of a storm. It was set to miss us, but took an abrupt turn over the last few hours. A low-pressure zone with a lot of rain, early for the season but not entirely unexpected. We'll be fine down here, shouldn't affect us in the slightest. But it's going to get messy up top. Can't run the helicopters and the roads will wash out. I'm expecting our trucks will get bogged down as well. Nothing we're not prepared for, but I wanted to make sure you're all in the loop. Nobody likes surprises, right?"

A murmur went through the group—everybody agreed. Milo figured any issues far above would hardly matter in the cavern.

"Data from the scan has finished processing," announced Joanne. "I could use some assistance with the analysis from Duck."

"No prob," said Duck with a smile, walking over to join her.

As the rest of the group broke up, Dale walked over to Milo, placing a fatherly hand on his shoulder.

"You convinced yet?" he asked for the third time.

Milo nodded. Either they were on the trail of Lord Riley DeWar, or it was all part of the most elaborate and useless hoax in history. Besides, Milo felt certain that DeWar wouldn't have taken the dangerous fifteen-hundred-foot drop to the bottom if he hadn't intended to explore the entirety of the cave. But whether or not he ever saw daylight again was another matter entirely.

While Duck post-processed the laser data, Joanne had moved on to other measurements. The cave guide gestured for Milo and Dale to come over to her.

"We've identified a minimum of three different branching passageways from this chamber," she said, unfolding a small handheld camera and clicking it on.

"Is that the thermal camera?" asked Dale excitedly.

"Yes indeed—your newest toy." Joanne smiled. "Took me forever to set up. Temperature differentials between the chamber and the passageways are extremely slight; I had to take a sliver of heat variation and level the false-color display to maximum. Take a look."

Joanne handed the thermal camera to Dale, who panned it across the chamber and the people within. The room itself was rendered in neutral reds; the people within were white-hot, their exhalations a brilliant yellow fire.

"Aim it over there," Joanne said, pointing to the wall on the far side of the chamber. Dale obeyed, trying to hold the camera steady. All Milo could see was the featureless blood-red of uniform temperatures, punctuated only by a few fading footprints on the rock.

"What am I looking for?" asked Dale.

"Give it a second," said Joanne.

A small patch in the corner of the screen slowly faded from red to a purple, then blue, as if a portal to another world had opened.

"The air in that passageway is slightly colder than ambient," the cave guide explained. "I've measured the temperature differential for this and the other two passages we've discovered thus far. It's the biggest."

Milo nodded. "Amazing. Kind of like the high-tech version of holding a candle up to a passageway to see if the flame flickers."

"Exactly. Only I usually use a Zippo."

"Well, if you were Lord DeWar," said Dale, handing the camera back to Joanne and slapping his hands together in anticipation, "which one would you pick first?"

"The biggest," said Milo with a grin.

"My thoughts exactly," said Dale. "Has anyone stuck their head in yet?"

"Not yet." Joanne snapped the camera's display closed and placed it back in a protective plastic crate. "Duck is still setting up—will probably be tomorrow before we make any further penetration. We've already accomplished a lot today."

"Nonsense," said Dale, a glint in his eyes. "Let's go ahead and take a peek. Just a few of us. If we hit anything requiring rope work, we'll turn around straightaway."

"I don't know," said Joanne, unconvinced. "Now that we're past the main shaft, the terrain will get more difficult with every step."

"Back by dinner. I promise."

Joanne thought about it for a moment. "I don't see why not. I'll let Duck know. Get your helmets and lights. We'll have to keep this outing small, that means no camera team."

"Probably means no Charlie either," said Milo.

"I'd be more comfortable if we added one last person to our party," said Joanne.

Milo wasn't surprised when Dale made a beeline for Bridget. Logan wasn't busy in the slightest, but no offer was extended him. Milo had a feeling that Dale wasn't happy with Logan's modern-explorer theory. His supporting role in the theory—the supposed discovery of the now-missing anchor—now seemed forgotten or forgiven.

Following Dale, Dr. McAffee came to join Joanne and Milo, making the final adjustments to her helmet strap and newly recharged headlamp. Though he was within earshot, Joanne instead radioed to Duck and explained the plan.

"*Okay,*" came the crackling response. "*Keep regular contact. Out.*"

Milo felt as though he were in a giant anthill. They'd only made it a hundred yards from the base camp, still close enough to see a faint refracted light from the balloons if he turned around and squinted. The curved cavern walls were claustrophobically narrow, forcing Milo to turn sideways to fit through, brushing them with both chest and spine. He was glad for the kneepads, as the ceiling drooped lower and lower with each step. The passageway twisted and turned, breaking off into smaller forking sub-passages. Finding their way back seemed easy enough, but Joanne still dutifully stopped at each intersection, marking the date and direction with thick white chalk.

Joanne led the party, followed by Milo, Bridget, and finally Dale. The passageway she'd chosen progressively shrank, like a withering artery slowly retreating from a belabored heart. Soon the ceiling was too low to even stoop, forcing them to crawl on hands and knees, pulling themselves ever deeper into the tunnels.

Milo quickly learned not to stop too suddenly. Bridget followed him closely, uncomfortably so, meaning that she'd bump her helmet into the seat of his pants if he didn't keep a good pace. She'd mutter an apology each time but wouldn't back off. He suspected she didn't like the claustrophobic stillness of the passageway any more than he did and had decided to keep as close as possible. It was almost strange how normal it felt being around her, a familiarity both soothing and exciting.

Milo's anxiety wasn't gone, but it was now buried under curiosity and fascination. The exploration was physically challenging, mentally exciting, intellectually engaging—wholly consuming in every way. He hadn't eaten anything in what must have been hours and he'd almost completely lost track of time. But he felt fantastic all the same, thrilled by his part in the grand adventure.

The passageway angled upward, the gritty flowstone beneath their knees turning dry. Above, the ceiling was filled with clinging calcium straws, small translucent tubes resembling upside-down candles beside the marble limestone walls and shimmering calcite drapery. He was reminded of a story he'd once read about early American masonic rituals. Potential members were often left abandoned in dark caves with nothing more than a candle and a book of matches. If successful, the men would emerge stark naked from the earth many hours later, having burned down the candle and every thread of clothing for light.

"Watch this," said Joanne. She took off her headlamp and pressed it upward into the straws. The fragile geology glowed like a candle-lit chandelier, illuminating the tight passageway with warm, inviting luminescence.

"It's beautiful," breathed Bridget, in awe. Milo couldn't agree more.

"I can't see it," complained Dale from the back of the line. But Joanne didn't pause, just kept moving. The foursome soon passed another fork in the passageway, one leading upward and a second leading further down. Joanne frowned at the steep, muddy slide and instead took the tighter passageway above it, dutifully marking the intersection with chalk.

The ceiling dipped again, now so low that Milo had to shuffle forward on his belly like a snake to catch up with the British guide, inadvertently smacking his boot against Bridget's helmet as he squirmed away.

"Hey!" said the doctor from behind him. Milo muttered an apology as he reached the passageway, feeling genuinely terrible about the accidental kick.

Ahead, Joanne had stopped. She silently gestured for Milo to come join her at the head of the line, right below where she'd just made a directional mark at a forking passageway, the arrow aimed at the larger of the two options.

"Take a look at this," said Joanne, tapping on the ceiling above her with a single gloved finger.

Milo immediately caught sight of what Joanne had discovered. Below the guide's white chalk mark was a second, much fainter mark. Milo took a closer look at the black smudge. Was it mold? No—it wasn't growing on the wall—it was a tailed triangle, a man-made drawing. His eyes widened with realization.

"What do you think?" asked Joanne beside him.

"What's happening?" demanded Dale from the back.

Milo raised his voice so that everybody could hear. "Joanne found something," he said. "I think it's a calcium hydroxide marking—it looks like someone painted an arrow with it."

"Is that another cave painting?" asked Bridget. "Like what we found in the galley?"

"Oh," said Joanne from in front of him, her voice indicating her immediate realization of the implications. "*Oh*. I've never seen one so old before, didn't know what I was looking at."

"I don't understand," said Bridget.

"Back in DeWar's time, they used calcium carbide gas lamps," explained Milo, loud enough for everyone to hear. "An upper reservoir was filled with water, which dripped a bit at a time into a lower chamber filled with calcium carbide. This produced acetylene gas, which was burned for light. They'd use the leftover hydroxide ash to mark passageways. Definitely not native art."

Dale cleared his throat. "He's right," he said from the back of the line. "Would have been cutting-edge technology in 1901. No doubt more evidence of DeWar. No way one of the local tribes could have made it this deep. Milo, my boy—you're becoming my good luck charm!"

"Let's continue, see if we find more," said Joanne. "Don't want to hang out here for too long—we'll run the risk of hypothermia if we stop moving. I can't turn around, but we can take some photos and samples on the way back."

"We're on the trail!" said Dale excitedly. "I can feel it!"

"Just be careful around this next bend," said Joanne from up ahead. "Looks like a bit of a drop to one side."

The guide was right—when Milo caught up to her, he found the passageway had opened up to form a natural bridge over another chasm, deep enough to where he couldn't quite see the bottom. Milo snuck a look back to see Bridget smiling behind him.

"I didn't expect this to be so . . . fun," she said. "So long as nobody gets sick or hurt, I'm officially on vacation!"

Milo turned to flash a grin when his hand suddenly slipped out from underneath him, the slimy flowstone betraying his grip. He grunted, losing his balance and falling over to one side, and slid over the edge of the natural bridge.

"Milo!" screamed Bridget. Milo was in freefall, but before he could even process the feeling of weightlessness, he slammed against the side of a curving wall, sliding and rolling through a tinkle of fragile calcium straws as he was unceremoniously dumped at the bottom of the chasm. His helmet had stayed on but the headlamp had come free, lying a few feet away from him.

Moaning and with his eyes watering, he barely saw the flashes of light from the rest of the party above him. Milo tried to say something reassuring, but the wind had been knocked out of his lungs by the impact. He could only manage a labored wheeze.

Dale, Bridget, and Joanne called his name over and over, shining their lights down from the bridge, trying to see him. But he was directly below and in the shadow of the natural structure, as good as invisible.

"I'm fine," groaned Milo, bringing himself up to a sitting position. "Everything is okay . . . nothing broken, I think . . ."

Milo checked himself again. Only his ego seemed bruised.

"Stay put," ordered Joanne, her voice echoing throughout the chamber. "We'll find our way down to you."

He nodded—an easy enough request to obey. Fighting his own protesting body, he reached over to retrieve his still-lit headlamp, placing it back on his helmet.

Milo turned to survey the small chamber, slowly rotating in a lazy circle. Just inches before him, the illumination fell upon the grimacing, empty-socketed face of a mummified human body.

CHAPTER 14:

AUTOPSY

2,350 feet below the surface

"There's a body down here," Milo shouted to the others, trying to keep the adrenaline-fueled warble from his voice. The back of his shoulders and head hurt; he'd jolted himself back six feet and into a boulder after first encountering the desiccated corpse.

"A *what*?" Joanne shouted from above, her voice distant and echoing. "I can barely hear you—did you say you found a *body*?"

Sucking in a long, slow breath, Milo closed his eyes for a moment, willing the shock to subside in his twitching limbs. Opening them again, he slowly scanned the entire room from end to end. No other ghoulish surprises revealed themselves—but he did catch glimpses of metal and cloth fragments half-buried in the muddy floor. Milo forced himself to look again at the cadaver, illuminating the hollow-eyed mummy in harsh yellow light. The instinctual fear began to fade, replaced by an increasing sense of curiosity. Before he knew it, Milo had shifted back to his hands and knees and approached the body with careful consideration, swiveling his head up and around to take in all angles. Stones jostled from the other end of the chamber as the others approached. His attention diverted, Milo let the body once again disappear into pure, unspoiled darkness.

Joanne emerged from a small, angular crevice in the far wall. As the cave guide stopped to survey the room, Bridget pushed her way past, rushing to Milo's side.

"Are you okay?" she asked, patting at his arms and legs, checking for broken bones or bloody patches. It was all he could do to not pull himself away—her touch felt electric.

Dale emerged last. "Milo!" he exclaimed. "We're going to have to put a bell on you—that was quite a tumble."

"I'm okay, really." Milo gave them a wry smile. "I hit a slick section on the way over the bridge, slid off the edge. The only thing damaged is my pride."

"Not exactly," corrected Joanne, frowning as she surveyed the chaotic, muddy trail where Milo had tumbled. The fragile calcite straws had taken the worst of it, hundreds snapped like twigs and scattered in every direction. Milo reddened as he looked at the scene. She was right, of course; in one clumsy moment he'd irreparably wrecked an ancient natural formation.

"I'm really sorry," said Milo.

"Oh, leave him alone," said Dale. "There's a whole cave of that stuff."

Joanne issued a stifled *harrumph*. "I suppose it *does* happen on occasion—better than breaking your neck. So where is this body?"

Milo didn't answer but simply swiveled his head toward the corner of the chamber, illuminating the pale, dry skin of the corpse. The figure leaned upright against the wall, impossibly thin from the mummification process. Its skeletal hands were palms-up, knees to chest, head angled with a mouth yawning open like a silent scream.

"Good lord!" said Dale, taken aback. "You weren't kidding!"

Neither Bridget nor Joanne gasped, but instead intently stared at the body from a distance.

"It's quite ghastly," admitted Joanne. "But I suppose we ought to look around a bit, make sure we're not trampling a larger archaeological site."

"Way ahead of you," said Dale, slowly making his way around the room-sized chamber. Milo joined him and the pair quickly began to identify other evidence—fabric scraps, rusty nails, even a stick of rotten wood.

"It was a camp," concluded Bridget as she picked up the surviving half of a corroded tent peg.

Milo wondered if the camp had been washed away by a flood—being on higher ground, the mummy could have survived unscathed.

"Should I have the next team retrieve the body?" asked Dale. "Take him home for identification and a proper burial?"

Joanne cleared her throat. "A recovery is certainly within the realm of possibility," she said. "But it won't be a pretty process—they'd likely have to break him—or her—into pieces for the smaller passages."

"At least he's dried out," mused Dale. "That'll make it a lot easier. Let's table this for now; I'd like to get Duck on the radio first."

As the rest waited, Dale grabbed his walkie-talkie and tried to reach Duck. No response came, and the device didn't so much as crackle with interference.

"There's too much rock," said Joanne. "You'll never reach him from here."

"Let's get a little closer and try again," said Dale, gesturing for the cave guide to follow him back into the crevice passageway. "Joanne—come with me. Milo and Bridget, you can probably hang tight, we'll be back presently."

Dale and Joanne disappeared, leaving Milo and Bridget in silence.

"Guess it's just you and me," he said.

Bridget just nodded. A pause fell between them. "Did you know we've been awake and active for nineteen straight hours?" she finally said.

"No. I guess I haven't kept track. I don't even feel tired."

"It's the darkness," said Bridget. "Disrupts the circadian rhythms. Without outside regulation, cavers find their cycles elongating . . . they'll work for days without rest, then sleep for twelve, eighteen, even twenty-four hours straight."

"That's actually pretty cool."

"Yeah." Bridget sighed. "But it comes with a price. Weakened immune system, reduced mental acuity, even auditory and visual hallucinations over time."

"I suppose you'll have to keep an eye on that, Doc. I'll let you know if I start hearing voices."

Bridget chuckled as she fished a digital camera and latex gloves out of her backpack.

"Document *everything*," she ordered, handing him the compact Nikon as she turned back toward the mummy. "May as well do a little investigation while we're waiting. We'll keep it basic—anthropological autopsies are *not* my specialty—but best get a rudimentary examination done before Joanne and Dale start sawing the poor thing to pieces."

With that, the doctor shuffled over toward the body, gingerly touching the face and appendages as she learned in for a closer look. She gently pressed the figure's skeletal knees apart, aiming her light down the exposed belly to the crotch.

"Well," said Bridget. "He's naked. And he's definitely male. Remarkable state of preservation; likely due to the consistent temperature and humidity."

"Was he stripped postmortem?" asked Milo.

"Hard to say," mused Bridget, shaking her head. "Could be any number of reasons why we found him in this state. Maybe he burned his clothes for the light, or maybe someone needed his clothes more than he did. Could have even been paradoxical disrobing . . . in the final stages of hypothermia, victims oftentimes strip themselves naked and burrow. Let's see if I can find cause of death."

Bridget gently pressed against the chest, pelvis, spine, and skull of the naked mummy, probing for clues.

"Ah," she said, finding a soft spot on the side of the skull, where dry, peeling skin covered a baseball-sized lattice of shattered bone.

"His head was caved in," said Milo, observing as her gloved fingers sank into the spongy wound.

"It would appear so," said Bridget. "But I can't tell much more . . . could have been an accident or violence. I don't see any defensive wounds on the arms."

"It's definitely not Lord DeWar," asserted Milo.

"I agree," said Bridget, eyeing him quizzically. "But what makes *you* so sure?"

"The chin," said Milo, pointing at the yawning lower jawline. "DeWar had a very prominent chin. The rest of the proportions are all wrong as well. Maybe one of his men?"

"Probably not—take a closer look at the eyes," said Bridget, using a pen to probe the depth of the empty socket. Milo made a mental note to bag the pen at the earliest opportunity; Bridget had a bad habit of chewing on the ends.

"What am I looking for?" asked Milo.

"The skin is withered, but you can still see the epicanthic fold," answered Bridget. "But he doesn't appear to have any Khoisan or Malagasy features. If I were to make an educated guess, I'd say this man was likely Asian."

Milo rocked back and forth on his heels in consideration. "To the best of my knowledge, there were no Asian men in Lord DeWar's party," he said, frowning. "A few Europeans and a number of African porters, that's it. Can you date the body?"

"He's definitely not black or European, and I can't date the body with what I have on hand," said Bridget. "Mummies are tricky that way, and I think we've already reached the limits of my ad hoc autopsy."

As Milo mentally processed the new information, Bridget retrieved the Nikon and continued taking photos. Silence fell between them again, leaving Milo feeling more than a little useless.

"It's hard for me to see you again," Bridget finally said, punctuating the stillness. She didn't look at him when she said it, didn't even put the camera down.

"Then why did you vouch for me?" asked Milo, finally uttering the question that had plagued his thoughts for hours. "Would I be here without you?"

"No," Bridget answered after a long silence. "But when I found out that Lord Riley DeWar was the subject of Dale's next expedition, I insisted he bring you onboard as the group historian. I know what DeWar meant to you, how he almost wrecked your career."

"Why didn't you just tell me?"

"I don't know. I just wanted to keep things professional; I don't want you to think you owe me anything. We've put each other through enough shit already. But I'd never forgive myself if I didn't give you a second chance at finding DeWar."

A heavy wave of guilt passed over Milo. He didn't know what to say. The silence turned long, too long.

It's hard for me to see you again.

She'd dropped the weight on him as though she'd carried it since their last goodbyes so many years previous. She clearly still cared about him despite everything he'd done. He most certainly cared for her, and no amount of time could truly erase their shared history, volatile as it was.

Another wave of repressed guilt washed over him. He'd hurt her before, and his very presence was hurting her again. It was unfair—he'd been in a position of power, her classroom instructor. Any of the comforting thoughts he'd clung to—that she initiated, that they'd desperately loved each other—was just crass self-justification. At the end of day, she was not the better for having him in her life.

"Thank you," Milo finally whispered. "And I'm sorry—sorry for everything."

Before she could respond, footsteps and light echoed from the passageway as the returning party crossed the natural bridge above. Soon

Charlie and Isabelle emerged from the crevice, followed by Dale, Joanne, and Logan.

"They were easy to find," announced Dale. "They were already on their way down the anthill."

"Whoa," said Charlie as he caught a glimpse of the body for the first time. "That guy is *gnarly*."

Joanne chuckled and moved to the back of the group, stooping down to probe at the metallic objects and cloth scattered across the floor, examining them one by one.

"What's the verdict?" asked Dale excitedly. "Have we found our missing man?"

"It's not DeWar," announced Bridget, wiping under an eye with one hand. "But I can't tell much more at this point."

"Why this room?" mused Dale. "I see no water sources, no shelter, and it would have been easy to find a way out, even in the dark."

"Maybe the sheltering instinct," said Logan. "Every animal tries to find a hole to curl up in when it knows it's going to die."

"At least it's not a *complete* waste of time," said Isabelle, though clearly unhappy. She trained her camera on the body. "That . . . *thing* . . . could make for some decent footage, but we'd probably have to blur the face for basic cable."

"I could pose with it." Charlie scratched at his prickly stubble in consideration. "Bridget—hand over the camera, I'm going to act like I'm photographing the find."

Bridget just rolled her eyes and refused to move or hand Charlie the Nikon.

"It's likely not a member of his party either," added Milo. "I hope this isn't a disappointment."

Dale thought for a moment before responding. "But you perceive, my boy," he finally quoted, "that it is not so, and that facts, as usual, are very stubborn things."

"Overruling all theories," added Logan, finishing the quote.

"To imagine that the English felt Jules Verne best reserved for children," said Dale with a smile.

Logan returned the smile as the camera turned toward him. "I prefer this one: Enough! When science has spoken, one can only remain silent thereafter!"

Everybody visibly cringed. Logan had practically yelled out the line. Unembarrassed, Logan beamed with pride much longer than was appropriate.

"I think I found something," said Joanne, standing with a shiny disk-shaped object in her hand.

"Toss it here," said Logan. Joanne threw it to him, and the geologist caught it.

"What it is?" asked Dale.

Before answering, Dr. Logan Flowers wiped it on his pants and tapped it against his helmet to listen to the sound.

"Its aluminum," said Logan. "And I'm pretty sure it's a coin."

"Can you still read it?" asked Dale.

"Yeah," said Logan, nodding as he scraped the last bit of grime from the glinting object.

"A coin?" repeated Charlie, confused.

"Definitely Japanese," added Logan.

"That *cannot* be right," said Dale.

"I think it's a wartime coin," said Logan, continuing to examine the shiny object. "It's dated 1938."

Baffled silence fell upon the group as they tried to make sense of the evidence, to come up with any other explanation than the obvious. Milo started to speak but cut himself off.

"Did we just find a lost Japanese caver?" demanded Dale.

CHAPTER 15:

CHRYSANTHEMUM

Dale reached over and practically snatched the coin from Logan's hands. Frowning, Dale examined the prize, turning it over with his gloved fingers and squinting for a closer look. Isabelle had already shouldered the camera to film. Behind them, Charlie shifted from foot to foot whenever the lens wasn't aimed in his direction.

"I don't see where it says 1938," Dale said, irritated. "And this script could be from any Asian alphabet. But it's definitely aluminum—I suppose I could agree with our esteemed geologist on that point."

Bridget, Joanne, and Milo all glanced at each other, not sure what to make of Logan's assertion.

"Look at the chrysanthemum flower on the front," said Logan patiently. "That's the Japanese imperial symbol."

"What the *fuck* were the Japanese doing down here?" asked Charlie in complete disbelief. "Did I totally miss something?"

"And the year 1938?" asked Dale, still unconvinced and visibly ignoring Charlie.

"Written in kanji on the reverse," answered Logan. "Below the bird image—it's a crow, by the way."

"Huh," said Dale, dropping his intense scrutiny of the coin and passing it to Bridget.

"You read kanji?" asked Bridget, giving the coin to Joanne after only a cursory examination.

"Not much more than numbers and a few words," admitted Logan. "Never formally studied it, picked up a little between anime and a few MMORPGs."

"Ugh, anime?" said Joanne, handing the coin to Charlie. "Those Japanese cartoons with all the weird sex? Tentacles and the like?"

"You're thinking of hentai," said Logan, defensively crossing his arms. "It's actually very different."

Charlie tried to stifle a snicker, but it came out as a snort. "Heads or tails?" he asked, flipping the coin in the air and catching it again.

"Languages are one of my many hobbies," said Logan, increasingly annoyed. "I'm fluent in French and Italian, and I read a bit of Russian and Arabic, and I'm currently learning the foundations of Thai."

"I didn't know that," said Bridget, her soothing tone a transparent effort to de-escalate. "You're a man of many talents."

"I started with Italian," said Logan, "so I could collaborate on papers about the Castelcivita cavern system in Salerno, Italy. From there, French was a natural progression. My grandmother is from Toulouse. Russian and Arabic came later."

"And Thai?" asked Joanne, still a bit unconvinced.

"That's for a website," admitted Logan with a mumble. "A, um, dating website."

Joanne shook her head and whispered something like *so dodgy* as the coin passed to Isabelle and finally to Milo. Small and smooth-edged, it couldn't have weighed more than a gram, even with the clinging dirt and corrosion. One side displayed a chrysanthemum-topped cloudburst surrounding a single Japanese character, the other a crow ringed by kanji script.

Milo gave the historical context of the find serious thought. Aluminum was once so precious as to comprise Napoleon Bonaparte's personal dining set, but by 1938 it was little more than a cheap base metal. Such coinage wouldn't represent the wealth of a nation, but rather its wartime desperation. But even aluminum would eventually fail as currency—in the waning days of World War II, the Japanese central banks had resorted to minting clay.

"Japs didn't hit Pearl Harbor until '41," said Charlie, scratching his head. "I thought you said this was a wartime coin."

"The Japanese had been fighting since 1931, starting in mainland China," said Milo, a little surprised that he needed to explain the well-known fact. "They'd been at it for a decade before Pearl Harbor."

Dale nodded, again frowning. "Well," he finally said. "We've found what we found."

"One man, alone," said Joanne. "I presume there were others with him?"

"Undoubtedly," said Bridget. "Their presence would also explain the wall anchor Milo found."

"The wall anchor he *lost*," added Logan. "But I suppose we can now have a working theory for the collapsed entrance . . . Japanese cavers of that time period would have had access to suitable explosives. Again, I'll need to run some samples up top to be certain."

"Whatever happened, they didn't retrieve or even bury his body," said Joanne. "I wonder why not? Maybe he was lost down here? Ran out of light, fell like Milo?"

"More likely someone bashed his skull in," added Charlie. "Went cave-crazy."

"Excuse me, but 'cave-crazy' is *not* a thing," interjected Joanne.

"Perhaps he was the last one left," said Bridget. "The rest were already gone—or dead."

Dale sighed and dropped to a cross-legged position, back against the wall, almost mirroring the posture of the mummified body.

"Milo," said Dale, "do you know anything about a lost Japanese caving expedition? Or *any* caving expedition to this region?"

"No," said Milo, shaking his head. "I mean, Japan conducted a number of field projects over the prewar decades . . . mountaineering, jungle treks, Antarctic exploration . . . I don't know of any Japanese caving expeditions in this area, certainly no missing or dead cavers."

The group's discussion almost immediately devolved into three separate debates, each entertaining their own theories. Eventually, Dale cut the entire group off.

"Here's the bottom line," said Dale. "We don't know a goddamn thing."

Interrupting the following silence, Logan cleared his throat. "We do know one thing," he said. "One lost expedition is eminently explainable. Two . . . is not."

The cavers made their way back to camp in silence. Fatigue hit Milo like a hammer, the hours of darkness and exertion, lack of appetite, and bruising fall joining forces in brutal harmony. The base camp chamber felt warm and inviting. Not for the unvarying temperature, but for the homey overhead lighting and the prospect of a meal and a sleeping bag.

Milo shed his pack by the entrance to the tent. Logan did the same. Everyone took a moment to draw clean water from the long, deep drainage crack. Pausing, Milo wiped off the worst of the mud and crystal fragments from his coveralls. He didn't make much progress with the muck before giving up—trying to stay clean was a losing proposition.

Walking back past the supply depot, Milo glanced at the weather report taped to the largest plastic case. As Dale had announced, it called for unseasonably heavy rains over three consecutive days, along with accompanying travel advisories. Milo looked up at the massive waterfalls, wondering if they'd grow. It was difficult to imagine them pouring with any greater ferocity.

As he made his way across camp, Milo's thoughts drifted to Bridget. *It's hard to see you,* she'd said.

Milo tried to think of something to say. Maybe *I'm sorry things got so bad between us.*

Or *Let's start over, learn to be friends again.*

Or *I still think of you every time I close my fucking eyes.*

The last one hurt to admit. Worse, it still might have the power to hurt Bridget as well.

Milo almost stumbled over a glint on the ground a dozen feet away from the muddy latrines. Bending down, he picked up a glinting bolt anchor. He turned it over in his hands, brushing clinging dirt free of the corroded metal, seeing the faint imprint of an imperial chrysanthemum flower on the neck.

He shook his head incredulously. He'd personally searched every inch of the floor; so had Bridget and the others. But now the missing anchor bolt was lying in plain sight.

Milo struggled to come up with an explanation but could only think of one—now that it was confirmed that a modern expedition reached the cave, whomever first found and concealed the bolt had placed it back out again.

CHAPTER 16:

THE PIT

2,150 feet below the surface

Milo made his way toward the gathering cavers, anchor bolt jangling in his pocket. He wanted to kick it into the latrine trench, bury it, throw it into the lake, or melt it to nothing. Holding it only reminded him that someone had hidden the truth from the group.

Last to sit, Milo was handed a plastic cup of wet, starchy noodles and tough, rehydrated beef. The meal wasn't half-bad; the sun-dried tomatoes dotting the mixture were a pleasant surprise, though a bit over-salted for his taste.

"We cooked this time," said Joanne. "But the duties will ultimately be shared among all."

"I don't think anybody's going to want my cooking," grunted Logan through a mouthful of soupy pasta.

"Everybody takes a turn," Joanne repeated. "And don't worry—most of the meals are of the just-add-water variety. No need for a Jamie Oliver-type chef down here."

"Let me know if you change your mind," said Isabelle, smiling dreamily. "Because I could *really* use a Jamie Oliver."

"Just be careful with the stove," said Duck, barely looking up from his meal as he ignored the producer's double entendre. "We cook with isobutane cartridges. Gets pretty hot pretty quick."

Dale let silence fall before changing the subject. "We'll probably need to turn in before too long," he said as he absentmindedly stirred his noodles. "No sense in overdoing it on the first day."

"Agreed," said Duck with a smile. "Everybody ready for the deepest sleep they've ever had?"

Joanne led the cavers in a hearty groan over the pun. Eventually, everyone slowly got up from their rocks, turning their cups over to Duck for washing.

Duck cracked his knuckles and looked up at the ceiling, watching the glowing orbs gently roll across the ceiling in the slight breeze. "The light is nice," he finally said. "But I kind of liked the old way better."

"How's that?" asked Bridget.

"We would always turn off the headlamps and flashlights to save power," said Duck. "Eat in total darkness. It was pretty cool . . . you've never really enjoyed a sandwich until you eat one in the dark after fifteen hours of busting sumps. In the right chambers, there's no wind, no noise, no light, no sound. Just you and your sandwich. The sandwich becomes, like, your entire universe."

"That was *almost* poetic," said Joanne, laughing.

"Cave sex is awesome for about ninety percent of the same reasons," added Duck, wistfully lost in his own memories. "Especially if you have a sandwich afterward."

Using his remote control, Duck set the illuminating globes to slowly fade over thirty minutes, dimming the ambient light until the gargantuan chamber was shrouded in complete darkness. Milo adjusted his sleeping bag in the tent he shared with Logan. Though he felt some natural fatigue as the light diminished, Milo couldn't help but tuck under the lip of the sleeping bag with his e-reader, speed-reading the first eighty pages of Jules Verne's *Journey to the Center of the Earth*. The updated translation was better than he remembered; he found himself smiling and highlighting passages, resolving to include himself the next time Dale and Logan started spouting quotes. But soon his eyes grew droopy. He clicked the reader off and fell asleep.

Milo found himself kneeling alone in the vast Tanzanian savanna, dark starlit sky above, alone on the eternal plains. The edges of the land curled up at the furthest reaches, as though the sphere of the earth had inverted, the ground beneath him no more than the thin surface of a bubble in the endless stream of the cosmos.

Milo silently followed a game trail into the long, dry valley before him. The winding path soon revealed the yawning maw of the cave in its most ancient form, unencumbered by collapsed rock or the fragile man-made edifices of Dale's camp.

Then he saw them—ghostly elephants threading through the distant trees from every direction of the compass, both colossal and ethereal, as, trunks clinging to tails, they slipped into the mouth of the cave like sand through an hourglass.

Milo looked down, watching as his unclothed limbs and torso elongated like the painted figures in the gallery. He strode over the plains, sliding through the grass, his naked feet padding over the billions of tiny holes, pinpricks in the membrane between worlds. A splinter stuck his foot, and when he bent down to pick it out it became a long, obsidian-headed spear in his hand, the length taller now than himself. The holes beneath his feet widened as albino locusts emerged to swarm around his feet. One bite, two bites, a dozen, a hundred, he felt their pincers pull at his skin. As he looked up, he realized the entire breadth of the landscape had transformed into a swarm of crawling insects, so vast in numbers they threatened to consume the very world beneath him. The pain of their pulling bites grew greater with every moment until Milo began to run, slowly at first, their fragile, brittle bodies crunching beneath his feet, and then faster and faster until he lost sensation of any speed, lush grasslands passing in a blur. Their prey having vanished, so too did the locusts, retreating into their shrinking holes.

His vision now unimaginably clear, Milo set his sights on an eland, a spiral-horned antelope, grazing across the valley. With each bounding step, Milo rose higher into the sky, high enough to pierce the constellation of stars, their twinkling orbs rushing past him like fireflies. Spear raised above his head, Milo plunged toward the earth, wind whistling in his ears like the cave's hurricane howl.

The eland bent before him, submissive, head down, front limbs curled to the earth, and he pierced it through the neck with the stone blade. Bloodlessly, it crumpled at his feet, the penetrating length of the rod vibrating with the force of the blow. Breathing hard, his legs trembling, Milo gazed up to find himself at the foot of a great oasis, surrounded by incalculable herds of elephant, giraffe, antelope, and water buffalo. Hippos and crocodiles floated within as lions and hyenas stalked from the outer perimeter, birds circling above.

Milo crept toward the oasis, the herds parting to reveal a woman's smooth silhouette before him. Facing away, she allowed him to watch as she waded into the oasis waters, long dark hair barely covering her nude form. He reached toward her with his impossibly long arm, almost touching her bare skin, when she suddenly swiveled to stare at him. The ethereal figure was now recognizably Bridget, her face impassive, one arm cradling full breasts, the other looped beneath an engorged, pregnant belly.

Waking up was a great deal less pleasant than falling asleep. Milo's exertions from the previous day had gathered in his joints and chest. Knees, arms, thighs, everything ached. The floating lights were a poor substitute for daylight, leaving Milo with the fuzzy, fatigue-laden sensation of the darkest, coldest winter solstice.

The tent rustled as Logan stepped in, naked as he brushed wet droplets from his hairy body and beard.

"Did you have sex dreams?" asked Logan, seeing that Milo was awake. "I had these *intense* sex dreams all night."

With that, Logan shook off, hurling water everywhere. Milo grimaced, trying to shield his eyes and mouth from the moisture. "You have to try showering in the waterfall," said the geologist. "It's like getting sand-blasted clean. Don't even need soap. Amazing. Cold as hell, though."

"Maybe later."

Drier now, Logan took a closer look at Milo. "Shit," he said, pointing at Milo's nose. "You're bleeding."

"I am?" asked Milo, feeling his face. Sure enough, a steady stream of sticky blood dribbled down his nose and across his mouth. It had already badly stained his sleeping bag below. Milo hadn't had a nose-bleed since he was in elementary school—embarrassing. He couldn't help but remember the images in the gallery, of crimson blood pouring from the faces of the dancing figures.

"Get cleaned up," suggested Logan. "I scored us some wet wipes, should do the trick. Joanne is going to hang back with Charlie and Isabelle at base camp, but you're with us—Dale says we're hitting the anthill in ten."

Dale led this time, followed by Duck, Logan, and finally Milo. He felt an overwhelming sense of déjà vu: the same claustrophobically hostile cavern walls, the twisting passageways, the forking sub-passages. The cavers dutifully followed Joanne's chalked directions, taking the most promising routes ever deeper at each intersection. Light from the base camp had long since disappeared; Milo was again reduced to crawling on hands and knees.

As the tunnel turned upward, Milo watched as the slimy mud beneath him turned dry once more. He expectantly turned his head upward to the chandelier of calcite soda straws. Stopping, he withdrew the flashlight from his pocket and pressed it into a collection of the fragile stalactites, watching in awe as they glowed like upside-down candles.

"Knock it off," said Dale, turning around from the front of the pack. "Joanne said you've already wrecked enough of those."

"Won't happen again," Milo mumbled.

Logan started talking about the straws' formation rates to anyone within earshot, and soon they were again at the natural chasm bridge. Milo could see the muddy furrows where he'd tried to save himself from sliding over the edge. This time, he gave the slippery section a wide berth, following the others across the bridge. No one commented on the corpse still lying shadowed and hidden below.

Duck hung back at the end of the natural span. When Milo caught up to him, the cave guide tapped at another smudged arrow at the intersection. The previous group had missed it in their scramble to reach Milo; this one pointed in a different direction. Marked with calcium hydroxide, the arrow had not been left by Joanne.

"Lead on," said Duck, pointing to the incredibly tight passageway.

"I could use some help with my pack," complained Dale from ahead. Logan and Duck sat up cross-legged to help Dale as Milo steeled himself for the crawl to come.

A hundred and fifty feet in and Milo was already miserable. The kneepads were no longer useful; now, on his belly, they only got caught on every jagged rock and loose stone. Hands in front of him, Milo couldn't turn around, could hardly even wriggle. Even breathing too hard made his spine touch the ceiling above. Every inch-long movement within the dark, airless passage required incredible exertion; every minute felt like hours.

"Just you wait," said Duck, now behind him. "Just you wait until we have to start pushing scuba tanks through these passages. Now *that* is all kinds of fun."

Though the ceiling remained low, the chamber ahead opened up to a disc-shaped void twenty feet across, large enough for Milo to drop his pack, flip onto his back, and gasp for air. Allowing the relief to wash over him, Milo couldn't help but sense a sort of inpenetrable darkness in the center of the room, an unquantifiable emptiness he'd not experienced before. Flipping onto his stomach, he scanned the room with his headlamp. To one side, a table-sized hole opened up the floor of the chamber. He crawled closer to it, finding that the edges of the hole were composed of crumbling, paper-thin stone hanging over sheer void. The hole was like a skylight and the pit below too vast to ascertain any sense of dimension.

"Don't come too close," said Milo as the rest of the party approached. "I think the floor might not support everybody."

Dale ignored him and crawled up to the very edge of the hole, sticking his head inside. "You're not kidding," he said with a long, low whistle. "That is a *big* chamber down there."

Dale glanced around the upper room until he found a bowling-pin sized rock. Grabbing it, he slid it across the cavern floor and into the hole as Duck punched the timer function on his wristwatch. Milo caught the whisper of wind as the stone dropped from view.

Ten seconds passed, twenty. By thirty, Dale and Duck were glancing at each other, shaking their heads.

"If we haven't heard it hit by now . . ." said Dale, not completing his thought.

"What if there's water down there?" Milo asked. "Could it have splashed down?"

"Still would have heard the *kerplunk*." Duck frowned as he clicked open his Zippo lighter above the hole. The flame didn't even flicker.

"No air exchange," said Logan. "And I'm not hearing any waterflow either."

"So where did the rock land?" asked Milo.

"Satan's featherbed," said Duck. "His old lady is looking up from the inferno thinking *where the hell did* that *come from?*"

"Should be using these sparingly," said Dale, retrieving a pack of road flares from his pack. "But here goes anyway."

The cave guide lit two and tossed them into the hole, one after another. For a moment, Milo could see the walls of the pit as the flares tumbled one after another, disappearing into the darkness.

"I can't see them anymore," complained Logan. Everyone else mumbled their agreement.

"What should we do?" asked Dale.

"I vote we drop Charlie in next," suggested Logan.

"Let's not get fixated on this little mystery," said Dale. "DeWar wouldn't have had the equipment to get down there anyway."

"There's no air exchange as far as I can tell," added Logan. "Means it's probably a dead end. Could be nothing more than a couple hundred feet down."

"Or maybe a couple thousand," said Duck.

"Unlikely," stated Logan.

As the rest of the party moved on, Milo found himself gazing into the inconceivable darkness of the pit, the skin prickling on the back of his neck as the pit stared back. A quote from *Journey to the Center of the Earth* leapt into his brain, leaving Milo to drift over every word.

An impression of void took hold of my being, Jules Verne had written. *There is nothing more intoxicating than the attraction of the abyss.*

CHAPTER 17:

THE SERPENT AND THE CATHEDRAL

2,475 feet below the surface

There were no more black-smudged arrows marking the winding passageways. Milo felt the absence was logical enough; the path now rarely split, and even then only one of the forking tunnels was ever large enough to fit through. He first tried keeping his backpack in front of him, shoving it along ahead, but eventually found the sensation too confining. Duck told him to instead tie the bag to one foot, leaving it to trail behind as they descended.

Duck still marked each intersection, but the action now felt perfunctory, even illogical. Milo had learned cave life demanded as much ritual as the strictest monastery. Every knot tied, every meal cooked, every lightbulb, battery, carabiner, rope, and camera went through a liturgical checklist before use. Back at the camp, Dale had attributed the methodology to Darwinism—as apostates rarely survived heresy, so too did cavers seldom survive mistakes in such a hostile environment. But instead of ten roughly equal commandments, there was just one law to rule them all . . . Thou Shalt Not Succumb to Summit Fever.

"Summit Fever is all about getting there, with nothing left to get you home," Dale had explained. Didn't matter if you'd just found Blackbeard's treasure or a trio of mermaids. If your air tanks were down by a third, if you'd gone through a third of your juice, a third of your flashlights, a third of your food, of your water, your physical strength . . . it was time to turn around and go home. Never make that final push for the peak, the deepest chamber, the final sump at the cost of your life. Better to come home to your family and try again next year.

Silence clung to the foursome as the passageway opened up, becoming smooth and tubular, with easy, gentle bends. They could stand up now, and Milo appreciated finally getting off his raw knees and stomach. The passageway descended for another quarter mile until the muddy floor dipped below the glasslike surface of still waters. Milo stooped down and brushed his fingers against the rocky shore of the newfound underground river. A mineral crust had developed around the edges of the river like the last ice retreating in spring. The water level hadn't changed in decades.

"Well, boys," said Dale, surveying the water's edge. "Looks like we've hit our first proper sump."

"What's that?" asked Milo, well aware that he was the only person in the group in need of an explanation.

"Sump? Just means an underwater passage," said Logan. "We'll probably wade it for a while, see if the ceiling stays above water. We may hit a point where the whole tunnel is submerged. If it's a quick dunk, we'll swim under it to the other side. If not, they'll need to use dive gear, leave the rest of us behind."

"They used to blow 'em up in the early days of caving," said Dale, first to slosh into the shallow waters. "Let 'em drain out. On the other hand, tribes worshipped them—their shamans believed they were the delineation between our world and the next."

Duck waved everyone back. "Let's rest for a bit," he said. "We should eat. Then I want to seal everything in our bags up tight, especially if the river gets deep. Everybody needs to stay sharp—the moving water will make every natural hazard twice as gnarly."

"Fair enough." The fragile mineral concretions crunched under Dale's feet as he retreated.

The group waded downriver for what seemed like hours. The structure of the tunnel reminded Milo of an abandoned Parisian sewer, almost man-made in its eerie symmetry. Logan explained how the limestone below them was flecked with copper, giving the waters a greenish, serpentine appearance. Milo decided he didn't mind his waterlogged feet, not even when the waters rose above chest level; the fact that he could stand upright was comfort enough.

They swam the final section. Milo dog-paddled, his sealed, buoyant backpack awkwardly holding him up as his helmet bumped and rubbed against the rocky ceiling above. Eventually the passageway widened again, allowing the cavers to swim into the cold, open waters of an unthinkably large chamber.

Dale dipped his head and took a mouthful from the subterranean lake. "It's pure," he said.

"It's filtered through a half-mile of earth," said Logan. "Cleaner than any bottled water in the world."

"I wouldn't be so sure," said Milo. "I saw Logan take a bath upstream."

"I heard that," grunted Logan from behind.

"This way," Dale said, leading the explorers to the side of the massive expanse. Milo followed, his feet touching the smooth stone bottom and dragging himself free of the lake and onto a low, sloping rock. He couldn't get a true sense of the scale from their echoing voices, knowing only that the chamber was surely gargantuan.

"Wow," said Milo, and not for the first time.

"I hope you appreciate how special this is," said Dale as he stretched out on the rock to rest. Dale's intense headlamp beam was still too weak to reach the length of the chamber. "A cave with this many large-scale rooms—it's truly unique."

"He's right," added Logan. "Quite the rare bird—I'm not sure if I've ever seen anything like it before."

Dale pulled out another road flare, lit it, and hurled it as hard as he could toward the center of the room. Improbably, it landed atop a truncated stump of a stone column, the molten white core of the blood-red fire illuminating the chamber like the Eye of Sauron.

Squinting against the flickering light, Milo found himself at the edge of a primordial cathedral, its stalactite-dripping ceiling three hundred feet above. The triangular room narrowed at the far end to a pipe organ of a hundred massive stone columns of various thicknesses, the largest of them stretching from floor to ceiling.

Most of the chamber was flooded, but rocks, having dropped from the ceiling in eons previous, formed disorganized huddles of pews. Most notable was the statue-like edifice before the pipe organ, a towering figure not unlike an angel. It loomed before them with outstretched stone wings, a single, lamppost-sized crystal formation pouring from its heart to the waters below.

Logan and Duck abandoned their packs to explore the perimeter of the chamber, beginning in opposite directions from the mouth of the serpentine river. Milo waded into the subterranean lake and began to swim, transfixed, toward the ancient edifice. Reaching its foot, Milo took his most powerful flashlight from his pocket and placed it at the base of the crystal. Instantly, the entire column glowed to life with an intense yellow light, harsh and distinct. A billion metallic imperfections sparkled within. With Milo's flashlight giving life, the edifice gained the distinct appearance of an angel holding a flaming sword, simultaneously colossal and beautiful and frightening.

Logan and Duck met at the pipe organ a few minutes later, neither having discovered a passageway out of the cathedral chamber. They again departed in opposite directions, this time slowly picking along a patch of wall and diving to the bottom of the shallow lake, probing through the clear waters with flashlights, searching for an exit.

After a long time, Milo withdrew his flashlight from the base of the crystal, and the flaming sword once again faded, the natural statue now a hulking shadow above him.

Logan was first to return to Dale and the packs, Milo following not long after. Duck still worked tirelessly, disappearing beneath the surface over and over as the other three watched.

Eventually, the cave guide turned and slowly swam the length of the chamber between the pipe organ and the flat rock, approaching the waiting party.

"I don't see any other passages," called out Dale. "Is it a dead end?"

Duck climbed out of the waters and collapsed onto his back. It was the first time Milo had seen him tired, out of breath—but the guide smiled broadly.

"I found an exit," he said. "There's a submerged passage underneath the columns—should we swim for it?"

CHAPTER 18:

THE SHRINE

2,625 feet below the surface

Milo, Dale, and Logan joined Duck beneath the pipe organ stone columns at the far end of the underground cathedral. Toes brushing the bottom, the four men paddled sluggishly, barely keeping their chins above water. Behind them, the red flare faded and died, the room-filling flame hissing mournfully as it shrank to embers. Milo's world became terribly small once again, no larger than the reach of his fading headlamp, the light disappearing into blackness before even reaching the far wall.

"What's the plan?" asked Dale.

"I'm going to swim it," said Duck. "I took a peek, and it's a simple dunk, no more than ten feet down and fifteen across to the next room. I'll check it out, make sure it's safe, and then come back for the rest of you."

"Whoa, hold up a minute," said Dale. "If you get stuck, can't turn around down there—"

But before anyone could say another word, Duck took three quick breaths in succession, priming his lungs before plunging beneath the surface. With a small splash, the caving guide disappeared, leaving a trail of bubbles.

Milo held his breath and submerged his face, letting his waterproof headlamp illuminate the lake. His eyes easily penetrating the crystal clear waters, Milo watched as Duck kicked, disappearing into a man-hole-sized hole in the wall. Then the bubbles vanished as well, leaving only stillness.

"What do you think?" asked Logan after Milo came up for air.

"I don't know," said Milo. "Looks pretty tight." He began to shiver.

Logan noticed him. "That's why it's good to be a little fat," said Logan, pointing toward Milo. "You'd think it would make it harder to fit through the squeezes, but it really doesn't. A little chubbiness compresses pretty good, and I can afford to lose a few pounds down here without getting too skinny. Skinny people like you and Bridget just turn to dust and blow away."

"Thanks for that," said Milo with irritation, his teeth beginning to chatter. He had a feeling that the shivering had a great deal less to do with the water temperature than the thought of swimming an ancient subterranean passage.

"Should he be gone this long?" asked Dale. "I thought he said he'd be right back."

The trio waited in silence, each moment passing with excruciating tension. Milo checked his watch, but realized the uselessness of the gesture. He couldn't help but imagine Duck stuck in the submerged passageway, struggling as he drowned.

After an interminable wait, the trio was rewarded by a flood of bubbles as Duck shot to the surface, gasping as water ran down his helmet. Milo had never seen the cave guide so excited—never seen *anyone* so excited, for that matter.

"You have to check out what I found," said Duck, his words tumbling over each other. "I've never seen anything like it. Follow me—and don't worry; it's an easy dunk, no risk of getting turned around."

Without waiting for an answer, he thrust himself under the water again and vanished. Dale waited a few seconds, shrugged toward Logan and Milo, took four deep breaths, and plunged in after.

"Ignore the fear," said Logan, eyeing Milo's worried expression. "Don't think about it—just go for it."

And with that, the geologist too gasped in air and thrust himself underwater, leaving Milo treading water alone in the cathedral chamber.

He experimentally ducked his head below the surface, catching a glimpse of Logan's kicking boots before the geologist dematerialized in a cloud of rising bubbles. Milo popped his head back above water, pulse pounding in his ears as he tried to repeat the deep, full breaths of the other men. He pushed himself underwater and kicked downward. Pressure built in his ears and he felt he needed to draw breath, though he hadn't even reached the entranceway to the flooded passage.

Milo kicked through the crystal clear water once, twice, three times as he thrust himself into the underwater tunnel, feeling the sharp rocks on all sides as they grabbed at his backpack and boots. Pain radiated in his lungs as they contracted, pulling suction against his closed mouth. His vision went gray and blurry, but he was still within the tunnel, couldn't even see the exit. His pants caught on a snag, forcing him to wriggle and yank loose, costing him precious oxygen.

Lungs convulsing, Milo flailed forward, dragging himself through the tight passage, his body screaming for air. He gasped involuntarily, sucking in a mouthful of water, gagging, muscles burning, face contorted. Just as Milo felt he couldn't stop his body from breathing in water, two hands plunged into the darkness before him, ringed with bubbles as they seized his backpack straps, yanking him out of the last few inches of the passageway and to the surface.

Gasping, Milo shook, unable to open his eyes as his stomach churned, his lungs burning, his body wracked with pain.

"You can throw up if you need to," said Dale, slapping him on the back. "Get all that water out—that's right."

Milo opened his eyes to see the three men surrounding him, concern written on their faces. Obliging, he vomited.

"It's okay," reassured Dale, ignoring the oily slick of regurgitation gathered between them. "You're doing great. Everybody has a shitty first dunk. This is your first one, isn't it?"

"Yeah. First one."

"You made it," said Dale, embracing Milo as he shivered, rocking him in the cold, shallow waters. "Nicely done. They get easier."

"Backpack got stuck," said Milo, teeth chattering as he slowly warmed again.

"I figured as much," said Dale. "Logan said you chickened out—but Duck and I knew you'd make a run at it."

"I went for it," repeated Milo, allowing the heat from Dale's embrace to wash over his body, fill him from within. "I made it."

Eyes clearing, Milo took in the new chamber for the first time. The dimensions were significantly smaller than the cathedral; this new room was no larger than a half-scale Olympic pool, almost entirely flooded but with a small peaked island in the center. The waters were deep, forcing Milo and the three other cavers to hold to one wall.

This new room was younger than the cathedral, at least geologically speaking. There were no colossal columns, no thick stalactites clinging to the ceiling. Instead, much of the roof had fallen away, created a submerged breakdown pile that resembled the aftermath of a rockslide, blocking any exit.

"No way to get through that mess," complained Dale. "Not without tanks. What were you so excited about?"

"Do you trust me?" asked Duck, again with a boyish grin.

Dale pursed his lips and nodded, but Milo could see the doubt written across his face.

"Then watch this," said Duck. He swam to Dale first, switching off his headlamp, then to Logan, and finally to Milo. With the last light off, the flooded chamber was plunged into absolute darkness.

Milo looked around, the surrounding blackness omnipresent and impenetrable. He held out his hand in front of his face and saw the dim outline, watched as little flickers of light danced across his peripheral vision, but knew both were illusions.

"Do you see it?" breathed Duck, his whisper gratingly loud against the silence.

Milo tilted his head in every direction, seeing nothing. Then, out of the corner of his eye, he caught a glimpse of a slight but increasing glow. Slowly, he turned to face the source, a warm golden light from deep beneath the waters, easily forty feet below.

"Did you drop a flashlight?" asked Logan, returning the whisper.

"I most certainly did *not*," said Duck. Milo could practically hear the smile in the answer.

"You mean . . . that light was there when you got here?" asked Dale.

"Almost missed it," said Duck. "Gasket on my main light failed, headlamp shorted out. I surfaced to switch it out with one of the spares when I saw the glow. Have you ever seen anything like this before?"

"Of course not," said Logan. "Nobody has. It's . . . impossible."

"I dove to check it out," said Duck. "Definitely a light source down there, but it's *way* too deep to duck, and I don't think anybody with air tanks will be able to thread through that breakdown pile."

"So you're saying we can't reach it?" demanded Dale, his voice rising.

"Not unless you know a way to get a bulldozer down there," said Duck. "There is a *lot* of ugly looking debris in the way."

"He's right," said Logan. "It's highly unstable and could easily collapse if disturbed. Quite unusual for a cave of this morphology."

"I hope I'm not the only who doesn't already know," said Milo. "But what are we looking at?"

"That's the thing," said Logan. "I have no idea—and as far as I know, nobody has ever seen something like this before."

"You think it could be lava?" asked Dale. "Molten rocks?"

"No way," said Logan. "We'd be dead within seconds of reaching this chamber. There's no methane, no bubbles coming up from the breakdown, no exotic gases, no heat . . ."

Milo briefly lost his grip on the wall, splashing into the water before pulling himself back up again. "Definitely not another expedition," he said.

"Bioluminescence," suggested Logan. "No other possible explanation. Wish we had a trained biologist down here."

"I didn't think we'd need one," admitted Dale.

"I tried to get it on camera, but the image won't turn out," complained Duck. "I can't get close enough for a sample either."

"Assuming it *can* be sampled," said Logan. "Or if it *wants* to be sampled."

The hair on the back of Milo's neck stood up, alarmed at Logan's characterization of the mysterious light source. Duck was the first to click his headlamp back on, followed by the other three, the mysterious glow extinguished as though it was never there. Unprompted, Milo pushed off from the wall, swimming over to the small island in the middle of the chamber as the other three remained to discuss the matter.

Milo dragged himself out of the water and onto the island, little more than an unbroken rounded stone, just fifteen feet across. Now close, he could see a small alter-like collection at the center, a mass of small, stacked stones. His pulse quickened. The arrangement was indisputably man-made, the rocks carefully selected from the breakdown pile and arranged into a cairn of nearly three feet in height.

"What are you?" breathed Milo.

Then he saw something that stopped him dead. The shrine was topped by three ivory masks. *Someone* had made it into this distant, deep room. The masks were not fertility idols; they were shamanistic animal representations, the first of a monkey, the second a leopard, and the third an antelope. Trembling, Milo reached out to touch them, as if that would somehow assure his mind of the reality of the impossible find. His fingertips drifted across the smooth, carved white. Any paint had long since faded, absorbed by the darkness. A thin veneer of calcite had begun to form around the edges, gently cementing the masks in place. They'd been there for thousands of years, maybe longer.

"What is it?" said Dale, calling out from behind him.

"Some kind of altar," said Milo without looking up. "Man-made. Carved artifacts too."

"From DeWar?" suggested Dale as he began to swim over. "Or maybe the Japanese? It can't possibly be native, can it?"

"Can't say for certain," said Milo, shaking his head. "But look at the calcification—I highly doubt it's modern."

Examining the artifacts closely, Milo realized the central, largest mask—that of the leopard—had been visibly moved. The thin calcite around it was cracked, as though it had been taken and then carefully replaced. Though every instinct as a historian demanded he leave the artifacts undisturbed, Milo lifted the mask. Beneath it was a large natural bowl, not unlike a stone mortar, glassy waters filling it to the brim. And within the pooling liquid lay a leather-bound book.

Before he could announce the book, Milo heard a disturbance from the waters behind him. He abruptly swiveled back toward the group. Dale, Logan, and Duck shrank back as the waters besides them bubbled and frothed with movement and light. A figure was rising from beneath the surface of the black subterranean lake.

CHAPTER 19:

SACRILEGE

Joanne rose up through the dark waters, coughing as her head broke the surface. Treading in place, she swiveled around, seeing Logan, Dale, and Duck to one side and Milo standing on the island in the center of the flooded chamber.

"Ahoy," said Joanne. "You blokes were hard to find—I must have been right on your heels until you hit that big room back there. Took me forever to figure out where you'd gone. How about leaving some directions next time?"

"Sorry," mumbled Duck with a genuinely apologetic tone. "I was going to do it on the way back out."

"Bad boy!" exclaimed Joanne. "I ought to tell your mother!"

"Why are you here?" asked Dale. "What's going on?"

"I have not-so-good news," said Joanne as she swam to the nearest wall. "The weather up top has deteriorated significantly; satellite modeling shows a tropical storm turning toward our location. It's a big one, maybe even a hundred-year storm, and could make things bloody wet and bloody dangerous down here. We've been requested to return at the earliest possible."

"Return?" asked Duck. "To base camp? Or all the way to the surface? Can't we just wait it out in one of the upper chambers, above the water table?"

"Not as such," said Joanne apologetically as she hauled herself partially out of the water, hanging onto the wall beside the three men. "Too risky. They want us all the way out for now. We could be contending with flooded passageways and fast-moving waters. If that weren't enough, the weather could make resupply missions quite difficult, and there's always the matter of keeping the hatch in working order. I think we'd all be more comfortable out of the caverns for a day or two, let this weather nonsense blow over."

"I suppose they have their reasons," grumbled Dale, scratching his face in frustration. "But just when we've started making some real progress! Milo, tell me *everything* on the way back up."

"I will," promised Milo, stealing one last glance at the ivory masks.

Joanne smiled and nodded, but Milo got the distinct impression that haste was of the essence. She'd already spent too much time tracking them down. Logan was the first to take a big lungful of air and duck beneath the surface, disappearing in a froth of bubbles.

"Milo—you're next," said Joanne, waving him over. "We really ought to go quickly, please."

"Just a minute," said Milo. He thought about mentioning the leather-bound book, but immediately thought better of it. Best to avoid the temptation to stay longer, especially given the approach of a massive downpour.

A hundred-year storm, thought Milo. He envisioned the serpentine river filling with water, drowning the cathedral chamber and the little island he stood upon. Maybe it wouldn't make a difference—the book was already waterlogged—but the coming flood might be just enough to lose it forever.

Milo opened up his wet backpack and pulled out a sealable laminated plastic bag. Moving quickly, he carefully scooped up the book and placed it within the sack, filled it to the brim with water from the stone bowl, and tucked the heavy container as securely as possible within his pack. The water added a lot of extra weight, granted, but at least it'd keep the book stable until they reached base camp. Submerged paper held up remarkably well over time, even in acidic seawater, leaving Milo with full confidence he could preserve the book once they'd returned.

"Milo!" shouted Joanne, waving him over urgently as Dale and Duck plunged beneath the surface in quick succession, unwilling to wait their turn.

"Coming!" he exclaimed, strapping on the backpack again and swimming across the chamber. Thrilled by his discovery, Milo felt no fear as prepared his lungs for the dive. Three quick breaths—hold—and he forced himself beneath the surface, kicking toward the underwater tunnel.

The book was important, yes, but not as groundbreaking as the mask-decorated altar. No scholar had ever even considered the possibility that a tribal warrior could have made it so far into the depths of a supercave. But what next? An established understanding of Stone Age African culture, technology, and human ability would be replaced with a monolithic question mark, a tangle of unanswerable questions. He knew full well the gaps left by such controversial finds were too often filled with vitriol and doubt, to say nothing of the inevitable ad hominem attacks against his already-tainted career.

Grasping rocks with his hands, Milo pulled himself into the passageway, pressure in his ears and burning in his lungs as he scraped and bumped along the low ceiling.

Milo could see himself descending into the dismissed ranks of other historical revisionists, like the archaeologists who supposedly unearthed Roman olive jars in Brazilian bays, or claimed that China had discovered North America in the 1400s. No—it'd be even worse than that—he'd be trying to convince the academic community that early African hunter-gatherers descended through a half-mile of vertical rock and swam flooded chambers, all without ropes, light, heat, or food. It would be a shaky claim indeed, especially when built atop the broken foundation of his career.

His backpack caught on the same rocky snag, abruptly jolting him to a stop. Milo knew what to do this time, twisting himself free and kicking off from the passageway, shooting upward again.

No rational scholar would accept the idea, Milo concluded. Maybe it'd be better if flooding from the hundred-year storm washed the masks and altar away. Milo felt it unlikely—the structure could have survived a hundred such storms, maybe more.

Pulse pounding and vision gray, Milo broke to the surface.

Milo found the long march back to base camp infinitely more exhausting than the trip down. As he answered Dale's increasingly frustrated questions, he felt as though he was slipping forward in time, his mind drifting as they waded, walked, and crawled up through the airless tunnels. One moment he'd be in the present, inches from the bottoms of Dale's oversize boots, the next a quarter mile further along, the group in another configuration, with no memory of the interceding journey.

The group eventually emerged from the anthill and into the base camp chamber. They were all soaked to the skin, caked with drying mud, heavy packs dripping and soggy. A pounding headache reverberated within Milo's skull, exacerbated by the echoing waterfall.

If Dale Brunsfield had been expecting a welcome reception—or even a single person to greet him—he was disappointed. Looking around, Milo only saw the empty camp, the dimly illuminated globes lazily tilting on the ceiling above, no movement other than the cascading froth of the falls.

The others dropped their packs at the edge of the supply depot. Logan sat down on a rock and put his face in his hands, drained by his exertions. Joanne slumped down beside him. Dale crawled inside his tent while Duck, frowning, began organizing a haphazard pile of ropes and carabiners beside the supply depot.

"How soon do we have to get out of here?" Logan asked without dropping his face from his hands.

"Ask me again in ten minutes," answered Joanne. "I'm so bloody tired I can't think."

"Definitely take ten," called Duck from the supply pile, loud enough for the rest to hear. "If you don't take time to recover, we'll never get up the shaft before the storm hits. Everybody needs to eat something too."

Pulling the Velcro straps off his kneepads, Milo winced as blood flowed back into his beleaguered legs. He unsnapped his helmet, rubbing at the raw, chafed lines across his neck and ears. Reaching inside his tent, Milo dropped his excess gear and lights, stretching and enjoying the brief sensation of weightlessness. He couldn't help but think of the leather-bound journal inside the laminate bag and wonder what secrets lay within.

"Milo my boy," called Dale from his tent. "Would you mind finding Charlie for me? Isabelle, too—would like to tell them about the glow we found, help them strategize for the upcoming shoot once we're back."

Milo nodded, trying not to feel irritated. Sure, he'd find Charlie and the film team, no doubt so they could swoop in and take credit. Legs stiff and aching, Milo trundled up toward the waterfall, following sounds of laughter. Headlamp in hand, he shone a light toward the grotto at the base of the shaft, clouds of cold mist obscuring his vision.

Bridget stepped out of this waterfall, wet hair sticking to the side of her face. She'd stripped down to a pair of shorts and a drenched college T-shirt that clung to her skin. Milo's stomach churned as he flashed back to his unwanted dreams.

Seeing Milo, Bridget's first expression was one of pure shock, which she recovered from almost immediately as she stepped barefoot into her open hiking boots.

"You're back!" she exclaimed, unconsciously crossing her arms over her chest and giving him an awkward smile.

"Yeah—Joanne came to get us," said Milo, backing away as his face visibly reddened. "She says the weather is getting pretty messy up there. Where are Charlie and the rest?"

Bridget looked around the virtually empty chamber. "They should have been back by now," he said. "Joanne told them to stay close. I think they were doing some more filming."

Milo turned around and looked across base camp.

"I don't think they stayed close," he said.

The third call over the radio went unanswered, as did the fourth, fifth, and sixth. Joanne had become visibly frustrated, shooting angry glances between Duck and the radio.

"I don't know what happened!" Joanne said again. "They said they'd be just around the corner!"

"If they went in a new passage, they didn't chalk it," Duck said. "I have no idea where they went."

"Goddamn it!" shouted Dale. "What's our timeframe?"

"We should have left the moment we reached base camp," said Joanne. "The storm has already hit the surface; we could start feeling the effects at any moment. They've already missed two scheduled drops—we don't need the supplies, but it's concerning that they can't send anyone to the top of the shaft."

Dale shook his head angrily.

"This is my fault," Joanne said. "I wasn't clear enough that they should stay put while I went searching for you."

"Can't change the past," said Dale, irritated. "But we need to find them and get ourselves out of here *immediately*."

"How bad is it going to get?" asked Duck. "How worried should we be?"

Dale swore as he yanked off his helmet and threw it almost halfway across the chamber. The blue plastic hit sharp rocks and bounced off into a dark corner. "This shouldn't even be an issue," he shouted. "This is why there are *protocols* . . . we had *plenty* of time to evacuate; now we have to spend it *looking* for people!"

"This doesn't help us," Joanne said, clearly on the verge of becoming angry herself. "Let's start moving—what's the plan?"

"We don't have time to do this search the right way." Dale's intelligent eyes darted back and forth as he thought, his frown still deeply etched. "And we won't have time to move any of our gear to higher ground."

"Then let's do it the wrong way," said Bridget. "I'd rather have wet equipment than drowned friends. Please tell us what to do."

"Listen to her," said Joanne. "You know she's right."

Logan nodded in agreement.

"Everybody pair up and pick a tunnel." Dale pointed to the myriad of dark passageways around the one leading to the anthill. "Bring chalk— red chalk—and mark your path."

Everyone nodded.

"Keep light on your feet," continued Dale. "That means make a best guess every time you hit an intersection. If you reach a passageway that's too small for a camera, turn around and try another one."

"Got it," said Duck, already turning to grab his pack and chalk. The young guide still hadn't put his socks on.

"I need you back here in one hour regardless of results," said Dale. "That means you do an about-face at the thirty-minute mark, no exceptions. We could be in for a world of hurt with this flood—they may have to fend for themselves. I'll go with Joanne. Duck, take Bridget. Logan and Milo are together. And above all—don't make the situation worse by taking a spill."

Milo could barely keep up with Logan as they half-ran down a narrow, winding passageway. It was as if the geologist had found some hidden reservoir of strength Milo did not possess, and used it to fling himself through the darkness. Every intersection, Logan would briefly eye the fork without stopping, scrawl a thick red chalk mark against the more promising of the two, and slip back into his punishing cadence. As the pair clambered across a breakdown pile, Milo slipped, dropping to his knees, wishing he'd put the pads back on before leaving camp.

"Keep up," Logan insisted. "We do *not* want to be in this section if it floods."

In an instant, Logan was beside him, helping him up, but then back to moving an instant later. Every few moments they'd belt out "CHAR-LIE! ISABELLE!" to a lonely, echoing response.

Looking at his watch, Milo clocked twenty-eight minutes of the exhausting search. The idea of turning around in a hundred and twenty seconds held no relief. Milo knew they'd have to return at the same pace, maybe even faster, to have any hope of reaching base camp by Dale's deadline. He tried to imagine the consequences if they weren't able to locate Isabelle and Charlie—would they be leaving the pair to drown?

Again, they reached a fork. Milo barely considered it before almost bolting toward the larger of the two, but Logan held up a hand for him to stop.

"Do you smell that?" asked Logan, tilting his head toward a small, rounded opening dwarfed by the one Milo had selected.

Milo checked his watch with impatience. "We have to get back."

"I smell . . . *gas*." Logan pointed toward the smaller hole. "I think it's coming from there."

Time ticking out, Milo and Logan both shouted Charlie's name but heard no response. But when Milo held an ear toward the hole, he heard the distant thumping of tribal drums.

Logan and Milo looked at each other for a moment before Logan crossed off the mark to the other chamber and together they wriggled into the hole. It opened within a few meters to standing size, the smell of gas and drumming growing ever louder, now joined by the flicking glow of firelight.

Rounding a turn, Milo stopped dead to stare. In the small, room-sized chamber before him, Charlie Garza danced nearly nude in front of a camera, his body covered with tribal makeup and illuminated by flickering gas-soaked torches. Isabelle filmed as a small portable music player belted out the tribal beat.

Behind Charlie was a long, smooth wall filled with cave paintings, crude men with long spears hunting animals. Milo's heart jumped into his mouth for the fraction of a second it took him to tell that they were all fake. Even from the distance, Milo could see the supposedly ancient paintings were made of lipstick.

CHAPTER 20:

EVACUATION

2,225 feet below the surface

L ogan led the charge back to base camp, Charlie close behind, Isabelle trailing with the heavy camera equipment. Milo brought up the rear, helping her through the tightest passages. Would-be television host Charlie hadn't had time to put more than his boots on; he'd hastily stuffed his clothes into Isabelle's pack and stomped along wearing little more than improvised paint and flesh-colored briefs.

The party was bunched up enough to where Milo could catch glimpses of Logan's clenched, scowling face at every bend. His frown deepened each passing second until the geologist could no longer contain himself.

"It's—*vandalism*," he finally spat. "It's all just *vandalism*."

"What?" demanded Charlie, wholly confused.

"It's just a little decoration," Isabelle said, defending her lipstick paintings. "In a thousand years, archaeologists will think it's just as important as the paintings in the gallery."

"In *ten* thousand years," retorted Logan, "it'll still be *shit*."

Milo felt compelled to agree with Logan, sharing his irritation as the group burst out of the last stretch of passageway—and into a maelstrom.

They were too late. The booming waterfall had transformed into a howling, deafening barrage of water. Having already flooded most of the subterranean lake, the aqueduct crack was now a rooster-tail geyser of water, spray shooting out intermittently down the length of the base camp. Waters surged down into the main anthill passageway as growing rivulets escaped from the channel and lake, steadily encroaching the camp.

Milo, Logan, and the television duo were the last to arrive. Joanne and Duck were already leading efforts to save equipment. Duck had stopped trying to take down the tents, and was instead yanking them out entirely, aluminum pegs already lost to the first waves of encroaching water. Joanne grabbed at the ropes and carabiners, hurling them across the chamber with all her strength, desperately trying to get them to higher ground.

Logan sprinted into the chaos as Milo and the other cavers jogged toward the supply depot, grabbing and dragging plastic cases and aluminum crates through the now ankle-deep water. Behind him, Charlie slipped, landing in the shallow, rushing foam, but quickly rebounded to his feet. The small plastic crate he'd been carrying washed away, disappearing into the anthill.

Milo felt a tap on his shoulder and turned around to see Bridget. She shouted something at him from just inches away, but he couldn't make it out over the roar of the flash flood. Frustrated, she just pointed toward the largest crate. Together they seized it by the handles, Milo barely able to keep pace with the doctor as she marched the equipment over toward the high ground that Dale had staked out.

Duck had secured a narrow shelf overlooking the illuminated chamber, safely above the gathering waters but up a steep slope. As Milo and Bridget struggled against the rocky incline, Milo noticed the shelf's manhole-sized window in the rock wall behind it, a passageway to an unexplored chamber.

Sliding the large crate onto the shelf and into Dale's hands, Bridget and Milo turned again and bolted toward the floodplain, passing the others as they struggled with as much gear as they could carry.

Milo instinctively knew there wouldn't be enough time. The waters were rising too rapidly and they'd only moved a third of the supplies, maybe less. Both Milo and Dale watched in horror as the tripod-mounted laser scanner tilted and slammed into the froth, its still-attached cable yanking a laptop computer off the rocks and into the torrent. As the mists grew, it was becoming hard to see more than a few meters away. As Milo's vision obscured, he began to lose his sense of orientation.

A snap echoed out from the shaft, loud enough to ring throughout the entire chamber. Milo looked up in horror as a truck-sized boulder swung like a clock pendulum in the shaft, colorful descent ropes tangled in its jagged teeth as it slammed against the walls. Another snap rang out and the hundred-ton rock tumbled into the froth, dragging with it thousands of feet of cascading rope, the fragile descent system all but destroyed.

Dale grabbed Milo's shoulder for support as the two waded through the roiling, knee-deep flow, determined to save one last pack before they were washed away forever.

"Does this explain why we didn't find DeWar's camp?" shouted Milo, leaning toward Dale, his mouth inches from his ear.

"It just might," responded Dale, his voice lost to the roar. Together, they reached a Pelican case far downstream of the now-obliterated supply depot. The rugged plastic box was snagged between two boulders along with a backpack, the currents bashing both ferociously into the rocks.

Milo heard shouting from the narrow ledge above—the guides were now pointing and yelling. He swiveled toward the waterfall. Even through the mist, he could see that the waters had gone from a clear, foamy white to a muddy brown. An earthen dam had burst far above, turning the downpour into a sediment-laden tsunami.

Dale dropped the Pelican case and began furiously wading back toward the ledge, the deluge around them turning swirling and dark. Milo reached back to grab the last pack and chased after him. He could feel rocks and debris churning in the current, ripping and bashing against his legs. The water was almost waist-deep by the time Milo reached the ledge. The men dragged themselves up the rocks. Charlie reached down from the ledge, using almost inhuman strength to pull Dale and Milo, soaked and exhausted, to safety.

Milo slumped to a sitting position as the guides shouted at each other. The muddy waters had cleared the mists, and the dull globes above still illuminated the entirety of the chamber. But something was desperately wrong—below and no more than thirty feet away, Isabelle clung to a partially submerged boulder as the raging dark surge swept by. Growing waves leapt ever higher, threatening to knock her from her fragile handhold. The boulder shifted, and Isabelle lost her grip, almost yanked downstream by the current before she caught hold of the rock again. Her sacrificed camera vanished into the muddy froth.

Dale swore and threw a rope across the chamber. Yellow-helmeted Isabelle grabbed onto it, holding tightly as the flood swept her underwater. Every person on the ledge grabbed onto the rope as it whipped and snapped under frenzied tension. Yanking hand over hand, they drew in the line—until it suddenly went slack.

Isabelle never surfaced.

Milo dropped the rope, looking at every member of the remaining party. Charlie was too shocked and battered to speak; Logan just buried his face in his hands. Dale and Joanne scanned the flood for another few moments before turning their attention to what little gear they'd rescued. Tears welled in Duck's eyes. Milo felt Bridget's hand slip into his, squeezing it. He couldn't bear to look at her.

Still dressed in his comical tribal costume and smudged makeup, Charlie turned to Milo with bafflement. In the confusion, Charlie seemed to not fully grasp what had just happened.

"Why'd you save that?" asked Charlie, pointing to the pack Milo had nearly lost his life retrieving.

Confused, Milo opened the satchel's top flap. Inside, he saw the soft, colorful fabric of Charlie's parachute canopy.

"Can I have it back?" asked Charlie.

Milo stared down the bigger man for a full ten seconds before hurling the pack into the flood.

CHAPTER 21:

IN A BAD WAY

2,150 feet below the surface

t took almost ten hours for the waters to recede. Milo stood silent sentry as the cold mists slowly retreated, the main shaft waterfall transforming once again from a muddy brown to clear, white water. Below, the collected pools slowly shrank along the length of the floodplain, once again revealing the glistening floor. Only one of the six ropes had survived, but there was no way of telling how much damage it had suffered in the vicious flood.

The ledge barely had standing room for the seven cavers. The small alcove behind them was little larger than a hotel bathroom, allowing only two sleepers at a time. The rest of the tiny chamber was stacked floor-to-ceiling with salvaged equipment. Milo supposed the tight quarters were fine; they'd only managed to save a single soggy sleeping bag anyway. One of the guides had fully unzipped it, stretching the bag over plastic sheeting as a makeshift mattress.

The cavers took turns on the ad hoc bed; each was allowed a

three-hour shift. Milo hadn't slept during his; he felt like he'd been up and moving for a hundred years. He finally gave up trying to sleep after about a restless hour.

Duck and Joanne congregated on the ledge beside Milo, whispering in low tones as Logan and Dale joined them. The foursome parted easily to accommodate Milo as well. He did a quick headcount and realized Joanne had left Bridget to sleep in the alcove by herself.

"I'm going in after Isabelle," said Dale, jutting his chin toward the anthill and the floodwaters still draining within.

"Good," said Duck. "I'm coming too."

Dale started to protest but was interrupted.

"This needs to be a fully manned search," interjected Joanne. "Ropes, whatever medical gear was saved, and as many of our people as possible—or else you'll be utterly useless should you find her."

"She's right," said Logan with a grunt. "Though I imagine we're essentially looking for a body at this point."

"We don't know that," Dale snapped.

"Sure we do," said Logan with lackadaisical certainty. "She probably lasted all of thirty seconds in the rapids. Even in the best-case scenario, she would be well into fatal hypothermia territory by now."

Milo glanced from the others back to Dale, whose expression was fury tinged with shock. Milo felt only guilt for so easily sharing Logan's cruel assumption.

"We don't leave people behind," said Duck, sharing Dale's glare. "What if it was you down there?"

"Then I'd be dead," said Logan with a shrug. "And I wouldn't give a shit. Because I'd be dead."

While the anthill was difficult before, it had now transformed into a slick, muddy river. All seven had abandoned virtually everything at the alcove save for lightweight packs that held only what they'd require for the next few hours. Joanne had carefully roped all seven to each other, forming a tight human chain as they traversed down the underground rapids.

Every member of the team fell eventually. It would start with a jolt and a quick yelp as their feet slipped out from beneath them. Plunging into the water, they were picked up by the current and slammed from rock to rock like a pinball until they snagged on something or were stopped short by the rope, the rest of the team straining to hold them.

Second in line, Joanne noticed a smashed Pelican case wedged between clusters of thick stalactites. Yawning open, the case spilled a week's worth of food across the wall and downstream; rice, dehydrated soups, dry pasta, and dented cans. Just below it sat the remains of the television camera. Though intact, it was wholly ruined, lens broken, casing smashed, dripping water down visible wires and circuit boards. Joanne pursed her lips as she retrieved the memory cards from the destroyed device.

"Want me to grab any of the food?" asked Dale, gesturing to the smashed container.

"We'll have to come back for it," said Joanne. "Keep moving."

Leading, Duck did not pause at a single intersection, instead following the river's route at each. Milo noticed that half of the chalk marks were now gone, washed away by the flood. He supposed it didn't matter—the rushing waters marked the only path that mattered.

Scanning the passageway as she walked, Joanne suddenly stopped the group with a wave of her hand, flashlight aimed at a smooth yellow sphere a few meters away. Milo recognized it immediately as the top of Isabelle's helmet.

The group scrambled down the slope, ignoring the slippery surface beneath their feet. Now closer, Milo could see Isabelle wedged within a breakdown pile, still wearing the yellow helmet, her blue-tinged face barely above the water, open eyes rolled back into her head.

"Be careful!" shouted Logan. "We could trigger a collapse at any moment—watch your step."

Ignoring Logan, Duck knelt down next to Isabelle and pressed his ear almost to her lips. "She's breathing," he announced with astonishment. "Holy shit—she's actually alive!"

Kneeling next to Duck, Milo surveyed the badly injured producer. Isabelle's right leg was twisted grotesquely under a large boulder. Only one half of her chest rose and fell, and she seemed totally unresponsive to the flurry of light and noise around her.

"Incredible!" exclaimed Joanne. "She's a tough cookie."

"If she made it this long, she's got a chance," added Duck.

"Get the rock off her!" ordered Bridget.

Before the group could rally, Charlie braced himself under the rock, teeth gritted and veins bulging as he slowly hefted the oblong boulder from underneath. It shifted with a low rumble, rolling free of her leg.

There was no hesitation from Bridget, no indecision. She issued a rapid-fire list of instructions, asking for pulse, spare webbing, bandages, tape, backboard, and blankets, ordering the team to ready any other medical supplies and cut Isabelle free of her clothes.

Milo was startled by how cold Isabelle's skin felt to the touch; she was freezing but not shivering. Then he remembered what Logan had said about hypothermia, the hours she'd spent in the water. It was nothing short of miraculous that she was still alive.

Duck flicked open a knife and ran the blade from Isabelle's pant cuff up through the thick canvas thigh and beltline as Bridget did the same with her fleece pullover. There was no consideration for privacy as he exposed her bruised, blackened chest and abdomen, her bloody, sliced-up hips and legs.

"She's bleeding internally," said Bridget, using the end of the knife to point where dark blood had pooled under the skin beneath the worst of her injuries. Within seconds, she'd rendered the producer virtually naked. Milo forced himself to not avert his eyes.

Without prompting, Duck rolled out a collapsible backboard, setting the thin plastic sled up beside Isabelle's twisted form.

"Helmet?" asked Joanne.

"Cut it off," ordered Bridget, flipping the knife around in her palm to pass it to her.

Joanne grabbed the handle of the sharp instrument and carefully slipped it through each of the four helmet straps, leaving only the loose shell on top of Isabelle's head.

"Need cervical stabilization," Joanne announced. Dale and Duck joined their hands behind the producer's neck, holding it in place as Joanne carefully slipped the helmet free of Isabelle's bleeding scalp and wet, stringy hair.

"Holy *fuck*," Duck exlaimed, examining the helmet as Joanne passed it in front of him. Milo caught sight of the damage—a baseball-sized circle on the side had been neatly punched in by a rock. The helmet had done its job, saved her from a collapsed skull, but she'd still likely suffered a concussion, maybe even a fracture.

"Get ready to lift her onto the backboard," said Bridget. "I want everyone around her in a circle—on three, *gently* but *firmly* lift her up and over. We don't want to exacerbate any spinal injuries or internal bleeding. Remember: slow is smooth, smooth is fast."

The team scrambled around the producer, waiting for the order. Bridget counted off to three and everyone awkwardly lifted, pulling Isabelle's body free of the rocks. The foot of her broken leg remained wedged, leaving the team holding her body in a dangerous limbo until Dale, swearing, cut her boot free.

Within seconds of cradling Isabelle in the collapsible backboard, Duck and Joanne were busy tying her down. Joanne paid the most attention to her skull and neck, padding it with her ruined clothing as Duck and Dale ran the webbing back and forth over her form, firmly strapping her forehead down last. The resulting contraption almost resembled an open-topped kayak, at least until Dale and Joanne covered every inch of the producer in synthetic fleece blankets, followed by a second round of webbing and straps, wrapping her up like a mummy.

Dale reached under the blankets and started rubbing warmth back into the freezing hands.

"Don't do that!" snapped Bridget, slapping Dale's hand away. "You'll send freezing blood right to her heart—it could kill her."

"Really?" said Dale, confused as he looked to Duck.

"Better listen to the doc," said Duck, shrugging.

"Is Isabelle going to make it?" asked Charlie, almost pleading.

"She's in a bad way," said Joanne. "But statistically speaking, she's already survived the hour after her initial accident—if we can get her out of here fast enough, there's every reason to believe she'll live."

"Thank God!" exclaimed Charlie with profound relief. Smiles broke out across the group—except from Joanne.

"There's no way we'll be able to get her back up to base camp," she said, dropping her head in resignation. "We can't fight the current *and* the tight squeeze, not with her on the backboard. We're sitting ducks if we get hit by another flood in these twisting passages. Besides, we're stuck on the wrong side of the main shaft until the surface teams rig up a new rope system. We have to go deeper and find a place to hold out— it's Isabelle's only chance."

CHAPTER 22:

CONFESSIONAL

2,625 feet below the surface

Milo woke to the sound of clanking metal, again jolted from inexplicable dreams. Duck and Logan waded into the flooded cathedral chamber dragging a set of six oxygen tanks in a rubber drybag, the two-liter bottles loudly ringing with every footstep.

Dale looked up from his sitting position at Isabelle's side, annoyed by the rough treatment of the volatile aluminum pressure vessels. It was Duck and Logan's second trip to base camp and back. The wading men were too exhausted to speak as they handed over the tanks and a few small packs of shrink-wrapped medical supplies.

Bridget looked at the returning men and shook her head before turning her attention back to the patient. Leaning over a cracked glowstick, she checked Isabelle's pulse and respiration for the half-hourly reading. Duck swayed from side to side as he watched, blinking his eyes too quickly as he tried to stave off collapse for a few more moments.

Milo shot a glance toward the geologist. Logan had developed deep, dark wrinkles under his hollow eyes, his expression distant, yet he seemed strangely at peace with the deteriorating conditions and physical exhaustion.

"I think we set an underground speed record," mumbled Logan. "We made it down here *fast.*"

"No such luck, bro," said Duck as he sank down onto one of the flat rocks that dotted the underground lake. "I set that record two years ago in Fool's Day Extension in Huatla, Mexico. Had the taquito-shits."

With that, Duck stretched himself out and closed his eyes, falling dead asleep in his filthy clothes before Logan could even respond.

"You need to rest and rehydrate," ordered Bridget. "Someone else can take the next run. Another run and you two will be just as incapacitated as Isabelle."

"I know what I'm doing," huffed Logan as he pulled himself up next to the sleeping Duck, flipped himself onto his stomach, and folded his arms under his chin. Bridget ignored his irritated retort.

"And you need to be more careful with the oxygen next time," added Dale. "You knock one of those nozzles on the rock the wrong way and it'll go off like a rocket, leave somebody with a tank-sized dent in their head."

Now fully awake, Milo dropped off his rock and swam over to where Dale and Bridget attended to their patient. Charlie sat beside Isabelle, holding one of her hands and whispering to her; he hadn't left her side for a moment since arriving at the cathedral chamber. Milo had no idea how long they'd been down there, probably just eight to ten hours, but it felt like days.

"You get a chance to look at the ropes?" asked Dale.

"Yeah," said Logan without getting up. "There's just one left, and it looks like shit."

"How is the patient?" asked Milo, dragging himself out of the water and crawling to join the circle around Isabelle. Strange how fully he'd adapted to the darkness; he hadn't even bothered to switch on his head-lamp during the swim over. The dim, struggling light from the single glowstick was more than enough.

"In and out of consciousness," said Dale, lifting up one of the blankets to expose half of her blackened, bare chest. Milo again forced himself to look. Bridget had placed a sort of crude flapper valve over the deepest chest wound, a small square of clear plastic taped on three sides, allowing air trapped between her damaged lung tissue and chest to bubble free. The previous batch of oxygen, fed to her through a nasal cannula tube, had kept her breathing, even allowing the collapsed lung to partially reinflate on its own.

Dale tapped the oxygen bottle as the pressure valve dipped into the red, the tank almost empty. He quickly worked to replace it with one of the new tanks ferried down by Duck and Logan.

"We're still going to run out in a few hours," said Bridget. "Hopefully she won't need the extra oxygen by then."

Dale just grunted in acknowledgement as he adjusted an IV line. Milo didn't bother to ask what would happen if Isabelle couldn't work up the strength to breathe on her own.

The IV line drew Milo's doubts as well. They'd salvaged the needles and tubes but not any of the fluid itself, forcing Bridget to work up a batch from salt, honey, water, and a few dissolvable painkillers, all boiled over their single remaining gas jet stove. The liquid mixture was poured in a taped-up plastic bag and hung on a backpack frame, the jury-rigged apparatus slowly dripping down a tube and into the largest vein in the inner crook of Isabelle's elbow.

"We'll need more IV fluid by then as well," added Dale.

"I can work up another batch," offered Bridget.

"I can't keep the bag clean if we keep refilling it," stated Dale, impassive. "Bacterial introduction is inevitable."

"We'll bomb her system with antibiotics the moment we hit surface," said Bridget, unfazed. "Right now we just need to keep her alive—infection is tomorrow's problem."

It was strange the way they ignored Charlie, but Milo couldn't blame them. The man was immobile, psychologically trapped by Isabelle's side as she flickered in and out of consciousness. Unsolvable problems went unspoken—Isabelle could be suffering brain trauma, internal bleeding, cerebral swelling, cervical dislocation, even organ rupture. And yet she breathed without pause, deeply, her heavy, drugged eyes fluttering open every once in a long while to take in what little of her situation she could process.

"You get any sleep?" Milo asked Bridget.

"A little," she answered. "Enough to stave off the nods for a few hours."

Milo grimaced. He knew what she was like when she was exhausted; in her current state he wouldn't have put her in charge of changing a light bulb, much less sustaining a human life.

"Can you two watch her for a bit?" asked Dale with a sigh. "I'm starting to lose it here. Hearing sounds, seeing lights . . . that kind of shit. I'll be worthless if I don't get a few minutes at least."

"She's as comfortable as she's going to get," answered Bridget, nodding. "The oxygen is a big help. I'm going to start rationing the dosage, stretch it for as long as possible."

Dale pursed his lips, considering. "Duck and Logan really came through on those tanks," he said. "Just wake me up if there are any developments."

With that, Dale slid off the side of the rock, waded to the far side of the chamber, and curled up on a small ledge.

Charlie gently stroked Isabelle's forearm, his lips moving inaudibly as her fingers gently twitched in response.

"I think she knows I'm here," said Charlie, his voice distant and hoarse.

"You should get some sleep too," said Milo. "We'll let you know if she opens her eyes again."

"You know she changed her name?" said Charlie, breaking his vigil to look up at Milo for the first time in hours. "She was born Zuzanna

Wieczorkowski. Brutal, right? Her parents came from Gdansk to San Bernardino in the early '80s, back when she was just a baby. She told me about it years ago, back when we first met. We spent a weekend together in Mexico once, got wasted on sangria in a cheap motel in Acapulco, talked all night and watched as the sun came up over the parking lot the next morning. Fuckin' *Wieczorkowski* . . . no wonder she changed it."

"Does she have anybody back home?" asked Bridget. "A spouse? Kids?"

"No way," said Charlie with a knowing chuckle. "Not Isabelle. She got married once for, like, a minute. It's the job. She got to travel the world, meet amazing people, and see more in a year than most people would see in a lifetime. But it all came at a price."

"I don't understand," said Milo. "What price?"

Charlie just shrugged. "It happened slowly," he said. "I didn't notice it at first. She was filming a Discovery Channel archaeology special in South America once, Skyped me from the site. Showed me an ancient artifact they'd just brought up. I said it was amazing; she said it was boring. Wasn't gold, like the last one she'd seen. Nothing captured her imagination anymore."

"I get it," said Bridget, nodding, distracted as she checked the levels of Isabelle's home-brewed IV. "She was burned out. What'd she think of this expedition? Was it something special?"

"This was just another assignment," said Charlie bitterly. "She only did it as a favor to me; she was already making plans for the next one. Isabelle didn't even think the cave would be that interesting, not after covering Son Doong caverns in Vietnam last year. She said maybe I'd bite it parachuting down the shaft and then she'd have a real story. We laughed about it."

Charlie didn't say anything more after that. Milo sat with him, silent, until Dale and Joanne replaced them for the next shift.

Milo found his own flat rock and tried to sleep. There wasn't anything else to do. With no recharger station, floating balloon lights, or extra batteries, all light was strictly rationed. They were left in near-darkness, illuminated only by the faint green of the fading chemlight beside Isabelle. Milo wondered how long it would be before he started seeing things like Dale.

A realization hit Milo: he wasn't bored. In fact, far from it. In the passing hours everything around him had become increasingly . . . interesting.

In the darkness and with virtually no visual distractions, Milo was inundated by remembered details about the surrounding cave—chemical compositions, geological terminology, species adaptation, hydrological forces. It soon felt as though he could dive into an undammed river of information, bathe in it, every bit of data at his fingertips, just waiting to be plucked and savored within the mind. Enjoying the sensation, Milo concluded that the effect of the cave might be not unlike that of an isolation tank—albeit considerably more perilous.

Not tired and unwilling to sit still, Milo removed the leather-bound journal from the sealed plastic bag, letting the waters drain out off the side of his rock and into the subterranean lake. The fibrous hemp within was entirely intact, allowing him to slowly peel back a few pages at a time, placing absorbent paper napkins between each. The ink itself was faded but legible, a testament to the insolubility of iron gall ink, and would likely be easily readable once the book dried. Milo finished by placing the journal on top of a smooth rock and weighing down the cover with a few additional stones.

He finished just in time to hear splashing from behind him. Bridget pulled herself out of the water and up onto his rock, dripping as she sat beside him.

"Can't sleep?" she asked.

Milo shook his head. "Feel like I should do something to keep myself occupied," he said.

"I haven't been this exhausted since med school finals," said Bridget. "Almost like I'm so tired I'm not even tired anymore."

Milo considered her for a moment, hesitating. "I don't quite know what to make of this," he said, "but I almost feel . . . energized. Focused, even."

It was Bridget's turn to look quizzically at Milo for a few moments before answering. "I actually feel the same way," she finally said. "And I'm remembering things too. Like the formula for the IV fluid. The recipe came from an offhand comment made by a professor at the end of class, not the sort of thing anybody expected on the test. I never even wrote the formula down. But when I thought about it, it came back to me so *clearly* . . ."

The two sat in silence, thinking.

"Want to see something amazing?" asked Milo.

"Sure," said Bridget, smiling.

"Follow me."

M ilo swam through the underwater tunnel, his thoughts clear and bright, his lungs full of clean air. With every stroke, he could feel the waters around him warming; Bridget followed at his heels. His powerful headlamp winked out, extinguished by moisture encroaching through the rubber seal.

But he didn't need his artificial light. The warm, golden glow was more intense now, streaming out of the breakdown pile in thick rays, erupting from the waters and dancing across the ceiling.

Milo and Bridget broke the surface of the water and inhaled deeply. A slight mist had collected at the surface, the bathtub-warm waters evaporating into the humid chamber.

A feeling of profound giddiness flooded through Milo, and with it an overpowering raw euphoria; a oneness with the glow. Dizzy with intoxicating sensations, he and Bridget locked eyes for a fraction of a moment before they threw desperate, shivering arms around each other, Milo clung to the wall with one hand as Bridget's yearning mouth locked onto his, limbs intertwined.

Milo's buzzing mind took a single step off the ledge and into oblivion, surrendering his perception into a somersaulting deluge of overpowering present and remembered past. Only his primal inner self remained, unbound to thought or consequence. Feverish heat surrounded him, an uncontrollable fire pouring from his skin and hers as they pulled desperately at each other's clothing. Milo swam across the surface of his own mind, primordial sexual memories of their lovemaking swirling into a single impossible moment.

Bridget and Milo almost dragged each other under, tumbling and circling as they half-paddled, half-floated toward the altar-topped rock in the center of the room. The last of their clothing fell away, boots already kicked off, Bridget's shirt drifting abandoned, Milo's trousers slowly sinking into the depths.

Irretrievably lost to the ecstasy, Milo was yanked suddenly into vivid flashes of his most precious memories—Bridget bathed in morning light as she slept in his arms; Bridget sneaking a look over her shoulder as she left his class; Bridget dancing in front of a mirror to a long-forgotten pop song as he watched, lost in his love for her. And then Bridget pulled him onto the island, tearing him from his memories, and in an instant straddled him with her naked form, pushing herself onto him, her fingers digging into his flesh of his chest as she threw her head back, her muscled body heaving in sync with his own.

Drifting, flying, floating, Milo allowed the last of his consciousness to disappear into the rapture of the golden glow.

CHAPTER 23:

ESCAPE

Bridget breached the water's surface like a mermaid, sputtering and laughing and snorting as she shook droplets from her soggy dark hair. Milo watched her nude form as she swam toward him, skin smooth and lustrous in the glowing golden light. Naked, he leaned against the stone altar and basked in the warmth of the underground room.

"I got your pants!" Bridget announced, waving them up and out of the water so Milo could see. "They were almost thirty feet down."

"Thanks," said Milo with a smile. "No way was I swimming that deep. You saved me from more than a bit of embarrassment."

"Embarrassment?" said Bridget, reaching the island and pulling herself out of the water. "Ha! Not half as embarrassing as literally every single thing Charlie did for the camera."

The pair immediately broke eye contact. Looking away, Bridget unrolled Milo's pants onto the rock beside all the other clothes they'd managed to fish out of the deep waters. A quick survey revealed they'd found virtually everything, missing only two socks and one of Bridget's gloves. The doctor sat against the rock cairn next to Milo, resting her head on his shoulder as they watched the slow dance of the golden rays shift across the smooth stone ceiling.

The light slowly faded as they watched, turning the golden sunset-like illumination to twilight. The mists around the water receded, the room slowly settling to cool darkness as Milo finished repairing his caving lamp.

Bridget pulled Milo's wrist away from his work and into her lap, slowly stroking his palm and intertwining her fingers with his as their clasping hands rested just atop her soft mound of silky dark pubic hair. Kissing the top of her head, Milo couldn't help but drink in the lovely contours of her strong, sculpted body, the curve of her waist, her muscled arms and taut stomach.

He looked down at his own body. The extended caving expedition had done wonders to his admittedly lackluster physique, the strenuous exercise and rapid weight loss emphasizing dormant muscles and freeing his abdomen from too much takeout and craft beer. He felt like the energy of his early twenties had returned; the sharp physicality he'd buried little by little with the distractions and resentments of modern life. Milo felt focused. He felt strong. But more than anything, he felt . . . alive.

Bridget smiled and kissed him on the cheek, her soft lips brushing against his growing stubble. "What the fuck just happened between us?" she asked, wonderment in her voice.

"I have no idea. Things feel so much simpler down here. Food . . . air . . . light . . . so little else matters."

"There's something else at work." Bridget turned to stare deeply into his eyes. "You felt it. I felt it. The glow, this room . . . it's like it took over, unleashed something buried deep inside."

Milo nodded.

"I wish I knew more about the glow, why it affected us like this," mused Bridget as she fiddled with her helmet. "I'm afraid that when someone comes back with the proper equipment it'll be gone. It's bioluminescent life; that much seems certain. But what is it?"

"We know it's a powerful psychoactive," said Milo. "My head started buzzing the moment I surfaced. Felt like I was skipping across a universe of my own thoughts and memories. I felt this . . . infinite joy. I've never experienced anything like it before."

"And a connection to everything," said Bridget, nodding. "Do you suppose that's why we made love?"

"Hard to say," answered Milo, putting his arm around her shoulders. "Seeing you brought up a lot of old feelings. Our judgment may have been compromised—but I never felt like I was acting against my will. I hope you felt the same way."

Bridget nodded, but didn't respond at first. "Even with all the chaos, the flood, Isabelle's accident, I don't remember the last time I could think so clearly," she finally said, not acknowledging the answer to her own question. "It's like all the noise is gone. Like I can be alone with my thoughts for the first time in years."

She paused for a few more moments, lost in contemplation. So much remained unspoken.

"Let's go," she finally said as she clicked on her light. "I want to get dressed and swim back before they send a search party."

The cavers in the cathedral room were all awake and standing by the time Bridget and Milo emerged from the submerged tunnel. Logan and Charlie were at Isabelle's side. Milo and Bridget quietly climbed onto the largest rock and joined Dale and Joanne standing next to Duck, who had his arms crossed and eyes closed as though he were about to perform a particularly difficult magic trick.

"Abby, Angel, Ashton," said Duck, rattling names off. "Calvin, Devin, Elisha, Giorgio, Henry, other Henry, Kelsey, Kevin, Lucas, Matthew, Max, Medha, Michael, Nick, Nina, Serena—"

"We get the point," interrupted Joanne, tapping her foot in frustration.

"What's Duck doing?" whispered Bridget, tapping Dale on the shoulder.

"He says he can remember the names of every classmate in his third grade after-school science camp," Dale replied. "I said he couldn't, so here we are."

"Weird, right?" said Duck. "Just came to me—out of nowhere. It's not just their names. I remember all their favorite foods and the first names of their mothers. Most of them said cheeseburgers and pizza, but one of the geekier ones said 'ants.' Like, you eat a few ants on a dare and that's suddenly your favorite food?"

"I've eaten ants," said Logan, raising his voice from the nearby rock where he attended Isabelle. Everyone swiveled to look at him.

"It's weird," maintained Duck. "Eating ants is super weird."

"Why?" demanded Logan, almost shouting to be heard from across the thirty-foot distance. "Insects are the protein of the future. I've eaten tarantulas, crickets, scorpions, even maggot larvae."

Dale just winced in disgust and turned back to the semicircle.

"While I have everyone here, I have an announcement to make," said Dale, addressing the cavers. "I've spoken with Duck and we've agreed that we need a new camp. The flooded-out chamber is no good, and we're too remote and waterlogged down here to be much good to anybody. Duck and I will hit the anthill shortly and look for a safe space to hold out. Logan has run the numbers—he thinks we've only explored about one to three percent of the total area of this cave to date. There has to be a better spot to hunker down than this."

"Hold out?" protested Joanne. "We can't just wait down here, Dale—we need to *leave*."

Around her, others murmured in support. Milo found himself fixated on the one to three percent calculation, unable to fathom the sheer size of the system.

"I agree that's the ultimate goal," said Dale, holding out his hands to quiet the group. "But we can't, not with Isabelle in her current state, not until our surface teams get their shit together, re-rig the main shaft, and come find us—the existing ropes are too damaged. We haven't checked in for almost twenty-four hours, which means they may have already started looking for us, or they're waiting until it's safe."

A few nods—they'd seen the boulder that took out the descent system and heard Logan's blunt assessment of the one remaining rope.

"But—" protested Joanne.

"He's right," interrupted Duck, cutting her off. "The surface teams know we're down here and they know what they need to do. We can't risk making for the hatch."

"At least allow me to go to the main chamber," said Joanne. "I can mark the path—leave instructions—see if there's still anything worth saving."

"Didn't Duck and Logan do that already?" protested Dale.

Duck shook his head. "We were running on fumes, bro," he said. "I was too tired to see straight, much less do a thorough check. There could be all sorts of stuff left in the base camp chamber, probably some supplies washed down the anthill too."

"Fine, whatever," snapped Dale, clearly done with the conversation.

"Very well," said Joanne, eyeing Dale with skepticism. "I'm taking Milo and Bridget with me. She says she can't do anything more for Isabelle, at least not for the next few hours."

Dale turned around and looked toward Logan. "Dr. Flowers—you okay with staying with Isabelle?" he asked. "You need someone else with you?"

"I'm a certified Wilderness First Responder," answered Logan irritably at having been asked. "And I have Charlie with me. The patient will be fine."

The trio moved in silence for most of the wet slog up the anthill. Joanne led, Bridget was on her heels, and Milo wheezed some distance behind as he attempted to keep up.

Joanne finally interrupted the quiet.

"Do you think what Duck said was strange?" asked Joanne, stopping for a moment in a narrow passageway as she turned to address the pair.

"How so?" asked Bridget. "About remembering things? I missed most of it. Not sure what to think." Milo noticed she'd said nothing about their own experience in the glowing room, where past and present swirled and a sea of memories converged in a single uncontrollable stream of consciousness.

"I'm remembering things too," Joanne admitted.

"Like what?" asked Milo. "Third-grade classmates and their favorite foods?"

"Not as such," said Joanne with a chuckle. "More like . . . the weather on every birthday I've ever celebrated. February in Birmingham is quite rainy, so perhaps not such a feat. But then . . . other things as well."

"Such as?" asked Bridget.

"Such as the first hundred pages of Charles Dickens's *Bleak House*," answered Joanne with a low whisper. "Word for bloody word. Like I can see the pages in front of me."

Milo and Bridget looked at each other, not sure what to say.

"I keep coming back to a single quote," Joanne continued. "Can't get it out of my mind. It reads: *Fog everywhere. Fog up the river where it flows among green airs and meadows; fog down the river, where it rolls defiled among the tiers of shipping, and the waterside pollutions of a great and dirty city . . . Chance people on the bridges peeping over the parapets into a nether sky of fog, with fog all round them, as if they were up in a balloon and hanging in the misty clouds.*"

"All I remember from that one is 'the universe makes a rather indifferent parent,'" said Milo. "I couldn't name a single character."

"Queer, isn't it?" asked Joanne. "Especially after Duck's little show."

"Maybe," said Bridget. "Maybe not. I think all of us have been experiencing similar symptoms. There's not much sensory stimulation down here, especially in the quieter chambers. Auditory and visual hallucinations are common in the depths, aren't they? Could it be that your bored mind is simply digging up old information for re-processing?"

Joanne shook her head in fierce disagreement. "I've been in a lot of caves," she answered. "Never remembered much Dickens before. This ability is something new."

The trio trudged up the last of the anthill without speaking. Joanne continued her rigorous policy of marking every intersection with chalk, this time reaching far above her head and marking with thick, unmistakable streaks well clear of the still-glistening flood-line. Exhausted from the climb, they emerged into the deafeningly loud, wet, muddy main chamber.

One of Duck's illuminated balloons still clung to the ceiling, dimly burning through the last of its flagging battery. The others had deflated, lying in collapsed, wrinkled piles in distant corners.

"Should we start searching?" asked Bridget, disappointment in her voice as she surveyed the massive room. The waters had scraped it clean, and the small ledge and alcove where they'd sheltered appeared thoroughly ransacked.

"Bollocks to that," said Joanne as she strode purposefully toward the main shaft waterfall. Reaching it, she experimentally tugged at the single wet rope still hanging from the distant ledge fifteen hundred feet above.

"You're not seriously considering trying it, are you?" asked Milo, unsure of the cave guide's intentions.

"There are no safety lines left," added Bridget. "And you have no way of knowing if the rope will hold!"

"There's only one way out of this complete debacle," said Joanne without turning to look at him. "Make contact with the surface, direct the rescue. They should have been down here by now—but if they're not coming to us fast enough, we'll have to go to them. I can rig three harnesses out of spare webbing. We'll use cord to make hand and foot loops, attach them to Prusik knot ascenders. The knots only slide one way—up. Slide the hand above your head; bring the foot after it. We call it frogging. It'll take time, but we'll be at the top of the shaft in a few hours, find out what the bloody hell is going on up there. We'll bring back food, medical supplies, and a proper team of rescue cavers."

"We're just going to leave?" said Milo angrily. "Abandon everyone?"

Joanne swiveled around and stuck a finger in his face. "If Isabelle stays down here much longer, she *will* die," stated the cave guide. "It's only a matter of time until an infection takes hold. Or a vital organ fails. Left untreated, cranial swelling will get worse. I'm no doctor, but I've seen my share of caving accidents. We have to bring her to hospital. And for the rest of us—we have *maybe* four days' worth of food left if we stretch it."

Bridget put an arm around Milo's shoulders, comforting him. "She's right," said the doctor. "Even in the best-case scenarios, Isabelle is dead within seventy-two hours. Every minute counts, and we need all the help we can get."

"Milo, you know where this is leading," said Joanne. "You study disasters like this one. Equipment will fail. Lights will go out. People will break down, falling victim to paranoia and hallucinations. What little remains of our expedition will become only chaos and death. Better to risk our three lives now."

"I'm in," said Bridget, jutting her chin and narrowing her eyes in steely determination. "Just tell me what to do."

"Milo?" asked Joanne, tilting her head at him.

"Fuck it," said Milo as he eyed the long rope disappearing through the mist and into darkness far above. "Let's go home."

CHAPTER 24:

SYSTEMIC FAILURE

725 feet below the surface

Trembling with exhaustion, Milo gingerly extended his gloved fingers to grip the top of the ledge. The cascading waterfall churned and roared, deafening him as water pounded rocks into sand fifteen hundred feet below. Salvation was mere inches away, but rallying the strength to grasp the overhang and pull himself over felt all but impossible. Every wet, mud-covered inch of his body burned with pain after climbing the near-endless height in complete darkness.

Though it saved their dwindling batteries, the darkness came with flickering hallucinations as his exhausted, understimulated mind struggled to cope with the vast nothingness of the shaft. Little flashes of light danced in the corners of his eyes, false glows that refused to move from the periphery of his vision. Every few minutes during the ascent he'd heard someone sharply call his name from just inches away. He'd jolt his head in the direction to see nothing but blackness.

The voices were always disturbingly familiar yet unidentifiable, spoken by long-forgotten friends.

Swinging from the rope within reach of the top, Milo tried to calculate the distance of each frog-like movement as he had ascended up the rope. Maybe eighteen inches? That would make for roughly a thousand repetitions, maybe more. His improvised webbing harness dug into his groin, leaving a long line of thick blisters across the sensitive skin of his inner thigh, and the constant movement left every joint inflamed. It was too dark to read his watch; Milo estimated they'd been at it for hours. Between his raw palms and exhausted abdomen, he felt like he'd just rowed across the Atlantic. He could barely think through the pain and fatigue.

Gathering the last of his waning strength, Milo hefted himself up and over the edge, flopping down on the widest section, just below where the sole remaining rope line met the thick stalactites. The rest had all snapped—four frayed ropes had broken at their topmost knots, but one had managed to shear off an entire thick stalagmite anchor. Looking around, Milo found the chamber surprisingly dry—the floodwaters had come from the waterfalls further down the shaft, leaving the chamber misty but untouched by fresh mud or debris.

Milo extended a hand into the darkness, palm against blistered palm as he pulled Bridget over the top, then Joanne. In silence, they breathed heavily and untied themselves from harnesses and rope, unraveling the Prusik ascension knots.

He couldn't help but grin like an idiot. After all, he'd earned his way out of the shaft, fifteen hundred feet of unceasing pain and exertion. Looking down into the vast abyss, he decided he'd never return. Perhaps it would be better to pretend that DeWar's journal and the three masks never existed than try to explain the find to his peers in academia.

Joanne swiveled her headlamp toward a small equipment dump, an abandoned pile of a dozen shrink-wrapped crates and Pelican cases only partially rigged for lowering. The cave guide dragged herself to her feet, inspecting the hastily abandoned equipment and supplies.

"There's no note," she said, confused. "Why would they just leave it here? Why wouldn't they lower it to us?"

Bridget and Milo shook their heads, unable to answer her.

"I'm going to try the radio," said Joanne. "If there's a rescue team nearby, they should pick up the transmission."

The cave guide announced herself into the walkie-talkie, pausing for a response. Nothing came, not even a crackle of interference.

"Maybe we can try again closer to the entrance," suggested Bridget as she got up to join Joanne. "We couldn't have possibly missed them in the anthill, could we?"

"No way," said Joanne, shaking her head. "They would have left a chalk trail, or at the very least seen ours."

The doctor shrugged and turned her attention to the ample supplies. Milo helped her open one of the largest crates, shuffling through uncooked rice and dehydrated meals to find a box of thick, chewy granola bars. Bridget grabbed two and passed around the rest.

Milo ripped his open with incredible anticipation, closing his eyes to concentrate all his focus away from his pain-wracked body and to the simple pleasure of eating. "Found chocolate!" announced Joanne, waving a small pack of Hershey bars. She opened one and broke off a thick chunk for herself before handing the rest to Bridget and Milo.

"You are my new bestie," said Bridget, gleefully snapping off a large piece.

"*I'm* my new best mate," said Joanne with a laugh. "I don't even care if I make myself sick."

"Still, I feel guilty about eating this with everybody else still down at the bottom."

"Believe me, they'll be thanking us once we organize the rescue."

"Chocolate for all!"

"Rescue first," corrected Joanne with a solemn nod. "And *then* chocolate for all."

All three lifted up their candy bars to toast the sentiment.

Revitalized, the three purposefully hiked through the tight, intersecting tunnels, barely glancing at the chalked directions. The muddy bootprints of the missing support team was trail enough. As they pressed onward, the reverberating, baritone roar of the waterfalls slowly gave way to claustrophobic silence. Within an hour, the trio emerged into the elephant graveyard, the fossil-flecked, high-domed auditorium with vanishingly distant walls. Milo slowly panned his light from side to side, again drinking in the forest of thick, crystal-filled stone columns, dripping stalactites, and spire-like stalagmites.

Then his light fell across a long, man-sized plastic tunnel, white sheeting supported by flexible PVC paralleling the deep crevasse, the open, unfinished end piled with loose piping and rolled plastic. The tunnel measured some eight feet in height at the peak and was nearly as wide. Piles of sheeting haphazardly covered the cave floor, with the tubular plastic piping left sitting on the fragile piles of petrified elephant dung and mummified bats. Before them, the tunnel extended far into darkness, disappearing under the mammoth limestone archway separating the gallery from the graveyard.

"What *is* that?" breathed Joanne in confusion.

"I was hoping you could tell us," said Bridget.

Milo racked his mind for a theory. "Maybe it's for the gallery," he suggested. "Protect the fragile petroglyphs from increased humidity or carbon dioxide fluctuations?"

"I don't know why they built the tunnel," said Bridget. "But I imagine we're meant to use it."

Joanne stepped into the tunnel first, the clean plastic sheeting crunching under her muddy boots, plastic walls ripping with each footstep. Bridget and Milo followed, uneasily taking in the sudden shift from natural morphology to the laboratory-like cleanliness of the white plastic.

There was no way to tell how long it was; the tunnel went far further than the reach of their headlamps. After a few minutes of gingerly making their way down the artificial corridor, Milo guessed they'd long since passed underneath the natural arch stone barrier between chambers and were now well into the gallery. There was no way to be entirely certain.

Ahead, Joanne squinted and leaned in to examine a long, rust-colored stain on one of the white walls. Bridget quickly caught up and gently pulled the guide away from the dark splatter.

"Please back away," said the doctor, holding up a sleeve to her mouth as she took Joanne's place, examining the stain for herself. Milo looked down, seeing a flurry of dirty bootprints and drag marks on the plastic sheeting below their feet.

"It's blood, isn't it?" asked Milo, a chill going down his spine.

"It most certainly is," confirmed Bridget, dropping the sleeve from her mouth. "It's dry now, so less infectious, but still potentially dangerous. You can tell it was coughed up by the marks from the water droplets."

"Why was someone coughing blood?" demanded Joanne, her voice now ice-cold and barely above a whisper.

"They must have collapsed here," said Bridget, pointing to the floor and the drag marks. "Someone pulled them away, back toward the entrance."

"Bridget, I need an *answer*," insisted Joanne. "We expected to find a rescue team, not a bloody plastic tunnel and body fluids."

"I don't have one," said Bridget curtly. "Not yet. I need you both to keep your gloves on. Touch as little as possible. We'll make for the hatch; find out the full situation when we link up with Main Camp."

In silence, the trio crept along the gallery chamber tunnel, careful to not brush the white plastic walls on either side. The tunnel was largely straight, but their lights still disappeared into the darkness without reaching the end. With no markers except for the blood splatter, it was useless to get any sense of sense of distance, no way to tell how far into the gallery they'd walked.

Milo began to notice a very particular smell building with each deliberate step. He looked over to see Joanne wrinkle her nose in disgust. The smell was sickly sweet, putrid. Only Bridget seemed unaffected, her movements tense and her silent attention fixed ahead. Milo's eyes began to water as his gag reflex contracted in anticipation.

Ahead, the tunnel opened up as it reached the entranceway. No longer a tunnel, the white plastic sheeting was now pinned directly to the ceiling and walls, encompassing the entire thirty-foot breadth and twenty-foot height of the room. The skeletal menagerie of hyrax, antelope, and other animals had been hastily swept into one corner of the room and enveloped with plastic covering like the rest of the uneven cavern floor. The thin layer of glittering dust that had previously clung to the air was now gone, leaving an eerie stillness in its absence.

Milo thought back to what Logan told him when they'd first stepped into the gallery entranceway.

It's a dead cave, the geologist had said. Encased in plastic and filled with the awful smell, the description felt disturbingly apt.

As he stepped into the room, Milo's eyes fell on a pile of lumpy black bags. A new wave of putridity washed over his senses, almost driving him to his knees as he fought down a retch. Eight bulky body bags were stacked against the far wall. Another five were scattered across the floor with obvious evidence of haste. Three final bodies had been put on blankets and dragged through the narrow metal door, abandoned uncovered on the cavern floor.

Milo's heart sank as his eyes fell across the closest of the uncovered bodies. Even with her sunken gray features and blood-flecked garments, he still recognized the blonde logistician who'd introduced him to Main Camp. It felt like he'd met her a lifetime ago. She'd died horribly, with thick rivulets of dried blood crusted at the corners of her mouth, eyes, and ears.

"These two are porters," said Joanne, gesturing to the other uncovered corpses. "Dr. McAffee . . . what happened to our people?"

"Don't touch anything," ordered Bridget in a whisper. "They're highly infectious postmortem. This has to be the work of Marburg virus."

"I wish I hadn't touched those crates." Milo gagged as he fought down another wave of nausea.

"Let's not jump to conclusions," said Bridget. "None of us have presented with any symptoms. Marburg is a fluid-borne virus; no reason to assume we've been exposed."

"I can't *believe* this is where they thought to secure the bodies," said Joanne. "Didn't they take a moment to think about the expedition party?"

"Probably the only way to keep the bodies away from wild animals and scavengers," said Milo. He shrank a little when the two women shot him an angry look. "Just saying."

Bridget pointed at one of the porters, at the gritty black substance dripping from his open mouth, down his cheek, across the blanket to the plastic sheeting below. Unlike the others, his yellow, bloodshot eyes were wide open and cloudy with decay. "He was alive when they dragged him in," she said, no emotion in her voice.

"Did they assume we died too?" asked Milo, the frightening thought hitting him with sudden urgency.

Joanne's eyes darted toward the closed steel door between herself and the surface. "We need to get out of this fucking cave," she said.

Careful to not so much as brush the walls, Joanne slowly edged down the narrow entranceway, the other two following close behind. Milo watched over her shoulder as she stopped dead before the steel door. Joanne reached out with a gloved hand and pulled at the wheel.

Nothing happened.

"What's wrong?" demanded Bridget as an increasingly desperate Joanne yanked the wheel a second and third time without results.

Milo glanced down at the base of the door, seeing black rings of hydraulic fluid dripping from around the rubber sealing. Just above it, one of the metal hinges was cracked. The warped door had been subjected enough external force to knock it out of alignment and destroy the hydraulic actuators.

Gasping with frustration, Joanne pounded on the impenetrable door. "You motherfuckers!" she screamed, but even the blows from her fists barely registered, deafened by earth piled up on the other side. Breathing heavily, her narrowed glance darted to the others as she collected herself.

"Why does it sound so muffled?" asked Bridget, fear entering her voice for the first time. "Why won't it open?"

Joanne just put her face in her hands, turned her back to the door, and slid down to a sitting position. "It's been buried from the outside," she finally answered in a whisper.

"A mudslide?" asked Bridget, her voice hollow. "Are they digging us out? Can you hear anything?"

Milo felt a knot thick grow his throat, fed by the most hopeless fear he'd ever experienced.

"I don't know," said Joanne. "I can't hear anything."

"It's not a mudslide," said Milo, his voice hoarse with fury. "Look at the door—it's been almost knocked off its hinges. Someone used a bulldozer. They buried us alive down here."

CHAPTER 25:

FRAGMENTATION

The cavers made camp at the top of the ledge, the roaring waterfall below now almost comforting in its familiarity. Milo couldn't sleep; his searching eyes were wide open to the black nothingness all around, hallucinatory flickers dancing in his peripheral vision. If not for the rumbling cascade and the rocky protrusions jutting through his thin sleeping pad, it would be as if he were weightless in the world, drifting in unfathomable emptiness.

Milo heard a rustling behind him, barely audible. Small hands smoothly ran up his spine, cupping his shoulders and sliding down to his chest. Bridget crawled into the sleeping bag beside him, clinging to his body in the darkness as she rested her chin on the back of his neck. It reminded Milo of the last night they'd spent together—an unexpected embrace in the middle of the night, though they had barely spoken in days. By the end of the following afternoon, she'd moved everything she owned from their shared apartment and left the city.

"Do you blame me for bringing you out here?" she whispered, her lips brushing against his ear.

Milo just shook his head, rustling his short hair on the soft nylon of the sleeping bag. "Of course not," he said. "You were trying to give me a second chance at what I've always wanted—nobody could have foreseen what came next."

"I didn't know how I'd react when I saw you again," she said, a little louder this time but still too quiet for Joanne to overhear. "Still think about you more than I probably should. When I travel somewhere amazing for the first time, or when I read an article I really enjoy, I think, *I can't wait to show Milo.* Like the part of my brain with you in it never quite shut off."

Milo took her hand in his, brought it up to his mouth, and kissed it. "Mine too," he admitted. "After you left, I felt completely unplugged from everything—had to teach myself to enjoy life again without you. I'm not sure if I ever quite succeeded. Always found myself wondering what you were doing—if you were happy, if you had anyone, if you still thought about me."

A silence fell between them.

"Are you?" asked Milo. "Happy, I mean?"

"Sometimes," said Bridget.

"I feel terrible about the way we left things," said Milo. "I always wanted to reach out, tell you I understood, that I wasn't angry anymore."

"If you had, I would have listened," said Bridget. "Or at least I told myself I would listen. But that was always our dynamic—you retreating into silence, me filling the void with resentment."

"When you put it like that . . ." began Milo.

"We really were a shitty couple, weren't we?" asked Bridget.

There was another thick pause between them before they both burst into stifled laughter.

"We were," said Milo. "But maybe someday we can become shitty friends instead?"

"I'd like that," said Bridget. "I should have told you that I missed you."

"I've missed you too," said Milo. He pressed her fingers against his lips again, but this time so she could feel his smile in the dark.

For the longest time, silence once again fell between them. He could feel Bridget stiffen again, muscles tense as her fears once again took hold.

"I'm not going to die down here," she whispered in his ear.

"We'll make it home," responded Milo. "I promise." And for perhaps the first time, he felt total certainty in the proclamation.

Milo's eyes closed. He dreamed of the eternal Tanzanian savanna, a sea of elephants, and the fertile oasis at the center of the world.

Milo stirred awake to the soft yellow light of a sunrise. Bridget had slept curled up in his arms but pushed him away as he shifted in the sleeping bag. He had little idea how long he'd slumbered, but felt refreshed, filled with new determination.

Blinking the sleep from his eyes, Milo swiveled his head toward the light. Joanne had taken her brightest headlamp, set it on the cavern floor, and smeared a dab of clear, amber honey over the plastic lens, filtering the illumination. Bridget stirred as well, stretching as she yawned, pulling her warm body away from Milo. Joanne sat on a rock staring at Milo and Bridget, watching as they withdrew their intertwined limbs from each other. It wasn't a disapproving look on her face—it was one filled with a deep, longing sadness.

"Helps, doesn't it?" asked Joanne, tilting her head toward the light. "A little yellow reminds the mind of dawn; makes it easier to get up. It's a trick we use on . . . hard days."

"Thanks," said Milo. Bridget even managed a smile.

"Did you sleep?" asked the doctor.

"A few minutes here and there," said Joanne as she absentmindedly picked up the lamp and smeared the honey off the lens and onto a finger, which she then licked. "But I wanted to make sure you two had your full eight. Can't say when we'll get the chance again. How are your blisters? Any pain or injuries beyond bumps and bruises?"

"I'll live," said Milo. "Still nothing on the radio?"

"I've been trying every hour," said Joanne with a sigh. "There must be too much earth between us and the receiver, even at the hatch. I can't raise anyone."

"Or nobody's listening," mumbled Bridget, her brief smile long since faded.

"I hate to state the obvious," said Joanne. "But we can't simply disappear from the rest of the group. We'll have to collect as many supplies as we can carry and rejoin our comrades. We're no use to anybody holed up at the top."

Milo pursed his lips in grim silence. With the hatch impassable, part of him knew it was only a matter of time until they were forced to rejoin Dale and the others. The supplies they'd bring back would be a big boost to morale, but he knew their situation would remain desperate as ever—especially for Isabelle.

"What happens when they get the hatch open again?" asked Bridget. Milo couldn't help but notice she said *when* and not *if*—the doctor refused to give up an iota of hope.

"I've left a note by the door," answered Joanne. "Told them we're all still alive but Isabelle has been badly injured and is in desperate need of help. I included the date, of course."

"Makes sense," said Bridget. "I can't think to add anything."

"I almost told them to go fuck themselves for stranding us," said Joanne with a smirk. "Bloody inconvenient, burying us alive."

Milo couldn't help but grin ruefully at the gallows humor. "Inconvenient" might well be the understatement of the century.

Milo's heart plummeted as he rappelled back down the seemingly endless shaft, wet rope whistling through his gloved hands. Every few seconds the rappel rack would jolt, hitting badly damaged sections of rope where the sheath had come entirely apart, revealing the fraying core within. They wouldn't get a second climb to the top again, not without a new line.

They'd been so maddeningly close to the surface, mere feet. But now he was returning to the dark, muddy hell of the deep. Last on the line, he plunged further and further through the misty waterfall, his feet finally crunching on the wet gravel below as he hit solid earth with a painful jolt.

Joanne emerged from the mist, balancing a heavy box on her back as Bridget followed closely behind.

"Never gone this long without a gonk day," grunted Joanne, shifting the crate from one shoulder to the other.

"What's that?" asked Bridget as she helped Milo unhook from his rappel rack, freeing the descent rope from his improvised webbing harness.

"Means a day off," said Joanne, grimacing. "A bit of time to relax, gather strength. We could really use one. Duck is the best at throwing one—on our first caving expedition together, he waited until we'd spent four days slogging through waist-deep mud, absolutely knackered and bickering among ourselves like children. And then he pulled out his hidden stash of bourbon and dark chocolate. But before he'd give us any, he made us do the Macarena dance. Really! The Macarena, like it was 1996 all over again. Made us sing the song and everything. And then we drank and laughed until everyone forgot their petty quarrels."

Joanne led the cavers out of the thick mists as though guided by preternatural sight, walking purposefully to the alcove where they'd first sheltered from the flood. She and Bridget had made good use out of the time it had taken Milo to follow them down the shaft. They'd already broken down most of the fresh crates abandoned by the porters, sorting and securing the contents within. But what was once base camp was now little more than a waterlogged floodplain barely illuminated by the exhausted light of the sole remaining balloon.

The guide let the final crate slip from her shoulder and slam on the rocky floor of the alcove ledge. It popped open, revealing a collection of tank tops and men's underwear.

Milo didn't see the point of grabbing another pair; he'd long since abandoned his own. Bridget experimentally pulled out a pair of large briefs, tugging on the elastic.

"You s'pose these are clean enough to use as dressings?" she asked, thinking out loud. "I'd really like to see Isabelle's bandages switched out."

"Your call," grunted Joanne. "As for everything else—we can't drag these crates; we'll have to pick through and grab high-calorie foodstuffs, spare batteries, and any medical supplies. If it won't keep us alive over the next seventy-two hours, it's not coming."

Milo figured any underwear would be better off applied to Isabelle's wounds than to his ass, but packed a few anyway. Joanne took a last sweep through the supplies, spotting a few final cans and batteries to cram into their packs. The last of the resupply scavenged or packed into the alcove, the trio trudged in silence toward the entrance to the anthill.

Though burdened with an overstuffed pack and following last in line, Milo still felt as though he could have completed the brutal descent with his eyes closed. Tired and sore, he remembered each duck, twist, and bend; knew by heart every section where he had to take off his pack, loop a strap around his foot, and drag it behind him through the dark, airless passageways. Without speaking, the trio passed over the land bridge, ignoring the mummified body below it. Milo slogged onward through wet, descending passageways, past the hole to nowhere and ever deeper.

Joanne stopped cold as she reached the banks of the serpentine river, her headlamp fixed on a note hanging from the low ceiling by a long strand of parachute cord, the message impossible to miss. The cave guide yanked the note off the cord and read the message out loud.

"It says *Established new camp*," Joanne read. "*Follow arrows. Dale.* Simple enough."

"Looks like we're not going to the cathedral," said Bridget, clearing her throat to speak for the first time in hours.

Milo swiveled his light around the tunnel until he saw the first over-sized chalk-mark arrow leading away from the main descending pas-sageway. Joanne nodded toward the mark and followed it through the narrow rock corridor.

Dry, stagnant air increased with every step. Now well out of the floodplain, the walls and floor had become dusty and dry, even the sta-lactites and stalagmites increasingly ancient and withered. No water had flowed through the still passageways in a million years or more, transforming the maze into a subterranean desert.

The winding path ended abruptly at an open expanse, and Milo real-ized he was looking across the unimaginable length of a great chasm. The flat, vertical walls on either side were quite close, only twenty feet of emptiness between them, but the immense span disappeared into the darkness long before the light from his headlamp could reach the other side. With his struggling batteries, Milo couldn't even make out the ceil-ing above or the distant floor far below.

Ahead, a dump-truck-sized rock with a flat top lay wedged between the canyon cliffs. It had dropped from the ceiling in ancient times, leav-ing deep grooves in the towering walls as it fell. But now it was wedged like a tension-set diamond, impossible in dimension. The cavers had rigged up a "nylon highway" of anchors and ropes from the passageway exit, up and along the vertical wall for a distance of thirty feet before reaching the flat-topped rock where they'd struck camp.

Joanne briefly eyeballed the ropes but ultimately ignored them, pre-ferring to instead free climb the sheer cliff despite her heavy pack. Milo and Bridget opted to clip into their webbing harnesses in case of a fall, following slowly behind.

Dale and the others didn't bother to get up from their thin sleep-ing pads as Joanne, Milo, and Bridget clambered up on top of the flat rock. Bridget went to Isabelle first, placing a comforting hand on Char-lie's shoulder as she sat down beside them. Milo joined the pair, look-ing down at the producer. It was difficult to see the true extent of her injuries as she lay wrapped up like a mummy atop her blanket-covered plastic backboard. Her eyes were open but unseeing, unsettling to watch.

"How's she doing?" asked the doctor.

"The IV fluid you mixed up lasted a while," said Charlie. "Another couple hours and we'll probably need a new batch."

"Good, good," said Bridget. "No swelling, discoloration, or hardness around the needle?"

"Nothing worse than when we found her," said Charlie as he adjusted a handkerchief to cover Isabelle's open eyes. "Dale checked her heart rate and blood pressure every hour, just like we discussed. No change."

"That's the best we could hope for," said Bridget, sneaking a glance toward Milo. The story of their journey to within meters of the surface was a terrible, burning secret to keep.

"She's started mumbling," added Charlie. "I can't understand a word of it—she's not conscious as far as I can tell."

"There are levels of consciousness," explained Bridget. "She may be trying to communicate—or it could just be unconscious manifestation."

"It sounds like . . . clicking," said Charlie. "A stream of consonants and vowels. I can't understand any of it."

Silence fell over the three as Milo glanced up toward Joanne and Dale. The female cave guide had taken their leader to the side, quietly whispering to him as he reddened in anger. The other cavers began to stir.

"You went *where*? Are you *insane*?" Dale shouted, loud enough that every caver suddenly turned to stare. Joanne didn't rise to the bait, instead simply crossing her arms as she gazed across the gathering party. Milo did a quick headcount, seeing everyone but Logan.

"Well, I suppose it's out of the bag now," said Joanne. "We went for the surface to get help. The rope held."

Milo and Bridget stared at each other, his mind flashing back to the gruesome find at the hatch.

"That's good news, right?" asked Charlie, desperation entering his voice as he rocked from side to side. "They're coming soon? When is help getting here? Did they already re-rig the main shaft?"

"We found an abandoned supply drop at the top of the shaft," continued Joanne, ignoring Charlie's rapid-fire questions. "But once we reached the elephant's graveyard, we found this . . . plastic tunnel—"

"None of this makes *any* sense," interrupted Duck.

"Our people on the surface were trying to build a passageway through the viral convergence zone," interjected Bridget. "There must have been some sort of outbreak up top. We found more than a dozen bodies just inside the hatch. Marburg virus, by the look of the symptoms."

"Get to the point," snapped Dale. "Who's coming for us, and when is rescue getting here?"

"Nobody's coming," said Joanne, her voice hoarse and solemn. "They bulldozed over the hatch. They buried us down here. We're stuck until they open it back up again. Dale's drone IR-scanned every inch of savanna within a ten-mile radius of the entrance—there's no other way in or out."

"Oh *fuck*," mumbled Charlie, looking up from Isabelle's side. "Oh fuck, this is a *nightmare*. They *bulldozed* over our only way out? What the *fuck?*"

"I'm certain it was temporary; just until they can get a handle on the pathogen," added Bridget, trying to inject some cold rationality back into the conversation. "Joanne left a note—she said we were still alive, told them our situation. They'll see it when they open the hatch."

"Might be a *hundred years* until they open it again," sputtered Charlie. "They must think we're *dead* down here. How do you even know you didn't bring the virus back?"

"Because we're not bleeding from our eyeballs," snapped Bridget. "I do this for a living, Charlie."

"Who was dead?" demanded Duck. "We have *friends* up there, man!"

Joanne shook her head. "I only recognized a couple of them," she said. "We didn't open up the bags. The bodies lying out were mostly porters. But it got Kylie too. She's dead."

Guilt washed over Milo as he remembered the blonde logistician's name. Charlie started moaning again, his guttural tones piercing the stillness, filling the echoing subterranean canyon with grief and fear. Milo allowed himself to slowly look from caver to caver, trying to ascertain their reactions.

Charlie was already useless, lost to his fear and shock. Joanne and Bridget had slipped into dispassionate professionalism, focused wholly on immediate, solvable problems. Milo couldn't tell if Dale was more upset at the fact that they were buried alive or that his orders had been flagrantly ignored. Duck was only afraid.

Finally, he looked back to Dale. And all he could see was anger.

"I told you not to go up there!" shouted Dale, red-faced and furious. "Why would you risk your lives like that?"

"To organize a *rescue*," hissed Joanne through clenched teeth. "For *all* of us."

Dale swore loudly as he reached into the interior breast pocket of his khaki vest, removing a small piece of crumpled printer paper. Milo caught a glance of it as Dale passed the paper to Joanne, recognizing the printout as a supply drop inventory list.

Joanne held up the inventory to her headlamp, close enough for Milo to sneak a look over her shoulder and catch the timestamp. It dated from the final scheduled drop, just before the deluge hit. Joanne flipped it over to read the handwritten note on the other side.

Eight sick
doc thinks Cholera(?)
Porters panicking
surface camp on LOCKDOWN
Suspending supply drops
SIT TIGHT

Milo's heart sank. Dale had known all along. By all appearances, the note was written not long before the situation on the surface turned critical. His mind spun through a web of potential scenarios, trying to piece together what had happened. Milo figured Dale wouldn't have had time to respond to the note before the flood hit. And it would have been easy to assume the worst when people started dying at the surface camp; they had no way of knowing how bad the flooding had become. After all, the dozen plus bodies dumped in the cave entranceway could have been a mere fraction of the total death toll.

"You knew." Joanne's voice had turned icy cold. "You knew and you didn't tell us."

"I didn't know it'd gotten that bad," admitted Dale. "There was nothing we could do about it from down here. I didn't see any sense in worrying the group. I told Duck; he disagreed. The flood hit before we could work it out."

"Are you serious?" demanded Duck. "Does this mean nobody's coming for us?"

"I could have expected this from Dale," Joanne snapped at Duck, pointing a single accusing finger. "But not you."

With that, she slammed down her backpack, spilling the looted supplies all across the flat rock. Duck dove to his knees, saving a box of dehydrated beef stew from plunging over the edge and into the chasm. By the time he looked up, Joanne had already hopped onto the rope line, swung herself down to the entranceway, and disappeared into the anthill.

"What's the big deal?" protested Dale. "We sit tight—just like the note said. They'll get things at the surface under control soon enough."

Duck glanced toward Milo and Bridget, shooting each a rueful, resigned smile. "I'd better go," he said. "Make sure Joanne is okay. She looks pretty pissed."

Bridget and Milo stood in silence, watching Duck as he easily downclimbed the sheer rock wall after her.

Without another word, Bridget turned away, walking across the long flat rock toward Isabelle. Charlie was beside the patient, fast asleep on a thin foam pad.

Milo walked over to Dale, who had begun sorting through the salvaged supplies from the aborted drop.

"You have anything to add?" asked Milo, sitting down.

Dale just shrugged. "You know everything I know."

"Getting rations ready?" asked Milo.

"Yeah," answered Dale. "Hope you're ready for a thousand-calorie-a-day crash diet. We'll need to make this last. Once we're out of food, all we'll have is each other."

"I really hope you're not talking about cannibalism," grunted Milo.

Dale just chuckled. "So you three made it all the way up the shaft on Prusik knots and a web harness?" he asked.

"We did," confirmed Milo. "My balls will never be the same."

"That's because they just turned to brass," said Dale, stopping the count to stare at Milo for an uncomfortably long time. "Welcome to the fraternity. If that feat doesn't make you a caver, nothing will. I had my doubts about you. No offense, but you come across as kind of an indoor kid."

"Thanks," said Milo, though not certain he entirely accepted the premise of the compliment.

Dale just nodded and cleared his throat. "Got something for you," he said, moving a few feet to the left and rifling through his pack. His hand withdrew an object carefully wrapped up in a small fleece blanket.

Milo unconsciously gulped as the blanket fell away, instantly recognizing the leather-bound journal he'd discovered atop the altar.

"I'm sorry we didn't have more time to discuss this or the masks," continued Dale, eyeing him intently. "Logan and I discovered the book in your bag as we left the cathedral chamber. You can imagine our surprise . . . it doesn't exactly look like the sort of thing you would have brought with you. Is this what I think it is—Lord DeWar's honest-to-God personal diary?"

"It would certainly appear so," said Milo, masking his own uncertainty. "It was completely waterlogged; I was in the process of preserving—"

"It looked pretty dry, so I went ahead and opened it, couldn't help myself," interrupted Dale with a knowing smile before Milo could try and convince Dale he'd planned to tell him about it all along. "Almost can't believe it's in such good condition, considering . . . they must have made diaries pretty durable back in the day. I read as much as I could. Starts out like you'd expect. Travel notes, observations of exotic animals and cave geology. All noblemen of that era seem to have considered themselves citizen scientists of some variety or another. They found the golden glow, Milo—same as us. We were following in their footsteps the whole time!"

"That's incredible," breathed Milo. "And then what?"

"And then the writing becomes . . . different. He's excited, almost euphoric. DeWar and his team start digging, trying to break their way into the next chamber. They're just about to make it through when everything changes."

"How?"

"I don't know. The normal entries end, and the rest is pages and pages of complete gibberish. I can recognize words here and there, but can't make heads or tails of it otherwise. I need someone who knows the man—really knows him—to take a crack at it, see if there is anything there or if DeWar just lost his goddamn mind."

"Did anyone else try?"

"Logan. He got pretty excited, said he had to zip out for a few minutes and that he'd be back shortly. Tried to take the book from me. I wouldn't let him. At this point I haven't seen him in a while."

"I'll read it," said Milo as he reached out to take the book. Dale didn't let it go, leaving Milo to struggle in an awkward tug-of-war until he finally looked up and locked eyes with Dale.

"I'm not goddamn stupid," said Dale, holding Milo's attention hostage. "Should I think it's just a coincidence that suddenly all of us have developed photographic memories at the same time? DeWar went on and on about memory anomalies too, at least until he stopped making any goddamn sense whatsoever. There's something happening to us down here. Duck suddenly remembers the name of every one of his childhood classmates. Charlie looks like he's quiet, but if you look closely you can see his lips moving. I caught him whispering—the man is going through every *Godfather* movie line by line. And did you see him move that boulder off Isabelle? It must have been eight hundred pounds if it was an ounce; I've never seen anything like that before. I don't know Bridget as well as I'd like, but Joanne's a million miles away and as quiet as I've ever seen her."

"And what do you remember?" whispered Milo. "Do you have it too?"

Dale nodded as he let go of the journal, allowing Milo to take it and hold it close to his chest.

"Yeah," said Dale. "I have it too."

Milo sat in silence, watching Dale's impassive face break down, tears gathering at the corners of his eyes. Whatever he remembered affected him deeply.

"I don't know what's happening," said Dale. "But what I do know is that there are things down here I've never seen before. Including ourselves. Three well-equipped expeditions went into this cavern, and as far as anybody knows, nobody made it back out. If Logan and Joanne are right, it's now *twice* that somebody has tried to permanently seal up the entrance."

A chill went down Milo's spine.

"Whatever we're up against, I have a feeling it's only going to get worse," continued Dale. "DeWar may have left the only warning of what's to come."

Milo gingerly opened the front cover of the leather journal. He'd done well with the formerly waterlogged tome—the rough hemp pages opened easily, barely sticking to one another. He ran his fingers down the elegant insoluble inking of the interior inscription.

JOURNAL OF LD. RILEY DEWAR
SUBTERRANE EXPEDITION 1901

Again, Milo shivered; he bridged the distance of more than a century with the simple brush of a finger, his mind swimming with the secrets that might lie within.

"I'll read it," promised Milo.

"Good man," repeated Dale. "Read fast. I don't know how much time we have left."

CHAPTER 26:

REVELATIONS

2,475 feet below the surface

Milo carefully walked to the edge of the camp. Sitting down, he leaned against the stone cavern wall, again marveling at the great rock wedged between two chasm walls as though suspended between the pillars of the earth itself. He dangled one leg over the infinite black nothingness, headlamp tilted down toward the journal in his lap.

Lord Riley DeWar was an engaging writer, comfortable in his trademark style of charming affability and genuine wonderment at the natural world. He and his twenty men began with a wagon train from the German-controlled colonial port of Dar es Salaam before journeying up the coast of Tanzania by local steamship. The young lord felt buoyed by both good luck and providence, his promised funding having materialized when needed, his men and horses vigorous and healthy. Arriving in the township of Tanga, DeWar directed his men inland toward Mount Kilimanjaro, the convoy trekking across the rolling Tanzanian plains.

Milo read DeWar's account of the cave for the first time, confirming Dale's theory. Having learned about the remote cavern entrance several years prior from German ivory hunters, DeWar came to believe it was part of the extensive Amboni cave system, theorizing an underground highway hundreds of miles in length, and quite possibly a source of vast, untapped mineral wealth.

The large party soon fell in with elephants, which DeWar described as *"prodigious grey beasts who moved atop the savanna."* He and his men shot a great many for sport, abandoning their bodies to scavengers but burying their sawed-off ivory tusks in a hidden cache. Attempting to cook one of the smaller pachyderms, he reported finding the meat *"most disagreeable"* when compared to the abundant antelope. Despite his hunting habits, DeWar had a naturalist's eye for animal life, describing and drawing multitudes of giraffe, ostrich, rhino, zebra, lion, and hyena. Often awestruck, DeWar would lapse into flowery biblical prose, describing the animal stocks as *"King Solomon's Menagerie,"* an unspoiled Garden of Eden.

After days of steady travel, DeWar arrived at the entrance of the cavern, a green, fertile opening surrounded by a massive confluence of elephant herds. There were too many to hunt; DeWar hid his men in trees and had them shoot off their rifles in quick succession. The frightened masses retreated, eventually allowing the explorers to approach the vast, yawning entrance.

Milo smiled as he read the description of air movements at the cavern mouth; DeWar compared the gentle winds to the soft breath of a lover. But the lord was considerably less impressed with the aboriginal artworks along the gallery, describing *"lowly, savage depictions of carnal knowledge, the natural beauty therein despoiled,"* though he did begrudgingly admit to admiring the *"properly bloody hunts."*

The lord's spelunking party soon reached the elephant graveyard. The earlier gunshots had startled one of the calves into the pit, where it *"cried most piteously atop a pile of long-dead young"* until cleanly speared through the heart by a porter.

Overall, DeWar's writings were a picture of barely restrained jubilance. As the rest of his party worked out a solution to reach the bottom of the main shaft, he patiently described a multitude of stalagmites, columns, and fossils, complete with hand-drawn images and cross-sections of crystals and calcite straws. He took a particular interest in the great colony of bats, remarking on their fine quality and the potential for lucrative guano mining.

Milo couldn't help but admire the long-lost lord. Like so many cavers, he too was a consummate equipment geek, devoting many pages to the impressive performance of his then-cutting-edge carbide headlamp and its gentle acetylene glow, though suggesting a multitude of improvements for future development.

Drawings revealed how DeWar had devised his descent down the shaft, though his descriptions strangely omitted any mention of a cascading, thunderous waterfall. He'd ordered a wooden lowering platform built, with long ropes and winch measured precisely to the plumbed and surveyed depths and a counterweight made from net-suspended rocks. To DeWar, the machine was a *"picture of efficiency,"* allowing virtually every member of the party to reach the bottom save the three porters manning the station from up top.

Observations dwindled as DeWar slowly normalized to the subterranean environment. Finding fewer and fewer novel geological features to comment upon, the journal lapsed into food consumption tables and the sort of petty grievances that plagued any expedition. As DeWar began the painfully slow exploration of the anthill, it became increasingly clear to Milo that the water level was much lower a century ago. Though DeWar's servants found a natural spring from which to provision and wash, the diary described almost none of the pools or rivers that now snaked many sections of the cave.

Writing less and less, DeWar would occasionally describe a fossil or a unique formation, sometimes wishing for a Darwin to accompany him or, as he put it, a *"true scientific mind, for I am but a humble explorer."*

Abruptly, there were no entries for three whole days, until DeWar picked up his journal again and began to scribble with the same vigorous, hurried style that characterized so much of his correspondence.

"*I have found it,*" he wrote. "*A great room in the furthest depths, beyond the termination of a long, twisting passage. I found the most monumental of natural cathedrals, within which resides a glittering stone formation, a guardian with crystal sword carved by nature herself. Beneath this majestic wonder is a narrow tunnel from which emits the most magnificent golden light. Below a pagan altar is the aura of angels, buried under an avalanche of broken stone. I will not rest until I have seen the source and laid my eyes upon this lost golden room.*"

Milo realized he was breathing hard, nearly skipping over words in his haste to read further. He took a deep, long sigh, steeling himself as he rubbed his eyes to continue. There were no more entries for another week, then another explosion of ink-splattered, manic enthusiasm upon the page.

"*My men work in a joyous state of exaltation,*" read the journal. "*We are like madmen in our efforts to clear this damnable rubble. No sooner do we make progress than the stones shift, risking the burial of my servants and porters. You will not believe me, good reader, but I labor beside them untiringly. We have required no sleep, nor lantern, nor food, nor water, we are sustained by the ethereal manna of this golden light. With great ecstasy, we are all lost within our fondest memories; cleaved betwixt two worlds, one of goodly labor and the other of remembered pleasures.*"

Blinking his eyes, Milo read the final lines.

"*Perhaps the oracles of old have mistaken the word of God; whereas the heavenly kingdom slumbers in the cool earth beneath us; and the tortured souls of hell, should there be such a thing, tumble in the abyss of the black sky above. I think we break through tomorrow. I shall be the first man through the passage.*"

Excited, Milo quickly flipped to the next pages, but found only gibberish. DeWar had entirely changed his writing style, packing four times as many now-tiny words into the same page, every scrap and margin of the fragile paper written over twice, three times with splattered ink.

Milo scratched his head, trying to come up with an explanation for the sudden turn to illegibility. His first thought was that he'd ruined the journal when trying to save it, that the ink had transferred from page to page. But the closer he looked, the more he could see the pattern—it was manic, yes, but intentional. Patterns slowly emerged; a kind of strange, brilliant logic and symmetry—

"How are you doing?" Bridget spoke softly as she sat down on the ledge, dangling her legs beside his own.

"I'm okay," said Milo. His voice felt hoarse, his eyes irritated and tired. Even his neck hurt from cocking his head over the pages.

"You've been here for hours," said Bridget. "You make any progress?"

Milo started to say something like *no, it hasn't been that long* but checked his watch instead. Bridget was right—he'd been reading the journal for nearly four hours, though it felt like mere moments.

"What'd you find?" asked Bridget. "Can I see?"

"Sure," said Milo, flipping the journal to one of the better drawings and passing it to her. Bridget admired the inked rendering of the giraffe, running her fingers down the corners of the page, careful not to smudge the antique image.

"Any clues as to what happened to our predecessors?"

Milo shook his head. "Not yet," he said. "DeWar made it a lot further into the cave than I would have thought. He and his men explored the main routes in the anthill all the way down to the cathedral chamber. The water levels were lower then—they didn't have to swim, they just walked into the glowing room. They were trying to dig through the breakdown pile to the source of the light—but then the narrative abruptly ends."

"Ends?" said Bridget. "So what happened? Maybe a cave-in while they were digging?"

"I misspoke," said Milo, flipping to the gibberish pages and turning to show Bridget. "It doesn't exactly *end*. The rest of the journal is completely filled with this stuff. Dale couldn't figure it out either."

"That's a little disconcerting," said Bridget, sucking in a sharp breath. "Did DeWar go nuts?"

"Maybe," said Milo. "That's what Dale wants to know. But I'm not so sure—I'm starting to see the underlying order to everything he wrote. At first, none of the scribblings made sense; but the longer I look, the more I can pick out."

"Like what?"

"Like only a fraction of it is in English. The rest is a complete hodge-podge of at least six languages that I recognize, maybe more. The sentence structure is completely experimental; he used whatever convention or word suited him at the moment. It's as though he picked the best word or taxonomy for each concept he's trying to relate."

"I don't understand," said Bridget. "*Six* languages? But why?"

"Let me put it another way," said Milo. "You know how some words simply don't translate to any other language? Like *schadenfreude*, German for taking pleasure in another's pain. No other language possesses the term, they only borrow it."

"Oh," said Bridget. "Like *je ne sais quoi* in French."

"Exactly," said Milo. "But the same goes for entire academic fields . . . chemistry, biology, physics, history, linguistics, and so forth. There are always words originating from a particular language or discipline that address a concept better than any others. And then on top of that, DeWar has reverted to a totally nonlinear sentence structure and whole sections with only mathematical formulas. I can't even get the gist of it."

"It sounds as though he were trying to rewrite the English language," said Bridget, confusion filling her voice.

"Not just the English language," said Milo, closing the journal to put it away. "*All* languages. And it wasn't a rewriting. It was almost more like a . . . grand unification."

"Is this what's next for us?" asked Bridget. "Are we going to start speaking in formulas? Lose our minds?"

Milo looked down past his feet, into the dark. Only the echoing nothingness below. "I don't know," he finally said. "I'll have to ask Logan what he thinks. He's better with languages than me . . . maybe he has some insight. Is he back yet?"

"No," said Bridget, swiveling around to double check. "He's still gone. Everybody else too; they're probably all sulking in their respective corners."

"I guess we'll see what they look like when they come back," said Milo. "Joanne was pretty pissed."

"Well, I hardly blame her," said Bridget with a shrug. "On a separate note, have you seen the blood pressure cuff? It's about time for another reading."

"No," said Milo. "But I can look around. Any idea where it ended up?"

"Couldn't say," said Bridget. "But Logan's stuff might be a good place to start."

Spontaneously, Milo leaned over and kissed Bridget directly on the top of her head, giving her shoulders a tiny reassuring squeeze. She felt thinner than he remembered, her muscles tense and knotted, betraying the stress behind her smile. Embarrassed, Bridget snuck a look over one shoulder to make sure nobody had seen the gesture.

Without another moment wasted, Milo stood up and walked over to Logan's area, not much more than an open backpack with a thin sleeping pad beside it. The search of the backpack revealed little more than still-soggy socks, a few pieces of climbing equipment, and a Tupperware container full of individually bagged rock samples.

Sighing, Milo sat down heavily on the sleeping pad, almost losing his balance as the camping mat slid backward. He saw a flash of smudged white chalk out of the corner of his eye. When he looked down, he saw part of the letter "D" peeking out from behind the pad. Drawing himself up to his knees, Milo lifted it up to see the rest of Logan's hidden message.

DON'T LOOK
FOR ME

PART 3:

SYNTHESIS

Truth is found neither in the thesis nor the antithesis, but in an emergent synthesis which reconciles the two.

—GEORG WILHELM FRIEDRICH HEGEL (1770–1831)

CHAPTER 27:

SEARCH

Depth unknown

Milo pressed his face against the cool cavern wall, open mouth seeking a thin trickle of water as it dripped down the eroded stones. His mud-encrusted scalp brushed against the crumbling rocks; he'd abandoned his helmet days ago. He tasted bitter clay as the water ran across his chapped lips and dry tongue, slowly filling his mouth. Milo forced himself to swallow, his throat tight against the gritty liquid. A second sip, and Milo swished and spat a few sandy particles onto the passage floor.

The tunnel was squat and winding, white calcite cracking beneath his feet. A low ceiling with bulging stalactites hung inches above his head. He could only see a few dozen feet in each direction before the next tight turn erased his sightline. Altogether, it would have been quite forgettable if not for Milo's maddeningly unshakable memory.

Swaying from side to side with exhaustion, Milo allowed himself to consider the tiny divot his mouth left in the muddy wall. His lips had irreparably altered the course of the drip, and now a single teardrop of moisture collected grains of dust as it traced a new line for the first time in a hundred thousand years or more. Perhaps an eon from now, or ten, or a hundred, a vast new void would be born from the newly eroding earth, unimaginable in dimension.

A young professor drinks from a crack in a subterranean wall.

A butterfly flaps its wings.

A woman is slowly dying.

Nothing changed. Or everything did. Who could say anymore?

Bridget snuck a glance at Milo before mimicking the action, the surgeon pressing her soft lips against the wall to drink. Milo's attention drifted, his mind unable to focus. It'd been so many days since he'd eaten that he no longer felt hungry, just lightheaded and listless, every footstep requiring total force of will, every breath a conscious directive barked at his atrophied body. The search party had abandoned their backpacks and water bottles, no longer able to trek under even the slightest weight. They were now nomads, reliant on the scarce oases of the cavern.

"I'd do anything for a Corona right now," said Duck. He'd stopped to watched Bridget sip at the trickle of water. "I'd literally drink that sweet amber nectar out of a hobo's ass crack."

Bridget snickered, the energy required by the slight laughter forcing her hands to her knees.

"Bend him over and pour that shit right on his Roger Rabbit tramp stamp," continued Duck, his words slurred. "Run it down his filthy hobo butt and I'd suck it right off his leathered ballsack."

Milo found himself laughing too. For a moment, Duck's hilariously disgusting imagery made it all go away: the headaches, the bruised knees, the loneliness, the fear, even the fact that they were the most thoroughly fucked people on the planet.

Out of all the sufferings, the headaches were the worst, eclipsing even starvation. Every one of them suffered them in silence. The pain would always start on the left side of Milo's head, a sharp, grinding ache centered behind his eye, like someone had taken a cordless drill to the inside of his brain. The agony radiated everywhere, snaking across his face, into his jaw and teeth, all the way down his neck and shoulders. It hurt so badly that his eyes would tear up, lids drooping and nose running. They'd last for hours before eventually fading into the general shittiness that plagued his every waking moment.

Despite it all, the trio pressed onward. Logan hadn't taken any food with him when he disappeared, perhaps the only reason they were searching for the lost geologist and not hunting him for sport.

"Let's keep moving," said Duck, pointing toward the unexplored passageways. "I have a good feeling about the next room."

"He always says that," muttered Milo.

Duck started off, Milo and Bridget struggling to follow. They'd begun rationing power in the hours after Logan's disappearance, and now only Duck carried a lit caving lantern, the rest had turned theirs off. The other two tried to follow his footsteps, relying on the dim, refracted light from his bobbing lamp to keep up, like trying to navigate through a room as seen through a keyhole.

"Friday, June 19th, 2015," began Bridget. "My immediate supervisor's retirement party. We went all out, reservations at Bacchanalia in Atlanta. Prix fixe menu. I had Kumamoto oysters, a Summerland Farm egg with raw fermented bok choi, and—"

"Whoa, whoa," interrupted Duck with a wave of his hand. "Slow down, woman. You know that's not how we play the game. What were the wine pairings?'

"Let's see . . . sparkling water with the oysters," began Bridget. "A pinot blanc with the farm egg. Followed by a ricotta tortellini with another pinot, Brie de Meaux with gelato, and poached rhubarb."

"What was the dessert wine?" asked Duck, licking his flaking lip as he greedily enjoyed the borrowed memory. "Don't stop now!"

"I was pretty hammered by the fifth course and drank whatever they put in front of me."

"Eidetic memory only works if you're paying attention," explained Milo as he stumbled over a loose rock, barely managing to catch himself before he fell.

"I can *taste* it when I think about it," marveled Bridget, not for the first time. "I can actually *taste* it. This will *never* get old."

They'd been at the exercise for hours. Brought about by the crippling hunger, the food fantasies had become a contest to find the very limits of their ever-expanding photographic recollections. Each round brought new details, growing to precise dates and locations, attendees, even the days' weather. Silly as the game was, it made the monotonous subterranean marching somehow bearable.

"Duck's turn," said Bridget, nodding toward the cave guide.

"Saturday, May 22nd, 2015," began Duck. "I was in Dominical, on the Pacific side of Costa Rica. Roadside ceviche, heavy on the cilantro. Uncooked tilapia chunks the size of walnuts. Had an Imperial with it— you know, the local beer with the black eagle on the label. It was raining, but, like, a *warm* rain. Surfed all morning, met and chilled with some Australian girls on the beach, danced all night."

"Sounds like a perfect day," said Bridget.

"Hooked up with one of them in the nightclub bathroom," said Duck. "And then her smokin' hot friend for the rest of the week. So yeah, pretty much perfect. Australian chicks are ballin'."

"Milo's twenty-fifth birthday," said Bridget, staring directly at him with a half-smile on her face. "He took me to meet his parents while they were on vacation in Banff, Canada."

Milo grimaced and shook his head. "Doesn't count," he said. "My parents were having some kind of argument and forgot the dinner reservation. We never even got seated."

"We still ate," added Bridget. "So it still counts."

"Tell it!" demanded Duck. "Finally getting the *good* stories outta you two. What'd you eat?"

"By the time we got back to the hotel they'd stopped room service," Bridget continued. "Milo and I drove a rental car into town, no idea where we were going. Finally found a closed minimart, Milo made them open back up so they could sell us some granola bars and a bag of corn chips—"

"And then we went back to the hotel and drank the entire minibar," continued Milo with his own half-smile. "I didn't tally the bill until the next morning. I've never sobered up so fast in my life."

"It was a small fortune," said Bridget solemnly. "But Milo was a complete gentleman and covered it all."

"But what I remember most is Bridget stealing a stale donut from the minimart," said Milo. "Right from under the clerk's nose."

"They were going to throw it away!" she protested.

"And then once we were back in the room, she stuck a candle in it," said Milo. "Made sure I got my birthday cake after all."

Duck stopped to turn around and consider Milo and Bridget. The light was too dim to blind them, but Milo covered his eyes nonetheless.

"Dude—you *for real* fucked up when you let this one go," declared Duck. "Stealing for her man? That's some straight ride-or-die shit. You nerds were meant for each other."

"His loss." Bridget smirked at Milo.

"Milo's turn," said Duck, nodding as he started walking down the passageway again. "Favorite dish. I want *details*, man. *Details*."

"I was about a year and a half old," said Milo, following closely behind. "Was in a hotel room for a family reunion in Colorado Springs. Had cookie dough ice cream for the first time. Finished it and then put the plastic bowl on my head like a hat. Seemed logical enough at the time."

"Hold up," demanded Duck. "You remember something from when you were less than *two years old*?"

Milo paused for a moment before answering. "I remember being born," he finally said.

Duck stopped again and stared up at the ceiling. Processing a flood of newly accessed memories, the cave guide's face went through six different contortions, beginning with visible confusion before swiftly transitioning through curiosity, surprise, confusion again, and horror before finally arriving at a measure of acceptance.

"I can remember my birth too," he said, eyes wide. "That's *so* heavy."

"I think I'm done with this game for a while," said Bridget, her face scrunched up into a frown. "Let's keep going."

Duck, Milo, and Bridget rounded the next turn and came to an abrupt stop. Any further progress was prevented by a ceiling-high breakdown pile; the passageway had collapsed centuries ago. Bridget stepped up to the rocky avalanche, briefly flicking on her own light to closely examine some of the larger gaps in the rock.

"Shit," said Duck, shaking his head. "I really had a good feeling about this section."

"You suppose he tried to crawl through?" asked Bridget as she stuck an arm through the rocks and wiggled it to see if she could fit between them.

Duck just shook his head. "No way his thick ass made it through there," he said, already retreating from the dead end.

As Bridget turned off her light and followed, Milo sat down on a flat rock on the edge of the pile and pulled a small sketchpad from the waistband of his tattered pants. He took a pen from behind the left arm of his dusty, fingerprint-stained glasses and began to sketch. The last mile of passageway came easily to his mind's eye as he drew the long, intersecting routes by memory. He'd left his other hand-drawn maps back at camp. Maybe some of the laser data had survived, but the scanner itself hadn't; they'd found the shattered remains of the waterlogged, football-sized head days ago. Besides, the data was trapped on a useless hard drive, all intact laptop batteries having been rewired to feed the lanterns.

Drawing was a talent he'd never possessed, but Milo easily managed a meticulous three-quarter perspective view of the cave, each winding passage and sharp ledge drawn with complete accuracy.

"At least we found some grub along the way," said Duck, patting the granola bars in the breast pocket of his shirt that he'd dug out of the mud. It took everything Milo had to not tackle the cave guide right then and there, rip the smashed, waterlogged bars out of his pocket, shove them into his mouth, and lick the plastic wrappers for what few calories might remain.

An hour later, the retreating trio had made their way back to the top of the route's biggest drop, a sheer cliff demarking the final stretch of the branching tunnel system they'd just explored. It was a negative slope, the topmost edge hanging over a void of empty space. A fist-width crack ran up the middle of the seventy-foot length, just enough of a grip for Duck to climb and set anchors for the other two. Maybe a week ago it would have felt like a towering, impassable obstacle, but now it was too small to even bear a name on Milo's wrinkled sketchpad.

Milo and Bridget put on their harnesses as Duck checked the short rope anchor he'd tied to the nearest thick stone column. Linking their climbing harnesses to a single carabiner, Duck next attached a heavy rappel rack in preparation for descent. At eighteen inches in length, the rack somewhat resembled an aluminum ladder, with removable rungs designed to slide up and down the metal frame. The cave guide ran a rope in and out of the rungs before throwing the long end over the ledge, the line uncoiling silently in the air before flopping at the bottom with a wet smack. There was no safety line anymore; every other rope was lost, damaged, or otherwise employed.

Once attached to the line, the rappel rack acted like a seizing pulley. With the rope snaking through the rungs, even a little tension drew the metal bars together, tightening their grip against line until friction brought the climber to a dead halt. It was the safest possible option, and would stop even an unconscious climber from falling. Keeping the rungs separate and the rope moving took a lot of muscle and attention; as Milo stepped over the side, he was forced to continually pry the bars apart with his gloved hand to keep the slick nylon sliding through during his descent.

For a single caver on a dry rope, the rappel rack was an oversized, heavy, and wholly redundant pain in the ass. With a full load on a wet rope, the system might just save a life. Two of the racks had been lost in the flood and a third dropped by accident during the search for Isabelle, tumbling end over end until it disappeared into the darkness of a deep, inaccessible chasm.

Attached to the single rack, Milo and Bridget's position was one of utilitarian intimacy, their legs intertwined and arms encircled as they descended. The surgeon had become frighteningly thin; Milo's hand clutched over the atrophying muscles that once so clearly defined her back and shoulders.

A few jolting drops later, the pair touched down at the bottom of the steep cliff, lost together in the darkness. Blind, Milo fumbled with the carabiner, freeing their waists from each other. He whistled into the void, and the faint glint of the rappel rack disappeared as Duck reeled the rope back in.

Milo sighed and leaned against the wall, feeling the early pangs of the next round of headaches.

"Christmas morning, 1993," whispered Bridget. Even through the dark, Milo could hear her smile at the memory. "Dad brought home cinnamon rolls—"

Milo glimpsed the flash of Duck's headlamp as the caver leaned back into his harness at the top of the cliff, the anchored rope taking his weight. It held for a fraction of a second before a sharp *ping* rang through the vertical chamber as the rappel rack gave way. Duck gasped a breathless "whoops" and then he was fully airborne, freefalling down the shaft.

A rush of air filled the chamber as Milo launched his body at Bridget, tackling her out of the way an instant before Duck slammed into the muddy floor beside them with a sickening crunch.

He lost his voice to speechless horror as Bridget screamed with angry, helpless fury. Dragging herself to her feet, Bridget flipped on her light and stumbled to Duck's side.

Duck had landed square on his back, empty eyes blinking at the darkness above. Milo threw himself to the ground next to the stricken man, preparing to bind broken bones, start CPR, any action that might save his life. Twitching, Duck struggled to breathe, his ragged inhalations shallow and gasping. He was conscious, but blood had already begun gathering at the corners of his mouth, coating his teeth.

"I fucked up, I fucked up," mouthed the cave guide, no sound leaving his lips.

Milo looked to Bridget with desperate eyes, a look she returned with equal impotence. Duck convulsed, trying to cough, spit up blood, breathe, but he couldn't.

"Help me get him on his side," ordered Bridget, stabilizing Duck's neck and upper spine and pointing toward his legs. Milo slipped his hands underneath his pelvis, feeling a spongy mass of pulverized bone and spasming muscle. He withdrew his hands, the sticky wetness of fresh blood clinging to his fingers, the smell of iron in the air.

Bridget shook her head, closing her eyes as she withdrew her hands as well, silently rescinding her previous order. There was nothing left to do but wait as Duck struggled to suck in a last few gasping breaths, clinging desperately to the dwindling few moments of life.

Milo leaned over Duck, one hand on the guide's chest, the other cradling his cheek as they stared into each other's eyes.

"You're back in Dominical," whispered Milo, his face mere inches from Duck's as Bridget softly cried behind him. "You taste the sea salt in your mouth."

Duck stopped breathing, his eyes widening as he took in Milo's words, blood gently trickling through his facial stubble, disappearing beneath the back of his broken neck.

"Tilapia the size of walnuts," repeated Milo, tears gathering in his eyes. "The Australian girls are waving for you to come back. Your ceviche is ready. You raise your beer. It's time to go to them."

As the last glimmer of life faded from Duck's eyes, the corners of his mouth imperceptibly lifted, the memory more powerful than the pain. He never took in another breath. Milo ran a gentle hand over Duck's eyes, closing them as he and Bridget silently sobbed.

CHAPTER 28:

LONG PORK

Milo and Bridget sat slumped against the cliff, Duck's motionless body illuminated by the fading glow of Bridget's headlamp. She leaned against Milo, her head on his shoulder, clinging to his arm. He knew it was his imagination, but felt as though he could still see the faintest hint of a smile on the cave guide's pale face. Duck seemed at peace, despite the still-seeping blood pooling on the muddy cavern floor like red oil.

The climbing harness was undamaged, the carabiner clip still securely locked to the heavy metal rappel rack. But there was no line clutched within the sliding rungs; they'd all popped free, hanging open like jack o' lantern teeth. Duck had run the nylon rope backward, and every rung popped free the moment he'd put his weight on the system. He'd never had a chance.

Milo's eyes drifted to Duck's hands. His gloved palms were raw and bloody from where he'd desperately grabbed the rope. Even if he hadn't been starving, no man possessed the strength to catch a thin nylon rope in freefall. It was just too sudden—a mistake born of fatigue and hunger, a high-pitched *ping* as the rack gave way, weightlessness, barely enough time to sputter a "whoops" before slamming into the rocky floor seventy feet below.

He pointed toward the rack, directing Bridget's eyes. She caught sight of the loose rungs and shook her head in disbelief.

"He'd threaded that rack a million times," murmured Bridget.

"Doesn't matter," said Milo. "He did it backward this one time. That's all it takes down here."

Bridget buried her face in her hands, pulling her hair back and shaking a few flecks of mud from the long, dark strands as silence fell.

"This is so fucked up," whispered Bridget. "Why were we even looking for Logan? He literally told us not to."

"Doesn't matter anymore—we're done searching," said Milo as he absentmindedly tapped the back of his head against the cliff wall. "We can't continue after what happened to Duck. It's time to go back to the camp, tell everyone the bad news. All we can do now is hunker down, hope someone comes looking for us."

Bridget started to try to get up but collapsed, closing her eyes as she leaned back against the wall. Milo tried to sneak his hand into hers, but she snaked it away.

"I'm going to disappear for a bit," said Bridget, eyes still closed as she massaged the bridge of her nose. "Bring me back when we need to leave."

"Where will you go?" asked Milo.

"I don't know," answered Bridget. "A time when I was happy; a time when I felt fed and loved and safe. Anywhere but here."

"I'll bring you back," he promised. But it was too late for her to hear; Bridget's eyes had already glassed over as she vanished into her memories.

Milo watched her for a few minutes before returning to his drawing, filling in details and relief to the interminable subterranean system. His hand hesitated over the tunnel—he hadn't intended to name it, but now felt as though he had to. He finally penned *Duck's End Passage* in a hasty scribble in the corner.

Milo tucked the pen back behind his ear and dropped his chin, staring at the ground between his knees as he pressed his back against the base of the cliff. His churning, grief-stricken consciousness incessantly reminded him of all the times he'd seen something terrible. Memories flashed in his mind's eye—the family veterinarian euthanizing his childhood dog as he pressed his fingers into her fur, feeling her heartbeat slow to a stop as she faded away. The funerals of all his grandparents. The live mouse he'd found in a basement spring-trap, entrails spilling from its split belly. A sudden motorcycle accident in Georgetown, the rider flipping over a BMW's hood before slamming helmet-first into the asphalt. Duck's slow-motion fall, perfectly seared into his perfect memory.

Groaning out loud, Milo slapped himself on the cheeks with both hands, forcing himself to stay awake. The memories were a burden, a curse. He couldn't contextualize them, rob them of power, intentionally misremember in any way. Every time his mind flashed to the waking nightmares, it was as though he were back again, the images just as shocking and horrifying as they'd been the first time, maybe even more so by their repetition. Milo wondered what would happen if he too placed himself within his favorite memories, become as glass-eyed and impossibly distant as Bridget. Could he ever leave, swim his way back to a fully conscious state? Or would the next cavers through the passageway find the unsolvable puzzle of two mummified bodies huddled in grief over a broken third?

Milo watched Bridget for the longest time, a passage immeasurable within the silent cavern halls. Every so often, her face would twitch with a glimmer of remembered joy. After waiting what felt like hours, Milo gently took Bridget by the hand, softly stroking her palm until life flickered back into her eyes and she looked him. Her face went ashen as she reoriented herself to her surroundings, forcing herself to divert her eyes from Duck's lifeless body.

"Where were you?" asked Milo.

Bridget just shook her head. "You weren't invited," she answered.

Milo couldn't help but wonder why—maybe because he reminded her of this cold, stony hell. Or worse, because her memories of him were not an escape.

"We can't bring him back to camp," said Bridget. "I don't have the strength."

"I'm not sure what we're supposed to do," said Milo. "I wish he was here to tell us."

"What would your explorers say?" asked Bridget.

Milo grimaced. "That's a very difficult question," he answered.

"Why?"

"Because we're all so hungry."

"You're not suggesting—" began Bridget, her voice choked with abject horror. "You can't *possibly*—"

"Of course not," insisted Milo. "We're not there yet . . . what I mean to say is, I would never—" *Eat him*, he didn't say.

"I'd rather die," said Bridget. "I'd rather die than desecrate my friend's body."

"We may not be the problem," said Milo, frowning. "We have to tell them he's dead, and somebody's going to put two and two together."

"Then let's bury him," said Bridget. "We have to bury him; we'll keep the location a secret. Nobody will think to look in here unless we tell them."

Milo just nodded. It wasn't as though the thought hadn't crossed his mind; everyone knew they'd have to deal with Isabelle once she relinquished her grip on the last threads of life. The same went for Duck—left to the wilderness like so many ill-fated alpine climbers, their bodies left in situ to the elements or buried under what little their comrades foraged. It would still be a greater dignity than the bodies at the entrance hatch.

They first went about the grim, silent duty of stripping Duck of supplies. Milo gently slipped off his cave lamp and shredded gloves while Bridget fished through his pockets, taking the carabiner and working rappel rack but leaving his harness, boots, and clothes untouched.

"Look," said Bridget, opening her hand to show Milo. She held several still-charged batteries she'd found in his pockets.

"I found something too," said Milo, feeling the familiar crinkle of a wrapper within the cave guide's breast pocket.

"What type?" asked Bridget, eyeing Milo's hands as he withdrew two granola bars.

"Peanut butter and chocolate," answered Milo. "Perfect, as if I didn't feel shitty enough already."

"I want to eat it now," said Bridget.

Milo just shook his head again. "We promised we'd bring back anything that we found along the way," he answered.

"You're such a Boy Scout," said Bridget, rolling her eyes.

Milo and Bridget dragged Duck by his boots, tugging the body toward a long, narrow trench less than a hundred feet from where he'd fallen. Any further and they'd have to contend with the maze of passageways, an impossible prospect. Together, they rolled his body into the shallow trench, Duck's coverall-clad form sliding into the coffin-width crack. Bridget crossed the young man's arms over his chest. Duck almost looked as though he were sleeping, if not for his deathly pale skin and sunken eyes.

"I feel like we should say something," said Bridget. "I think he'd want us to remember him."

"I don't think we could forget, even if we wanted to," said Milo with a wry smile.

"Just . . . say something," said Bridget. "Something nice."

Milo nodded and cleared his throat as he collected his thoughts. The longest pause fell between them.

"The darkness was Duck's light," he finally said. "He radiated charm and good cheer despite the miseries all around him. He was the warm heart of our expedition, a man who honored journey above destination, people above prize."

Bridget nodded in agreement, stifling resurgent tears.

"Dwayne 'Duck' Spurlock was just twenty-five," continued Milo. "He gave his life not for his own ambition, but to find a man who'd abandoned us at our hour of greatest need. He was selfless. He was kind. He was our friend."

Bridget reached over and placed a soft hand Milo's shoulder before bending down and picking up a fist-sized rock, which she then gently placed at the center of Duck's chest.

"Thank you for everything," she whispered. "I'm sorry this happened."

Milo followed suit, picking up two rocks from beside the trench and gently placing them on top of the young caver's body.

"Duck, there's a quote I'd like to say," whispered Milo to the still body. "In his novel *Journey to the Center of the Earth*, Jules Verne wrote the following: '*Where there is life, there is hope . . . as long as man's heart beats, as long as a man's flesh quivers, I do not allow that a being gifted with thought and will can allow himself to despair.*'"

Milo reached for Bridget's hand. She took it this time, squeezing his in acknowledgement.

"*At every instance we may perish,*" said Bridget solemnly; Milo recognized the beginning of the quote from another passage of the same book—she'd read it as well, perhaps as a child. "*And so too, every instant we may be saved.*"

"We must choose to live," promised Milo, his voice rising as he turned to address Bridget. "We must choose to live, if for no other reason than to tell his story."

CHAPTER 29:

DEATH RATTLE

2,475 feet below the surface

Dry, stagnant air collected in Milo's lungs as he stumbled down the descending passageway. He turned sideways, exhaling the air from his lungs to slip between the narrow walls. True to his clear memories, the winding path ended abruptly at a vast open expanse, his dwindling lamp giving no sense of the true length of the great chasm.

Bridget belted a halloo across the expanse, which was returned with a diminished, echoing response from an unseen Joanne. Milo nodded. The makeshift camp still stood atop the massive rock clutched between canyon walls, but to conserve batteries, the party had long since surrendered the outpost to darkness.

Milo's lamp flickering behind her, Bridget led the way back to camp, scaling the nylon ropes and anchors from the passageway termination and thirty feet up and along the vertical wall before reaching the flat-topped rock. There was no greeting, the permeating darkness made all the more encompassing by the surrounding void. Milo's light fell across two empty sleeping bags, abandoned white-gas containers, and week-old discarded wrappers before reaching Joanne's hollow, vacant face.

A sound—Milo jolted his lamp to the side, the light spilling over Dale Brunsfield for the first time in days. Dale now spent most of his time on solo explorations, never explaining his intentions or whereabouts. He'd simply mumble an excuse and disappear for hours at a time. Unlike Logan, he'd always managed to return, though his comings and goings had become increasingly erratic and unpredictable. Milo couldn't help but wonder if Dale still expected imminent rescue, or if he'd finally resigned himself to the hopelessness of it all.

Dale didn't even look up at the light, just held up a hand to shield his eyes. He held Lord Riley DeWar's leather-bound journal in his lap, the pages opened to a section midway through the schizophrenic, indecipherable scribblings as though he'd been reading. Useless in the dark, of course, but Milo couldn't help wonder if the tactile sensations—turning the fragile pages, running fingers over the ink-splattered indentations—somehow assisted the photographic memory they now all shared.

"Don't interrupt him," croaked Joanne. She sounded sick, but no worse than the rest of them. "He's concentrating. He doesn't want to talk to you right now."

Milo nodded, gulping down another wave of grief as he prepared to speak.

"Duck's dead," blurted Bridget, unable to wait.

A flinch darted across Joanne's impassive face, and then a second as she replayed the statement in her thoughts, as though seeking any alternate interpretation or flaw in the two-word statement.

"How?" she asked, still not looking up at Bridget or Milo.

"Rappel rack failure," answered Bridget. "He fell."

"You mean he fucked up," said Joanne, turning to stare at Bridget for the first time, her dead eyes glinting in the lamplight.

"Yeah," Bridget answered softly. "He did."

"Regret to hear that," interjected Dale, slapping the leather journal shut as he looked up at the returning pair. "He was a good man."

"Did he . . . suffer?" asked Joanne, a single tear welling in one of her eyes.

"No," answered Milo, speaking for the first time. "It was practically over before he even knew what happened."

Dale nodded and turned back to the journal, flipping through the pages to where he'd left off. Bridget strode over and knelt down next to Dale, trying and failing to get his attention.

"Don't you have anything else to ask me?" pleaded Bridget, placing one hand on his unmoving shoulders. "Don't you care?"

"I need to get back to this," said Dale, stiffly. "Milo abandoned DeWar's journal to search for Logan. He should have stayed and kept at it. Someone needs to solve this riddle. Lord Riley DeWar is the key to everything, you know."

Bridget tried shaking Dale's shoulder but he wouldn't even look up. He just kept staring at the pages as though enough concentration alone could force the book to reveal its secrets.

"Got something for you," said Milo, reaching into Duck's frayed bag. "We found it in the anthill on the way back."

He carefully removed Dale's robot, the exposed circuit boards and wires visible within the dented shoebox-sized casing. Both tracks had been ripped off by the flood, and a delicate appendage at the top held the remains of a shattered camera lens.

"It was hung up in a calcite curtain," Milo continued. "Bridget spotted it all the way up, practically in the ceiling. We must have walked right under it a half-dozen times."

"Good," said Joanne, no emotion in her voice as she acknowledged the find. "Might be able to find a few amps in the lithium-ion batteries. Should be good for a few hours' light."

"Or it'll short out whatever you wire it to," grunted Dale, again without looking up. "Bring food next time or don't bother coming back at all."

At least she's trying, Milo could have said as he fished out the two granola bars. But he didn't.

Milo and Bridget backtracked out of the canyon chasm, following the nylon ropes across the gap to the ledge. Once again on solid ground, they carefully made their way into one of the side chambers, to where they'd relocated Isabelle. The producer still clung to life, unconscious in her blanket-covered plastic litter. A body-wide infection had taken hold, but what should have been her final hours had stretched into days. She breathed light and shallow, her face flushed and red, heart struggling to pump thickening, dehydrated blood.

Charlie remained curled up beside her, not even a blanket separating his body from the cold cavern floor. Like Joanne and Dale, he was almost completely unresponsive, barely even blinking at the reintroduction of light to the dark room.

"Any changes?" asked Bridget as she leaned over Isabelle's flushed form.

Charlie didn't even shake his head, just stared off into the distance as though he were alone. Unlike Bridget, he hadn't retreated into a happy memory—he had descended into nothingness itself, leaving behind a figure more void than man.

Bridget pulled back the blanket, exposing Isabelle's blackened, gangrenous skin. Drying pus collected around her seeping wounds, and the angry bruising had turned hard and dark. There were no more painkillers, antibiotics, or improvised intravenous fluid. Even if help had arrived days ago, there was still little chance Isabelle would have ever seen the sun again.

"Charlie—say something," said Bridget, louder this time. "Tell me you're still here with us."

When Charlie didn't respond, Milo shuffled closer to the man, gently shaking his shoulder. Charlie still wouldn't even acknowledge them.

"He's completely catatonic," Bridget said, shaking her head in anger. "Not that it matters; Isabelle doesn't need him anymore. She has hours at most. Part of me hoped she'd pass before our return."

"How about you?" said Milo, sitting down next to Bridget. "This is a stupid question—but are you okay?"

"No," answered Bridget. "I've never been less okay in my life. I feel so fucking useless; I can't even make Isabelle comfortable. The merciful thing would be to bash her head in with a rock, end her suffering."

Milo and Bridget simultaneously glanced toward Charlie, wondering if he'd react to the stark, uncompromising assertion. He said nothing.

"Hey *Charlie*," Bridget shouted, leaning over Isabelle's body as she spoke. "Duck is dead. You got anything to say about that?"

"We're all fucking dead," spat Charlie, briefly turning his head toward them and then turning it back.

Bridget trembled with anger and disgust. But she still broke off a piece of her granola bar and passed it to Charlie, who ate it without thanking her.

Bridget split the last piece between Milo and herself. Milo chewed slowly, trying to enjoy the rush of chocolate and sugar. He only felt like he was going to throw up, his stomach assaulted by the sudden influx of dense calories for the first time in days. Sipping out of his water bottle, he willed the sweet morsel to stay down.

"I need to sleep," announced Bridget, standing up to walk over to the rope lines leading to the flat rock. "Tell Charlie to wake me up when Isabelle dies."

"You want company?" offered Milo.

"No," Bridget answered. "I really don't."

Milo sat at the edge of the great suspended rock where they'd struck camp, feet dangling over the side. His mind wandered, wondering how it would feel to drop into the chasm, wind whistling; one final thrill as he plummeted into the abyss for the last time. Maybe he'd have time to pick a memory before he hit the bottom, experience one last happy moment before it all came to an end.

He still had no idea of what lay at the bottom of the chasm. With his luck, it would be a shallow sump, enough to arrest his fall but fracture his legs and spine, leaving him suspended between life and death, fully conscious to all suffering as he drowned alone in the dark.

Feet still dangling, Milo put his hands behind his head, shifting onto his back, and fell into a light, fitful sleep. He used his brief inter-missions of consciousness to try to steer his dreams toward the fertile valley dreamscape, but he found only more darkness and rock. Indistin-guishable voices, some familiar, some alien and ancient, whispered and screamed at him from the void.

Milo awoke to a great commotion. Charlie stood on the ledge facing the suspended rock, waving and shouting. One flashlight after another clicked on, slicing through the darkness as they collected on Charlie like a spotlight, blinding him with harsh white illumination. Still ges-turing with one hand, Charlie held the other to his forehead, stanching a head wound as blood trickled through his fingers.

Joanne and Dale sprang to their feet, almost vaulting across the flat rock toward the edge. Bridget tripped, slamming a hand onto Milo's shoulders as she caught herself. But Milo hardly noticed the blow.

"What happened?" shouted Bridget, her voice easily carrying across the rope-bridged gap between them.

"I can't find Isabelle!" snapped Charlie, angrily clamping a palm to his own bloody forehead.

"Isabelle?" said Joanne. "She's awake? She's moving?"

"She's not just *awake*," shouted Charlie, dropping his bloody hand to reveal the deep cut on his face. "She's fucking *gone*."

CHAPTER 30:

ORACLE

Depth unknown

Milo crawled through the tight tunnels, ignoring the overwhelming fatigue as he pushed his emaciated body ever further. Charlie led the desperate search for Isabelle, Bridget and Joanne on his heels, Milo huffing and wheezing at the back of the pack. He couldn't believe how *fast* Charlie could move on all fours. The starvation that afflicted the rest of them hadn't slowed him down an iota.

The last thing Dale said was that he'd wait at camp, a familiar face in case Isabelle returned on her own. Milo knew she wouldn't, just as he knew Dale would likely disappear again once the rest were out of earshot.

None of the party acknowledged their dwindling batteries, all four setting their headlamps to the highest power output. The missing woman had left quite a trail, shedding clothing and filthy bandages along the way as she dragged her battered body into the depths. She'd sliced open her bare knees on a spider's web of sharp calcite ridges not far from camp, leaving smudged bloody drag marks in the dust behind her.

Bridget stopped, flopping onto her back to catch her breath as she clung to a smooth, knobbed stalagmite like a hand railing. "We should have caught up to her by now," she wheezed, eyes darting for the next clue. "Charlie—how long were you out? How much of a head start did she have?"

"I don't know!" said Charlie, slowing to let the rest catch up again. "A few minutes maybe, a couple hours at most? Can you keep track of time down here? I sure fucking can't!"

"Think, Charlie," ordered Joanne, her voice low and gravelly. "How long?"

"I seriously don't know," answered Charlie, raising both arms in protest. "Two hours, max?"

"Did she take a light with her?" asked Joanne. "A lantern, a headlamp, anything?"

Charlie shook his head. "Shit," he said, "I didn't even think to check. She could have grabbed one, I guess."

Joanne sighed angrily and X'd a large chalk mark on the wall next to a forking tunnel, a smeared splatter of blood on the ground clearly indicating Isabelle's route.

"How is this my goddamn fault?" demanded Charlie. "I didn't hear a thing, slept right through it. I ran out to tell you guys as soon as I came to, nearly knocked myself out in the process."

"You're saying there were no signs whatsoever?" asked Joanne, making no effort to conceal her complete disbelief. "One minute she's in a coma, the next she's vanished?"

"What, am I not allowed to *sleep?*"

"Mm-hmm," said Joanne, raising her eyebrows. Whatever her assumption, she clearly now thought it confirmed.

"She probably linked up with Logan," muttered Charlie. "I bet they're having a good laugh at all of us right now."

"Isabelle isn't having a *laugh*," said Bridget, almost shouting as she smacked the knobby stalagmite with her palm in frustration. "She has internal bleeding, broken bones, brain trauma, to say nothing of the infection that's in the process of *killing* her. The very idea that she is even up and crawling is antithetical to everything I've ever been taught as a medical doctor."

Milo turned and reached to adjust the crusted, bloody sock Charlie had been holding up to his scalp. Charlie's perfectly curated four days' beard was now two weeks long, his $300 haircut caked with scabs and mud, faded tribal tattoo encircling a still-powerful bicep. Though the filthy sock was a poor choice of wound dressing, all of their clothing was now in an equal or worse state, the last of their bandages long since lost or discarded.

"I think I have a concussion," complained Charlie. "Everything hurts and I can't think clearly."

"Could also be the hunger. Any nausea?" asked Bridget.

"I guess," admitted Charlie. "But there's, like, nothing left to throw up."

"As much as I would like to chalk this up to Charlie's normal grousing," interrupted Joanne, "should we consider stopping to deal with his possible concussion?"

"I'll check him when we get back to camp," grumbled the doctor. "Odds are he's fine."

"I don't feel fine," Charlie complained. "Isn't there some kind of treatment for this? Medical advice? Anything?"

"You're in luck," said Bridget, turning from Charlie to track Isabelle's trail down the next empty passageway. "At-home treatment for mild concussions means no food or water for twelve hours while you stay within a dark room. Also, Charlie shouldn't think too hard about anything, but I can't imagine that's ever been a problem."

Joanne thought about that statement for a moment, genuine amusement spreading across her face. "If I may be so bold," she said. "In terms of Charlie's knock about the head, one might even describe our current predicament as somewhat . . . ideal."

Milo broke out into chuckles despite himself, as did Bridget. Joanne joined in, laughing much harder and longer than the other two.

"It's seriously not that funny, guys," Charlie protested, rubbing his forehead. "This really hurts."

Joanne's raucous, croaking laughter gained manic volume and intensity with every moment, continuing even after Milo and Bridget had fallen to worried silence. Milo stooped down, his light revealing Joanne's tear-streaked face. Her laughter turned abruptly to choking, uncontrollable sobbing. But the tears weren't wet saline—they were streaked with dark blood. She rubbed her face with her hands, staring at her red-stained fingers with horror. Fear turning to fury, she yanked her headlamp off her head and slammed it into the ground, hitting it again and again until the waning light flickered and died for the last time.

"Oh *shit*," said Bridget, eyes widening. "She's infected!"

"Just a second—" began Milo, but he was cut off by a wave of Joanne's hand as she composed herself once again. Collapsing, the guide pointed at the passageway, wordlessly insisting the rest of the party continue without her. Unresponsive to Milo's questions, Joanne buried her face between her knees and sobbed.

"We've got to quarantine her, help her, something!" Milo said.

"One problem at a time—we need to move *now*," repeated Bridget, her voice harsh with urgency. "She's not going anywhere without a light. Joanne—*stay here*, do *not* move. We will be back for you shortly."

As Bridget stood up, Joanne switched off her own lamp, conserving its precious battery power. The trio abandoned Joanne to the darkness, her eerie sobs echoing through the tunnels as they trudged ever deeper.

Bridget had taken over the chalking regimen, the two men now trailing as she led. The clues grew fainter with every step, now little more than smudged bloody drag marks every dozen feet or the nearly imperceptible stain of unwashed fingers as they brushed against a white calcite wall. Their pace had long since slowed from the initial dogged sprint; Bridget and Milo no longer expecting to find Isabelle's ghostly form around the next constricted passage or crawlway.

They slowed their approach as the tunnel opened up, the trio sensing the vast void long before their flashlights first fell across the flooded grotto. The undiscovered antechamber resembled an ancient throne room, a hundred feet between encircling walls, the high ceiling rendered invisible by a clinging mist. Large enough for its own weather system, the cave's trapped, stagnant humidity had condensed into wispy subterranean clouds.

"What's that sound?" asked Charlie. Straining his ears to listen, Milo soon heard it too—a distant dripping into hollow calcite flutes, the tinkling notes like music.

"Anyone else feel like we're intruding?" asked Bridget with a whisper.

A chill went down Milo's spine. "One can hardly blame the peoples who believed in the supernatural power of these caves."

"Like, cave spirits?" whispered Charlie, his eyes darting around.

"Not spirits," corrected Milo in a murmur. "Not even *a* spirit. More like . . . *The* Spirit."

"I think I found Isabelle," Bridget whispered, her steady flashlight aimed squarely at a flowstone pedestal in the center of the chamber.

Milo aimed his lamp in line with Bridget's. What had first appeared to be a natural formation was instead a low stone platform supporting a crouched figure. Milo and Bridget tiptoed through the reflective, ankle-deep grotto waters, flanking from either side. Charlie hung back, still holding the dirty sock to his head as he stumbled forward.

Milo forced himself to hold the flashlight steady as Bridget gingerly approached Isabelle's motionless form. The producer sat in an upright position, her naked body a head-to-toe blotting of ugly bruises across pale, fragile skin. Knees to chest, her head was angled, eyes shut tight, mouth yawning like a silent scream.

Bridget extended her fingers to check for a pulse. She barely needed to bother—Milo's heightened senses detected no movement or heat radiating from Isabelle's lifeless body.

"She's dead," confirmed Bridget in a gravelly voice, withdrawing the two fingers from Isabelle's carotid artery.

"Why is she sitting like that?" whispered Charlie, barely able to speak through his horror.

Neither Bridget or Milo answered, instead panning their lights around Isabelle's remains in search of any additional clues.

"No headlamps or flashlight," said Bridget. "She must have found her way here in the dark. We'll do an inventory back at camp to be sure."

Milo shivered. To him, Isabelle's nude body resembled a Buddhist mummy, a flesh-body bodhisattva, the incorrupt human form. Facing the end of their lives, devoted monks trained to die in meditation, frozen forever in lotus position as their followers preserved their bodies with clay, salt, and gold. Their uninterred remains would be publicly displayed as the ultimate expression of faith—or, to some, religious suicide.

"She can't be dead," whispered Charlie, unable to tear his eyes away from her body. He collapsed to his knees in the water surrounding the pedestal, prostate before Isabelle.

Bridget gently clasped Milo by the arm, pulling him aside. She spoke to him in low tones, shielding their conversation from Charlie.

"This isn't a coincidence," she muttered. "We know where we've seen this exact pose before."

"The mummy of the Japanese caver," confirmed Milo. "Why would they die in the same way?"

"I know she's alone in the dark, but Joanne is going to need to wait," said Bridget. "We need to go back to the Japanese mummy, take a closer look. Something connects their two deaths—something we missed the first time."

CHAPTER 31:

SECOND OPINION

Bridget and Milo retreated from the grotto with solemn, deliberate steps. She stopped at every intersecting passageway, rubbing her own chalk marks into nothing with a chafed palm. She didn't have to explain why, not to Milo. Unlike Duck, they'd left Isabelle's body untouched, respecting her final gesture. But all the same, it was best to conceal the path to her remains.

They'd left Charlie kneeling in the reflective waters at the edge of the natural pedestal. Milo had asked Charlie if he could find his own way back, if he had enough batteries, enough water. Milo didn't ask him the only thing that really mattered—whether or not Charlie had enough strength left, if he cared enough to save himself, even if only for a few hours longer. Grief-stricken, Charlie didn't answer, not even with a ghost of a nod. But Milo and Bridget couldn't force him to come, nor could they stay.

Joanne was gone by the time they reached the passageway where they'd abandoned her. There was no way to tell how long she'd sat and laughed or cried before vanishing, only a single bloody handprint remaining. Despite the darkness and her sickness, her steps still led in the direction of their emergency camp. She'd somehow found her way back without any light.

Bridget and Milo soon found themselves within familiar passageways, their footsteps echoing as they ascended the anthill. Hours into the trek, they approached a section of incline coated with a thin layer of slippery flowstone. Milo recognized the pattern of fragile calcium clinging to the ceiling. A bit of additional crawling and he was once again suspended atop a land bridge, seeing again the muddy slide.

Milo rolled and dropped over the side, enjoying the fraction of a second of freefall before his boots caught the sharply angled mud below. He slid down the slick surface through the field of broken calcite straws before skidding to a stop at the bottom.

"Slow down," ordered Bridget, easing down the same route after him on her butt. "You'll break an ankle or worse."

"Sorry," said Milo. He hadn't even thought about the little stunt. Dropping off the side and sliding down felt so intuitive, as though he'd done it a thousand times before.

Angling their twin headlamps downward, the pair again illuminated the hollow-eyed mummy in harsh yellow light. Milo felt almost amused at the fear he'd first felt staring at the shrunken, gray corpse.

"I'm glad we didn't bury him like Dale wanted," said Bridget, scowling as she examined the body. "Digging him up again would have been a giant pain in the ass."

Milo looked over the mummy, then slowly scanned the length of the room. "So we made it back," he finally said. "What are we missing?"

"I don't know," Bridget answered, crossing her arms and pursing her lips. "I thought we searched the room pretty thoroughly the first time."

"Maybe an autopsy?" suggested Milo. "Could you do one if you had to?"

Bridget thought for a few moments before answering him. "I could, but it wouldn't be pretty," she said. "Not sure what we'd learn given the advanced state of decay."

"How would we start?" asked Milo. "Hypothetically speaking, of course."

"Internal examination," stated Bridget without hesitating. "Dissection of the chest, abdominal and pelvic organs. Maybe the skull as well."

Milo gave the doctor an apologetic smile. Horrified, Bridget glanced between him and the mummified corpse.

"We weren't speaking hypothetically, were we?" asked Bridget. "Because I'd *really* rather not."

Shrugging in resignation, Milo pulled a black garbage bag out of his pack. He used his knife to slice along the seams, spreading the full length of the plastic onto the cave floor like a thin, shimmery blanket before handing the blade to Bridget.

"At least we'll have a clean place to work."

"*Nothing* about this process will be clean," responded Bridget. "But I'm not walking out of here empty-handed."

Sighing, Bridget squinted at the body before using both hands to lance the knife into the mummy's left shoulder joint, severing tendons and fibrous muscle until the entire length of the arm fell free, the limb unclenching from the corpse's knees for the first time in nearly eighty years. She repeated the action with the other arm before turning her attention to the bare pelvis. Grunting, she held the body for stability as she sawed through the thick groin tendons until the legs popped free with a sickening crack, exposing the pale, sunken abdomen.

Milo and Bridget lowered the body face-up onto the plastic sheet, its arms and legs attached only by a few cracking sections of dry, leathery strips.

"Don't forget—this was *your* idea," said Bridget, pointing to the now broken joints with Milo's knife. He realized she'd noticed his uncomfortable expression.

"I thought it'd be more . . . precise," admitted Milo.

"Anyone recovering his body would have chopped it up into pieces anyway," explained Bridget. "So take comfort wherever you can get it. And believe me, I am *not* enjoying this either."

Steeling herself, Bridget carved a Y-shaped incision into the chest, beginning high on each shoulder, meeting just below the sternum and dragging the cut all the way down to the pubic bone.

"They never do this right in the movies," Bridget muttered. "Have to start the dissection above the armpits, or else the chest won't open up properly."

Milo stifled a retch and turned away briefly.

"You and me both," agreed Bridget. "And by the way, my anatomy professor would *freak* if she saw the mess we're making of this poor guy."

"I suppose we're doing the best we can under the circumstances," Milo responded between gags.

Bridget just nodded as she peeled back the skin, revealing the yellowing, discolored ribs below. The sternum cartilage was almost completely gone, and the soft lower organs underneath were decayed to unrecognizability. Milo helped hold the body in place as Bridget individually broke the ribs on either side, yanking them back to expose the mummified internal organs of the upper torso.

"I really wish I had gloves for this," she complained as she wiped bone fragments off her hands onto her thick pants. "In fact—I wish I had an X-ray machine right now. Or better yet, an MRI. And a shower for afterward."

Milo winced as he examined the desecrated body. "The anthropologists are going to throw a shit fit when they see this," he said. "I'm investing in pitchfork polish when we hit topside—those stocks are going to hit the roof."

Ignoring him, Bridget carefully prodded the body's shriveled, blackened heart and collapsed lungs. She gently pulled back the paper-thin liver, exposing the stomach and withered intestines below.

"I'm not seeing anything obvious," said Bridget with another sigh. "We may not learn anything else without medical instrumentation and diagnostic tools."

"Was he starving?" asked Milo. "Could you tell us that, at least?"

"Probably not," admitted Bridget. "But I can tell you if he died with anything in his stomach."

Bridget reached into the mummy's thorax, knuckles bumping against the sharp-ridged interior of the spinal cord, cradling the stomach in her hand from underneath. Holding the knife like a delicate paintbrush, she gently ran the blade down the length of the stomach twice, drawing an intersecting X. The flaps opened easily, the lining still flexible and pliant despite the many decades of decay.

The headlamps couldn't quite reach the interior of the organ, leaving Bridget to scrunch her face as she fished inside with bare fingertips. She withdrew two long, slender objects that almost resembled withered, jointed sticks.

"What are those?" asked Milo, thoroughly mystified.

Bridget tilted the find so Milo could see the instantly recognizable nailbeds at the ends—they were severed fingers.

"Are those . . . ?" asked Milo, concern in his voice.

"They are indeed," Bridget confirmed. "His last meal was two human digits. Not his own of course; he wasn't missing any."

"Holy *shit*," whispered Milo, grimacing as his eyes took in the blackened skin, the ridged, yellowing nails still held tight within their beds.

"They're partially digested," added Bridget. "Whoever killed him didn't catch him in the act. At least a few hours transpired . . . between the . . . the, uh—"

"The cannibalism and the head wound?" said Milo, completing her sentence.

"Yeah," said Bridget. "That. Can you help me try to put together what happened? Maybe this is confirmation bias, but I'm completely convinced we've found an important clue. Isabelle may well have sacrificed her life to lead us this far."

Milo nodded, closing his eyes to focus. In moments, a wave of profound giddiness flooded over him as he concentrated. Dizzy at first with intoxicating euphoria, he and Bridget once again locked eyes before his mind took a single stomach-wrenching turn toward oblivion, uncontrollable fear enveloping his perception as the surrounding room shifted, the walls around him freely warping into impossible configurations. Every detail of the chamber took on staggering importance, each scarred rock, footprint, every imperceptible man-made and geological disturbance magnified, his mind running through a thousand parallel scenarios as it recreated the final moments of the dead man's existence.

"**M**ilo!" shouted the echoing voice, penetrating the depth of his unconscious mind. He slowly came to, as though swimming up through the darkest subterranean lake, each furtive push toward the surface blocked by rocky overhangs and constricting tunnels.

Again the woman's voice called his name, dragging him upward. He felt a pressure against the side of his face—a slap? There it was; the reflective surface of the imaginary waters, now within tantalizing reach. He kicked at the waters again, lungs bursting as he pushed himself toward—

Milo slowly opened his eyes, groggy and weak, Bridget cradling him in her arms. He unconsciously wiped at his nose, his hand coming back with a thick smear of red blood. Everything hurt, especially his aching head.

"What the fuck just happened?" mumbled Milo, coughing. His lungs burned, like he'd actually been underwater fighting for his life.

"You've been out for nearly half an hour," said Bridget, peeling his eyelids back to check his pupils. "Your nose started *gushing* blood—Jesus, Milo—at one point, you stopped breathing for almost an entire minute."

Bridget helped Milo up to a sitting position as he pinched his nose against the last of the dripping blood. The entire front of his shirt was covered in crimson, easily visible even over the weeks' worth of caked filth.

"Milo!" repeated Bridget, smacking him on the shoulder. "Talk to me—are you okay?"

"The scratches on the wall, the marks on the body . . . it was all so fucking *clear*."

As he spoke, his returning headache began to throb, a sharp grinding behind one eye that radiated pain through his jaw and teeth. He winced as a new trickle of blood dripped from his nose as he once again teetered over a vast abyss of limitless information.

"Whoa, whoa," cautioned Bridget, her voice pulling him back from the edge again and into full, painful wakefulness. "Whatever you're doing, ease the hell up."

"What's happening to me?" croaked Milo.

Bridget shook her head, still taking in Milo's rambling, nonsensical speech.

"It could be a byproduct of our eidetic memories," she theorized, her tone betraying her uncertainty. "Maybe a heightened ability to process and evaluate new information, bringing subconscious cues to a higher level of processing . . . I imagine it could become too much for your conscious mind to handle. For the lack of a better word, maybe you short-circuited?"

"That makes sense," said Milo, more than a little relieved that she hadn't dismissed him outright. "It was like the glowing golden room with the altar, only I wasn't drowning in memories, I was drowning in information. I can't help but feel like the explanation to everything is right under my nose. Every corner of this room screamed out at me at once; begging me to pay attention, put the pieces of the puzzle together."

"I hesitate to say this," said Bridget. "But we've come this far. Can you try again? Safely, I mean?"

"Maybe," said Milo. "But I'd need you—your voice was the only thing that kept me from losing myself. You were my anchor."

Bridget started to speak but stopped herself as she considered the implications.

"I changed my mind," said Bridget, shaking her head. "I can't ask you to do this. I can't lose you."

Milo buried his hands in his face, teeth chattering. "Like you said—we've come this far," he finally said. "We have to try something. Talk to me. Walk me through it; pretend you're guiding a meditation."

Wordlessly, Bridget held one of his hands, using the other to place him in a sitting position next to the mummified body.

"We'll give it a try," said Bridget. "But if you start to get into trouble again, I need you to pull back. I don't care how close to an answer you are. Can you promise me that?"

"I promise," answered Milo.

"Then start by closing your eyes," said Bridget, her voice soft but clear. "Visualize the room."

The chamber instantly sprang into Milo's mind in incredible detail, every square inch perfectly illuminated by voluminous light. He could see the land bridge over top, the muddy slide where he'd fallen, the mummy returned to where he'd first discovered it.

"Where are you?"

"I'm in the room," confirmed Milo, teeth gritted in concentration. "It's back to the way we first found it."

"Empty your mind," said Bridget. The grinding in his brain faded, pain retreating from his jawline. "Allow your subconscious to evaluate everything that is seen and unseen."

The room was no longer screaming for his attention. Milo found the stillness within.

"What do you see?" asked Bridget.

"A thousand details—broken stalagmites no thicker than a needle—pebbles disturbed by soft footfalls—even the marks from where his fingernails brushed against the cavern walls."

"What does it mean?"

"It's a trail, Bridget. And I can follow it."

CHAPTER 32:

DATA GAP

Bridget stopped at a passageway intersection to mark their route, ignoring Milo as he impatiently shifted from foot to foot, waiting for her. She started to smear a thin chalk arrow across the cool, wet wall but the white nub crumbled to fragments in her fingers. The doctor gently blew the powder off her hands, the tiny particles glittering as they clung to the air under the illumination of her dimming headlamp.

"Doesn't matter," Milo said, answering her silent worry as he spoke for the first time in hours. "You know we'll remember the route—chalk, no chalk, there's no difference anymore. Let's keep going."

"It's not for us," argued Bridget. "It's so they can find us down here, assuming anyone ever looks."

Milo turned his attention back to the tunnels without responding, but the trail had faded from his mind over the hours. As hard as he concentrated, he could no longer see the faint depressions of bare feet, the brushed-aside stones, the fragile and broken soda-straw calcite formations.

"Shit," said Milo, alarmed. "I think I lost the trail for good this time. Should we backtrack?"

"Don't ask *me*," sighed Bridget, sitting down and taking off her backpack. "I never saw it to begin with—I've just been following *you* this whole time."

Milo thought for a moment. "I'm going to try and pick it up again," he said. Summoning single-minded focus, he closed his eyes and pushed his perception outward, allowing his subconscious total reign over his mental faculties. He opened his arms, hands outstretched, fingers hesitating in the air like an orchestral conductor. Lost to his waking dream, Milo caught flashing glimpses of jostled stones, padded mud, faint marks, and gently disturbed dust—

"You look like a weird magician or something," Bridget interjected, failing to stifle a snorting giggle.

"I lost it again," said Milo, chuckling as he rubbed his dry eyes. It felt strangely comforting to laugh at the ridiculous pose he'd struck as he tried to conjure the trail. "Can't hold all the details in my mind anymore."

"Sorry for messing you up," said Bridget, giving him an apologetic half-smile. "But we may as well keep going. You can always try again if we hit another intersection."

The tunnel snaked ever deeper like a drainpipe, the earth beneath them wetter with each passing step. It became difficult and then impossible to avoid the water dripping from the ceiling, the droplets soaking through Milo's muddy hair and tracing dirty streaks down his face and neck.

"We must be underneath a body of water," said Bridget. "Either that or this chamber is still draining out from the flood."

Milo grunted in acknowledgement as they rounded the next turn, their boots squishing clay beneath their feet. The passageway before them angled sharply downward as it narrowed. Bridget craned her neck to look over the edge of a steep, muddy chute that disappeared into the darkness below. A thin trickle of silt-laden water ran down the length, pooling deeply at the bottom.

"Think we can get down?" asked Milo.

"I know *I* can," said Bridget, eyeing the slippery, rock-studded descent. "You're welcome to give it a shot too."

Grabbing the first of the smooth stalagmites, they lowered themselves onto the slide. Milo squinted at the rocky handholds leading down into the darkness. It'd be like descending a pegboard, but using stalagmites the size of saplings.

Fifty feet passed, and then a hundred. Milo and Bridget rested every few seconds, carefully positioning themselves for the step down. With each movement, the passageway further narrowed and was soon reduced to little more than shoulder width. Milo's head knocked against a rough ceiling as they finally squeezed through the last tight section, the passageway again opening to a long, wide hallway.

"Check this out." Bridget bent down, eyes fixed to the ground. She reached into a clear puddle and gently retrieved a scrap of limp, blackened fabric. A partially melted, tarnished brass button still clung to the cloth by fraying threads.

"Might explain why our friend was naked," said Milo. "Looks like he burned his clothes for light."

Bridget wrinkled her nose as she carefully replaced the fabric. "Hard to imagine the desperation he must have felt. Wandering down here, alone in the darkness."

Milo nodded. He knew their waning batteries would soon put them in the same critical position. He shone his headlamp down the length of the passage, light playing across the flat cavern floor, narrow walls, and eroded, crumbling ceiling. Many of the smaller rocks had already come loose, lying scattered across the ground, growing in scale and frequency until the lamplight reached a fully collapsed section. The ceiling had fallen in decades previous, turning the corridor into a dead end.

"I think this is as far as we can go," said Milo, pointing to the cave-in with disappointment. "I can't see a way through."

Bridget frowned as she approached the rocky avalanche. Climbing the loose debris slope, she stood up on her tiptoes and shined her light into a narrow gap near the top of the pile.

"There's a way through." Her voice was muffled within the rockpile. "Come take a look."

Curious, Milo joined her on the slope, shining his light into the tight crawlway she'd discovered. Improbably, it appeared to run through the entire length of the caved-in section, leading to a new chamber on the other side.

Milo didn't like the route. Not only was it the tightest space they'd considered traversing yet, the collapsed rock could shift again at any moment. As he inspected the interior, Milo's light fell across a small black object about the size of a postage stamp. He reached into the avalanche to retrieve it for Bridget.

"Holy *shit*," said Bridget, examining the find. "I think that's a human fingernail."

"This is not a natural cavity. Someone *dug* through the collapsed section by hand. Maybe they were trapped on the other side after a cave-in?"

"So not a dead end after all," Bridget mused. "Our Japanese friend must have come through here." As she spoke, a deep rumbling resonated throughout the chamber. Both nervously glanced upward as thin lines of dust trickled down around them.

"I don't want to hang out here long," said Milo. "It sounds like rocks are shifting."

"What do you think—can we climb through?"

"Probably—but it could collapse again at any moment."

"We made it this far. Boost me in."

Milo braced himself against his rocky footholds as he pushed her up into the hole. She wriggled up and through, accidentally kicking him in the face with a muddy boot.

After an interminable wait, a small hand emerged from darkness, grasping Milo's wrist and pulling him upward as he struggled to fit his shoulders through the gap. Though not large, Milo was forced to hold his breath almost entirely to crawl on his belly through the ten feet of hand-dug tunnel. Gasping, he finally pushed his way out the other end, sliding headfirst out of the squeeze and down a low scree-slope of loose rocks and dust. He flopped on his back and panted, getting his breath back as Bridget stood over him, scanning the new chamber with her light.

It wasn't much different than the other side, at least to Milo's initial glance as he climbed to his feet. Though spared from the worst of the collapse, dozens of large rocks ranging in size from baseballs to refrigerators had fallen from the ceiling. Bridget crouched beside a boulder, light shining on the smooth, yellowed texture of a shattered human skull.

"This isn't the only body," said Bridget, pointing over her shoulder. "I count five in all. There are Imperial insignias on their clothes."

"I think we've found our lost Japanese expedition," said Milo. "Looks like this is where it ended."

"They must have been trapped in the collapse," continued Bridget. "At least three of them were killed instantly when the ceiling came down. But one or more survived long enough to dig their way out."

"Why skeletons?" asked Milo. "Why aren't they mummified?"

"It's wet in here," said Bridget with a shrug. "Even the smallest populations of microscopic organisms could have taken hold, stripped the bodies to bare bone."

Milo pinched the bridge of his nose as she spoke, refusing to allow the full horror of the room enter his mind. His peripheral vision flickered, his consciousness preparing a flood of hallucinatory imagery of crushed bodies and screaming men. It could have taken weeks for the one survivor to tunnel through the collapse in the darkness. He experimentally brushed a hand against the rough walls, his fingertips returning with a thick veneer of wet dust. The cave was slowly digesting the collapsed section, eroding it into nothing.

"Let's not linger," said Milo, shining his light at the loose, rocky ceiling of the passageway as it extended into the darkness. "One good sneeze and that entire section could come down."

"I get that our friend burned his clothes for light," said Bridget as she stood up, brushing the excess mud from her knees. "But what about his boots? The mummy had bare feet."

"My guess is that he ate his belt and boots after supplies ran out," said Milo as he slowly moved from one skeleton to the next, examining them under the harsh illumination of his flashlight. "Wouldn't be the first starving explorer to resort to shoe leather. But he didn't stop there. Some of these bones have knife marks—and one of them is missing two fingers from the left hand, probably the same fingers we found in his stomach. Undoubtedly cannibalism. Maybe he suffered the head wound in the initial collapse, but he could have fallen over the side of the land bridge just as easily."

"There's a satchel over here," said Bridget, calling Milo over as she opened up the stiff, decaying remains of a large canvas bag. Milo took a final glance at the partially fingered, skeletonized hand before tearing his attention away from the bodies. He watched as the doctor cast her light over yellowed labels, rusted tin cans, metal tools, and dusty bottles within the satchel. Then something caught his eye—modern, unblemished cans and plastic bags underneath the petrified Japanese supplies.

"Goddammit," swore Milo, pointing at the recent additions to the bag. "Some of this is our stuff!"

"That *asshole*," said Bridget, picking up a package of instant rice to get a closer look. "You think Logan holed up in here? Nothing was missing from camp—he must have scavenged these from the flood zone after he took off."

"Has to be Logan's," Milo said. "He might even have others. We should keep looking. But if we come across Logan, I don't know if I'm going to hug him or kick his ass."

"You can hug him all you want," said Bridget as she eyeballed the stolen supplies. "*I'm* kicking his ass."

But before they could say another word, a faint noise drifted from the tunnel behind them. Milo and Bridget froze. The light from an approaching headlamp appeared from the darkness, growing gradually brighter as a figure emerged from the darkness.

CHAPTER 33:

THE VOID

Milo watched in shock as Dale Brunswick emerged head-first from the hand-dug tunnel. He barely cast a glance toward them as he slid to the bottom of the rocky slide. Groaning as he drew himself to his feet, Dale reached back and pulled a ragged backpack from the hole and slung it across one shoulder. Short, patchy white stubble had grown across his formerly clean-shaven face since Milo had last seen him.

"One must feel some admiration for these men," said Dale, an almost lazy tone to his voice. "Despite their allegiance to a ruthless empire, they died scientists and explorers."

"Where's Logan?" whispered Bridget. "Is he with you?"

Dale just shrugged as he slumped against the cavern wall and ran a hand through his ivory hair. "No idea where Logan is holed up," he said. "Haven't seen him since he pulled the Houdini act."

"How did you find us?" Milo demanded, suspecting he already knew the answer.

"Happy coincidence," said Dale as he reached into the decaying canvas satchel to select one of the plastic containers he'd stashed. "Found the bodies a few days ago on one of my runs. Seemed like as decent a place as any to camp."

Dale ripped open the wrapping and unscrewed his canteen top, pouring powdered milk into the container. Giving the bottle a couple of good shakes, Dale opened up the canteen and took a dripping swig of the sour mixture.

"You've been hoarding food," stated Bridget. "While the rest of us starve."

Dale considered them without answering before raising the canteen for a second sip. For the first time, Milo could see the thick rivulets of dried blood running from Dale's nose, dripping down the front of his filthy shirt. But Dale had barely brought the bottle to his lips before Bridget reached out and violently slapped it from his hand, spraying the white liquid across the chamber as the canteen clattered to the bare cavern floor.

"Start talking," ordered the doctor. "What haven't you been telling us? You didn't just *find* this place down here, did you? You've been *looking* for it. You knew they were down here since before any of us set foot in this goddamn maze."

Dale just nodded, a wave of distinct irritation crossing his face before fading once again into a strange placidity. "Are you familiar with Unit 731?" he finally asked, waiting until silence had fallen before speaking. "Do you know how they earned their infamy?"

"Of course," said Milo, instantly recognizing the designation. "They were Imperial Japan's secret military biological and chemical warfare brigade during the Second World War. Their crimes were the stuff of nightmares—tens of thousands of soldiers and civilians subjected to brutal human experimentation, live firearms testing, and weaponized pathogens."

"Everyone with even a *passing* knowledge of medical ethics knows Unit 731," added Bridget, fury still etched across her face. "They'd vivisect living patients, force pregnancies, test flame throwers and grenades on captured soldiers, systematically rape women and children, infect prisoners with bubonic plague, smallpox, botulism, anthrax—"

"Certainly," interrupted Dale, folding his arms over his chest. "And in doing so, they created the most scientifically rigorous and complete studies on trauma and infectious disease in history. A legacy that generations have stood upon, albeit secretly."

"And at the expense of countless human lives," snapped Bridget. "It matters where this data came from."

"Data has no inherent morality," said Dale. "And all *you* know is what made it into the textbooks. What's less known is that Unit 731 was no more than a bureaucratic term, a budget line-item for a larger *idea*, an idea that existed long before Japan's invasion of China in 1931. Their work wasn't just applied epidemiology and weapons efficacy experimentation; they possessed an equal mandate to boost the performance of the Japanese foot soldier."

The CEO glanced at Bridget and Milo suspiciously before speaking again.

"This effort went far beyond studying the effects of burns, bullets, shrapnel, and frostbite—all inflicted under controlled conditions by the doctors themselves, of course," continued Dale. "These men developed an interest in the traditional medicine of conquered cultures. They hunted ancient knowledge. They captured Taman warrior-shamans of Borneo to study their blowpipe poisons. Their jungle-trained shock troops stalked the reclusive Ruk cave-dwellers of central Vietnam, seeking an uncontacted tribe who slept upright, climbed cliffs and trees like apes, and whose secret incantations could supposedly kill. In Papua New Guinea, soldiers and scientists trekked uncharted rainforest in their search for the headhunting Glass Men, losing twenty to disease and arrows in the process—"

"This is a lot to take on faith, Dale," said Milo. "I've never seen a word of this in any book I've ever read."

"It was of the highest priority to Imperial Japan, and conducted with the utmost discretion," continued Dale. "Their covert actions are *still* a state secret. You have to realize this was a worldwide effort. They investigated remote groups that the Germans dismissed outright in their parallel efforts. Ultimately, it was regarded as somewhat of a failure. There were a few minor discoveries that eventually worked their way into the Japanese wartime medical practice, nothing that could have tilted the war to their favor. But what they found beneath the plains of Tanzania was . . . special."

"What happened to the Japanese team on the surface?" said Bridget, interrupting. "They must have had support equipment, personnel—"

"There were three Japanese expeditions to the deep," Dale went on. "Led by Lieutenant Sadao Kawabe, who'd cut his teeth on the caves of occupied China. In the first two trips below, his men reported feelings of euphoria, heightened physicality, and increased memory. They all disappeared on their third and final trip below." He gestured to the broken and crushed bones around them. "I followed their maps to this passage."

"You never answered my question about the men on the surface."

"Imperial Japan was not very good at making the right sort of friends," said Dale, failing to hide a sly smile. "Oral history from this region suggests there were indeed a few dozen men waiting up top . . . too few to fend off the inevitable attack from San warriors defending their most sacred and closely guarded secret. Despite superior firepower, their men were overwhelmed and slaughtered. The last survivor on the surface blew the entrance of the cave to protect their operation and fled with his few remaining notes. Despite incredible initial reports from the subterranean expedition, the loss of their primary team and subsequent wartime realities canceled any further exploration. What few records remained were archived in Japan and later confiscated by American occupation forces in a grand sweep of Unit 731's human experimentation data."

"Why didn't western intelligence pursue it after the war?" asked Milo.

"Japanese data was deprioritized, due to a combination of cultural arrogance and the translation expenses. Money changed hands in the early 1960s, and a great deal of the research found its way to one of my family pharma holdings. It languished there for decades until a medical researcher brought it to my attention."

"And DeWar's map . . . it was a fake, wasn't it?" breathed Bridget. "You concocted the entire rationale for this expedition."

"An unfortunate and incredibly expensive necessity to conceal the origins of this discovery. Yes, the map is a fake. It was based on Unit 731 surveys."

"So what were we? Lab rats?" snapped Milo. "You led us down here just to see what would happen?"

"Of course not!" protested Dale. "I resent that accusation. I'm an explorer, a citizen scientist—and I've come to believe this cave is the single greatest discovery since the polio vaccine."

"It's like our minds are shredding themselves from the inside out," whispered Milo, furious. "Every terrible thing I've ever seen or done, every regret I have, I experience it all over and over again like it's the first time. People are supposed to forget things, Dale. Just look at us— we're falling apart."

"You're missing it," Dale muttered, irritated at having to explain himself. Now angry, he stooped over to pick up his milk-filled water bottle, slapping the cap shut with an open palm. "Can you even imagine the potential? This place may be the key to total recall, the ability to unlock memory, incredible physical ability, high-level reasoning, the total capacity of the human mind itself! Our abilities are increasing every hour—you've experienced it yourself. Imagine sitting before a grand piano for the first time—and then playing Liszt's *Rondeau Fantastique* from memory, every keystroke extrapolated in real time. Imagine painting like Picasso, sculpting like Da Vinci, composing like Mozart, programming computers like Bill Gates—hell, trading stocks like Warren

Buffett. We're not talking about the next designer drug. This will revolutionize the *world,* pour forth the genius capacity of every person on this planet."

"A few casualties notwithstanding," Milo said. "Duck—Isabelle—all those people at the surface—and maybe even Logan too."

"I never intended for that to happen," said Dale, eyes cast downward. "They're unbearable tragedies, all of them. I'll carry that weight to the grave, and I'd take their place if I could. I suppose I should have known nature has a balance. For every cure, a disease. For every apple, a snake."

"*Fuck* you," spat Bridget. "*You* led us in here without disclosing the risks. I thought I knew you, Dale. I thought we were friends."

"Listen to yourself!" shouted Dale, face reddening with newfound anger. "This is so much more important than this bickering—can't you see it? Our world demands we evolve *now* before it's too late. We live in a world with nuclear consequences, shepherded by minds that haven't physiologically changed since the Stone Age. We make our decisions with the same primitive processes as every other upright ape—anger, sexual fixation, self-involvement, no ability to separate fact from opinion or superstition. Our collective decisions will ripple for *millennia,* and yet our leadership cannot think past the next election cycle, the next fiscal quarter. We live in a world populated by false gods and invented monsters, our societies motivated by petty grievance and tribalism. Even the tools designed to demolish the walls between us have been turned inward upon themselves, co-opted by marketers who sell our own selfish fantasies back to us one click at a time. We have lost our last grasp at any central thread of truth; every day we find our humanity reduced from a common species to a mere nationality, an exponential fracturing that continues through age, gender, ethnicity, education, class, and religion, dividing us until we are rendered entirely alone. But even alone, we find no truth; our every inconvenient or uncomfortable fleeting thought immediately flushed down the memory hole by more and more electronic *garbage.*"

Dale gazed from Bridget to Milo and back again, carefully studying them both.

"Think about it," Dale ordered. "Please . . . think about it. Tell me I'm wrong."

"You've been down here too long," snapped Bridget. "You want to, what, switch off human nature? Replace it with a pharmacy?"

"Haven't we already?" said Dale with a barking laugh. "Would you even know who you are without caffeine? Without alcohol, without cannabis, without antihistamines and painkillers and mood stabilizers and tranquilizers? Would anybody? Hell, even *sugar* is an addictive drug in all but name, and a relatively recent addition to our diets at that. Our lives are defined by the substances we take—tell me, when was the last time you hooked up for the first time without the help of a few drinks? Or made a new friend? Every milestone in social interaction is heightened or moderated by drugs; we are inextricably hardwired to experiment with our own neurochemistry. To medicate is human; we've been doing it since the first goddamn monkey picked up the first goddamn fermented apple."

"We got the answers we came for," said Milo, reaching over to squeeze Bridget's hand, breaking her angry stare-down with Dale. "I think it's time to go."

Bridget was just starting to voice her agreement when Dale dropped the ragged backpack from his shoulder, yanking DeWar's leather-bound journal free as the bag hit the ground with a heavy clunk. Dale shoved the journal into Milo's chest, almost knocking the historian off his feet. He knew the tough, fibrous construction of the journal could handle the rough treatment, but it made him wince all the same.

"Read it," said Dale, his voice pleading. "Please. Find the key, find out what's happening to us so we can bring it to the world."

"What does it say?" Bridget asked. "What happened to Riley DeWar down here? Why can't *you* read it?"

"You think I haven't tried?" said Dale, almost begging. "I've obsessed over every page. Please, Milo. Only you know DeWar. I need you to try again—read the journal. This is the entire reason I brought you down here."

"I'd like to," said Milo, shooting Dale a smartass look as he pointed to the bloodstains on his ruined shirt. "But homework seems to give me a bit of a headache these days."

Dale slowly shook his head as he gazed at Milo's chest. "Please," he repeated. "Try again. It will explain everything, I'm sure of it—I need to understand what's happening to us."

"Don't do it," protested Bridget. "Milo—you're not seriously considering this, are you? Just getting this far has taken enough of a toll already."

Milo held the journal in his trembling hands, running a single finger over the embossed leather binding. The first wave of now-familiar euphoria washed over him, the intoxicating madness. Every page of DeWar's inscrutable, fantastical scribblings flashed into his mind's eye, the words drawn from a dozen languages. The historian could see it all—every equation and diagram, every hurried inkblot, wrinkle, and stain.

"Open it," whispered Dale.

"No," said Milo, dropping the book to the floor, the leather slapping against the floor loud enough to make Bridget jump. "I don't need to open it. I've already memorized every page."

And with that, Milo once again plunged into the frothing avalanche of his own mind.

CHAPTER 34:

THE LECTURE HALL

Suspended in empty space, Milo was no more than an untethered intellect drifting within a shapeless void. Fear gripped his mind; he'd never allowed himself to go this far before. Though previous excursions had unlocked deep access within his consciousness, this was different, a true nothingness, no remaining connection to his physical form.

Alone in the blackness, Milo found himself in the awkward position of not knowing what to do next.

I need a place to work.

Searching his mind for options, Milo played with the idea of a cubicle—*no, think bigger*—or better yet, a scientific laboratory, a library, maybe even the familiar comforts of his Georgetown apartment.

Perhaps a lecture auditorium?

The image of Gaston Hall leapt into Milo's mind, conjuring the 700-seat jewel of Georgetown University into being. His consciousness floated over the viewing gallery, looking across the commanding coffered ceilings, the gilt-detail frescos, the sunlight-pierced arched windows.

Alone within his mind's projection, Milo felt wholly at ease creating an imagined representation of his body; selecting the English-cut suit he'd always wanted, the gray jacket complete with notched lapel and oh-so-fashionable ticket pocket.

I could use a few visual aids, thought Milo as he stepped up to the podium, tugging at the hem of his crisp wool jacket.

No sooner had Milo completed the thought than chalkboards and easels, projections screens and posters materialized in every corner of the room, each bearing pages of Lord Riley DeWar's tight, scribbled handwriting and sprawling equations.

I could use some help.

As Milo concentrated, the doors to Gaston Hall burst open to accommodate a flood of former colleagues and professors followed by a veritable sea of historical philosophers, codebreakers, translators, doctors, and explorers, all neatly lining up to stare at Milo with expectant faces.

He leaned forward to the podium, tapping the microphone, the echoing *thump* of his finger reverberating through the revered chamber.

"Let's get to work," announced Milo.

hump.
Thump. Thump.
He's not breathing.
Thump. Thump. Thump.
Goddamn it, Milo—wake up.
THUMP-THUMP-THUMP.
Milo! Wake up! Now!
Gasp.

The room came groggily into focus, the dim rays of Bridget's head-lamp like glass shards in his eyes. Spikes of pain radiated through his skull. Blood flowed freely from his nose, bubbling across his lips and collecting in his stubble. He felt weak, barely able to lift a single hand to shield his face from the light. His chest and rib cage hurt worst of all; it felt as though he'd been sacked by an all-pro defensive tackle at the one yard line.

Milo tried to speak but could only croak, lifting his head just enough to see Bridget crouched over him.

"He's back!" announced Dale from outside of his narrow vision.

Milo slowly turned his head to see Dale sitting on the ground beside him. Bridget had hung a lamp from the nearest rock, dimly lighting the chamber in yellow tones.

"Can you hear me?" said the doctor in a whisper, gently pulling back Milo's eyelid to examine his dilated pupils.

"Yeah," confirmed Milo, turning his head to cough his airway clear, spitting blood onto the sand. "I can hear you."

Bridget sighed with relief, closing her eyes in silent prayer before opening them again. "You were in that trance for hours," she finally said. "I thought you'd stopped breathing at one point."

"I feel like hammered shit," groaned Milo as he attempted to sit up from the hard, cold ground.

"Just relax," said Bridget, gently pushing him back. "Don't try to get up. Take your time before saying anything else."

"Did you do it?" whispered Dale. "You decoded it, didn't you?"

"Every scribbled word," whispered Milo, locking eyes with Dale.

"What was inside? What happened to him down here?"

"It wasn't like that," said Milo, shaking his head. "It was so much more than a travelogue. He didn't use it to record events; he used it to write these . . . *insights* . . ."

"Insights?" repeated Bridget. "I don't understand."

"Conceptual insights," said Milo. "It's hard to explain. His jour-nal was almost like a book of ideas, all decades ahead of their time. He extrapolated from existing research, solved theorems, conducted thought experiments. His journal held initial theorization on some of the most important scientific discoveries of the early twentieth century."

"Like what?" demanded Bridget.

"Like . . . all kinds of things," Milo replied. "DeWar outlined the third law of thermodynamics, the concept of the atomic nucleus. Drag and lift formulas for fixed wing aircraft. He even quantified stellar synthesis, the cosmological process by which all heavy elements are formed within solar bodies. Dale . . . he may have been the first person to hypothesize the Big Bang."

"Incredible," marveled Dale, his voice distant with awe as he soaked in the revelation. "All deduced by a single playboy lord, a man wholly undistinguished as a scholar."

Before Milo could respond, a low rumble began to build in the eroded ceiling, the little trickles of dust turning into pouring streams as rocks began to fall around them. A second collapse had been triggered.

"*Run!*" screamed Bridget, breaking for the tight, fragile tunnel. But it was too late. Boulders cascaded from the ceiling with a grinding roar, blocking the only path of escape. Milo sprang to his feet, chasing after Dale and Bridget as the three plunged into the unstable passageway, holding hands over their heads to block a deluge of fist-sized rocks. The entire chamber shook ferociously as choking dust swirled around them, reducing their visibility to nothing. With a deafening crack, the floor beneath Milo's feet split open, sending him cartwheeling into the void below. In his freefall, the last thing Milo heard was Bridget's scream.

CHAPTER 35:

WARRIOR'S PATH

Milo knelt in the savanna grasses of his vast dreamscape, dark starlit sky twinkling above the eternal plains, all of the earth before him no more than a grain of sand in the endless stream of the cosmos.

But he was not alone this time. Bridget crouched beside him, her dark hair drawn back into dreadlocks, her slender neck pale in moonlight. As he drew himself to his feet, two splinters penetrated his heel, and Milo bent to draw them from the earth. In his hands they grew to a pair of long, obsidian-tipped spears, the lengths now taller than himself. Milo separated the twin weapons, passing one to Bridget.

As before, holes beneath their feet widened as albino locusts emerged in a growing swarm. One bite, two bites, a dozen, a hundred; he felt their pincers pulling at his skin. The entire breadth of the landscape teemed with seething insects, so vast in number they threatened to consume the very world beneath him. Milo allowed the pain of the bites to grow until Bridget cried out—and then he began to run. She matched his pace, striding slowly at first, the brittle bodies of the white locusts crunching beneath their feet. Together they ran *faster and faster until he lost any sensation of speed, lush grasslands passing in a blur, the insects retreating to their shrinking holes.*

His vision now incredibly clear, Milo watched a lion as it stalked the low wetlands. With each bounding step, the pair rose higher in the sky, soaring through the misty froth of stellar constellations. Spears raised, Milo and Bridget plunged toward earth, wind whistling in their ears like a hurricane's howl.

The lion swiveled with fangs bared to meet them, defiant as it reared and swiped, its roar shivering through the swamp's low trees. Milo slammed the spear into the beast's shoulder, piercing the thick hide deeply as Bridget drove her weapon into hardened skull, the thick wooden shaft of her weapon shattering in her hands. The wounded animal bellowed, Milo clinging to its matted mane, one hand on his spear as he violently forced the glass tip toward his quarry's beating heart.

Bridget dodged flashing teeth and claws, lost to a cloud of dust as the lion pounced the air where she'd just been. Spinning around to face the beast, she lunged with obsidian spearhead alone, the blade clutched in her fist like a knife.

The lion charged. Milo leapt forward, grasping the mane as he physically wrenched the animal's snapping maw upward. Bridget issued a piercing scream, baptizing herself in blood as she slashed the lion's throat with the obsidian spearhead. Milo threw himself free, tumbling over the grass as the animal collapsed, sighing one last foamy breath with Milo's spear still vibrating in its back.

Breathing hard, legs trembling, Milo and Bridget looked first to each other, and then to the foot of the great oasis where they found themselves, incalculable herds of elephant, giraffe, and antelope surrounding them. Hippos and alligators floated within as leopards and hyenas stalked the outer perimeter, birds circling above.

His hand reaching to clasp hers, they together parted the tall grasses, tiptoeing to the sandy edge of the oasis waters. Milo and Bridget embraced and sank to their knees, ground soft beneath them, she soaked with blood, he

panting and sweat-slicked. Pushing him to the sand, she straddled his body,
pressing herself into his firm flesh.

But then she stopped—beside them, the oasis had begun to drain, waters
vanishing to a swirling whirlpool. The hippos grunted and made for shore
while the crocodiles sank into the mud. Bridget pulled herself away from
Milo; they crouched together as the last of the water disappeared. All that
remained was the black pit, unimaginable in scale, with thick golden ropes
leading from the banks to the center of the earth, the long woven chains glow-
ing bright as the rising sun.

B ridget leaned over Milo and put a hand on his forehead, her mud-
caked face revealing profound relief as he slowly stirred. Moving
his arms, he felt soft sand beneath his fingertips, momentarily remind-
ing him again of his vivid dreamscape, flashes of the eternal plains
briefly drowning out the pain.

"You are officially unkillable," said Bridget, eyebrows raised as she
spoke. "I wasn't sure you were even *alive* down there."

"What happened?" croaked Milo. "Last thing I remember was running—the entire chamber was coming down around us."

"The floor collapsed out from underneath you, dumped you into the
chamber below," said Bridget. "You fell at least sixty feet, maybe more.
Dale broke his wrist in the cave-in and it took us almost three hours to
climb down to reach you. You're just lucky you landed on a sandy hill
and not bare rock."

Milo looked around. With the limited light, all he could tell was that
he'd landed hard on the crest of a steep sand dune, then tumbled another thirty feet before coming to a rest. Around him, massive rocky
formations from the cave-in dotted the sand, all nestled within their
newly formed impact craters. It was a miracle he hadn't been crushed.

Dale approached from below, slowly shuffling up the sandy hill to
reach him, arm cradled in a tidy sling. "Hallo!" called Dale. "He lives!
No worse for wear, I hope?"

"We'll see," said Bridget, restraining her optimism. "He took a pretty serious tumble."

Looking around for the first time, Milo realized the rolling dunes were within an immense underground canyon, sheer walls on either side, a winding, subterranean stream cutting through the middle. Through the darkness, he could barely make out the newly formed gash in the ceiling from where the unstable chamber had collapsed, dropping him into the ravine below.

"One of the falling rocks sliced you up pretty good," added Bridget. Surprised, Milo checked his arm. She'd stitched it up well, especially given that she'd used thread from the frayed remains of her pants. Though his arm was still painfully swollen, he'd already regained a surprising amount of mobility, if not strength.

"Thanks," said Milo, genuinely impressed at what she'd accomplished given the conditions.

"Can you believe the *size* of this place?" said Dale, his voice echoing as he gestured to the canyon with open reverence. "Just goes *on*, and *on*, and *on* . . ."

"So what's our situation?" asked Milo, slowly drawing himself to a sitting position. He supposed he felt more or less all right, at least not considerably worse than before the impact.

"Down to one light," answered Bridget, standing up beside him and offering a hand, which he took. "Yours broke when you hit the dune, but I was able to save some of the batteries. Nothing left in the way of supplies. No water, but we have the stream, so dehydration isn't an immediate problem."

"Anything else?"

"Yeah," said Bridget. "I kind of landed on you when I came off the wall, fell the last ten feet or so. Feel terrible about it and wanted to get it off my chest."

Milo tried to laugh, but his bruised ribs and cracked sternum wouldn't let him. It came out almost like a wheeze instead.

Dale cleared his throat before Bridget could answer. "You're not going to believe this," he said, kneeling beside Milo, "but look what we found down here." Dale held up a glinting obsidian knife, the razor-sharp edges hewn with the careful taps of an experienced hand.

"Don't tell me," said Milo. "You made this yourself based on a documentary you saw in seventh grade?"

"Not even close," Dale said, chuckling. "Take another look across the stream."

Milo turned to watch as Dale's light played across the sand dunes and sheer wall. At the base of the rocks lay an uninterrupted collection of low altars stretching in both directions, some built tall like the one he'd discovered beneath the flooded cathedral, others no more than a thin slab of simple rock. Skeletal bodies lay atop each altar, most naked but all adorned with stone tools, ivory masks, crude leather pouches, and gourds. The oldest among them held short-statured skeletons with low, wide skulls and thick brows—ancestral precursors of humanity.

"These are San warriors—the first people," whispered Milo, his voice filled with awe. "They must be the tribal warriors who came to this cave in ancient times. Are these the ones that never made it out? My God—some of these altars are prehistoric, probably built tens of thousands of years before the birth of Christ."

"This could be one of the greatest archaeological finds of all time," said Dale. "According to legend, once in a generation a carefully selected warrior would enter the cave to meet his destiny. If he survived, a powerful medicine man would emerge. The Imperial Japanese heard stories that these transformed men could see in the dark, run for days at a time without resting. They were legendary in combat and were said to possess perfect memory, able to instantly recall events and topography from years, even decades previous. Sound familiar?"

His injuries briefly forgotten, Milo brought himself up to his feet, transfixed as Dale and Bridget helped him wade across the stream to reach the open altars. With Dale's lamp as his guide, he trembled at the sheer number of burials; the mounds following the immeasurable length of the subterranean canyon.

"Some of these bodies were placed here decades after they died," whispered Bridget. "They were probably collected from all corners of the cavern system. It would explain why we haven't found more bodies. Most of the ones I examined died violently—probably from falls and such. But I couldn't establish the cause of death for all."

"Some likely drowned," said Milo, allowing his hand to drift to the cool edge of the nearest stone altar, careful not to disturb the body. "Others from dehydration, starvation, disorientation, or insanity."

"At least we're not completely stuck down here," said Bridget. "As far as I could tell, this canyon goes on more or less indefinitely. I have no idea if it leads anywhere worth going."

Milo nodded, his mind eased by the trickling of the gentle stream. Bridget gently took the obsidian knife from Dale and returned it to the withered hand of a short, skeletonized warrior, his body lovingly decorated with ostrich hide and ivory beadwork.

"Almost beautiful down here, isn't it?" asked Bridget with a sigh. "I can think of worse places to wander aimlessly until we run out of light and starve to death in the darkness. But if we tried for the surface again—"

"Even *if* we had enough batteries, which we don't—" added Dale.

"—I don't think we could make it, not in our current condition," continued Bridget, finishing her sentence. "What should we do? This feels like the end, Milo. We're running out of options."

"Warriors entered this cave," repeated Milo, grimly nodding his head. "They made it through four thousand vertical feet of darkness. Some of them made it back out again, and we need to figure out how—it's our only hope. I want to see what Lord Riley DeWar found down there."

The trio removed their boots and slung them around their shoulders by the laces as they slowly trudged the sands of the subterranean canyon. With every step, Dale's lamp fell across more burials, some little more than the crumbling dust of ten-thousand-year-old bones.

Milo reached over to touch Bridget's hand; she returned the grasp. There was a certain comfort in their mutual resignation. He allowed his mind to wander, taking in the beautiful vastness of the chasm, the cool texture of the wet sand between his toes.

Putting a finger to her lips, Bridget waved for Milo's attention and then pointed high up into the air, stopping the trio for the first time in hours. Squinting, Milo could barely make out a faint light at an impossible distance above them.

"What the hell is that?" asked Dale, trailing closely behind.

"It's our camp," murmured Bridget. "Charlie and Joanne are still up there, stuck on that suspended rock. I just hope Joanne made it back safely and that she's smart enough to self-quarantine—but we can't help either one of them from down here. There's no way we could climb to reach them, it's just too dangerous. Should we try to call out, let them know we're all right?"

"We're all right?" grumbled Dale. "Not from where I'm standing."

"No," answered Milo with his own whisper. "To them, we'd only be ghosts in the abyss."

They followed the dying light like a guiding star until the last of the distant camp's dwindling lamp slowly winked out for the last time. Far above, the sounds of plaintive human grief spilled into the unfathomable void as Joanne cried into the darkness like a forsaken angel.

CHAPTER 36:

BREAKDOWN

2,595 feet below the surface

After miles of gently winding between sand dunes, the stream drained into a hole in the canyon wall. The trio of cavers followed it, soon emerging into the familiar waters of the serpentine river. Newly deposited silt rose up in blossoming clouds behind every footfall as they waded downstream. It was as though the river had turned chameleon, the copper-flecked greens transmuting to earthy hues as they trekked ever deeper. Milo couldn't help but remember what Dale had said: that subterranean waters marked the final delineation between the world of man and next.

They sloshed through in waist-deep waters for hours. Milo regretted he'd once compared the system to a Parisian sewer. No, the serpentine river was no French drainpipe; it was a thing more ancient and astounding altogether.

Holding their breath, the three swam under the lowest ceiling until the passageway opened to the full breadth of the flooded cathedral, spike-studded ceiling now three hundred feet above. Before them stood the statue-like stone edifice, the towering figure in shadow like a winged angel, a frozen crystal pillar pouring from its heart and into the waters below.

"Indescribable, isn't it?" asked Dale.

"Every time I see this formation, I think of the Book of Genesis," said Bridget, staring at the natural figure with reverence. "Chapter three, final verse . . . *so the Lord drove out man, and he placed at the gate of the Garden of Eden an angel with a flaming sword.*"

"Lord Riley DeWar would agree with you," Milo murmured. "He wrote about a stone figure with a crystal saber, carved by nature herself."

"He had quite the talent for the dramatic," added Dale. "Pity he never returned to write about his underground exploits."

As they paused, the trio watched the motionless stone under the dimming illumination of Dale's headlamp.

"Are you ready?" asked Milo, looking toward the stone pipe organ that stood atop the flooded passage to the inner sanctum.

Bridget pursed her lips before nodding. "Keep track of your pants this time," she said. "I'm not swimming after them twice."

Milo caught Dale stifling a smirk before they all dove, kicking through the crystal clear waters, sharp rocks nipping at Milo's clothes and boots as he pulled himself through the flooded tunnel to the next chamber, Bridget and Dale following inches from his heels.

The three surfaced simultaneously, bursting from the water with ragged gasps. The room remained untouched by the flood, the small peaked island at the center of the chamber still adorned by the altar and ivory masks. Below them, the massive boulders of the collapsed ceiling rippled beneath diminishing waves.

Milo and Bridget swam to the island, pulling themselves ashore as Dale treaded water behind them. The warm golden light beneath had grown in intensity since their previous visits, rays bursting from between the rocks and erupting from the surface of the subterranean lake.

Dale clicked off his headlamp. "Got to conserve every milliamp," he said. "We have a few hours of power left, tops."

The first wave of familiar dizziness washed over Milo. The chamber was sauna-warm, feverish heat crawling across his skin as his perception flooded with a deluge of memories. Roughly grabbing him by his neck, Bridget pressed her mouth to his as Dale turned away, Milo's evaporating mind almost succumbing to the rapture of the golden glow. But then she pulled away.

"You think we can make it to the other side of the rocks?" whispered Bridget, leaving Milo dangling over the edge of cognitive abyss. She pointed straight down, toward the submerged golden light.

"I don't know," he admitted. "But I think we ought to try."

Bridget nodded and peeled off her shirt to a sports bra and unzipped her pants. "What?" she demanded, realizing both Dale and Milo were watching her with a somewhat bewildered expression. "I don't want to get my clothes caught up on the rocks—besides, it's too hot in here anyway."

"Good thinking," said Milo, shrugging as he unbuttoned the shredded remains of his shirt, joining her as he stripped down to his underwear.

"Are we ready for this?" asked Bridget, hands pausing over her half-removed trousers. "Really ready? Milo, we're sailing off the edge of the world here. We could get stuck, drown. Even if we make it to the other side, we could go insane or die instantly. Whatever is affecting us might be filtered through forty feet of water. We have no idea what total exposure does."

Milo looked deep into Bridget's eyes, weighing every crease on her worried face, every dark strand of loose hair, every moment the two had ever shared.

"We're out of options," Milo whispered. "There is something at work down here that we don't understand. Seeing this through is our only shot at staying alive. Could you really turn around, so close to learning what lies on the other side?"

Bridget closed her eyes and turned from him, hiding her face. "Yes," she finally said in a very small voice. "I'd turn around if it meant I could keep you this time."

Milo grasped Bridget with both arms, rocking her, holding her so tightly he thought they might both burst. "Never again," he swore. "I'll never take another step into the unknown without you—we have to see this through together."

Dale cleared his throat, tears in his eyes as he stood on the edge of the island. He hadn't so much as unbuttoned his shirt.

"You're not coming?" asked Bridget.

Dale just shook his head. "I don't have a chance at surviving that swim, not with the busted wrist. I'll wait for you as long as I can, and then I'm going to push for the surface, alone if I have to. All I can do is wish you both Godspeed. Please don't make me leave without you."

Bridget nodded, her face buried in Milo's chest. Together, the pair began to breathe faster and faster, hyper-oxygenating their blood in preparation for the final dive. Pulling away, they abandoned the last of their clothes as Milo counted down.

"On three," he whispered. "One . . . two . . . *three.*"

Milo and Bridget leapt from the rocks and into the water, Dale's still figure disappearing into the froth of bubbles behind them. Kicking hard, Milo passed ten feet, twenty, pinching his nose to equalize his ears. By thirty feet, his lungs were bursting within his pain-wracked chest, his pulse pounding in his ears like hammer.

Forty feet under the surface of the black lake, Milo's fingers touched the bottom. He pulled himself across the broken, jagged rocks, wriggling into the biggest gap between them, his body scratched and dragging against the stones, the golden light now blinding.

Palm grasping for a handhold, Milo felt a sudden slick softness. He yanked back a fistful of the strange texture. Silhouetted by the light, the dark shape before him suddenly twitched, blocking his path as it rotated to reveal a thick human body. Milo panicked, irreplaceable bubbles running from his mouth as Dr. Logan Flowers's swollen, wide-eyed face turned toward him.

Desperate hands clawed across his back—Bridget had made her way into the passage behind him. Unable to turn around, he shoved himself further forward, toward the dead man. He'd read drowned cavers were always stuck in the tightest, worst sections, impossible to extract. Trapped, Logan's corpse now blocked the only path.

Summoning all his strength, Milo grasped Logan's torso underneath the armpits, pulling with all his might. He could see it now—the geologist's limp arm caught between two rocks, rending his entire body immovable. Bracing his legs, Milo bubbled in frustration as he pulled again, air streaming between gritted teeth, joints popping, spine exploding in pain. With a dull pop, Logan's bloated arm separated at the shoulder, ripping free in a brown gout of liquid decomposition. The path unblocked, Milo slithered through, Bridget close behind.

The pair burst into a flooded corridor, finally free of the rocky debris pile. Clinging to the ceiling, they pushed themselves along the hundred-foot length, gaining speed with every desperate thrust.

And then they were clear of the rocks and into open waters, the blinding illumination their only guide. The last of his dark vision closing, Milo involuntarily sucked in little gasps of water as he kicked and clawed for air, making for the surface.

With one final push, Milo broke the waters, emerging into a world of pure golden light.

PART 4:

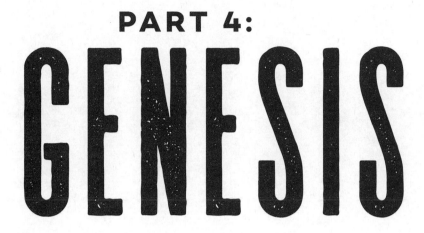

GENESIS

And the earth was without forme, and voyd, and darkness was upon the face of the deepe.

—Genesis 1:2 (KJV, 1611)

CHAPTER 37:

EGO DEATH

Depth unknown

Milo burst through the glassy surface and into a world of golden light, his convulsing lungs sucking air in ragged gulps. He dug his fingers into the nearest muddy wall but was ripped away, a roaring current dragging his struggling body deeper into the cave. Gritty, sulfuric droplets burned in his eyes as the blinding cavern around him slowly came into focus. But he understood nothing of what he saw—the insanity had taken hold, no mere giddiness but an explosion of unquantifiable ecstasy and the joyful annihilation of his consciousness. The river and tunnel swirled in a kaleidoscope, the lenses of his eyes focusing, irises contracting, retinal cells capturing photons, optic nerve dancing with electrical impulse, brain awash with neurochemicals, but his cognitive ability to perceive had evaporated.

Vanishing into his own mind, Milo struggled to tread water against the current. His pulse pounded as he fought to maintain control, the golden light penetrating his mind like a thousand jagged needles. A smothering blackness erupted from within, paralyzing his limbs and tearing away all sensation. Unable to see Bridget or process the avalanche of psychedelia, Milo's eyes rolled up into his head as his skin erupted in fiery pain. Throat closing, he could not even scream as he lost his final connection to thrashing arms and twitching legs, the fast-moving waters pulling him beneath the surface once more.

It was as though he'd pulled a giant red lever that caused the entire universe to wink out all at once, a *Star Trek* transporter beam pulling him apart cell by cell, every neuron in his brain firing independently of the whole, his mind's eye obscured within a surging gray-matter electrical storm.

Convulsed in seizure, Milo rocketed over the crest of a massive subterranean waterfall and plummeted into the churning froth below.

CHAPTER 38:

REBIRTH

Milo's mind slowly stirred within his motionless body. He was no longer drifting in a fever-dream of formless void; he was underwater, trapped beneath the outwash of the churning underground waterfall. Panic gripped him—he couldn't move his paralyzed arms and legs. Pressure crushed his chest as he struggled to swim for the surface, only managing shuddering twitches. Screaming within the confines of his own skull, Milo forced nerve signals to his useless limbs, begging them to obey his command. His body jolted at first, then thrashed, muscles and mind joining to fight the paralysis. One hand responded, then the other, his arms and legs haltingly falling to his will.

Swimming upward through the froth of bubbles, Milo slipped past a dark human form suspended in the white, swirling waters. Bridget's unresponsive body floated facedown, still lost within her unconsciousness. He wrapped his numb arms around her waist as he kicked hard, desperately pushing the pair toward the surface. They burst free of the waters, and Milo dragged her limp body from the underground river and onto a low, sandy shore.

Bending down, he pressed his ear against her mouth, listening for breath, but heard nothing.

He drew himself to his knees and pounded the doctor's chest with both fists until she finally gasped, tilted her head to one side, and threw up into the sand.

Milo and Bridget lay on the low shoreline, staring at the white calcite walls of an immense limestone cavern as gentle waves lapped their feet. The waterfall they'd fallen over cascaded off a thirty-foot ledge and into the pool beside them. Time passed like a dream as Milo and Bridget rested, their sinewy, muscled forms glowing under the illumination of gathering golden ropes.

The curving walls above them were a rainbow of fossil layers, the light playing against stony Cambrian trilobites—horseshoe crabs— that had scuttled the ocean floor a half-billion years previous. Above the crabs were beautiful spiral-shelled nautilus, Silurian-period sea scorpions, primordial fish, and brachiopods, the final ceiling layer impregnated with the primitive four-footed amphibious reptiles of the late Paleozoic era.

The source of the light was a curious thing indeed, a soft emanation from wet, flowing tentacles that clung to the rocky ceiling like leafless vines. The mold-like growths followed the highest arcs of the chambers, extruding in every direction like a fibrous root system, splitting and forking over and over again until the spreading fingers were no thicker than threads.

Milo and Bridget had surfaced not into another chamber, but another world. In proportionality, the expanse perhaps resembled the altar-room, wide and circular with an island at the center, waters lapping at the sides. But the scale was not the same by any measure, stretching more than a mile in each direction, the outer perimeter lost to a low, distant haze. The waters held within the chamber were not a pond or even a lake, but a veritable sea. Thick golden ropes emerged from every feeding tributary, clinging to the ceiling as they met at the highest point above the central island, binding together to become a massive, drooping nuclei a hundred and fifty feet across, the heart of gold illuminating the subterranean world like a newborn sun.

Though three thousand feet below grassy savanna and a dozen horizontal miles from the entrance, the world around them was profoundly, inescapably thick with life. Smelling the slight tinge of sulfur in the air, Milo could feel the warmth of heat-bearing geothermal vents from deep below the enclosed sea, feeding the cavern with warmth. Long, translucent tubeworms gently danced in the flow of the gritty, mineral-rich waters alongside thick-shelled white clams, the organisms clinging to the surface of every submerged rock. Pale snails climbed waving tubeworms as ancient shrimp and primitive, translucent octopi darted to shelter before every footfall. On the walls and ceiling, colonies of flightless albino locusts crawled in swarms, feeding upon the glowing molds. Milo concentrated, turning his focused gaze to one new species at a time, using the fleeting moments to memorize their alien features.

Bridget and Milo watched the teeming life for what felt like hours, their bodies slowly recovering from near-drowning. Milo looked to Bridget and then himself. They'd become their most ancient human forms, at least in a sense. Unclothed, the two had shed everything but the most necessary physiology, their bodies honed and hardened into lean, natural muscle.

Bridget sat up and reached over, gently plucking one of the flightless locusts from the wall. The doctor turned the insect over in her fingers, considering the organism before carefully placing it into her mouth, crunching it beneath her teeth, and swallowing. She selected a second locust from the wall and handed it to Milo. Trapped between thumb and forefinger, the insect squirmed to escape his grasp. He bit the locust in half, the sweet, bitter innards bursting as he crushed the hard outer shell. The taste was mild and the texture ultimately palatable; and soon he found himself harvesting a second and a third, his contracted stomach slowly filling with still-twitching proteins.

Milo asked Bridget how long they'd rested upon the shores. The words came out as a jumble of languages and equations.

But Bridget understood him. And she answered in her own string of elegant numbers, her dynamic, living cipher beautiful in its simplicity. Naked of equipment and without the stellar sky as timekeeper, she'd kept track of the interminable hours by heartbeat alone. But what other chronometer could there be in this lost world? Milo instinctually knew that within the chamber they could eat when hungry, sleep when tired, make love upon mutual desire, beholden only to ancient rhythms. Even his memories were no longer a flood; they were now crystalized, organized, each at easy and immediate reach, as though he could pluck and examine a single remembrance like a shell from the sand.

Milo spoke about the golden *arachnocampa luminosa* glowworms, a form of gnat found within the caves of New Zealand and Australia. Their tiny, pinpricked bioluminescence turned ceilings into starry blue constellations within the deep. He asked Bridget, "could the root-like formations be some distant, primordial relative of the glowworm?"

Bridget contradicted him in a flowing, elegant thesis derived from a dozen tongues and pure mathematics. The golden ropes above them were no scattered insects; they were long, branching filamentous structures of colonized organisms, perhaps like the bioluminescent foxfire of ancient European forests. The strange, sunless ecosystem was a sort of subterranean refuge, a relic population left behind by the epochal retreat of the seas and the changing climate above. As mountaintops above desert plains become "sky islands," preserving colonies of tall trees and alpine flowers from ages past, the cave sheltered the remnants of a distant era, a clockwork ecosystem set into motion tens of millions of years before a single tumbling meteor changed the planet forever. So too had the endless network of golden roots once spread throughout the cave, perhaps once kissing the shadow of the distant entrance before its long retreat into the deep.

Together, Bridget and Milo stood and walked the first stretch of the immense shoreline of the great chamber, their bodies bathed in the light of the second sun. The ecstasy threatened to take hold again, their minds pulsating with new intensity as they came across the scattered bones of two dozen men amid the fragments of a makeshift camp. Flesh stripped from skeleton, tools and fabrics reduced to nothing, Milo saw little more among the many bones than the shards of broken eyeglasses, the rusted imprint of an iron spike, and the decaying leather of a hobnail boot—at long last, the remains of Lord Riley DeWar's lost expedition.

Milo turned to Bridget and—in the bath of light and ecstasy, and without words—begged her for logic, for answers among the mystery.

In response, Bridget silently extended a single finger toward the lonely subterranean island below the second sun.

W ith the pulsing, swirling ecstasy once more growing within him, Milo could no longer see the golden underground world nor Bridget beside him; he could only feel the cool water against his naked skin as existence itself heaved and cracked. And yet he swam, each moment threatening to tear him from the waters and cast him again into the universe-before, the realm of pure void.

His senses fading into the disintegrating reality, Milo's fingers brushed sand once more. Trembling, he realized he'd reached the shore of the tiny island.

Milo slowly drew himself to his feet in the ankle-deep waters surrounding the archipelago. His perception had shrunk to virtually nothing, seeing neither the distant chamber walls nor the iridescent globe above. All he could see was Bridget and a single calcified human skeleton slumped within a throne of hand-hewed stone—Lord Riley DeWar.

Bridget spoke first, struggling to speak with simplicity. "He looks so lonely."

"The last living member of his expedition," said Milo. "The loneliest man on earth."

The doctor looked to the stone island, to the crude rocky seat, to the skeleton. "I don't see any broken bones, no obvious trauma. There's enough food and water in this chamber to last lifetimes. Why did he die down here? Why didn't he just . . . go home?"

"I don't know," said Milo, his mind already soaking in clues from his surroundings, subconscious churning as it evaluated every inch of the throne and body from a thousand perspectives, ringing voices and images erupting in beautiful symphony within his mind. He dropped to his knees and brushed away at the tips of DeWar's skeletonized fingers, revealing faint lines of the explorer's careful script scratched into the stone itself.

AND THE EYES OF THEM BOTH WERE OPENED.

"Both?" asked Bridget. "There's only one body here."

"He's not speaking about himself," said Milo. "It's from Genesis. Chapter Three, the story of Eve and the tree of knowledge. *She took of the fruit thereof, and did eat; and she gave also unto her husband with her, and he did eat. And the eyes of them both were opened.*"

"It's reductive," asserted Bridget, narrowing her eyes. "He encountered something he couldn't possibly understand, so he retreats to religious allegory?"

"Nothing DeWar did in his final hours was reductive," whispered Milo. "We know this from his journal. I think the inscription is the same shorthand he used for everything—finding expedient language for the grandest of concepts. Nothing we've seen is an accident, is it? The cave paintings—the elephant graveyard—the ancient mausoleum—every human-made marking, every artifact. We're just miles from Olduvai Gorge of the Great Rift Valley—"

"The Cradle of Humankind," Bridget confirmed. "The greatest paleoanthropological site on the planet. DeWar had the chance to scrawl one final insight into the stone—and he chose this. Why?"

Milo opened his mind, the sudden onslaught of imagery driving him to his knees once more, ears ringing and vision overwhelmed with subconscious deduction. He struggled to maintain hold of the pictures rushing through his mind, the flashes of the hilltop grasses over the vast Tanzanian savanna and oasis from his dreams.

"Milo!" exclaimed Bridget.

"I can almost see it," gasped Milo, holding his face in his hands. "The moment DeWar discovered—the moment when *she* found the fruit."

"*She?*"

"Eve—but not our Eve, not the religious construct. *The* Eve, the early hominid that found this cavern. That's what DeWar wanted us to know. This cave isn't the cradle of humanity—it's the womb."

"What are you saying?"

"Imagine—the first woman standing transfixed before a long, branching golden tendril clinging to the ceiling."

"Back when the golden organism claimed the entire cavern," said Bridget. "When it reached all the way to the original entrance."

"She reaches up to the stone ceiling and plucks a glowing nodule from the vine. She holds it to her face as a mist of spores drift from the globe, entering her mouth and nose. She collapses, eyes dilated, trembling in ccstasy."

"The psychedelia would have been overwhelming,"

"But only at first. The neural pathways of her mind struggle to rewrite themselves, somehow cope with the sensory overload—just as ours have. Her gifts were the same as ours—memory, deduction, even mental mastery of the physical self. Only hers were given to an ancient mind."

"An ancient mind now capable of abstract thought—of language, of medicine. And thus *homo* became *homo sapiens,* ape becoming *thinking* ape," whispered Bridget. "Apex predator of every ecosystem on the planet."

"But what are the golden threads?" said Milo as the pounding revelations began to fade, exhausted of insight. He turned to face Bridget, seeing her softly lit face once more as they together looked at the incandescent tendrils and their bulbous fruit above. Together they slumped to the sand at the foot of the skeleton, holding each other as the world around slowly materialized into being once more.

"Possibly the single greatest accident in the history of the cosmos," said Bridget. "Most likely a bioluminescent slime mold, a colonizing single-celled eukaryotic species of the kingdom Protista."

"Not the fruit of the gods per se?"

"Nor a Promethean torch or Eden's tree of good and evil—at least not in any understandable sense."

"But it is special," insisted Milo. "It *has* to be special."

"It *is* special," said Bridget. "Species find their defense mechanisms by genetic accident; small mutations in biological coding resulting in toxic compounds, waxy barriers, foul odors, bitter flavors, thorns, molecules that bind to sensory thermoreceptors—"

"And psychedelics."

"And psychedelics, yes. Animal and plant life will use any advantageous mutation that might protect and perpetuate their genetic lineage. At some point in the distant past, an anomalous strain of our light-emitting mold began to synthesize a molecular compound analogous to a neurochemical. Serotonin would be my guess. Variations of similar defense mechanisms naturally occur across a number of ecosystems. But this specific molecule is uncommonly psychoactive, and once through the blood-brain barrier, it breaks down the brain's ability to differentiate informational priority. Quite the effective deterrent to most species of the animal kingdom, as you might imagine."

"The mold weaponized the mutation," Milo said, marveling. "Turned it into a defense mechanism through a million-year process of natural selection."

"It's really that simple, isn't it?" said Bridget. "A naturally occurring defense mechanism. Most animal species would experience disorientation, seizure, even death at higher exposures. It's a neurotoxin, for lack of a better description. But for our early ancestors, this was nothing short of what first made us truly human. It's the genesis of everything we now know, everything our species has achieved. She may have been just one woman—but our world stands upon her shoulders."

"My memory palace—my newfound powers of deduction," whispered Milo. "Charlie's physical self-mastery. Joanne's incredible sight. Your medical intuition. All fruit of the same cognitive tree."

"But what happened to DeWar?" Bridget asked.

"I can only speculate," said Milo. "I believe his men spent their final hours on the beach, lost to their most treasured memories. And DeWar could have spent a thousand lifetimes exploring an unfathomable universe of knowledge. He placed his journal on the altar before returning to his lonely throne to meditate. His body ultimately failed his mind; it was only a matter of time. We have that choice too—to stay and build kingdoms in our imagination."

"And what would have happened if Lieutenant Sadao Kawabe had found this? Brought it back to his superiors?"

"It could have changed history—for all we know, he could have brought back the deductive knowledge necessary to split the atom."

"Dale wants to bring this to everyone—all seven billion of us," said Bridget. "He believes we're a Stone Age species in a world of nuclear weapons and climate change, our minds bound by primitive selfishness while wielding tools we can't possibly understand. He thinks this will transform us all for the better."

"And you?" asked Milo. "What do you believe?"

"I believe in the first people," said Bridget. He watched as she gazed into the blackness of her mind, eyes blank. "Eve took nothing from the cave. She gave her people only knowledge. She didn't stay to explore her inner mind until death; she didn't drug her tribe with some molecular neuro-mimic. She was the first shaman, the first medicine woman, the teacher of all teachers to come."

"And I believe DeWar stayed because he didn't have anyone to leave for," said Milo as he reached out to squeeze Bridget's soft hand. "I do."

CHAPTER 39:

MEDICINE WOMAN

Milo held Bridget on the sandy beach of the cavern's lonely island as she slept. Time passed like a dream, their sinewy, muscled forms intertwined under the illumination of the gathering golden ropes. He allowed his vision to drift up the rainbow walls of fossil layers, the thousands of petrified organisms around him tickling his brain with words like *metazoan, Ordovician,* and *trilobite.* Playful hallucinations of armor-plated placodermi fish and the first reptiles of the Carboniferous period swam across the walls, their forms remembered from textbooks and coursework so many lifetimes ago.

Bridget stirred within his arms, her lean body pressing into his. Yes—someone to return for, someone for whom he'd willingly sacrifice his passage through the gates of infinite insight, maybe even enlightenment itself.

She was awake now—for how long he did not know. The doctor frowned, again visibly forcing herself to use plain-spoken English and not her full range of languages and equations, as though already preparing to reenter the world above. It came more easily now, with Bridget once more sounding like herself.

"Did you dream?" Milo struggled to constrain his question into simple words, insisting that his mind translate.

"Everything—I dreamed *everything*," began Bridget. She attempted to explain in words twice, three times, each beginning with a stuttering false start until she gave up. From her lips and hands spilled a beautiful soliloquy in words of a half-dozen languages, all exactingly placed within a spiraling algorithm of logical extrapolation. She'd spent her brief dream not just within her own mind, but her body, cell by cell, neuron by neuron, exploring the webbed connections within and without, traveling upon the face of intersecting biological function—neurology, immunology, genetics, and ecology. Her journey was a vision of bodies and minds and the world around them, an examination of the threads that connected them all, thick and delicate alike.

"We have to get back to the others," said the doctor, finding her words once more. "I know how to help Joanne."

Milo looked across the unimaginable length of the great expanse, visualizing the vast graveyard in the darkness below. Now far from the deepest glowing chamber, he and Bridget had again reached the suspended rock, its heavy bulk wedged between the grooved, towering walls as it had fallen a million years before. Milo free-climbed the thirty feet of nylon ropes connecting the passageway to the rock, immune to the psychological pull of the nothingness below.

And then his headlamp fell upon Charlie, who had holed up in a sleeping bag that leaned against one of the walls in the darkness. He'd wrapped a T-shirt around his nose and mouth, his naïve protection against the pathogen. But Milo had to admit he was courageous—despite the danger, Charlie had remained by Joanne's side, unwilling to leave her to the sickness.

Joanne was in rough shape. She'd balled herself up in a sitting position in a pool of bloody spatter and pink drool, barely conscious. Motionless, her bloodshot eyes and flushed skin radiated feverish heat from her curled body. Dried vomit collected on the dry stone and the corners of her mouth.

Charlie held up a single hand before his eyes, shielding himself from Milo's feeble light. Bridget pounced on him without warning, grabbing his face to inspect it closely. She held his cheeks tight between her palms as her thumbs pulled down the bottoms of his eyelids. She nodded approvingly to Milo—miraculously, Charlie wasn't infected. And yet something about Bridget's animalistic diagnosis disturbed Milo; it appeared her medical insight was now irreparably interwoven into her intuitive, instinctual subconscious.

The doctor opened the flap to her pack, spilling out a small pile of the flightless albino locusts from the great chamber. Most had survived the perilous underwater journey and now crawled in every direction as they attempted to escape.

Bridget crunched a single locust between her teeth before feeding the other half to Charlie. He chewed, slowly eating the insect despite his surprise. Charlie visibly brightened—the influx of protein had reactivated dormant energy reserves within his body.

Milo concentrated, preparing to make himself understood to Charlie. "Are you okay?" he said, his voice strangely deep and uneven.

Charlie squinted at him before answering. "Yeah," he finally said after a long pause. "Lots of time to think down here, work through some shit. Seriously considered jumping off this rock after the lights went out. One last epic rush, you know? But every time I got ready to do it, I kept on coming with just one more reason not to. Like maybe seeing my dad again. Or birthdays with my little nieces and nephews. Sunrises off Baja Mexico, hang gliding in La Jolla, shit like that. Jesus Christ . . . I figured you two were never coming back. Where the fuck have you been?"

Milo tried to speak, to come up with a way to describe the demolition and reconstruction of his mind, traversing the void, DeWar, his vision of the early hominids—but couldn't.

"Never mind," said Charlie with a sigh. "Doesn't matter. By the way, you guys are acting super weird right now—like you have to think about what you say really hard before you say it."

"Talk to me about Joanne," said Bridget. "How bad is she?"

Charlie gestured over to Joanne. "You're seeing the worst of it now," he said. "She's in trouble, bad trouble. Barely moving, throwing up. Sometimes she cries a little."

"And Dale?" asked Milo.

"He came by maybe a day ago, not that time means anything on this goddamn rock. Stuck around just long enough to gank the last of my supplies and make a run for the surface. Wouldn't even tell me what happened to his arm. Thanks for the bugs—you guys got any more light?"

"You're looking at it," said Milo, pointing to his single fading headlamp. "We're down to our last battery. It's on the lowest setting—we have a couple of hours left, tops."

"That's not nearly enough to get to the surface," groaned Charlie, squeezing the bridge of his nose in frustration. "Won't even get us out of the anthill."

Silence fell among the foursome as Bridget turned her attention back to Joanne, tracing a path away from the guide's collapsed body. Spotting a small pool of dried blood, Bridget chipped it from the rock with her fingernails, rubbed it into a powder between her palms, and inhaled deeply, the red dust sucked into her nose and mouth.

"What the *fuck* are you doing?" demanded Charlie. "Are you *insane*?"

Bridget considered him with narrow, confident eyes. "It's old blood," she said. "Old, dead blood holding old, dead virus. My immune system will recognize the threat and develop antibodies, inoculating me against the pathogen. The Chinese protected themselves against smallpox with this method hundreds of years before the first European vaccines."

"But how—" began Charlie. Bridget cut him off.

"I *see* it," she hissed. "Turn off the light—I can't help her—not yet. I have to wait for the immunity to gain a foothold first."

As Milo reached up to turn off his headlamp, Bridget stared unwaveringly at Joanne, squatting and rocking on her heels as she took in every mumble, twitch, and sigh. And then the light went off, leaving Milo to count his heartbeats alone in the darkness.

Seventeen hours of darkness passed before Bridget spoke again.

"I need light," she announced.

Milo clicked on his headlamp, the dull glow of the final battery barely reaching the edge of the suspended rock. But it was enough to illuminate the four cavers: Charlie slumped against a sheer wall, Joanne still curled in her filthy sleeping bag, Bridget crouched in wait as Milo stood over them all.

"The virus isn't even alive, not like us," said Bridget, her finger tracing a single crook-like pattern into the dust beneath her feet. "It's just a single strand of loose RNA, a scrap of floating genetic code. The code gets inside cells, reprograms them to make more of the virus."

And then she jerked her head up, looking to Joanne.

"Joanne's temperature has skyrocketed—she's locked in a cytokine cascade," Bridget continued. "The fever is a feedback loop within her immune system. Her capillary walls are breaking down, bleeding her from the inside out. She's dying."

"What will you do?" whispered Milo.

"I have to get her fever under control first." Bridget cocked her head as she again considered Joanne's motionless form. "Keep it from cooking her brain from the inside out. And then I have to make sure she doesn't bleed to death internally. If this works, she might—*might*—have a chance."

Charlie spoke. "Using what? You saw it yourself—we are out of supplies, out of light, and out of time."

"She has to fight this virus from within. All I can do is try to guide her. Charlie—I need you to build a fire."

Charlie began to protest, only to be cut off by a disinterested wave of Bridget's hand. He begrudgingly went to work, gathering a small pile of sodden clothes from Duck's pack. He flicked a lighter once, twice, and then held the tiny glow to the clothes until they caught. The flames danced, adding motion and dimension to the tall chasm walls.

Bridget began to speak, her voice rising to a lilting tone. The words were familiar, flowing languages and equations, but spoken in a manner altogether more ancient, the notes resonating deep within Milo's subconscious mind. Dizzy, he bent to his knees and covered his ears—this powerful, hypnotic meditation was not meant for him.

Slowly at first, and then faster and faster, Bridget chanted to Joanne, her body radiating heat and motion. The meditation extended first to minutes, than hours, as Bridget slipped into a standing trance-state, her eyes rolled back into her head, revealing only the whites in the flickering firelight. Bound by the words, Joanne violently flipped to her back and writhed, her muscles seizing and shaking.

And then Bridget seized Joanne by the face, heat boiling over as the doctor clasped her with one hand over heart and the other over spine, faces pressed together as Bridget sucked air from Joanne's open mouth.

Just as quickly, Bridget dropped the cave guide and plunged her hands into the fire, sweeping them through the licking flames, cleansing herself. A pungent aroma of burning hair and skin wafted across the suspended rock as the fire slowly receded to embers.

Reeling from the seizure, Joanne shivered, half-crawling out of her sleeping bag. She whispered, asking for water.

Charlie walked to Joanne, passing a half-full canteen. She slurped it down in a single draught. Grasping the guide around the shoulders, Bridget presented the albino insects, gesturing for them to be eaten. After some convincing, Joanne finally took one into her mouth.

"I've never seen anything like that," said Milo. "That didn't even look like medicine—it was like some kind of *ritual*."

"She's lost a lot of blood internally," said Bridget. "And she's not out of the woods yet. We were able to access her immune system—it will lessen the inflammatory response and reduce her fever. It should keep her out of septic shock, at least for the moment. The reduction in nausea will let her eat and drink, at least a little."

"Why is she shivering?" asked Charlie, pointing.

"Her hypothalamus thinks she's cold. It will constrict her capillaries, minimize further blood loss in her extremities. Joanne is still very sick, but this may give her body enough time to mount a defense, flood her system with antibodies, hopefully bring her viral load under control."

"Incredible," marveled Milo.

"The healers of ancient tribes—" said Bridget. "They could *speak* medicine directly to the mind. I can see it all, it's all so *clear*. She won't be able to move under her own power, but in a few hours we'll be able to carry her and start traversing back to the main shaft."

"You mean—we might be able to get out of here?" said Charlie, hope entering his voice for the first time. But Milo shook his head. Charlie had spoken too soon. Within moments, the last of Milo's fading headlamp flickered and died for the final time.

CHAPTER 40:

FIRE IN THE DARKNESS

2,475 feet below the surface

Charlie spoke first. "Now we're all equally fucked," he said.

Milo had to admit he wasn't wrong. The darkness was all-consuming, almost liquid as it enveloped the four cavers in murky, impenetrable black.

"What now?" asked Milo, his voice echoing into the nothingness.

"I could get a fire going again," said Charlie. "But we've just about run out of shit to burn."

"A torch won't get us anywhere near the surface," said Bridget. "Joanne's the only one who really knows what she's doing down here. Our memories are good—hell, they're perfect. But it's not enough. Even a perfect mental model won't get us out of the anthill in the dark."

One stumble, one false footfall, one wrong passageway, and we'll all end up dead at the bottom of an unmapped shaft. It took the last of our battery power to make it back."

"We could return to the great chamber," suggested Milo. "A torch might get us there if we moved fast enough. Down there we'd have light, heat, food. It's enough to sustain life—at least for a while."

Bridget shivered. "If you call that living. Even if we could find our way back, there's nothing in the glow for us anymore. What could we do? How long could we possibly last?"

"I hate to say it, but we could be worse off," said Charlie.

"How so?"

"At least on this rock we won't starve to death ankle-deep in a puddle at the bottom of some unnamed tunnel. When the time comes, we can always take that long walk off a short ledge."

"I don't want to end up like Duck," said Bridget with a shudder. "It was all so awful."

"Maybe he was the lucky one. It went fast for him—painless. He probably didn't even have time to realize how badly he fucked up."

The party lapsed into silence, leaving Milo alone to his darkness as he considered his fate. Then he heard the faintest click, a second, a third—more confident now—each echoing throughout the chasm.

"Who is doing that?" demanded Charlie. The clicking didn't stop; it grew in strange volume and force. Again, Charlie shouted into the void, demanding answers. Nobody responded—until Joanne spoke.

"I am," she croaked. Milo heard shuffling as she emerged from the sleeping bag. As she stood, she made another click, and then another, each one louder than the one before; and soon they were not just loud but joyful, each one echoing into the oblivion of the massive subterranean chasm.

"Seriously, what are you doing?" said Charlie again.

"Can't you see?" said Joanne with a laugh. "Can't you see the beauty around us?"

"What beauty? What the *hell* are you talking about?"

"I can see the chasm—the suspended rock—*everything*." For good measure, Joanne made the noises again, as though more clicks would somehow cut through Charlie's confusion.

"Is she *echolocating*?" asked Bridget, disbelief in her voice as the answer dawned on her. In a jolt, Milo realized the idea wasn't as foreign as it first sounded.

"No way," said Charlie. "I thought only bats and dolphins could do that."

"People can too," said Bridget. "There are blind men and women who use canes, tapping feet, and oral clicks to understand their surroundings. They can navigate streets, hike the wilderness—even mountain bike. But learning the technique takes *years* of practice."

Excited, Milo experimentally clicked a few times himself. He heard the echoes, but the sound triggered nothing within his mind.

"Whatever is happening, it's like a flashbulb to me," said Joanne. "Every click—it becomes a great rolling wave of light, trailing off in every direction as the echoes fade."

"Joanne—I need you to think very carefully before you answer this question. Can you lead us to the surface?" asked Bridget.

"I don't know," said Joanne, her voice still weak. "I can see—but I can't walk. I don't have the strength."

"What do you see?" asked Milo.

"Beauty—everything—a world of shadows," said Joanne. "I see a world of shifting winds and mist."

"Winds and mists are good enough for me," said Charlie. "If she can lead us out of here . . . hell, I'll carry her myself."

The four cavers shuffled through the anthill for hours, Charlie leading with Joanne clinging to his back, every clicking step giving her another flash of vision within the tight, intersecting tunnels. Occasionally a glimpse of the tunnel would leap into Milo's mind, a familiar footfall triggering his photographic memory. But no matter how hard he listened and concentrated, Joanne's clicks were only clicks to him.

The cavers saw the distant red flame and heard the waterfall before they reached the massive chamber at the bottom of the great shaft and the muddy plain where they'd once struck camp. Dale's final flare had burned down to embers, the faint remaining light illuminating the domed, stalactite-thick ceiling a hundred feet above. Long since receded from the flood, the diminished waterfall slammed against loose rocks in a pool, the outflow draining down a deep, narrow crack. Joanne reveled in the overwhelming noise, eyes closed, every echo of the waterfall's cascade illuminating her misty vision.

Dale Brunsfield lay facedown in the pooling waters at the edge of the waterfall, fifteen hundred feet of severed rope coiled around his body. It didn't matter how far he'd made it up before the line gave way—fifty feet or five hundred, it had been enough to kill on impact. Gentle waves shifted the corpse with unnatural animation, a cruel imitation of life.

"Look at the flare—it's still burning. He's been dead less than an hour," said Charlie, pointing.

Bridget covered her face in her hands, as though she could simply shut out the gruesome scene and return herself to familiar darkness. "What was he going to do—leave by himself? Abandon us down here?"

"He thought we were dead, or as good as dead. I know this sounds awful, but at least he tested the rope for us. This could have just as easily been the four of us lying at the bottom of the shaft."

"Some test," whispered Joanne, slipping from Charlie's back and standing on her uneasy feet for a moment before slumping to the muddy floor.

Together, Bridget and Milo grasped Dale's corpse under the armpits, flipping him over and dragging him from the waters. His body was spongy and he was deathly pale, even under the crimson light of the flare.

"He must have bounced off the rock wall a few times on the way down," said Bridget, her gaze drifting over him. She took one soft hand and drew it over his face, closing Dale's eyes for the final time.

"Not to be overly pragmatic, but how the fuck are we going to get out of here?" said Charlie, squinting at the endless shaft above them, fifteen hundred feet of vertical rock face separating them from the upper passages.

"That's a question for later," said Bridget, sitting down next to Dale's body. "First we need to bury our friend."

The flare had long since died, plunging the four back into suffocating darkness. Milo and Bridget began to build the cairn just feet away from where Dale had fallen, lifting his body into the largest side chamber next to the churning waterfall. The alcove was not much larger than a closet, but it would more than suffice as a natural mausoleum, the grave site protected from any future flooding.

Can't get buried no deeper for no cheaper, thought Milo, remembering the old caver's aphorism from one of the books he'd read on the surface. Together, they placed Dale's body into the pocket below the inscription Milo had discovered at the base of the waterfall a lifetime ago One after another, they selected clean, smooth stones from the pooled waters, slowly walling Dale into the tiny chamber.

Bridget hefted the final stone, preparing to place it at the top of the rock wall. Charlie stopped his work—he'd been sorting through the fifteen hundred feet of rope by touch alone, cutting away the frayed sections while braiding together the remaining good lengths for strength.

"This is the last one," said Bridget, voice echoing in the void. "Should we say something? I know he abandoned us, but he was still a friend."

Joanne grunted. "I'm done giving any goddamn eulogies," she said. "Who will say ours when *we* die down here?"

"Wait—" said Milo, touching Bridget's arms. "Don't seal it up yet."

Everyone probably expected him to speak, but he didn't. Instead, he went person to person and pack to pack, gathering up the few digital memory cards and written notes. He added the last of his hand-drawn maps to the tiny pile, binding them together with the tattered remains of a rubber band. Milo slipped the data into the hole. He touched Bridget's arm again and she placed the final rock.

"Now what?" said Joanne.

"Now we climb," said Charlie, snapping the last braided rope to test the knot. It cracked in the air.

"Seriously?" said Milo, incredulous.

"Sure," said Charlie. "This shaft is fifteen hundred vertical feet—a classic big wall climb. I did Zodiac on El Capitan last summer; it's about the same height. It took sixteen pitches, but we reached the summit."

"It's not exactly apples to apples, it is?" Bridget objected. "We're talking about fifteen hundred feet of wet rock, in the dark."

"Sure—but we're not carrying much of anything either. We'll be able to move faster."

"You need to be a hundred percent blunt with us. Do you have the endurance to do this?"

Charlie sighed. "I don't know about you, but I feel like I've never known my body better. I feel so connected—so alive. I think we can do it. We won't have enough rope or anchors to lay the whole route. A two-man team would be best. I'd like to have Bridget, but Joanne needs her more. I'll lead off, set anchors—I'll show Milo how to ascend right up the sections of rope, and then we'll break down the system for the next pitch. If our people at the surface opened the cave back up again, we'll coordinate with them to get Bridget and Joanne. If it's still closed off, I don't care if Milo and I have to dig our way out—I'm not dying down here."

"What's the catch?" said Joanne, probing.

"Well . . . Zodiac took me three days."

"*Three days?*" exclaimed Bridget.

"Yeah," said Charlie. "So best if we get started soon."

The pain was even more all-encompassing than the darkness. Every one of Milo's fingers had split open, every joint ached even more than the empty hunger in the pit of his stomach. Every handhold, every foothold, every inch gained came with a fresh wave of pure misery. In the black of the void, Milo couldn't tell if he was a foot off the bottom or a thousand. The waterfall churned around him, soaking him to the skin, chilling him to the bone.

If the ancients could do it, so can I, thought Milo. But he only felt wetness and dark and pain.

Charlie's self-mastery was astounding. He knew exactly how strong he was—when to push, when to rest, easily moving up the sheer face. Strong as he had become in the depths, Milo couldn't keep up. The braided rope between them yanked taut again and again; smacking Milo in the face. He was holding Charlie back.

Milo reached up, feeling for a wet, loose handhold. And then it happened: his hand slipped from the rock, plunging Milo downward. One of his flailing arms snagged a gap between slick stones, catching him fast before his harness snapped tight. His entire shoulder popped from its socket, ripping muscle and tendon into shreds.

The pain shattered him. Jolts of green electricity split his nonexistent vision, blasting through his refuge in Gaston Hall, lighting the savanna of his mind ablaze. Milo screamed into the darkness.

Within moments, Charlie was hanging beside him, holding him, yanking his useless hand from between the rocks and lowering him until the rope went taut. Milo tried to move his dislocated arm, but couldn't even wriggle a single finger, much less attempt another handhold.

"Cut me free," gasped Milo, shivering. "Cut the rope—let me drop. My arm is fucked. I'm done for, and you need the line."

"Please, Milo!" begged Charlie. "Just—just try to make it a little further!"

"*Cut it!*" screamed Milo, agony in his voice. He used his good arm to pull a small folding knife from his pocket, pressing it into Charlie's open palm.

Even over the din of the waterfall, Milo could soon hear the sound of knife slicing through a first rope, a second. A flood of relief washed over him; it'd all be over within seconds. He clutched his good arm to his chest, leaning back in his harness, waiting for the final thread to snap, consigning him to ten seconds of weightless falling—and then the release of nothingness, finally free of his pain.

Snap.

Milo opened his eyes, confused. He was still tied to a wall anchor, his rope intact. Charlie had sliced through the line at his own harness, and now clung to the wall with nothing more than his own strength.

"I'll be back for you," promised Charlie.

"Don't do it," begged Milo. "You can't free-ascend the shaft—you're *fucking crazy!*"

"I'll be back," repeated Charlie in a whisper. "Milo, I'll be back for you. I swear I will. Just hold on for a little longer."

M ilo drifted through time, lost in his mind, lost to his pain. Visions of past and future selves appeared and disappeared before him: the arrogant young upstart; the chastened, heartbroken academic; the pain-wracked, stranded castaway; the man he could have someday become; the children he would never have. For a moment, he thought he heard DeWar's gently mocking voice drifting up from the depths, questioning his foolish decision to leave the great chamber.

The idea of Charlie free-climbing the shaft was impossible, suicidal. One tiny slip and Milo wouldn't even hear his twisting body as it whistled by, slamming into the rocks a thousand feet below.

Milo's useless arm hung by his side. He'd given away the knife, couldn't even cut himself free. With only one working hand, the rope and harness knots could not be untied. He wondered how many days it'd take before he died of exposure, the powerful waterfall pounding against him, tearing him apart piece by microscopic piece. The same forces that carved the cave over a hundred and fifty million years ago would ultimately reduce his body to nothing, not even leaving a shattered skeleton underneath a crude rock cairn to mark his life.

A single orb of light descended from above, breaking through Milo's delirium. The light became brighter and brighter, illuminating the seemingly endless shaft and waterfall. And then he saw it—a man-sized metal basket lowered by steel cable, disappearing into the depths below. Even from a thousand feet above, Milo could hear Joanne and Bridget's echoing cheers.

Lost to pain, exhaustion and relief, Milo passed out, still hanging from the wall.

Milo didn't remember the basket coming for him. Once minute he was tied to the wall, the next he was in the metal cage as it rocketed up the shaft. Slumped against the aluminum bars, he could only experience the world in blinks and whispers.

A sensation—human hands reached to grasp him as he slid from the basket and onto plastic sheeting at the top of the shaft.

Charlie's voice cut through confusion of sound and lights—"Yeah, he's the last one."

Milo was loaded onto a collapsible stretcher, thick webbing strapping him into place. Men surrounded him, alien-like in their makeshift biohazard suits, masked faces, duct-taped rubber yellow gloves, and blinding headlamps. He stared up at the featureless ceiling of the white plastic tunnel as it passed.

The bodies at the entrance were gone, the metal hatch unburied and removed. Wind roared through the now-open passageway, howling like a hurricane. Still strapped to the gurney, Milo went out of the mouth and into the dark, starlit savanna, as though the eternal void of the cave had followed him into the world.

With no particular ceremony or discussion, Milo was bundled into the back of a plastic-lined military truck. The last thing he saw before the rear doors closed was a single rusted bulldozer slowly clanking toward the cavern entrance, its blade pushing a thick mound of dirt and rock over the open mouth.

EPILOGUE:

EXODUS

In the day ye eate thereof the tree of life,
then your eyes shal bee opened:
and yee shall bee as Gods, knowing good and euill.

Eve tooke of the fruit thereof,
and did eate,
and gaue also vnto her husband with her.

And the eyes of them both were opened,
and they knew that they were naked.

—Genesis 3:5–7 (KJV, 1611 Abridged)

One year later
Kennedy Center of Performing Arts
Washington, DC
23 feet above sea level

M ilo Luttrell leaned back in the plush third-row seat, adjusting the jacket of his English-cut suit. He patted the ticket pocket, feeling the two VIP entrance passes within the soft gray fabric. Bridget sat to his left, absentmindedly touching the string of pearls around her neck as she watched the screen onstage, across which splashed a beautiful montage of Tanzanian savanna and oasis. She wore a shimmering yellow dress of a golden hue not unlike the glow they'd discovered deep within the earth.

The crowd murmured, beginning to clap as the conference keynote speaker entered from the wings. The lights dipped as the music swelled, a single spotlight drawing Charlie Garza to the center of the stage. He wore a tight athletic turtleneck that showed his broad shoulders and muscled arms. Behind him, the slide flicked over to a scene of ruin: a single rusty bulldozer idling before the collapsed entrance of the cave. It next showed the destroyed surface camp, the still-smoldering tents, trailers, and cremated bodies scattered across the grasslands. Charlie's profile stood tall in the foreground, arms crossed, a look of steely determination in his eyes—a hero.

"This is a story of courage," began Charlie, voice booming from hidden speakers as he scanned across the two thousand seats, every one of them filled. "This is a story of perseverance. Of sacrifice. When disaster struck my expedition into an uncharted Tanzanian supercave, my team of eight men and women were stranded nearly three thousand feet below the surface of the earth, with no hope of rescue. We soon learned the caverns had already claimed other explorers—in 1901, Lord Riley DeWar and nearly twenty men entered what is now known as

Brunsfield's Cave, never to return. In following their footsteps, our lives nearly ended in the same dark tunnels."

The crowd murmured as Charlie paused for effect.

"But what I learned in those depths enabled me to save myself and three of my comrades," he continued. "These lessons in leadership and the capacity of the human spirit changed my life—and it can change yours as well."

Milo shot Bridget his best well-what-did-you-expect look. She just scowled, already irritated and ready to leave. Charlie continued the self-serving speech, but Milo had stopped listening.

He and Bridget had been hounded by the press for months since their emergence from the earth, journalists of all stripes demanding answers to the disappearance of a renowned Wall Street pharma magnate, the brief flare-up of an ancient virus, and the illegal nature of the expedition itself. Charlie soon appointed himself the survivors' spokesman and adopted the mantle with great gusto, to the profound relief of the other three. He got his television deal—and a book deal—and a long-term outdoor apparel deal, meaning the rest were more or less left alone.

Bridget quit her job not long after her homecoming; concentrating her efforts instead into NeuroGenysis, her burgeoning Maryland-based biotech startup. Just months in, the industry was already buzzing about her cognitive mapping initiative, a project equal in scope and ambition to the first sequencing of the human genome. The potential medical implications were groundbreaking, to say nothing of the expected benefit to artificial intelligence research and the science of human potential.

It took Georgetown a little longer to fire Milo, by failing to renew his contract under the auspices of "moving the department in a new direction." By the time they let him go, Bridget was ready to take him on as her corporate Chief Operating Officer, her fourth hire as President and CEO of NeuroGenysis. Any jitters felt by founding investors at his unconventional background and relative lack of corporate experience soon evaporated once exposed to his singularly uncommon intellect and powers of deduction. Milo's photographic memory never failed to impress, whether he was memorizing the names and faces of a thousand conference attendees within seconds or reciting textbook-precise explanations of NeuroGenysis technologies. Combining his abilities with an unblinking devotion to Bridget's vision, Milo had already become quite a force for the nascent company.

The phone in Milo's pocket buzzed, ringer set to silent. Milo surreptitiously snuck a peek at the screen.

"It's Joanne," Milo whispered to Bridget. "Probably for you—do you want to take it?"

Bridget thought for a moment before answering. "This could be about the offer. Yes—I ought to talk to her."

Phone still vibrating within his pocket, Milo took Bridget by the hand and led her past rows of knees and to the aisle, darkness and soft carpeting masking their escape from the speech.

"Where is Joanne these days?" asked Bridget.

"Thailand with friends, last time I heard," answered Milo. It was only the latest in the barrister's far-flung travels, her response to the suffocating persistence of British press photographers. As much as her social circle loved joining Joanne on her lengthy vacations, they were not yet used to her disconcerting habit of disappearing into deep, dark places without so much as a battery-powered penlight.

Charlie continued with the overproduced, pompous speech as Bridget and Milo exited the rear doors of the opera house, stepping into the long, high-ceilinged corridor. They hadn't made it in time—the phone had stopped buzzing.

"You'll have to keep it short with Joanne when you call her back," said Milo. "Don't forget—you have the phone interview with Lillian at *Forbes* in twenty minutes."

Bridget grabbed Milo by his elbow, pulling him toward her so she could give him a peck on the cheek. "Thanks," she said. "I like a man who is cognitively incapable of forgetting appointments and anniversaries."

The pair stepped out of the Kennedy Center and onto the grand, airy balcony that looked over the Potomac River. They stood at the railing, Bridget closing her eyes as she took in the soft summer breeze. Milo wrapped his hands around her waist from behind.

"Should I call Joanne back?"

"In a minute. Let's enjoy the sun for a moment longer."

THE END